Praise for *J*

◆ ◆ ◆

"In . . . her affecting and adventurous new novel, [Katherine J.] Chen creates a rich, visceral world. . . . This is not your grandmother's St. Joan. . . . If every generation gets the Joan it deserves, ours could do worse than an ass-kicking, avenging angel fighting simply for the right to fight."

—*The New York Times Book Review*

"A secular reimagining and feminist celebration of the life of Joan of Arc that transforms the legendary saint into a flawed yet undeniable young woman."

—*USA Today*

"Joan of Arc has long enthralled novelists, who have portrayed her as a virginal warrior with holy visions. In her afterword, Chen describes trying to reconcile these conflicting representations of fighter and saint. It wasn't until she imagined the brutality of Joan's youth in a medieval war zone that she could realistically capture her protagonist's humanity. Chen's Joan has a scrappy, resilient childhood filled with both abuse and love. She grows up learning to fight, but always for justice on behalf of the people and country she loves."

—*The Washington Post*

"The only miracles enacted in these pages are the ones the writer herself pulls off: In *Joan*, Ms. Chen retrieves the worn fragments of Joan of Arc's story and assembles them into a narrative that's eerie, austere and just this side of plausible. To do so is no small feat. . . . Surely many readers will feel that Ms. Chen has summoned up just the Joan of Arc that this anxious, repressive age demands."

—*The Wall Street Journal*

"In this compelling novel, Katherine J. Chen presents her vision of Joan of Arc: one of courage, resilience, vulnerability and passion. This is a beautifully written novel that will have you thinking about this iconic woman in new and complex ways."

—*Ms.* magazine

"An epic take on the life of Joan of Arc, Chen's *Joan* reimagines the martyr as a secular, fierce, intelligent young warrior and woman, humanized and ripe for our time."

—*Parade* magazine

"We all know the story of teenage Joan of Arc, who was burned at the stake by the English, but this electrifying novel fleshes her out as a passionate young woman who defied convention (and then some!). . . . A vivid and very real slice of historical fiction that tears along towards her fateful ending."

—*Good Housekeeping* (UK)

"[A] revolutionary reimagining of Joan of Arc . . . Chen masterfully transforms the two-dimensional martyr into a multifaceted woman and warrior."

—*Booklist* (starred review)

"[A] smartly written rendition of the life of Joan of Arc . . . [Chen] does a wonderful job depicting Joan's soldier mentality and fierce heart. Like the passionate protagonist, this is a force to be reckoned with."

—*Publishers Weekly*

"For readers who love Hilary Mantel's Wolf Hall trilogy, *Joan* offers similar pleasures with its immediacy and somewhat contemporary tone. It's an immersive evocation of a character whose name everyone knows, all these centuries later, but whom, perhaps, none of us knows at all."

—*BookPage*

"The historical Joan was *then*, but Chen's Joan is *now*. . . . She exercises an author's right to weave issues such as parental abuse, patriarchy, discrimination, social inequity, religious tyranny, and a variety of other moral and philosophical concerns into the events and obstacles that continually destabilize her young heroine's imagined life. . . . A story of moving and often poignant power."

—*Bookreporter*

"If, like me, you've always thought of Joan of Arc as a pious teenager in a suit of armour, then this clever, tender novel, full of humanity, will make you see the 'Maid of Orleans' in a new light. Katherine J. Chen's Joan is a scrappy, determined and very real heroine."

—*Red* magazine

"[An] excellent historical novel . . . a fictionalization of the remarkable life of the legendary Joan of Arc . . . It'll transport you to another time and place as you follow Joan's rise from a vulnerable little girl with an abusive father to a fierce warrior who sent France's enemies packing."

—AARP

"*Joan* by Katherine J. Chen brings one of history's most iconic heroines to life."

—*The Daily Beast*

"Like Hilary Mantel's Wolf Hall trilogy, *Joan*'s lush descriptions and gorgeous prose made me feel like I was right there, present in the middle of the story, even though it unfolded centuries ago. I don't want readers to miss this one."

—Anne Bogel, host of *What Should I Read Next?*

"Simply spectacular . . . Chen breathes new life into this historical figure in a way that turns this time-worn tale into a brand-new adventure. . . . Joan in this book is more real than any other rendering of her I've yet encountered. . . . You will never think about Joan of Arc the same again."

—*Napa Valley Register*

"Readers will love this Joan. . . . The writing in this book is beautiful. Chen has turned Joan into a flesh-and-blood teenager, a passionate and determined young woman."

—*The Free Lance-Star* (Top Reads of 2022)

"Chen is interested in the human Joan, not the visionary, and the voice she creates for her is unforgettable: blunt, sarcastic, affectionate, and insightful. . . . This is the richest characterization of a historical figure I've encountered since Hilary Mantel's Thomas Cromwell in *Wolf Hall,* and Chen's achievement belongs in that august company."

—*Historical Novel Society* (Editors' Choice)

"[A] very human portrait of Joan of Arc . . . Making her real requires imagination and empathy, and Chen brings both to the task of putting solid flesh on the charred bones of a legendary figure. . . . Chen's take on the Maid of Orléans feels similar to that of Lauren Groff's version of Marie de France. . . . An elegant and engaging work of historical fiction."

—*Kirkus* (starred review)

"An intense character whose motivations are far more complex than the religious fanaticism that's often associated with Joan . . . a good choice for historical fiction readers who are curious for a unique perspective on the saint, one which may serve as an entry point to learn more about her life."

—*Library Journal*

"To embark on a novel about a woman of such fame requires courage and vision. . . . Chen achieves the task brilliantly. . . . The result is a powerfully feminist, secular retelling of Saint Joan, perfect for our areligious age."

—*World Literature Today*

"Chen interprets Joan of Arc as a fascinating combination of history and imagination, a creation unlike the saint most people know. . . . Firmly rooted in the here and now, she is a real, fleshed-out person. . . . Chen's Joan is strong, loyal and inspiring, a tribute to the irresistible combination of truth and imagining. She is a Joan for today and several centuries of tomorrows."

—*The Emporia Gazette*

"Chen's vivid historical novel of Joan d'Arc asks what makes a saint. . . . The way Chen secularizes Joan by portraying her as a dynamic child and self-made warrior makes her relatable to readers today."

—*International Examiner*

"Katherine J. Chen has not only found a foothold to stand among the many portrayals of Joan of Arc's life, but she has also found something new to say about the role of a woman at war that will resonate soundly with modern audiences. . . . Told in clear, beautiful prose, the resulting story depicts the fires of faith in Joan's life as both a secular and spiritual being, at once flawed and heroic. Chen's novel is captivating and exemplary of how to develop an historic female character."

—*Historical Novel Society*

"There are certainly glimmers of *Wolf Hall* in this tale of an outsider on the rise, and in the seething Machiavellian court politics. . . . Chen earns the comparison [to Mantel] thanks to her vivid, visceral and boldly immediate storytelling. . . . It's Joan herself who constantly bounds off the page, a proto-feminist genius born into the wrong age. Thanks to Chen's efforts, she is now a hypnotic heroine for our time."

—*The Daily Telegraph*

"Chen's brilliantly imagined novel breathes new life into this famous tale. Her Joan is a riotous tomboy, a hot-headed adolescent and a decidedly unsaintly soldier—and is all the more inspiring for it. . . . A triumph of historical fiction."

—*The Mail on Sunday*

"A brilliant exploration of how an otherworldly peasant girl became a leader of violent men and a national icon . . . In graceful prose . . . Chen suspends Joan in a liminal space where her historical visceral reality, her agency and the mystery of her unearthly gifts can coexist. . . . Chen helps the reader suspend disbelief by presenting Joan as a beguiling, fully human mix of wariness and confidence, and fiercely protective of those she loves. . . . For here at last is the true Joan, glorious in the flower of her strength, leading her men to victory after victory."

—*The Guardian*

"This is a big story, and the author also keeps our attention by ringing changes that make this a Joan for our times. She is at war with misogyny as well as the English. She is an inspiring feminist heroine, courageous and kind, humane and hopeful, a girl in armour who shows what a girl in armour can do. . . . She's like Shakespeare's Henry V on the eve of Agincourt, meditating at night among the troops."

—*The Times Literary Supplement*

"A propulsive, gripping must read book about a young woman who was unafraid to become a leader of men in a deeply patriarchal society . . . Chen does justice to her legend and this will transport and move you."

—*Glamour* (UK)

"In this inspired, lyrical reimagining of Joan of Arc's life, the author transports us inside the head of a young woman whose divinely inspired military gifts were viewed with awe and suspicion. She celebrates the magnitude of Joan's achievements after surviving a difficult and miserable childhood, and it's a picture that makes clear why Joan is still venerated after her cruel death, aged 19."

—*Woman & Home* (UK)

"What Joan is in this book is a true kickass heroine, and I think Katherine Chen has knocked it out of the park with this one. I absolutely loved it. It comes with the stamp of the greatest of all, Hilary Mantel. That's all you need to know."

—JOHN MITCHINSON on *Monocle on Culture*

"[Chen's] Joan is naturally strong, and a scrapper. If her ability to learn medieval warfare seems uncanny, then it is made perfectly credible. . . . [*Joan*] eschews both post-modernism and anachronism, as well as the real-life ending of Joan, in fire. Chen's Joan is fresh, unusual and vivid."

—*The Sydney Morning Herald*

"Katherine J. Chen breathes new life into the story of one of France's most famous heroines. In a gripping tale of thrilling historical fiction, *Joan* offers a glorious feminist reimagining of the life of Joan of Arc."

—*Marie Claire* (Australia)

"Chen writes history in an embedded manner that is evocative of Mantel's Cromwell in the Wolf Hall trilogy. . . . If you're a fan of immersive historical experiences, beautiful prose and characters who will stay with you, then don't miss *Joan*."

—*The AU Review* (Best Books of 2022)

"Written in gorgeous lyrical prose . . . this feminist celebration of the historic figure is thrilling storytelling."

—*Woman* (New Zealand)

"While we've enjoyed some great reimagining featuring Circe, Ariadne and Marie de France, it's finally time for Joan of Arc to tell her side of history and reclaim her slab of badass-ery. And we're so here for it."

—*Pedestrian* (Australia)

"This Joan is no pious maiden but a strong soldier and smart military strategist and logistician; and yes, she really did pull an arrow out of her own neck."

—Margaret Atwood (on Twitter)

"It is as if Chen has crept inside a statue and breathed a soul into it, re-creating Joan of Arc as a woman for our time."

—Hilary Mantel

"Measured, austere, profoundly physical—I loved it."

—Jo Baker, author of *Longbourn*

"A glorious, sweeping novel . . . richly imagined, poignant, and inspiring."

—Jennifer Saint, bestselling author of *Ariadne*

"A bold, brilliant, and provocative re-imagining of one of history's most famous warriors, *Joan* reads like a thriller, while remaining rich with detail about the traumas of the fifteenth century."

—Gareth Russell, author of *Do Let's Have Another Drink!: The Dry Wit and Fizzy Life of Queen Elizabeth, the Queen Mother*

"Visceral and piercing—I was blown away."

—Allison Pataki, *New York Times* bestselling author of *The Magnificent Lives of Marjorie Post*

"Meticulously researched and skillfully told, *Joan* reimagines a legend many of us thought we knew. Beneath the legend lies the truth of an extraordinary life and a woman whose courage, love of country, and military mind both separated her from and bound her to a land and its people. In Chen's capable hands, Joan becomes fully flesh and achingly real."

—#1 *New York Times* bestselling author Lisa Wingate

"*Joan* is an epic novel with the mythic power of a fairy tale. In clear and powerful prose, Chen catapults you to fifteenth-century France, where she reimagines Joan of Arc as a vulnerable and sensitive young woman whose clarity of moral vision and purpose transform her into a warrior. . . . Gripping, resonant, and illuminating."

—#1 *New York Times* bestselling author CHRISTINA BAKER KLINE

BY KATHERINE J. CHEN

Mary B

Joan

Joan

Joan

A Novel

KATHERINE J. CHEN

RANDOM HOUSE
New York

Joan is a work of historical fiction. Apart from the well-known actual people, events, and locales that figure in the narrative, all names, characters, places, and incidents are the products of the author's imagination or are used fictitiously. Any resemblance to current events or locales, or to living persons, is entirely coincidental.

2023 Random House Trade Paperback Edition

Published in the United States by Random House, an imprint and division of Penguin Random House LLC, New York.

Random House and the House colophon are registered trademarks of Penguin Random House LLC.
Random House Book Club and colophon are trademarks of Penguin Random House LLC.

Originally published in hardcover in the United States by Random House, an imprint and division of Penguin Random House LLC, in 2022.

Epigraph from *Joan of Arc: La Pucelle,* selected sources translated and annotated by Craig Taylor (Manchester, UK: Manchester University Press, 2006), pg. 84.

Library of Congress Cataloging-in-Publication Data
Names: Chen, Katherine J., author.
Title: Joan: a novel / by Katherine J. Chen.
Description: New York: Random House [2022] |
Identifiers: LCCN 2021034296 (print) | LCCN 2021034297 (ebook) | ISBN 9781984855824 (paperback; acid-free paper) | ISBN 9781984855817 (ebook)
Subjects: LCSH: Joan, of Arc, Saint, 1412–1431—Fiction. | LCGFT: Biographical fiction. | Historical fiction. | Novels.
Classification: LCC PS3603.H4485 J63 2022 (print) | LCC PS3603.H4485 (ebook) | DDC 813/.6—dc23
LC record available at https://lccn.loc.gov/2021034296
LC ebook record available at https://lccn.loc.gov/2021034297

Printed in the United States of America on acid-free paper

randomhousebooks.com
randomhousebookclub.com

4th Printing

Book design by Simon M. Sullivan

To Joan

(1412–1431)

I will make a war cry that will be remembered forever.
And I am writing this to you for the third and final time;
I will not write anything further.

Joan of Arc
(from a letter dictated to the English)

CAST OF CHARACTERS

◆ ◆ ◆

JOAN AND HER FAMILY

JOAN, *a girl from the village of Domrémy in Armagnac France*

JACQUES D'ARC, *Joan's father*

ISABELLE ROMÉE, *Joan's mother*

CATHERINE, *Joan's elder sister*

JACQUEMIN, *Joan's eldest brother*

JEAN, *Joan's second brother*

PIERRE, *Joan's younger brother*

DURAND LAXART, *Joan's uncle*

SALAUD, *Joan's dog*

OTHERS IN THE VILLAGE OF DOMRÉMY

HAUVIETTE, *Joan's friend*

JEHANNE, *Hauviette's mother*

The priest

FRENCH ROYALTY

CHARLES VII, *the Dauphin, the eldest surviving son of the French king and the dispossessed heir to the French throne*

Marie of Anjou, *the Dauphine, Charles VII's wife, and Yolande of Aragon's daughter*

Yolande of Aragon, *the Duchess of Anjou and Queen of Four Kingdoms, the Dauphine's mother, and Joan's ally*

Jean de Dunois, *"the Bastard of Orléans," the illegitimate son of the former Duke of Orléans, and Joan's friend*

Charles, *Duke of Lorraine, an early supporter of Joan's*

Charles VI, *the Dauphin's father and King of France until his death in October 1422*

Isabeau of Bavaria, *the Dauphin's mother and much-despised Queen of France*

CLERGY AND COURTIERS

Robert le Maçon, *a trusted advisor to the Dauphin and Joan's ally*

Georges de La Trémoille, *the Dauphin's favorite at court and Joan's rival*

Regnault de Chartres, *the Archbishop of Reims and Joan's rival*

Colet de Vienne, *a royal messenger of Yolande of Aragon*

SOLDIERS

Robert de Baudricourt, *the captain of the garrison at Vaucouleurs and a reluctant supporter of Joan's*

Bertrand de Poulengy, *a knight and Joan's traveling companion from Vaucouleurs to Chinon*

Jean de Metz, *a squire and Joan's traveling companion from Vaucouleurs to Chinon*

Étienne de Vignolles, *better known as La Hire, an infamous soldier and Joan's friend*

Jean d'Aulon, *Joan's squire*

Raymond *and* Louis, *Joan's young pages*

FRANCE'S ENEMIES

Henry V, *King of England until his death in August 1422*

Henry VI, *the young son of Henry V and Catherine of Valois (the Dauphin's elder sister) and heir to the English throne*

John the Fearless, *the former Duke of Burgundy, an enemy of the Dauphin's; assassinated by the Dauphin's men in September 1419*

Philip III, *Duke of Burgundy, John's son, and England's ally*

John, *Duke of Bedford, regent of England, and Burgundy's ally*

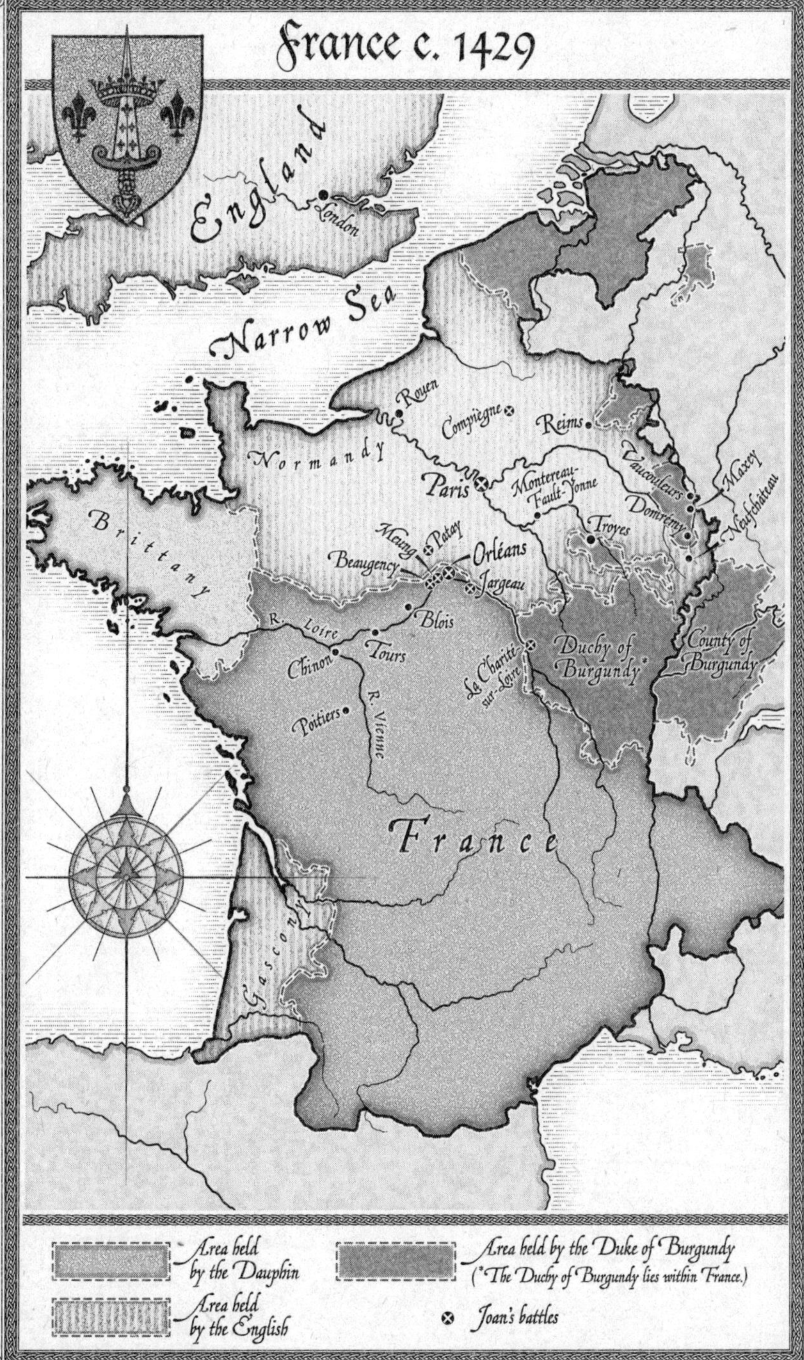
France c. 1429
England
London
Narrow Sea
Normandy
Brittany
Rouen
Compiègne
Reims
Paris
Montereau-Fault-Yonne
Vaucouleurs
Maxey
Domrémy
Neufchâteau
Troyes
Meung
Patay
Beaugency
Orléans
Jargeau
Blois
R. Loire
Tours
Chinon
La Charité-sur-Loire
Duchy of Burgundy*
County of Burgundy
Poitiers
R. Vienne
France
Gascony
Area held by the Dauphin
Area held by the English
Area held by the Duke of Burgundy
(*The Duchy of Burgundy lies within France.)
Joan's battles

Part One

‡

The kingdom of France has been at war with England for nearly one hundred years, the result of an ancient feud steeped in land and blood.

The current King of France is Charles VI, also known as Charles the Beloved or Charles the Mad. He is a delicate man who suffers from intermittent psychotic episodes and believes he is made of glass. The current King of England is Henry V, who is the very opposite of poor mad Charles. A hardened and energetic warrior determined to subsume France under English rule, Henry is a monarch to be reckoned with and feared, a man with a true fixity of purpose. Under Henry V's military leadership, England enjoys a succession of victories, including the Battle of Agincourt in 1415, and controls Normandy, Paris, and nearly all of the territories north of the Loire River.

In the vacuum left by an incapacitated French king, two individuals grapple for power: Charles VII, the Dauphin, or the eldest surviving son of the King of France, and his father's cousin, John the Fearless, the influential and ambitious Duke of Burgundy. In May 1418, John seizes Paris, driving the Dauphin out of the capital. However, only a year later, Charles VII finds himself embroiled in John's assassination during a meeting of truce on a bridge in the town of Montereau-Fault-Yonne. This is a grave political misstep, setting off a disastrous series of events for the Dauphin. As a result of his father's death, John's only son, Philip III, the new Duke of Burgundy, swears vengeance on Charles VII, his cousin, and pledges to aid the English against the French. There are thus three forces at play during this time, with England and Burgundy allied on one side, and France on the other.

In 1420, in a great political coup, the Treaty of Troyes is signed between Henry V of England and Charles VI of France. By this treaty, the disgraced Dauphin falls out of the line of succession to the French throne, and a marriage is arranged between Henry V and Catherine of Valois, Charles VI's youngest daughter. The Treaty of Troyes declares that the son (and future descendants) of Henry V and Catherine of Valois will rule over both kingdoms, and that Henry will replace the Dauphin as heir to Charles VI's throne.

These events drive the now "illegitimate" Dauphin, a young man of seventeen, to take sanctuary in the Loire Valley, where he establishes his own court. This is a time of turmoil. A town seized one day by the English may be recaptured the next by the French, and vice versa. Though Charles VII has his supporters—those who do not recognize or accept the terms of the Treaty of Troyes, believe his claim to the throne is valid, and have no wish to live under English rule—it is a miserable period for France and its people. The Dauphin has much against him. His mother, Isabeau of Bavaria, no longer recognizes him as her son. His sister Catherine is allied in matrimony to his English enemy. And England has taken a great deal of French land, albeit at no small cost to its own purse. Though he is heir by blood to the French throne, the Dauphin must end the war with England and Burgundy if he is ever to fully assert his kingship and reign in peace.

This is where our story begins.

I

◆ ◆ ◆

DOMRÉMY, SUMMER 1422

HER JOB IS PICKER-UPPER OF STONES. Not pebbles but rocks of heft and edges and sharp corners. As the boys of Domrémy gather in the field, Joan is bent-backed over the ground, digging missiles out of the earth with blackened fingernails. From her skirts, the ends gripped in a tight fist, she makes a bundle weighted down with hard treasures.

At her brother Jacquemin's whistle, the others come padding over, a shuffling and uncertain army of which he is captain, being the eldest—sixteen—and tallest. From his mouth, a stem of wheat curves in a long arc like a single whisker. He looks out at the scorch of afternoon sun in a clear blue sky and stretches a leg, shakes a foot as if to wake it. Above them, a hot wind exhales, stirring a few hairs on every head. A stillness eases into the grass. One boy opens his mouth to yawn.

She shows Jacquemin her collection, and he nods. As captain, he has first pick of stones. He takes two of the largest for himself and flicks his eyes in the direction of the rest of his men. She goes slowly, deliberately, down the line. What she distributes is not randomly given. She examines each outstretched hand, assessing whether it is one accustomed to splinters, cuts, and scrapes, to dusty fights in yards and haystacks, or as yet uninitiated in the rites of boyish scuffles and hard labor. You don't want to give a boy a rock that is bigger than his palm, that he cannot clutch in his fingers and throw with precision. So, she gives her brother's friends, the square-shouldered boys of twelve and thirteen, rocks she thinks suit them: stones blunt and heavy.

For the smallest of this makeshift army, a boy she knows only by sight and by name, she saves the best. He is aged seven years to her ten and chewing the fingernails of one hand carefully, even thoughtfully, while the other dangles at his side. When she holds out her prize, he does not take it, so she has to grip the hand that isn't in his mouth and press the two rocks allotted to him into his palm. As far as rocks go, one is ordinary. But the other is smooth and narrow and easily held. Unlike the rest, it features a jagged edge. She'd smiled when her hand had grazed its sharpness in the warm earth.

"They may not show their faces," Jacquemin tells them, already bored. He tosses a rock like a juggler about to put on a show, catching it with a small flourish.

"They are cowards," he adds.

But even now, behind them, at the edges of the clearing: a rustle, a stir so subtle they jump, and she can hear her heart beat inside her ears. The enemy has come, and for a moment, just a moment, they are struck dumb by what they see. It is as if they are looking into a mirror, and for every boy from French Domrémy who is here, there is his counterpart, his twin, from the Burgundian village of Maxey, their neighbor less than half an hour's walk away on a fine day, their sworn enemy. Ten against ten.

As number eleven, she stands out: a girl dressed in faded red wool with dark hair in knots swinging past her shoulders. Jacquemin says, in a low snarl, "Get out of the way, Joan," and she glowers at him before moving, at her own pace, to the periphery of the battleground. She leans against a tree, folds her arms, regards the scene. Her brother does not know it, but in her pocket she has kept back three stones, and when she looks down, she spots a thick branch, like a club, at her feet. It is good to be prepared.

They are, on both sides, a ragged bunch. You can tell where their mothers or sisters have patched up their tunics and trousers, the discolored squares sewn onto knees and elbows, where fabric easily wears thin. You can hear, almost, the collective grumbling of stomachs. Boys are always hungry, though their portions are often larger, and in her house, you have to eat quickly if you want your share of bread and pottage. She knows this, having three brothers (two older, one younger) of her own. When food is scarce, they talk on and on about what they would eat if they could: the cuts of dripping beef, the smoking fillets of fresh-caught trout, the banquets they would hold if they were lords. Sometimes, when they are in good spirits, they let her crouch nearby and listen, and her mouth waters, for her appetite is no less than theirs, and she, too, is always hungry. But usually, they chase her away, and if they cannot chase her away because, like a wall, she will not shift from her place, then they will stop talking until she grows tired of the silence and leaves of her own accord.

No one knows with certainty how these mock battles started or why the boys of French Domrémy and Burgundian Maxey should take up stones when their fathers are able to hold a watchful peace between themselves. But here they are, these boys, on the field. Here they are, face forward, wiping final threads of milky snot onto their sleeves, ruddy-cheeked not from anger but from the warmth of a summer day. Here they are, flint-eyed, faces blank, jaws set. Only a few, she thinks, look like born fighters: you can always pick them out; it is the way they stare across at their enemy without blinking, their stillness and quiet, how they lift and hold their heads. The Maxey boys come ready. From their pockets, they show their hands, palms full of dark rocks. She wonders which of their sisters helped them pick out these stones and whether missiles selected by another girl, a Burgundian equivalent of herself—perhaps her name is also Joan—will be as good as the ones she has found in this place, though she thinks not. She has picked the best stones for her brother's army.

How does a battle begin? Which side will strike the first blow? Or does it commence all at once, like the meeting of hands for prayer? This is a question she and her uncle Durand Laxart have turned over during his many visits. Despite his low birth, his lack of learning, her uncle is a thinker, a teller of stories, a wanderer who has lived the life of a dozen men in his forty or fifty years. No one knows his precise age. When he smiles or laughs, showing off his good teeth, each one intact, not chipped or missing or a blackened stump, he could easily pass for thirty. He says he has been a ship's boy, a cook, a tanner's assistant, a one-hour, one-day, and one-month laborer, in the fields, on the docks, even, he claims, on the scaffold as the hangman's helper.

So, how does a battle begin? He has told her stories of battles, legendary battles, that start with a song. A scream. A curse. A prayer. But on this fine summer afternoon, on a good-sized plot of neutral land wedged between their two villages, the battle starts with a question.

"Who is that?" the leader of Maxey asks, pointing in her direction.

She answers before Jacquemin can: "Are you talking to me, Burgundian filth?" Perhaps it is the rocks concealed in her skirts that make her bold. Or the stick she knows is lying within reach of her foot, which she can roll into her hand at a moment's notice.

Jacquemin shoots her a death glare, a look that says, *Go before I tell Father you were here, and then you'll be sorry,* just as the enemy captain spits on the ground. He spits with such force, you expect a front tooth or two to roll in the grass. He is a safe distance away—his spit lands nowhere near her—but Joan is startled. Usually her voice alone is enough to ward off her brothers, to make them shrink back. She moves closer to the tree, anchoring herself against it. "Armagnac cunt!" the Burgundian captain shouts, and a rock is tossed in the air—she can't tell from which side. Not necessarily thrown, she observes, at any particular target. She hopes, for the boy Guillaume's sake, that he hasn't wasted his prize with the sharp edge so soon.

Stones fly, launching themselves through the air like angry, whizzing birds. Every time a rock hits a target, a shoulder or a stomach, there is a yelp of pain.

When the stones are exhausted, fighting follows, though it is more like a brawl, each boy gripping another of similar height and weight and rolling through the dirt as one body. Teeth sink into ankles. Thumbs press into shut eyes. Everywhere, a tangle of gangly limbs, a wobbling, lurching dance through clouds of kicked-up dust. The high-pitched shrieks of younger children splinter the shouts of older ones. She would join, except she doesn't know where to begin, and she can't tell the enemy from her own side anymore. Next time, she thinks, it would help for the boys from Domrémy to mark themselves somehow, perhaps to wear a piece of cloth tied around their arms in the same color. Or the Burgundians could dress as horned devils. That would do the job, too. At the thought, she smiles.

When they'd first arrived, Joan had noted the dark borderline of trees that rimmed the land and said, Look, Jacquemin, look up. In the voice that never failed to put a murderous glint in her father's eye, she'd told her brother, You should have begun collecting stones weeks ago. Every mock battle, its date and hour and location, is determined by the captains well in advance. We—she includes herself in this we—could have found the best rocks and put them in sacks to raise, by rope, to the tops of the trees. Then each boy would climb to a covert branch, and from his perch, he could ambush the enemy as soon as they arrived. The boys of Maxey, they'd believe the sky or God was pelting rocks at them. They'd piss themselves. They'd run.

But her brother had only glared at her. A lad of few words. Her father thinks this is one of his strengths; she thinks he's just slow. "If you want to stay . . ." he'd said, not finishing the sentence. He'd extended an arm and gestured carelessly at the field. Look for rocks.

From a distance, she spots Maxey's captain in a deadlock with Jacquemin, which makes her want to reach out to her brother with a long arm and shake him. Not five minutes have passed, and already you need my help! But she bends. The stick fills her right hand. She runs in the direction of the enemy's exposed back, the head like a wisp of orange flame, catching the sunlight. She raises the stick to strike, as well as to fend off anyone who might think of attacking—

A scream stops her.

She hasn't yet reached the fight, but the branch tips out of her hand. She turns and stares in the direction of the noise, not knowing at first what she is looking at. Then she sees: in the midst of the fighting, there is a patch of silence. The quiet feels strange; it does not belong here. I a corner of the field where two boys should still be throwing fists a kicking, one boy has detached himself. The other is lying or ground. She observes, even from this distance, the white terror e moving boy's face as he stumbles backward and nearly trips over his own feet. He covers his mouth, wipes whatever is there across the front of his shirt, as others, too, begin to look up from their pummeling. Her gaze returns to the boy who doesn't move.

Already she knows who it is before her eyes can make out the face. Guillaume: seven years to her ten. The light that heats the back of her neck is the same light as before, but different. There is an edge to it now, like the point of a sharpened knife held against her skin. The boys step aside to let her pass. Perhaps they think, because she is a girl, she can do something to help.

Now the enemy is moving again: faces bewildered and pale, fleeing in the direction of Maxey, where they will close their Burgundian ranks and admit to nothing. No one calls out or runs to stop them. By the time she nears Guillaume, they are gone, cutting through grass and the shadows of trees as nimble as thieves in the night.

When she reaches him, she exhales with relief; he is alive. Then she kneels, and it is as if she has swallowed one of her own rocks. She tries to convince herself that the wound isn't as bad as it appears, that a flesh wound, a clean cut, can release a surprising amount of blood. She sees that Guillaume's eyes are open, that they are the gray-blue of clouded skies and fixed on a spot in the far-off distance.

Behind her, she hears Jacquemin swear revenge. She turns; this is not the time for blood feuds. Now it is she who gives flinty looks and blunt directions. "Get help," she orders. Her brother makes a sound, a stifled cry like a dog that has been stepped on, and begins to run. Three of his followers tag behind him. Those who remain look like they might be sick. They turn their eyes away; the blood, she would guess, frightens them. There is so much of it.

Theirs is a small village, so no face remains a stranger for very long. She has seen Guillaume sitting on the threshold of his cottage while his mother tends to her garden, considered the best in Domrémy. She has een him pick up a gray cat, which their family keeps to fend off mice, d rub his cheeks, first one, and then the other, against the scruff of its k. For his age, he is small, and the cat must be heavy to carry for long periods at a time, but he is always draping it, like a sack of flour, over his shoulder, always petting its ears and trying to cradle it like a baby, though the animal won't let itself be cradled. She thinks: A boy who is so tender with animals can't be a bad person, can he? From her skirts, she tears a strip of wool and presses the cloth to his head, and the wool turns dark, nearly black, until her own fingers are sticky. The patch of grass, from the back of his skull to the bottom of his neck, is leaking red, as though the ground itself were being dyed, a bolt of mossy-green fabric dipped in a tub of scarlet. She hears a strangled sound catch in his throat, which she feels echoed in her own throat. It is as if they are, the two of them, linked together in this brief moment; what he feels, she also feels, this dizzy and dazed confusion, a growing nausea that can't be vomited up. Her hands, now cold, now hot, now cold again, tear a bigger piece off her dress, and she presses, pushing it against the wound. To keep from gagging at the smell of blood, she tells him words she knows are empty before they have even left her mouth. *It is only a small cut. Hold on. Help is coming.*

She wants to ask Guillaume how it happened. Was it a rock, a piece of wood, or just fists? Did the boy who did this have a weapon concealed? But she doesn't ask. She is thinking, because she knows he will die, My face shouldn't be the last one he sees in this world. It should be his mother or father or sister here. Even the cat. Not me, someone he barely knows.

She feels she is memorizing the picture of him, a body that has grown over seven tender years from infancy to boyhood, from swaddling bands to trousers. His face has not yet lost its baby roundness. His skin is smooth and probably soft, his hair springs up in yellow-brown tufts, the color of sunlight on a dirt field. His blood, too, looks new, and his hands are clenched in fists, as if he is still fighting. But now one loosens, and her hand extends to meet it. She is surprised to feel something drop into her palm. When she looks down, she sees rocks, the ones she gave him, both unthrown. She folds her fingers over them. She wants to ask, even as she fights back tears, Didn't you think of using them, stupid boy? Fool, coward. I saved the best for you.

They are only three years apart, though his hands couldn't be more different from hers. No calluses. No roughness. These are the hands of a child who is loved and spared hard labor. The one blemish she can spot: a pink scar, a thin line that runs for about an inch from the inside of the top of his thumb. The cat, she suspects. Except for his leaking head, he is all a boy should be: whole and sound, healthy and strong. For a moment, panic seizes her; she is afraid her hands, rough and large, the hard and solid grip of her fingers, will hurt him.

The moment the last breath goes out of him she can feel it. It is like a disappointed sigh that no one, apart from herself, has arrived to see him off.

Then, all at once, the men are here, and she is rising slowly to her feet. She is being pushed back and away, and two of the men, close friends of her father's, are staring as though there is something wrong with her. They think she has been hurt because her hands and wrists, her skirts where she had knelt, are covered in blood, and her dress is torn. Did Maxey do this, they ask, as if what happened here were the work of an entire village. But she says no, it is all Guillaume's blood, and she shows them the cloth she used to try to stanch the bleeding. They seem to understand; they nod and pay no more attention to her.

It is Guillaume's father, called from another field, who carries his son back to Domrémy, to his mother, grandmother, older sister, and to his cat. The dead boy's head falls over his father's arm, leaving a crimson snake trail in the grass.

She is the last to leave. She stands, staring up at the sky, as though waiting for the glinting sun to explain to her what has happened. She feels that it is important for her to make sense of this. A boy has died. She watched him die. What did he die for?

When she comes back to herself, she sees that one of her hands is balled in a fist. She is surprised by the effort it takes to open her own fingers, to reveal the rocks she had earlier passed to Guillaume, which are now returned to her. She has been holding them so hard, they have made pink-red indentations in her palm, like tiny bird tracks. She tosses the ordinary stone away. But her prize, the one with the sharp edge, she keeps. She slips the rock into her pocket. She considers, surprised by the calmness with which she reasons, that if Jacques d'Arc, her father, had been Guillaume's father, then Guillaume would have thrown the rocks to save himself. He would have used his fists, and it is possible he would still be alive.

Her father has said to her brothers (while she was listening out of sight), We will never see a great battle here, not in Domrémy. Can you imagine Agincourt or Crécy taking place in these fields? Not in a thousand years! And he laughed, picking at his teeth with dirty nails the color of blackest earth.

But if we consider how battles begin, then this one, between France and Burgundy, between Domrémy and Maxey, between rock-throwing children born in different villages, began three years ago. It is a tale everyone knows, a tale simple in nature, of vengeance, of how the Dauphin, in the town of Montereau-Fault-Yonne, had John the Fearless killed because John was gaining too much power for himself. And now John's son, Philip, the present Duke of Burgundy, says he will not rest until the Dauphin is dead.

The Dauphin is still alive, but in this place, a boy has died. This, her uncle Durand has told her, finishing another of his battle stories, is the way of war. One day, all is well with the world. The affairs of kings are solely the problem of some ancient and royal bloodline that has nothing to do with the poor cottager who eats cabbage for every meal. The princes are feuding, but the earth is being tilled, the grass is being cut, the sheaves are being tied. Until one day, the yawning guard climbs the stairs to the battlements and, peeping over the crenellated edge, sees an army ten thousand strong waiting for his surrender. One day, the cottager wakes in the dead of night with the tip of a sword pressed against his ribs. It is not always parents and grandparents who die first. A father, sweating over his work, hears a shout to come and come quickly and, running, he steps as through a nightmare, into a clearing to see a face familiar to him from its birth. The face will never wake again. It is cold to his touch.

II

◆ ◆ ◆

AT SUPPER, THE MOOD IS BLACK. From her seat, as far from the head of the table as she can sit, Joan keeps her head down to escape the stream of oaths flying like an arc of sour piss out of her father's mouth.

It is not the boy, Guillaume, he is grieving, though there may be a little of that, too, since he is also a father to sons. Mostly, however, it is anger. It is the indignity of knowing that Domrémy has lost a battle, even one between children. The humiliation is what he can't stomach. If he were there, if he were only there, he keeps repeating, to face those tit-sucking whoresons drunk on their famous Burgundian wine, those curd-eating milksops who kill a man and then don't take the credit for doing it; he closes his right fist in his left hand: what he would have done if only he were there . . .

"But that wouldn't have been permitted, Father," Jacquemin says practically. "You are too old." His intent is to soothe, but its effect only makes his father's skin jump, the blue vein like a swollen rivulet in the side of his neck throb. He has no need for words. He answers his eldest with a curled lip, eyes hard as splinters of bone. In war, what is not permitted? What tricks? What traps? What subterfuge? Tell me. In fact, I dare you to say it to my face again.

Jacquemin looks down, cowed. So, her father goes on. And on.

He is the only person Joan knows who can hold a conversation entirely with himself. No sooner does a thought enter his head than it travels to his lightning-quick tongue, and it is not always curses that come out. He is sometimes perceptive, occasionally eloquent. We have suffered, he says now, no raids from the companies of mercenaries that have ravaged the French countryside for longer than I have been alive. Heaven has looked kindly on our small village. Our cottages have not been burned. We've had no need to seek refuge within the fortified walls of cities. We've not had our livestock taken, our women defiled, our children killed, the corpses of grandmothers and godparents set alight before our eyes, if we could not give over our life's savings for the right to bury them. These things, he continues, have happened to others, and there is no reason to believe that Domrémy, though we take our name from the blessed Saint Remigius, is better or worse than any other place in France that has suffered. You hear stories like this all the time: cloisters broken into, silver chalices pissed in, altar cloth used to wipe the stinking sweat of an Englishman's brow. But this, what happened today, is to our shame. We cannot justify it, for it was no army, no company of Burgundian or English or even disgruntled French soldiers come to wreak havoc upon us. He pauses, and the silence holds the full weight of his displeasure. It is weakness, he concludes. Weakness.

For a moment, her father simply lets the word hang heavy in the air. Then he wets his lips, takes a drink, continues: It is the coddling of mothers that brings about such frailty in boys, for all women are weak and soft. They were born to be such. His eyes dart quickly to his wife and two daughters. Women, mothers, sisters, daughters, wives, they cannot help it. That boy, Guillaume—he spreads his hands flat against the table, on either side of the bowl containing his supper, for this is his final judgment—well, we shouldn't be surprised he was felled. This is what happens when you don't put a child to use as soon as he can pick up a stick or bend his back in the field. His father was always petting him, like that cat he carried around. An unnatural boy. Christ in heaven, he says. He carried the cat, and his father and mother carried him. They threw their arms around him every time he so much as scratched his nose because it itched.

She thinks he's finished, but he isn't. It is never enough for Jacques d'Arc to simply insult the dead and abase the bereaved. So, it's weakness of boys, this much is established. But it's also France. It's weakness that drips, like rain from the eaves, above to below. The weakness of our rulers, the King and the Dauphin. Joan moves her mouth, mimicking his expressions, her head turned away as she pulls faces. Her mother and sister see what she is doing, but her mother looks down, while her sister looks up, as if aiming a prayer at their wood-beamed ceiling. Neither of them smile.

But Jacques d'Arc, it seems, cannot escape weakness. Here, too, is the very weakness he hates, at his own table.

As she tries to get her sister to look at her and laugh, Joan feels her hand slip and the bowl in front of her teeter on the edge of the table before fate intervenes, brushing ghostly fingers across the rim and coaxing it over. She watches the bowl, as if in a slow dream, wobble and fall with a crash.

An accident—only an accident. But she knows a miracle must be performed. And quickly.

In the time before her father reaches out and thrashes her, she must somehow make whole the bowl that has been ruined. The serving of pottage the bowl contained must be scooped back inside, as though it had never been touched or disturbed. And her father has already risen from his chair.

So, she is on all fours, her hands working frantically, lumping the clay pieces together in a small and, she hopes, neat little mound that will satisfy the high standards of Jacques d'Arc. She is using her palm to ladle as much stew as she can into her mouth, so that she can't be accused of wasting food, not in such uncertain times as these, when there are consecutive bad harvests throughout the country. Also, she is eating from the floor because, in spite of her grief or owing to it, she is starving. In her haste, she has swallowed a bit of the bowl itself, a hard and tiny crumb, so the bowl will never be whole again, even if all of the pieces are carefully put back together. Fresh rushes are spread on the floor, and somehow she has chewed a bit of them, too. There's the taste of grass in her mouth, along with everything else she has gulped down already.

The room has turned sideways. It takes her a moment to understand why, until she pins down the source of her pain: her ear, her left ear, is inside her father's fist. He's pulling it, dragging that tender scrap of flesh until she's sure all the tiny bones inside must be squeezed to a useless mush, like the pottage she's spilled. If ever he lets her go, she will probably be deaf on the one side, which she wouldn't mind, not so much, because he is always shouting and usually at her.

From this position, as her father is trying to separate her ear from her head and she is nearly weeping with pain, she can see the rest of her family at the table: her three brothers, Jacquemin, Jean, and Pierre; her sister, Catherine; her mother, Isabelle Romée. She knows, from experience, that she won't get any help from them. Standing up to Jacques d'Arc and saying, "It's just a bowl and a bit of stew and your daughter a child," throwing yourself between his fists and the small person he is beating, these will only prolong the episode. And there will be more black-and-blue eyes to go around, more swollen heads and bruised hips to rub and moan over the next morning. Let no one say the family of Jacques d'Arc does not learn from its mistakes. Better to sit still and pretend the beating is happening somewhere far, far away, to just wait it out and hum a pleasant song in your head to drown out the cries while you finish your supper—and keep your bowl on the table.

When he releases her, the room spins about Joan's head, and she trips, arms flapping, into the closest wall. Her ear is hot to the touch; it feels as if he's set the whole side of her head on fire with a candle. She can't tell if that ear is still working, but she can hear her father's shouting. He's taken a page from the Maxey captain's book of insults and is calling her names: little bitch, mangy cur, thankless, whining pup that should be put in a sack and drowned in the nearest stream, if only he had a sack big enough to stuff her body in. Why are all of these images about dogs, she wonders. Doesn't he know that dogs are God's best gift to man? Her own dog, a muddy stray she found shaking and wet under a bush one morning, is her closest friend. She's named the dog Salaud, or "Bastard." It isn't meant to be an insult. To her, the name signals their closeness, that the two of them are of the same stock: unwanted, the wretches of the world, easy to kick around.

Near the door, Salaud is barking. She wills him, with every taut and leaping nerve in her body, to please, please shut up, or there's every chance Jacques d'Arc will take a knife from the table, stamp across the room, and slit his throat.

But, happily, Salaud will live another day. Her father is still swatting at her head, like it's a fly he's trying to smudge out of existence, and the most she can do is cover her face with her arms to dampen the blows.

Tomorrow, there will be bruises. She can feel them already, planted beneath the film of her skin and primed to sprout blooms of indigo and cornflower blue. He takes a swipe at her chin, and the punch knocks her, as she hopes, straight into the door. He lunges, charging like a whole mountain range on legs. But she quick-steps around the door—she is in such a rush to leave that she almost rolls into the fresh air—and her dog slips out between her feet, as though they had planned this escape together. She doesn't stop, not for anything, not even to crow in triumph. Though her jaw feels loose (possibly it is broken), she's giggling over her shoulder, spit dribbling down the length of her chin as she runs, and Salaud catches up in a few bounds. He's nipping at her shoes, as if it were all a game and he's annoyed that until now, he's been left out of the excitement. She looks down, he looks up, and without pausing, she ruffles the mud-colored fur sticking up on his head. Behind them, a trail of dust rises up as dense as a layer of fog. When they reach the dirt road that winds through the village, Joan lets out a whoop, a victorious wolf-cry, and her dog's tongue flaps out, like a flesh-pink flag heralding their tiny victory. If these are not moments to live for, she wonders, then what are? For the moment, she has forgotten about Guillaume, about the dress her sister washed for her, which, when it was rinsed, leaked blood and stained Catherine's palms as if she had been eating fresh berries. Her body is throbbing with pain, but she is never more alive than when she slips like an eel out of Jacques d'Arc's grasp.

◆

SHE DOESN'T STOP RUNNING until Hauviette's cottage, at the other end of Domrémy, is in sight. Hauviette is always laughing, always bright like a moving sunbeam. Like Joan, ten years of age. Unlike Joan, who is serious, with an angular jawline, and constantly grinding her teeth, she is marked by the village as a beauty. She is auburn-haired and hazel-eyed, a child made in the glorious colors of autumn.

It is almost worth it—the ear mashing, the hair pulling, the backhand slap of the mouth—if this is what is waiting for you at the other end: Hauviette's mother, Jehanne, smoothing your hair and rubbing your shoulder, calling you poor lamb, poor babe, her breath sweet as fennel, her dress giving off the scent of crushed herbs; Hauviette herself, giggling, treating the visit like a happy distraction and cleaning the crescent-shaped cut on your hand, where a piece of the bowl managed to slice through your skin, a little too enthusiastically; Salaud, who snuck in before the door could shut him out, and who has fallen asleep beneath the table, snoring; and your own heart quickening, for once, not from dread of new pain about to be visited upon your body but something else—from goodness, from the shock of charity and kindness.

Not that this is anything new. Jehanne and Hauviette are used to her visits. They have an old strip of linen—called Joan's linen—set aside for her wounds. They have a bowl—called Joan's bowl—to wash her face of blood so they can see just what Jacques has done to her this time.

What surprises her is that they don't mention Guillaume. She expects they will want her to relate to them what she witnessed, though she can't remember much about the fight itself, only the boy's dying moments, which are vivid. But they are quiet. They don't speak except to make comforting noises as they fuss over cuts and her badly knotted hair. Jehanne says, when the silence stretches on, "I thank God and His angels nothing happened to you, Joan." And it thrills her that there are people in the world, though few in number, who care that she is alive and would feel an absence, even an ache, were she to fall ill or be found dead.

For her, Guillaume's death is like a scrape or a bruise. Touch it, and it will hurt. So, she doesn't touch the memory; she tries not to think about what happened, because thinking makes her stomach churn and she knows she needs to hold down her food. One should never waste food. Yet every time she closes her eyes, the sight returns. Sunlight pools across the dead boy's cheeks like melted gold, and when the light dims, his face is white as polished bone. She imagines words the boy never said. She reaches into her pocket and pricks her finger against the sharp edge of Guillaume's rock.

Before she leaves, for she must eventually leave, she is slipped two pieces of dark bread. Salaud follows her out into the night, his small rib cage pushing against her ankle.

Someone is standing in the lane, waiting for them not far from the cottage door. A glimpse tells her it's Catherine. In a village this small, it is hard not to be a creature of habit. Her sister knows where she would run to for help.

When she takes Catherine's hand, the joints of her sister's fingers are stiff from cold. How long has she been standing here? It is summer, but the nights when the skies are starless and black as pitch can still make one shiver.

Tonight, there is a moon, like a perfect Eucharist wafer, pressed into the sky. It seems almost reachable, as though if you stuck your tongue out far enough, you might taste the body of Christ in the air. What would He taste like? Joan guesses: whatever the opposite of pottage is, that boiled, viscous mush, sometimes brown, sometimes gray, that makes up nearly every meal. Whatever the opposite of dry black bread and curdling milk is. She has heard, from her uncle Durand, of a spice called cinnamon. He says no one knows where cinnamon comes from. But a merchant once told him there is a creature—adept, despite its great size, at hiding itself—called the cinnamon bird that builds its nests from cinnamon sticks. People have disappeared off the face of the earth trying to follow these birds. The cinnamon the merchant sells passes through many hands, nameless and secret, before it finally comes to him, and there is never a great quantity to be sold; he must fight and argue for the honor of transporting it and showing it off among his wares. So, Joan thinks, perhaps the body of Christ has the flavor of this spice, rare and desired among men: of cinnamon.

They can't go home, at least not tonight. This is understood between them, for if she is a fugitive, flying from her father's justice, then Catherine, too, has betrayed him by slipping out in the darkness to find her.

Instead they walk, silent, to their usual spot, beneath the great tree of Domrémy, known in the village as the Faerie Tree. The elders say tiny winged creatures live in the branches, and they may do mischief or they may grant wishes, depending on their mood, which one should never take for granted.

Joan settles against Catherine's body, exhales, and recalls the two pieces of bread Jehanne gave her. She offers one to her sister, who shakes her head, so Salaud gets both.

Catherine, third-born of Jacques d'Arc and Isabelle Romée, will turn thirteen later this year. She is the only beautiful one in the family; others in Domrémy say Joan and her brothers are nothing to look at, and Joan, in this instance, is inclined to agree. Catherine is so beautiful, even their father, who people say could knock Satan on his back in a fair fight, won't dare to hit her face, for fear of misshaping her nose or chipping a tooth. Just like cinnamon, how did Catherine come into this world? No one can tell, not with parents such as theirs. It seems both a lucky and an unlucky accident: lucky for Jacques and Isabelle, unlucky for Catherine. If she were a noblewoman, knights would compose verses to honor her; they would bankrupt their households buying chests of rubies and gold for a glimpse of her enigmatic smile and white neck.

Yet it is her goodness, not her beauty, that makes Joan love her. How long would Catherine have stood alone in the lane, if Joan had not left Hauviette's cottage when she did? How many times have they sat, just so, beneath the Faerie Tree, Catherine's arms draped around Joan's shoulders to warm her, as they waited for sleep to come or for first light to dawn?

As for Joan, no one in the whole village wonders from whom she springs. First to be thrashed and beaten by Jacques d'Arc when he is in a bad temper, she is also her father's daughter: ugly, dark-eyed, large. Put them side by side, and her unwieldy shoulders are simply a miniature of his, her thick ankles a girlish copy of his ox-bull legs. They are alike in other ways, too: always thinking, aware of what is happening, what has just happened, and what might happen next. They are constantly ready for a quarrel and a challenge.

The truth is Jacques d'Arc has done well for himself. He's not a native of Domrémy but moved here to marry her mother, a woman of property, whose uncle was the prior of a monastery—this impressed him. His house, which he owns, is the only one built of stone in the entire village. It is whitewashed and square, with a sloping roof, and located next to the church, which may be an accident or may be intentional; she can imagine her father saying, See my house, it is second only to God's in importance. He owns nearly fifty acres altogether: cropland, pastureland, land in the woods known as the Bois Chenu, where he charges others in the village a hefty price for allowing their pigs to forage. In every delegation sent to speak with town officials from nearby Vaucouleurs, he is at the head and ready with his speech. Though he can't read or write or properly hold a pen, he is a natural negotiator, an easy talker. He's not like some who bow their heads and direct their words at their shoes. He will look his betters in the eye. He has a brain for figures, a cleverness with money, which has caused many to speculate how much he has saved over the years. Most say it must be at least two or three hundred livres, possibly four, though his friends, of whom he has several, claim it is nearly a thousand. He is an expert at what he knows and has an instinct for his work: the crops, their rotation, the quality of soil, how to use the earth without exhausting it, how to portion out acres for pasture so that one's oxen don't keel over from hunger in the wintertime. It is impossible to cheat him. Try, and he will give you a fist of reasons not to do it again.

He is a hard father to his sons and demands that they—Jacquemin, Jean, and Pierre—work as much and with the same vigor as he does.

But he is harder still on Joan. There is a rumor that in the month before she was born, Jacques d'Arc lost his wits in a way that was unusual for him. Drinking with friends and neighbors, he boasted the child to come would be another son. Catherine, though pretty, was a fluke, he claimed. He could have only sons, and this next one would be strong as Saint Christopher. Someone, whose name is now lost in the telling, took him up on the promise, and, at her father's insistence, a not-insignificant sum of money was laid down as a wager. A pledge was made that, upon the child's birth, Jacques would bring it, whatever *it* was, to be shown to everyone.

Joan arrived. Imagine his dismay at this red-faced, kicking infant. A girl. For an hour after her birth, he walked around baffled, as if God had forsaken him.

"What a set of lungs," the man who won the bet said to him good-naturedly before he took Jacques's money.

"What fists! Look how she beats the air as if she hates it," another added.

It quickly became a game. "What eyes, as beautiful as her father's," an old man cooed nearby. "What feet, or are those hooves?" others called. "What hair as black as devil's spit." "What arms as thick as the mooring rope for ships."

And all the while, she was passed among the hands of the drinkers to be peered at like she was some oddity. But they were gentle with her; they knew how Jacques d'Arc held grudges, how he'd never forget either the money he had lost this night or this early betrayal, the blow Joan had, as a babe, already dealt his pride.

Then someone who'd drunk too much of her father's ale, who slurred his words and could barely stand up without slouching right down again, shouted, "You haven't really lost, Jacques. She's a little bull, she is. Just the bull is a girl."

His friends told the man to shut his mouth or they would shut it for him. But no one denied it. "Is there a female equivalent of Saint Christopher?" one man asked, genuinely curious. She, Joan, was a healthy child—and strong. Just a pity she wasn't a boy. Even Jacquemin, when they cast their minds back, had really been a beanpole of an infant, hadn't he? And Jean a stubby mite of a thing.

Now Joan wonders if every time her father looks at her, he thinks of the money he lost. How much was the bet, she wants to know. Two livres? Three? Though it's probably not about money in the end. It's about Jacques d'Arc being made to appear the fool. It's about losing, which a man as proud as he is never likes to do. It's about the definition of children being sons.

Above the Faerie Tree, Joan hears the susurration of wings, and a bird glides like a restless piece of night that won't settle against the sky. She thinks of Guillaume. The soul is supposed to take flight when the body expires, only this, she has recently learned, isn't in fact true. The soul doesn't rise but, rather, sinks to a place called Purgatory, where the sins committed on earth are atoned for, and the soul is cleansed in purifying flames, both hot and cold. Guillaume is there now. She pictures him crouched in a cave, the floor engulfed in blue-and-white fire, all alone.

Though what has Guillaume done to deserve this? The priest of Domrémy claims even love can be a sin. If you love something too much, if you feel you can never part with it—say, money, or jewels, or your cat—this is also wrong. Everything in the world is merely temporal. Only God endures. Your greatest passion must be for Him alone.

She has been instructed by the priest, by Catherine and her mother, that the prayers of the living can alleviate the suffering of those whose souls must dwell for a time in Purgatory. So, she decides she will pray for Guillaume. She will pray for him at least once every day. And she will do more than pray. She will sneak a bowl of milk and a piece of cheese from the cupboard for the cat who has lost his master and friend.

Soon, the dead boy's body will be rolled into a white shroud. It will be placed on a bier of wood, the only covering a black pall. His final resting place is a plot in a churchyard. But death is not the end. There is the matter of reparation, of costing out the total price of his family's loss against his value, both real and projected: the man Guillaume would have become, the labor he would have performed, the wife he would have married, the children he would have had, the litter of cats he would have raised. She imagines each limb of the boy being measured, each hand and foot weighed, his naked body, now washed and clean, searched for disfigurements or scars. She sees, with her mind's eye, numbers being scratched across a vellum scroll, then added, several calculations checked and cross-checked. The result may be something like this: for each ankle, two chickens; each thigh, a pig; for his arms, which when grown would have worked his family's land, an ox; for his head and his heart, a horse of good age and a shiny new plow.

But how is love weighed? She has heard Guillaume was born late to his parents and there is a difference of seven years between his elder sister and the son they wished for. From her pocket, she pulls out the smooth rock and runs her thumb along the edge. It is so dark she cannot see her own hand, but the rock is there. She feels it, how light it is in her palm. What has happened makes her sad. Not for the first time today, she is in danger of crying, when she thinks how what is warm and good isn't enough to save a boy's life—not a father's protection or a mother's tenderness—but beatings, a body hardened to pain, the ease with which one rolls a stick, like a club, into one's hand and is willing to hurt another, might. Love, possibly, isn't enough either, not in this world where nearly all the stories she hears from her uncle are about wars both past and present. Who has lost. Who has won. Who is maimed and how many are dead. She makes a promise, whispers it into the dark, imprinting it in the night sky as the boy's face is imprinted in her memory. The promise is this: If she, Joan, has a choice, then she will choose to be a thrower of rocks. She will live.

III

♦ ♦ ♦

THERE IS A JOKE IN THE VILLAGE: that Joan is welcome to rest at every hearth in Domrémy except her own; that Jacques d'Arc lives in the best house, a house built of stone, but one can count on one's fingers the number of days in a year Joan sleeps under his roof.

There is always something to do in a village, and Joan's day begins when her chores are finished. Then she is out the door before anyone (her father) can catch her. She will help load a cart bound for market, even if she barely knows the cart driver. She will coddle babies for the half hour that their mothers need to run an errand or rest their eyes. If she sees a hole in a cottage, she will gather sticks for mending it. She will slap on clay over the twigs, and the hole will be gone.

Some villagers find it amusing to guess where Joan will appear next, her shabby dog trailing her everywhere she goes. They'll hear the bells ringing for Vespers or Compline, and they'll chuckle and ask whoever is standing nearby, "Is that Joan banging away? Sounds like it."

Last autumn, she had followed a group of farmers bound for the Bois Chenu, the woods in which her father owned land.

"What are you going to do there?" she asked when they noticed her trailing behind them.

They looked at one another, and the youngest of them answered her roughly, "You think you're a little lordling, don't you? Who are you to be asking us questions about what we are doing?" But his friend touched his arm and said, "Calm yourself. What are you getting so angry about? She is only curious and bored." And, turning to her, he said, "Well, sweetheart, we have made a deal with your father, Jacques.

He has given us permission to take our pigs into the woods and let them forage on acorns, and we have paid him for the right."

She listened, nodding, and waited for them to lead the way. The men continued, every so often looking back to see if she was still following them. When they arrived in the woods, the farmers let their pigs loose to forage. But it wasn't long before they saw they had been cheated. The trees were mostly bare, and there were hardly any acorns left for the pigs.

The farmers crossed to a thin post, a wooden marker Jacques d'Arc had tied with a piece of string, and said to Joan, "We were told we cannot go beyond this boundary."

They were angry and grumbling, ready to turn back and make their complaints directly to her father, when Joan picked up the post, kicked the dirt over the hole to obscure where it had been, and moved it deeper into the woods, just beyond a patch of trees thick and heavy with acorns. She did this partly to help the men Jacques had cheated—and partly because she just wanted to make her father angry.

Gaping, the farmers followed her and watched her climb the nearest tree and shake the branches. Acorns showered their heads. The next tree she climbed with one hand, the other holding a long stick she had broken off a fallen trunk. She began to beat the branches with the stick, and even more acorns rained down on the pigs, who were no longer jostling one another, now that there was enough food to go around. The pigs moved from tree to tree, trailing Joan, and the men even began to tease her, pointing at a particular acorn hanging at the far end of a limb and saying, "That one! We want that one!" They did this until they felt they had gotten their money's worth and called her to come down before she broke her neck; they said not even a lizard could be more agile than she was.

Her father heard what happened, not from Joan—she would not be so stupid as to tell him—but from a loudmouthed neighbor. When she stood in front of him to account for what she'd done, Jacques stared curiously at her. Had this child been sent solely to torment him? To unravel all his tricks so that no scheme of his could be realized again?

Before he beat her, he told Joan she had ruined his plan. Didn't she know he had wanted to cheat those farmers, his neighbors, for reasons of his own? No, she didn't know, but what reasons did he have, she asked him, before the first slap landed and she saw stars.

The next day, the farmers found out where she was, which wasn't, of course, at home. She was up a tree again, and they had to shout at her to come down so they could properly thank her. They each shook her hand, even the man who had called her a little lordling, and saw her arms were raw with welts, which made them pity her more. They had brought her a little reward, a few scraps of meat, to share with her dog.

This is only one story about Joan. Others in Domrémy have seen her sit in a field that doesn't belong to her father, where she has settled and not moved for a whole hour, thinking or dreaming whatever it is a young girl dreams, until the owner of the field made his appearance and asked what she was doing on his property, staring like a simpleton at the clouds. She has pushed boys into a stream for capturing songbirds from bushes and torturing them and been heard talking to her dog, to the Faerie Tree, to a beetle on a leaf. Once, someone spotted her with her head in the water and shouted, "What, are you trying to drown yourself, Joan?" and she came bubbling up, a silver fish leaping and wriggling from her hands.

Today, the morning after the boys' battle with Maxey, she is keeping busy. The bruises from the previous night are coming up, and it is startling how effective pain is at keeping the memory of death at bay. Also, the sun is out. The day is clear. It surprises her that the weather is not in mourning, that people are already moving about, though some small groups of men and women huddle together, whispering and talking behind their hands. She hears babies crying. Mothers scolding young children. Men shouting at oxen and mules. The only place not full of noise is the place where death has already visited. Some believe what happened was an accident; others think Guillaume was targeted, being the smallest boy. But the fact remains, she hears someone say, that he is dead, and money should be paid. Even if it was a tussle between children—Oh, is that what it was, Joan thinks, the throwing of rocks, the kicking and stamping of ankles, stomachs, and ribs—and he tripped and fell and hit his head on a stone, well, he must first have been pushed, or he was frightened and stumbled. He was not a violent boy, but violent or no, the result is the same. He is gone.

It does no good to weep or to mope, and it is always wise to keep out of her father's sight. So, she carries grain to the mill for one of her godmothers, each arm wrapped around a bulging sack. She has so many godparents she has lost count. Another joke: Joan will put Domrémy's miller out of a job because she is stronger than he is and less of a cheat. The miller has heard the joke and doesn't find it amusing.

She stops by Hauviette's cottage and helps Jehanne clean while Hauviette makes chains out of flowers and sings. Outside the dead boy's door, she feeds crusts she's saved to the mewling cat, and then moves on, looking for something else to occupy her time. A few people will give her a penny for the services she renders them, even if they haven't asked for her help. Others pat her shoulder or head. Still others offer food: a cup of fresh milk, which she finishes in one gulp, not wasting a drop, a few pieces of black bread, a bowl of warm pottage, or vegetables to take home to her sister and mother. She has returned with onions, heads of cabbage, and fistfuls of herbs: lovage, sage, and thyme. Sometimes, she is full enough that she doesn't need any supper. Her father is always complaining that she is a parasite who will eat him out of house and home, but this isn't true. Mostly she eats one meal, her dinner, at the expense of Jacques d'Arc; the rest she forages on her own.

The blacksmith lets Joan watch him work. She sits on a barrel near the fire, but not too close, as he hammers out horseshoes and oxshoes and nails. He usually gives her little jobs, like passing him a tool from his worktable or fetching a cup of water or patting down his forehead with a damp cloth when sweat drips into his eyes. The range of a blacksmith's work in Domrémy is limited, but occasionally there are more lucrative projects, such as when a plow needs mending or a housewife must order a new cauldron. This morning, he is in a good mood because he has received two commissions, so he lets Joan press the bellows. Smoke blows into her face. Sparks settle, like stars, on her dress, and the blacksmith swats them away with his huge hand. Like everyone else, he has heard what has happened. He asks gruffly, "You watched the boy die? Is this true?" She nods, and he passes her his hammer, points at a white-hot piece of metal on the anvil's edge, and instructs her to beat it. She takes the hammer greedily, which makes the blacksmith chuckle, and for the next few minutes, it's like all the feast days of Christendom and celebration rolled up into one. She beats and beats, feeling happy. It is rare that she has such an outlet for her energy. At first, the sound, piercing and brittle, seems to shake through her whole body. Her hand vibrates. But then she gets used to it. She doesn't know what she is making, and she doesn't care. She pauses, a little out of breath, sweat dribbling from the tip of her nose, and wonders if this is what her father feels when he hits her. If so, no wonder he enjoys it so much.

"The metal is already dead, Joan," the blacksmith says. Then he adds, "Though that is what I'd do to a Burgundian, if any from Maxey or elsewhere should dare to come here." He is no longer smiling. When she leaves him, he drops two nails into her hands. They are still warm. She looks down, asks him what she should do with them.

"There is always some use for nails," he says. "But don't let your father know you have them or that I gave them to you."

She nods, pocketing the gift. They are both serious, and this transaction is solemn. Her father, if he knew, would probably crucify her.

People talk about why Jacques d'Arc has a special dislike for his second daughter, as if the words "second daughter" did not already provide the answer they were looking for. She, Joan, also wonders, and has come up with an explanation beyond the lost bet and her girlhood. She thinks it is because he doesn't know what to do with her. His sons, Jacquemin and Jean and even Pierre, who, at six, is younger than she is, can be put to use. Catherine, he plans to marry well. If he is smart, he may be able to make a profit out of his eldest daughter's marriage, and what is marriage really, in the mind of Jacques d'Arc, but a business transaction, a chance for acquiring further capital and property? What, however, can he do about Joan?

What can he do with this girl-child, who is as strong as a young bull but slippery like a shoal of minnows? When she runs, as she does now, not because anyone is chasing her but simply for her own amusement, the nails in her pockets rattle like little invisible bells. Her single braid is the tail of a black cat whisking around a tree, a bend in the lane, a corner. In Domrémy, it is common for people to say, "I thought I saw her, Joan, just there—standing in a stream, coming in, going out, up on So-and-so's roof, hanging off a branch—not a moment ago. Is she still there now?" Yet by the time they look, she is already gone. Unless she falls into dreaming, she will never sit for long in any place. She is not quiet. Often she will shout at her brothers or at other boys standing in her way, and her voice sends sparrows flying from treetops. After beatings, she stands up and runs, returns bruised but intact hours later, and she is still capable of laughter, of mischief. Some grown men shake—actually shake!—when Jacques d'Arc crosses their path, and even his sons will lower their eyes as soon as he enters a room. But not a slap or a shove will take the glint out of Joan's eye, the eye that looks her father up and down, as if to say, *Strong but getting on a bit. Not worth the asking price.* "Tell me," Jacques d'Arc has said to his friends, "what does one do with a daughter like that? Unless she changes, and she is not likely to change, no man will put up with such a woman—so then, is it possible she will have to become a nun? But what convent will take her?" His mind is already calculating; he will probably have to bribe them. Joan has overheard this conversation and doesn't find it funny. She rubs the space between Salaud's eyes, and he licks her hand. She will not go anyplace where they don't have trees for her to climb. She will not set foot in a house, even if it is a house of God, that doesn't welcome dogs.

IV

◆ ◆ ◆

A NEW MORNING, and her head is itching, as if it were on fire. She and Salaud make a good pair, scratching and yelping whenever they pick at a spot too hard. He has fleas. She has—Catherine takes one look and makes a face at her. "Oh, Joan," Catherine murmurs. Joan's ailment is common enough, even among the crowned heads of princes. It is lice.

Catherine leads her sister to a stool and instructs her to sit and keep still, while she picks out the white flecks, like snow, and their mother runs to Jehanne for an ointment. Joan could almost take delight in it, the way Catherine wriggles and squeals every few moments. "They have feet! They actually have feet!" she cries. And it is all Joan can do not to giggle at the tiny dance Catherine does with her own well-shaped feet around the stool. But it is taking too long, and she has lost track of how many strands Catherine has already sifted through. "Don't we have a pair of shears?" she finally asks, and when the shears are produced, she says, "Just cut it. Won't it be easier?" "But your hair," Catherine protests. "It's your hair!" So Joan grabs a fistful and cuts off a generous amount to show her sister what she means. A dramatic gesture; perhaps she does not need to cut quite so much at once, but it is done, and now the rest of her head must also be shorn. A fire is built to burn her lice-infested hair. This is not the first time she or another member of the family has had this problem, but she pledges: From now on, I will wear my hair short.

Across the room, three heads peep around the doorway, and from a distance they consider safe, her brothers watch. They smile at the sight of Joan, arms crossed, wincing when the tip of the shears brushes too close to her scalp.

She casts what she hopes is her most deadly look at them, but this just makes Jacquemin cling to the wall so he doesn't fall over laughing.

"Go on, laugh," she says. "When Catherine is done, I shall come for you."

"Just be glad it is not a tooth worm, Joan," Catherine says. "Or an ear worm." And she wiggles a finger next to Joan's ear, while Joan tries not to smile, to keep her expression angry.

When their mother returns, she stares open-mouthed at her youngest daughter. "You look like a boy!" she shouts. But it is too late. Joan shrugs. A foul-smelling liquid is rubbed into her scalp to drown the remaining lice. She pinches her nose, gags, makes a choking noise.

The sound of choking reminds her of death, of Guillaume. Her head, now shorn of hair, is closer to Guillaume's head. Yesterday, the boy was buried, and she believes she can smell his blood in the air, though this is probably of her own imagining.

Outside, her brothers are waiting to prance around her and pull more faces. She lets them. None of them were friends with Guillaume, and what her father thinks, they think, too. The boy was weak. He should have taken better care to defend himself. He should have fought. She has not told them about the unthrown rocks. She does not want to shame a person after he is already dead. But in the hour before supper, she had heard a sniveling sound, like a mouse scratching the wall, coming from the next room. She had seen Jacquemin alone and crying into his fists. When he'd caught her staring, he had told her to get out. So, they did not talk anymore about it. But he must have recovered, because now he is jumping and smirking: his usual self.

On Jacquemin's forehead, there is a bump the size of a small egg, smooth and pink, from when he butted skulls with the Maxey captain. If this is what Jacquemin walked away with, she'd like to see the welt on the other boy's face. Jacquemin has a hard skull, filled, she thinks, with rocks. The three boys sidle up to her and jostle her; they ask if she has lately eaten figs and sweetmeats, which are known to be the cause of lice; they touch the remaining stubs of her hair and pretend it stings their fingers. When they say she was ugly before but now she could be an ogre's wife, she no longer scowls at them. She doesn't pummel them with her fists or kick her feet like a bucking horse but shoves each of her brothers aside to make her way past them. When she does, her touch is uncommonly gentle. Though she will never admit it, she doesn't want any of them to trip and fall and crack their skulls. She doesn't want any of them to end up like the boy who is now dead.

◆

Death, war, hatred of Burgundians—these are all temporarily forgotten. People gawp at a new Joan making her rounds of Domrémy. When she shows up at the church to sweep the floor, the priest stares. His face twitches. He is calling on the strength of the archangels, the minor angels, the saints, the many-faced cherubim and the many-winged seraphim, on Christ and the Holy Virgin, and the saved residing in the valleys and gardens of Paradise, to keep him from laughing. So, his face continues to twitch, and at one point, he covers his mouth with both hands and coughs, as if he is trying to smother himself.

Hauviette has heard of her misfortune. She arrives armed with a chain of snow-white daisies, which she throws with a giggle over Joan's bowed head, ready to receive the benediction. "There," Hauviette says. "Better now?"

The blacksmith says to her, not quite laughing, but not trying to hide his smile either, "If I had the material to spare, I could make you a helmet."

The blacksmith is her friend, but Joan still glares at him. Beneath the soot and grime of his face, he turns pink. He passes her a hammer: a silent apology. She takes it, and his giant finger points at a pair of horseshoes. No words are necessary. She thinks of water that turns red, blood that when dried feels like a second layer of skin on one's hands. The body buried. How everything, one's limbs, one's bones, one's blood, returns eventually to the earth, to nothing. She thinks if one's skull is soft, better to wear a helmet.

Her arm is strong, never sore or tired. She beats.

◆

It is already past the hour of Vespers, eventide, but these summer days are long, and the light does not go without a fight. The sky is splattered blood orange and blue and violet and, in certain parts, a crisp leaf green.

She sees these colors through a perfect square, an unshuttered window, not in her own home but Guillaume's. The women have gathered here to console, to pray, but mostly to commiserate. They are more serious than the blacksmith and the priest. They look at her, noting the rough terrain of her head; with sharp eyes, they take in her dress, which has lately been washed, as if to search for traces of blood. There are none. Catherine is thorough.

Something has happened, which is why the women are gathered here in Guillaume's cramped cottage while the men sit in Jacques d'Arc's house of white stone. In Maxey, a demand for reparation was made and turned down. Not only dismissed but thrown back in the face of Domrémy's men: among them, the father of Guillaume; among them, Jacques d'Arc.

Guillaume's mother, who has always looked old and tired, looks older and more tired. Joan scoops up Guillaume's cat, and Salaud, at her feet, instantly begins to fuss. When the women stare at her, as if to say, *Christ, Joan, who cares about the cat,* she turns away from them. The women shift their focus back to one another, but Joan gazes out. Her vision is filled with the changing colors of the sky.

The truth is, she doesn't have the heart to face these women, still in the throes of grieving. Not that they are crying. None of them, not Guillaume's sister or grandmother or any of the rest of the women, are crying. They are whispering among themselves, and whatever language they speak is as incomprehensible to Joan as the rustling of wings, the murmur of a breeze.

She knows this is her mother's natural tongue: the speech of suffering, the patois of prayer and commiseration, of one human being imparting to another these questionable words of comfort—all affliction comes of God. It is Christ's grand design, like a scattering of seeds. Every forest, lane, and village, every town and city and unswept alley of the kingdom, her mother has explained to her, is covered in such seeds of misery, so the only thing to do is to learn to accept the pain. Accept and submit to God's will, whatever you lose.

She, Joan, doesn't speak this language. What's more, she does not want to learn. She pushes her bruised face into the fur of Guillaume's cat, which, she discovered after asking the dead boy's sister, has no name, has never been given one. So, Joan is turning her mind over, trying to think of a good name.

She tries to copy Guillaume: flip the cat on its back and cradle the animal like a baby, because she does not want to be here among these women, quiet though they are in pain, and who exchange prayers for things impossible to put into words with the ease of swapping recipes. The cat is soft in her arms. It mewls, and the cry is like a human cry. Some sounds one does not hear so much as feel, and she feels this cry in her heart.

The cat gives her a slow feline blink; its gray-green eyes look watery, or maybe that's just a trick of the light. But she would rather believe that animals, too, are capable of grief, of memory and therefore of remembering better days. I know, she thinks. She wants to whisper this into the cat's ear. I am not your master, though I would happily be your friend. And you miss the boy you used to see every day. You miss being called by your name, for I am sure he gave you a name, even if no one knows or remembers it now. Well, I shall try to think of one, and I won't give you a bad word for a name, like I did my poor Salaud.

She sets the cat down. She inches slowly along the wall, though she doesn't have to. No one pays any attention to her, not even Hauviette or Catherine, who are huddled around Guillaume's sister.

She slips out and, crossing the lane, decides to spin back toward her own house like the funnel-shaped storms she has heard about that can splinter church steeples and halve great oaks. By the time she reaches her threshold, she is dizzy and light-headed. Anything to try to forget. Anything to dispel the ache death has left behind. The pain she feels is dull, not bright and fresh like a cut. She squats down. The men have left the door open so a cooling wind can enter, and she can hear movement within. A glance, and she counts six of them, not including the priest, who no one really wants there, for he is standing on one side of the table while the others are crowded together at the opposite end. Still, even Jacques d'Arc draws the line at throwing out clergymen.

The men are restless. They are making fists and unmaking them; they are rubbing their faces, kneading their thighs as they sit, and some cannot remain sitting for long; they push back their chairs, just short of kicking the furniture, because it is Jacques d'Arc's furniture, and pace up and down the room. Luckily, someone has had the sense to remove, from the tabletop, the pair of shears used to cut Joan's hair this morning. Her father's friends look angry enough to stab anything, even themselves.

"Well?" Jacques is first to speak. This is all he has to say. He does not need to add, We need a plan; he does not have to explain, All my plans are schemes, traps, tricks, and snares, and I have a few in mind already, so which shall we try out first?

When no one answers, he offers, as if it were a bowl of delicious stew, "Or shall we attack?" He adds, "This is now a matter for men, not boys."

The priest throws up his hands. "Wait, wait . . . This is what I feared. We cannot . . ." He stumbles, then speaks slowly, as if he is addressing children: "We must take this matter to the nearest court . . ."

Her father is ready for this. It is as if the priest is in a play and does not know that he has just performed his part to perfection. "What?" her father answers him. "Court? This has gone beyond the court. We'll find no justice there."

The priest flushes with anger. "The Lord says, If anyone insults you, does you injury, assaults your honor—"

"Yes?" her father cuts in. "I should turn a knife in his ribs, yes? I should beat his brains in? For this is *my* interpretation of what the Lord says."

A sound interrupts their argument: a third voice. For a moment, she thinks she has missed a woman in the room, because the voice is high-pitched. Then she realizes what she hears isn't words but a wailing.

The sound comes from Guillaume's father. He is cupping his narrow face with both hands, his jaw wedged open. It is painful to look at, the contorted expression, the tears large and wet and shining, and some of the men turn their own faces away, perhaps because they are embarrassed or they think it is shameful for a man to cry like this in front of other men, or at all. Even the priest lowers his head to mutter a swift prayer, willing the scene to end.

Only her father doesn't turn away. He rises from his chair and stands in front of Guillaume's father. He grips the man's shoulder. And when his friend cries harder, each sob a strangled, throaty gurgle, Jacques's grip tightens, until she is sure he will snap his entire shoulder off like a piece of dried crust. He is staring at him, as if to sear a message into the man's soul. She feels she will never forget this moment. In the hand that rests on the man's shoulder, her father has planted a promise; it is a promise the priest cannot hear. We will avenge your son. We will make sure he has not died for nothing. Yet no words are spoken aloud; none are necessary.

Whatever Jacques does, it seems to work. Guillaume's father straightens. He stops crying. Someone passes him a cup of water, which he drinks, and he wipes his leaking nose with his sleeve.

The priest has been outshone, though this is generally what happens when Jacques d'Arc enters a room.

She rubs the ear so recently clutched in his fist. But, she thinks, he's still a brute.

"It is . . . a symptom of these times," the priest says uselessly. "This tragedy . . ."

Whatever has passed between her father and Guillaume's father has tired Jacques out. She watches him return to his place at the head of the table to sit. He rubs his face. He leans forward, and his voice when he begins is softer than before. "When I was young, a mere child . . ." The men collectively chuckle. "Yes, I, too, was once a child," he says, nodding to his audience and sympathizing with their disbelief, as Joan listens on the doorstep. She has never heard her father talk about his youth.

"My grandfather lived to a hundred, God love him. And he was kinder to me than my own father. He would take me often upon his back, and while he worked, he would sing songs he'd heard. He possessed an excellent memory. Recite him a poem, a ballad, and he could repeat it back to you without missing a single word. He told me about the glory days of France, the great battles and the warriors who fought in them, until the stories he told were as clear to me as visions. As a boy, would you believe it, I dreamed of Charles Martel, Prince of the Franks, until my father struck me a blow one morning when I would not wake and said, If you go on this way, Jacques, you shall have to beg your bread."

There is a murmur, and her father nods. He exhales, lacing his fingers together.

"I never tired of hearing these stories, and my grandfather never tired of telling them. How Charles Martel at Tours defeated an army of thirty thousand Saracens though he had only half their number. During the fighting, a rumor spread that the enemy camp was being plundered of its ill-gotten treasure by a separate force attacking from the rear. See how a rumor is like an arrow, only better. Once it is loosed, it multiplies in the ears of a hundred, a thousand, then ten thousand men. The fools believed what they heard. They turned their horses around, some in the middle of attacking, and were all cut down from behind. And then my grandfather would say to me, after the story had been told, he would say, Jacques, though these are the tales of great men and do not concern the likes of you or me or anyone else here, we live in the same land as Charles Martel, and yes, we may step, without knowing it, where he and his army did when we go about our work each morning. So stand up straight, boy, do not slouch or hang your head, and be glad of what you have, though it may be little. Be glad the earth you till is the same earth turned by the warhorses of the great French knights, for the ground you stand on, the very air you breathe is different because of what came before."

Jacques pauses. The men are quiet and solemn-faced. They are listening, waiting to see where her father will lead them with this story, and they are ready to be led. She, too, is listening so hard she is holding her breath.

"Then, seven years ago—hard to believe it is already seven years—I heard of Agincourt, that most terrible of battles. At first, it was a game of patience. The English waited three hours for the French to attack, and when there was still no charge, they changed position, replanted their stakes, and fired their arrows. The French knights had no choice. They charged. Though some say the charge came too soon, that the attack was disordered, and there were not enough men.

"The English King spared no one. When I was young, I had felt that the strength of France was the strength of us all. I did not think the descendants of Charles Martel could ever lose, not in this way. And then lose and lose again.

"But you know," he continues, "the harvest that year, poor though it may have been, was still brought in, and the groundwork laid for the next harvest, which, if I remember, was not half bad. And though my wife lost a child before it was born only two months after Agincourt, the following year, I was blessed . . ."

She nearly gives herself away, leaning into the doorway to catch, though it must be impossible—an admission of affection? But no, in her head, she counts backward. It is seven years since Agincourt, and she is already ten. The blessing is not her, Joan, but Pierre.

"We are none of us soldiers. We are none of us the descendants of Charles Martel. We are as far from the kings and princes of the realm as the fish that swim in the sea are to birds that fly," he says. "But we are still men. We are fathers and husbands. We are, some of us, landowners. And though it has been hard, though we live in a time of strife and war and our losses cannot compare with the losses of the kingdom, even we simple men cannot be expected to sit and scratch our heads and wonder what we should do when a child's life is taken from us unnaturally. If the boy had died from illness, if he did not eat the bread and drink the water that was placed before him and slowly faded, then we should feel only sorrow and pity for his parents. But how can I forget the lessons my grandfather hoped I would learn from his stories? How can I forget the duty we owe to the land we live on and to ourselves? Will we let our village take this mildly? Are we shameless enough to say, France has lost many battles of late, so let us also hide our faces and take this child's death in silence? Will the only expression of our grief come in the form of tears and howls and moans? Well, this may appease the priest's conscience. It will not appease mine."

The men are quiet. Though they say nothing, neither for nor against him, she knows her father has won. A lull follows in which she collects pebbles and drops them in lines in front of her. Here are the French. Here the English. She takes a fistful of grass, casts what she has grabbed over the French ranks. Here are the arrows unleashed by England's archers, by the deadly longbow, which is their specialty. On that island, they are all masters of this weapon. She has heard that on the day of Agincourt, the sky was stained black with arrows. And when they dropped, the ground turned white with feathers, the arrows' fletching; it was possible for a person to look about him on the field and imagine he stood ankle-deep in snow.

From her neck, Hauviette's chain of flowers snaps with ease. The head of each daisy floats over the pebbles and the strewn grass. And here is the flower of chivalry.

The meeting ends, but not before Jacques has treated his guests to cups of ale, so everyone can leave happy.

When he sees the men off, she is still squatting on the doorstep. As they pass her, most of them jump. No wonder. She is frightful to look at. Only the priest smiles. He thinks she is making a pretty portrait with flowers and rocks.

"Ah, I think I see a lady's face," he says, pausing to stare over her shoulder. "And you have decorated her hair with daisies."

When he is out of sight, Jacques emerges. His gaze slides down to where his daughter is, still nudging pebbles east and west, north and south. He, too, looks at what she is making, and for an instant, she registers what seems to pass for comprehension. Is that a battle? But if there is recognition, then it is a flash like a lion's eye behind a bush, there and then gone.

And to prove no understanding exists between them, that no such shared insight will ever bind them, not in this lifetime or the next, he strikes the rocks she has positioned with his foot. He stomps on each white daisy, twisting his heels in. Then he ambles away, a bounce in his step, without a word.

V

◆ ◆ ◆

SHE IS STILL CROUCHING, peering at the destruction left in her father's wake, when the tip of a shiny boot carefully inserts itself into the circle of her Agincourt. The boot does not belong to her father. It hovers over a crushed daisy, marveling at itself.

"I was walking this way," a voice says from above, bright as birdsong, and indeed, it is a voice that at any moment may burst into singing. "I saw your father's house, and I thought, He's really gone mad this time, poor Jacques, for he has installed at the door one of those stone demons that usually decorate the walls of cathedrals and abbeys to ward off evil spirits. They are called gargoyles, and I have seen ones with goat heads and horned devils curling their beards with a taloned finger. I have seen some with human faces grinning like idiots and others in mid-scream. But I have never in any of my travels seen a gargoyle quite like you."

She moves, and the movement is stonelike, a crouched statue, mossed over, finding its feet again. One leg has fallen asleep, so she rises unsteadily. Durand Laxart reaches out a hand to help her, but she is not really made of stone. To show she is flesh and blood, she throws her arms around her uncle's neck. She inhales the damp warmth of his shoulder and permits herself to be squeezed until she's out of breath with joy.

"I first took you for a statue," he says when she's done hugging, clinging, and burrowing her bristly head into his chest. "Then I said to myself, No, it is a boy. A poor begging boy moving from door to door because he is hungry for a crust of bread. Then when I came closer, I saw the boy was wearing skirts, and I rubbed my eyes with my fists to make sure the devil was not playing tricks on me. And then I saw it was you."

"Me," she says simply, grinning.

He puts off asking what has happened to her hair. That will come out later. Instead, he looks down at the wreckage of greenery at his feet.

"What have you done here?" he asks.

"It is Agincourt," she replies.

A pause. He studies the scene carefully: the spray of pebbles where Jacques d'Arc broke the French lines and, it seems, the English lines, too.

Her uncle nods and appears so solemn that even his expression darkens as he speaks: "I did not think you were there, Joan, on that cursed day, so terrible for the kingdom of France. But now—now I know better. You would have been only three years old, but you have captured what happened at Agincourt perfectly."

It is one of those things one should not really joke about. So many dead. The flower of French chivalry trampled into the mud. Seven years later, outrageous ransoms are still being paid by a bankrupted nobility.

Nonetheless, they are laughing.

◆

THEY WERE NOT ALWAYS such good friends. When she was a squalling babe, capable only of kicking up her heels and mashing her fists against her gums, her uncle had paid no heed to her. He shrank away whenever her mother or one of her godmothers hauled her, screaming, into the room. He had no children and neither envied nor aspired to the permanence of settling down. How could I face the same hearth, he said when people asked him why he did not marry, the same roof and dirt floor, the same sad cauldron and sad-faced wife, day in, day out? How could I go against my own nature and sleep for decades in the same rotting straw bed, infested with the same nest of ticks? So, he doesn't. Sometimes he does not sleep even two nights in the same place. The faces of his women are continually in flux. If they are ever sad, he is never around long enough to wipe away their tears.

This is how their friendship began: four years ago, when she was Pierre's age, she had shot out the front door like a dog about to be whipped just as Durand Laxart happened to be strolling in the direction of her father's house.

She ran hard, but her father possessed longer legs and was quickly closing the distance between them.

He saw her not so much running as tumbling to get away from Jacques d'Arc. Their eyes locked. Later, he would say he witnessed the precise moment when her fear turned to determination. She did not ask for his help. With one arch of her brow, one glance, she demanded it.

It was an instant of extraordinary beauty. When he recalls the memory, he can't help smiling. The leap, so perfect, into his arms, and he, seeing her pursuer did not stop, had no intention of stopping, and looked as if he might thrash him, too, turned his back to Jacques and sprinted away. She'd tucked her feet up, each small hand clutching a fistful of shirt, like the reins of a chariot, as she stared over his shoulder. Then, several panicked heartbeats later, a light voice in his ear, as calm as if she were Hannibal crossing the Alpine pass, she said cheerfully, "We are far enough. You can stop, Uncle."

He set her down, and they went to drink from a nearby stream. When the water touched their lips, cold and sparkling, it was as if to baptize a new union between them. He offered her a hand, wet and dripping, and she, smiling, still out of breath, took two of his fingers in her own, for that was all she could grip. She shook them, like a dog shaking a bone.

Now they are as two soldiers on an old campaign. The campaign is always the same: to avoid capture by the enemy; and the enemy is always Jacques d'Arc.

He'd taught her to swim. She remembered the day, a mild afternoon in springtime; the two were on the banks of the Meuse, and she edged away from the gently rippling water. "I can't," she said. "I just can't."

Back then she was afraid of anything that wasn't solid beneath her feet. But her uncle reached down and said to her, "My little dove is afraid, is she?" And she fell into his outstretched arms, realizing too late her error. The arms snapped closed behind her, and he dropped her, shrieking, into the water. But when she had stopped kicking, stopped flailing her arms like small whips, turning the water into a froth of white foam, she realized he was holding her up, her chin bobbing just above the surface. First, she learned to paddle like a dog. Later, to hold her breath underwater. Still later, to glide like a darting tadpole, a minnow with shining scales.

He taught her other things, too, after they became friends. He knew he shouldn't pick favorites, but he chose Joan and not her siblings because she was the quickest, the only one who would listen to an entire story carefully from beginning to end, even if she was skeptical. Because she would look at the sky and see that it did not terminate at the farthest cottage in Domrémy. Because she believed in cinnamon birds.

The world is a globe, he once told her. When formerly he had worked in the household of a lord, he met an astrologer, who was the oldest person he ever saw, and the astrologer showed him a book of the planets and the stars. "The planets are like people," the astrologer said. "Here is Saturn," and he pointed to a man with a scythe. "Can you believe it, Joan?" he'd asked, and she had nodded solemnly. She could believe it.

He'd taught her that there are different kinds of people in the world. "They do not all look like me or like you, so handsome and stunningly beautiful," he said seriously. "There are islands where little people live. Though they are small, they age very quickly. One who is as old as you, Joan, would appear a wrinkled crone."

She always listened to his stories, even if she didn't think they were wholly true.

"Where have you been?" she asks him now. She blushes, shy after betraying so much pleasure at his arrival. It has been at least three months since she last saw him.

"I've just rolled out of a fine lady's feather bed," her uncle replies.

"Else, how do you think I could afford these?" And he sticks out a foot to show her the polished boot. "The leather is soft as a woman's . . ." He reddens.

"Hair?" she offers.

"Yes, soft as a woman's hair. That is what I was going to say."

They leave behind the ruin of Agincourt to walk together. Above them, the blazing sky succumbs to night, blotted blue and purple and a crimson so dark it is nearly black.

They are standing in a field that in another week, at most two, will be ready for harvesting. This is also why her uncle is here: to help with the reaping, sheaving, threshing, and winnowing. There is always a need for more hands, and a bit of money to be made this time of year.

They stand side by side; her shoulder reaches just above his waist. When he inquires, politely, whether her new hair is the work of her own hand, she sighs.

"Lice," she says.

They catch each other's eye. Lice, like Agincourt, shouldn't be funny, but they break into a fit of laughter, though it hurts her to laugh.

"I shall miss Catherine braiding my hair," she says. "I liked that."

"Who doesn't?" And he runs a hand through his own thinning hair, as a joke. "But it suits you in a way."

She sees that he is serious. "It itches less," she concedes.

A pause, then: "Here is something to make you feel better. Did you know when Duke William of Normandy first arrived on the shores of England—oh, this was four hundred years ago—King Harold had his spies report back what they saw. And his men informed him that the enemy was a large contingent of priests. Nothing to be concerned about."

She glances up. How can this be, her look says. How can one mistake an army for priests?

"It was because the Normans shaved and did not grow their hair long, so anyone who saw them assumed at first that they were holy men. One could say something good came of having their hair cut, don't you think? Well, good for the Normans."

"Priests," she says thoughtfully, "with swords and shields?" King Harold's spies fell for that?

Her uncle appears at a loss for a reply. "People were more trusting then," he says.

He glances down at her. She catches, what, a flicker of pity? She has not yet seen her reflection in a stream, but if her uncle, who is used to her usual wounds—one eye swollen to twice the size of the other, or both narrowed to dark purple slits—looks like he might cry, then it must really be bad. And having just arrived in the village, he has not heard what happened to Guillaume. Another defeat, Joan thinks, to add to Agincourt.

"I am used to it," she says to cheer him up. "I am French, after all."

They giggle. This is another joke between them that shouldn't be a joke: France is losing the war, and badly; therefore, it stands to reason that any subject of France is more likely to be thrashed and pummeled than a Burgundian or an Englishman. And Joan is no exception. Is it any wonder? Just look at the English King. She has heard Henry is a tall man, over six feet in height, and cruel. On his cheek is a scar from an arrow wound he suffered as a youth. The arrowhead had to be extracted with a special tool. Look at Philip, Duke of Burgundy, cold with rage. And then look at the French King. Our King who is mad, who takes all measures, including the careful placement of iron bars in his clothes, to prevent himself from breaking because he thinks he is made of glass.

Her uncle kicks a clod of earth. "Things could be worse, Joan."

Really?

To prove his point, he tells a story from the recent past, a mere three years ago. Henry, King of England, set siege to the great city of Rouen, capital of Normandy. "What is the point of telling a story if one already knows the ending?" she interrupts. She is impatient. Everyone knows Rouen fell. Ah, her uncle says, but not before holding out for five whole months, nearly six. And when food grew scarce, the people ate the likes of your precious dog, Salaud. They ate horses and cats, too, until there were no more animals to be found, until even a rat was a rare and much-coveted delicacy. The city's leaders, to conserve resources and because they believed that help was on its way, issued a summons: all those who drained the city's resources, that is, the elderly, beggars, be they young or old, the ill, must leave their homes and seek shelter in another place, away from the city. They thought Henry would let them leave. What threat did these people—the sick, the frail, many, mere children—pose for someone as powerful as him? But Henry did not let them go, and they were caught in the ditch that lay between the gates of Rouen and the field where his troops had set up their camp. These prisoners could not reenter the city, and they could not move past Henry's army without risking death. Imagine living in a ditch: waking in it, pissing in it, sleeping each night in the same strip of earth that will become your grave. And to show he was not entirely without mercy, that he could still take pity on his enemy, on Christmas Day, the English King doled out bread to each of them, but not one survived the ordeal. They still starved.

There are no happy stories, just stories that make you feel grateful you weren't born somewhere else, somewhere like Rouen.

A moment of quiet follows, and Durand sighs into the lull. "Now," he says, "does my story make you want to embrace your father and give him a big kiss?"

She elbows her uncle, not in the ribs, which she can't yet reach, but in the thigh. She watches him wince; it isn't an expression he makes solely for her pleasure.

"You are getting strong," he says, rubbing his leg.

"You are getting old" is her answer, and again their eyes meet; again, they laugh. The sound sends birds sweeping into the air. The noise they make is so loud, the vast field begins to feel like a very small room, and they are stamping around in it, drunk on the smell of earth and golden wheat. Salaud circles them, barking.

She can barely see herself in the dark. Since her birth, she has never known a time of peace. If it isn't the French being beaten in battle, it is news of marauders, who are sometimes French themselves, setting fire to villages and performing fresh atrocities. Like it or not, she is always thinking about the war. She is always hearing stories, though some are made up. Go out and fetch a bucket of water, and if it is too quiet, her ears will strain for the sound of footsteps coming from behind. When the church bell rings, it could be ringing for Vespers or it could be ringing because a company of brigands with torches has been sighted in the distance. She cannot look at a field without picturing how it would appear razed, the grain destroyed, and the long winter months still to be weathered. One can die at the end of a sword, from bad humors in the body, which create worms, or from hunger, and these days she cannot look at a bowl, even when it is full, without also seeing it empty. They say a dragon lives in the Bois Chenu, the dark wood where once she shook acorns down from trees. She knows a wood can be the home of a dragon, but more likely, it is where a small army, Burgundian or English, may hide itself before attacking. A wolf's shadow can also be a man's.

Durand says every misfortune is likewise an opportunity. Consider the Black Death, how many that plague killed. But after those long years when it seemed God Himself had given up on the world, the price of labor went up. Every plowman was worth his weight in gold. The common man bought land and suddenly, almost in the blink of an eye, found himself a landowner. One went to bed terrified; the air itself was rancid with the smell of corpses, of death. But if you woke up the next morning, you might live to see a new world. And your place in it will have changed.

Can't war be like this, too? One man's loss is another man's gain, and you don't have to be English to come out the winner. Think how precious food is. Grain and flour. Salted meat and salted fish. Fresh apples. So, go into supplies is what Durand has heard in the course of his travels. Go into transport. Go into building work. There is always something to construct in war. Gatehouses to be fortified. Ditches to be dug. If you have a good pair of hands, someone will find a use for them.

"Have you ever fought, as a soldier?" Joan asks.

Her uncle shrugs. "I've been on battlefields. I've seen corpses." His answer is evasive. Then he turns to her. "Define what you mean by fight. There are plenty of roles other than a soldier in war."

She doesn't ask how any of what he says applies to her. The skills she knows—the collection of kindling, the quick and unthinking motion of the wrist that snaps a chicken's neck, the skimming of cream, the practiced humming that appeases flustered babes—would any of this help her in war? She can't read—though she doesn't know anyone, besides the priest, who can. But she has a pair of hands. She is hardy and, save for occasional bouts of lice and fleas, strong. Sometimes she cannot see her future. Other times, when her uncle recounts a story, an image will come to her, and she will feel, for the length of the tale, that things could be different. How? She doesn't know. But it is possible, just possible, that not all roads have to end in a field like this one.

The war has widened the scope of the land for her. It has taught Joan the names of places she didn't know: Orléans, Crécy, Sluys, Poitiers. New towns means new people. There will always be those like her father and the captain from Maxey. But there will also be people like Durand, like Catherine and Jehanne and Hauviette, who will make you a chain of flowers when you are bald and hurting, and take you into their arms without the intent of killing you. France is a kingdom. It is large. Just think.

This is the hour the spirit world comes out, her uncle tells her. Like the feu follet. Have you ever walked past a lake and seen strange lights, green and blue, floating across the water, when there is no boat or fisherman in view? Well, if you have, that is the feu follet, and if you catch sight of these lights, then you must turn away. You must run in the other direction, for if you follow them, you will never find your way back again, and no one will recover your body.

At this hour, hobgoblins dance beneath the leaves, avoiding spots where the moon shines. Lutins hide in the knots of tree trunks and may work their magic for ill or for good. And in the damp darkness of caves or beneath bridges, the Dames Blanches await travelers and unsuspecting passersby. Their spirits can slip into any crack of rock, any cliff-side. You may turn a corner and come face-to-face with a hooded woman dressed in white, her body glowing, her face pale. She will ask you to dance or to stand on your head and walk on your hands, to pick her some fresh flowers and sing your favorite song, and you must oblige her if you want to avoid a curse.

In the gathering dark, as they stand in this field, anything feels possible. The dark is for imagining. And you can see horrors. You can scare yourself with tricks of the mind and dancing devils. Or you can plan out your whole future in the pitch of night. You can dream with your eyes open.

The key is to stay alive. If you still have breath in you, there is every chance tomorrow will be better. One day, she thinks, I'll leave Domrémy. Some people are born in a place, and they are never able to see past its fences, its hedgerows, and its fields. They reach the last furrow of the last acre, the edge of the forest, and turn around, go home. They live beneath the same patch of sky and wait for clouds or good weather or rain to come to them. But not me. She tells herself, I'll search out my own weather. I'll plunge into the unknown wood.

In the dark, she smiles. She will live to a ripe old age. She will say, when she is old, I survived this and this and this, but first, before anything else, I survived my father's fists.

◆

THE HARD WORK of the day ended, the mood is one of idleness. Joan is tired of the ground, where she has crouched for hours, tying sheaves and gathering from the field the leftover wheat the men have missed. So, she is in a tree, nibbling one of the cakes the women of Domrémy have prepared. She is a resting panther on a thick branch, blinking dark eyes behind a thicket of sage-green foliage and observing the village from up high: the young girls dancing, barefoot, in the grass, their shining waist-long hair catching the sunlight; the boys gaping at the girls and her own idiot brothers among the open-mouthed. The women chatter and laugh, though their hands remain busy. They spin flax and look away from their work to check that their smallest children are where they have left them. Joan stretches on a limb as if it were a bed; she licks a crumb into her mouth and lets it dissolve on the tip of her tongue. Most of the noise below is coming from her father and the other men who are drinking and eating. Their laughter is like storm clouds rolling in, rumbles of thunder.

And her uncle? Her uncle is making Hauviette's mother, Jehanne, giggle. He looks like he might sweep her up in his arms if they were alone and if Jehanne's husband were not giving him dark looks a few feet away. From his smiles, his not-so-innocent glee, Joan guesses he is telling her a story, perhaps the account of how he once inserted himself among a group of bricklayers and earned a full week's wages without lifting a finger or how he acquired his latest pair of shining boots.

From a distance, she hears whispers rise, a stir, and catches a single word: *Maxey*. She narrows her eyes. A stranger has come, and he is walking in the direction of the men. She is surprised. For all the bluster about shame and weakness, a boy dead, a family's only son buried, nothing has been done. Not even another rock battle has been scheduled.

Her father jumps to his feet. He strides forward to greet the man, who looks about forty, with a swaying paunch and thick, flabby arms. His tunic is a light blue, and the cloth so worn, the threads seem in danger of snapping and exposing his chest. He is a large man, larger than her father, yet the number of people who stare makes him bashful.

Jacques offers him cakes and ale, which the man turns down. To everyone else, thinking to themselves, What is Jacques d'Arc doing with someone from Maxey, our sworn enemy?, her father says in a congenial voice, "It is just business. Please excuse us."

He leads the man to a tree; in fact, it is her tree, and they are standing right under her branch. She is intrigued by what will happen. Will she be witness to a killing? A real murder? She takes another bite of cake, swallows hard.

"I am glad you came," her father says. He has lately surprised her with these other sides of himself; apparently, he is capable of simpering. "It is an embarrassing position I find myself in."

The man nods, though he looks more embarrassed than Jacques.

"Still, it is my own fault. I admit to that," her father continues. "What man does not occasionally give in to his baser instincts and lay too much on a wager? That night luck was not on my side. I haven't lost everything, of course. I thank God I didn't throw away all of my wits, even having drunk as much as I did. But I can't let my family go hungry when winter comes, and I don't want to sell to anyone in my own village. It is hard enough on my pride that I have to do this."

"You have children?" the man asks. For the first time, he appears at ease, as if this fact has made her father less of a snorting bull.

"Yes, no less than five. Three boys, a lovely girl. She is just there, do you see her with the other young women? I do not need to point her out to you. I know you will spot her. She is the most beautiful girl in the village. I intend to marry her well."

"And the fifth?" the man asks.

"The fifth is . . . around somewhere. She is like one of those imps you tell your children about to frighten them so they will be good and say their prayers at night." Jacques laughs, throws up his hands. Not my fault! Don't look at me—I had no part in that! "If you saw her, you would see why her mother and I, we despair . . ." He sighs dramatically. From her branch, her hand twitches. She wants to throw the remainder of her cake at his head.

But the man offers a weak smile. "I understand," he says. "I have children myself. They are six, five, and two." He counts on his fingers. "Two boys and one daughter."

"Well, shall we talk money? What will you give me for my pigs . . ." Her father slings an arm around the man's shoulder, as if they were old friends. He steers him away from the tree. She hears murmurs, a few numbers thrown out, rejected, the price driven up.

When they return, it seems a deal has been struck. Her father is smiling, and this stranger, who she has decided is not as clever as Jacques d'Arc (who is?) but probably kinder, seems to be working out the sums; from her father's fine mood, it seems likely his guest has agreed to pay the cost of a few acres for two sickly runts or a pair of watery-eyed sows. She watches them shake hands. As he waves goodbye, Jacques appears on the verge of skipping. He repeats his offer of a cup of ale, but the man shakes his head, says he should be getting back before he is missed.

It is then that the last bit of cake slips from her fingers and lands, a soft, misshapen clump, at her father's feet. For a moment, she thinks he won't notice. But he is a wolf, with a lupine awareness of his surroundings. He looks up. She looks down, remains perfectly still. She doesn't know whether Jacques, at his age, can still climb trees. Or if he'll simply pick up the tree by its roots and shake her down like a leaf.

For a long moment, they gaze at each other. If this is a staring contest, he loses by blinking. She hears him groan, as if to say, *You again! So that is where you were!* But today she will be spared. His friends are calling him back, and he returns to them in a fine mood.

Later, when she is sitting in the sun outside her home, a shadow covers her. She glances up: A thundercloud? No, it is only her father.

"How much did you hear?" he asks. She listens closely, weighing each word as if they were coins falling into her hand. Is that uncertainty in his voice? She thinks so.

She meets his eye and dares herself to smile, though she is pretty sure it comes out a sneer. Well, didn't Durand call her a gargoyle? "Nothing," she says. "I heard nothing."

Her father grunts. He tosses something at her, making her flinch. But she hears Salaud sniffing, and when the pain doesn't come, she dares to open her eyes. Jacques is gone, but at her feet is a cake, whole and new. She checks, double-checks, smells the cake to make sure it hasn't been smeared with dung or spat on. Her fingers break off a fragment; she casts it up, and Salaud snatches the piece in midair.

Sometimes life will surprise you. Possibly, she thinks, remembering her uncle's story, this gesture is not unlike what Henry, King of England, did outside the gates of Rouen on Christmas Day, when he gave out loaves to those caught between the city and his army. Yet one must take the bread, even if it comes from the hands of one's enemy. One must nibble the cake that has dropped from the hand of Jacques d'Arc and hope, against the odds, that it is a sign of better things to come.

It is the end of summer, and a rumor has reached Domrémy that Henry, England's warrior-king, is dying. He has contracted dysentery and now lies, in shock and pain, on his deathbed; if this is true, and not a false rumor, then England will lose its greatest ruler since Edward III and his son the Black Prince crossed the Narrow Sea. It was Edward, with his greed and his love of power, who began this cursed war.

Life may be full of suffering. But sometimes a ray of light shines through a crack in the wall, and one can pass a hand through a rainbow and see one's own skin turn the color of the heavens.

Perhaps, if Henry is no more, the English will slink back to their miserable island, and the war will end. Perhaps, now that she knows her father has made another bad wager and lost money, he will stop beating her. Victories, however few and far between, however incidental, bear remembering.

She gulps down the last bite of sweetness.

There are some days when one feels like singing, and this is such a day. Durand has taught her a poem by a famous troubadour; she walks down the lane, arms outstretched, bellowing music from the pit of her stomach while Salaud jumps at her heels. When she passes, villagers still look at her twice. Her hair grows back slowly, sprouting dark tufts, not soft like spun wool, but angular and hard. She sings about joyous mornings and birdsong, about flowers and days of good weather when one's belly is full and sleep comes easily at night.

When she is finished, she thinks she hears a smattering of applause. But perhaps it is only the wind rustling through the branches or a pair of animals darting through a bush, cracking twigs beneath their paws. Perhaps it isn't a pair of animals at all but Jehanne and her uncle rolling behind a hedge, having fallen into each other's arms at last. Does it matter? When your tongue holds the residual sweetness of honey, when you have all your teeth in your head and a seeing pair of eyes, when you have seared into your memory the image of Jacques d'Arc confessing that he has lost money on a bet, is it important who hears you and who claps their hands? No, not really.

Her uncle, when she sees him next, is flushed and pink, his own hair tousled, which would confirm her theory of what he has been up to. He says, "Your head looks like a caltrop, Joan, those spiked balls one throws on the battlefield, to make horses and charging men go lame."

"You can do that?" she asks him.

"In a battle, you can do anything" is his reply.

VI

◆ ◆ ◆

WHENEVER THERE IS A FAIR, people will comment, as though they were alive then to see it, "If you had only been to the fairs of times past—now, *those* were real occasions, worthy of being remembered. This is nothing compared to what they used to be." And they will count the deficiencies: How there were formerly jongleurs singing in every street and dancing bears. How there was a lion—a real lion—at the Fair of Saint Jean in Troyes. And today, we have no lions anymore, not even among our own princes and lords. Ha-ha!

These same people will talk about the famous cloth markets, where merchants from Lucca and Bruges greeted each other as old friends or old enemies in the common tongue of the fairs, which was of course French, and where there was cloth for purchase of every weave and color imaginable. Of reds alone, there numbered several shades, and the best, the most blinding vermilions, hailed from the guilds of Italy, particularly Florence. As long as you had money, there was nothing you could not get your hands on: a cotton or linen in a particular shade of green, a citrine yellow finished with gold brocade, the wool of Cambrai or the wool of Ypres. Expert fingers unfurled their bolts and showed you your every desire, as if it were a map only they possessed.

And the spices . . . If you couldn't afford saffron—and if we are honest, how many of us can—you could at least see it, the small clump of crimson threads, as untidy as a bird's nest, resting in a merchant's palm, that is worth more than four healthy sheep combined.

But these people, these lovers of the past, forget what happens between two points, from the Byzantine city of Constantinople to the

French city of Provins: the pack trains of braying, tired mules, the creaking wheels of caravans, the horses gone lame three-quarters of the way through a journey of craggy trails and nonexistent roads. They forget the challenges of driving a cart through mud to a destination one mile away, to say nothing of a few hundred. And all for what: to transport a sack of peppercorns, an iron case of ivory, a barrel of Auxerre wine. They forget that in between this fair and the Fair of Saint Jean two centuries ago, the Black Death happened, and millions perished.

The world has changed, but it will startle you what can endure the passage of time, the worst of plagues, and the worst of wars. One's appreciation for indigo, for furs, for a shiny new pot doesn't wane just because another town has fallen to the English. By night, the same town may be retaken by the French (one can only hope). This fair, today, is meant to say, *Life goes on, and the people of Vaucouleurs go with it.* There is a war. The roads are more dangerous than they were fifty years ago, but does this mean the good citizens of France should go without salt and hemp? That tired housewives shouldn't be spoiled by the husbands who love them and wear pretty silver bracelets or drink quality wine shipped from Épernay? No, of course not! There is still a place for beauty; there is still time to sigh over a goldsmith's craft, to forget one's troubles over a bolt of silk, before all is lost.

The Duke of Lorraine, an aging and shrewd man in his fifties, has ensured safe passage for all traders and visitors. He has promised to reimburse any merchant who is forcibly deprived of his goods while traveling to or from the fair and to make a public spectacle of punishing—that is, executing—the thieves responsible. In these uncertain times, there is nothing quite like the hanging or mutilation of a common criminal to make people feel safe again, to put them in a mood to spend money they don't have and buy what they don't need, of which the Duke will receive a small and very reasonable fraction in taxes.

This trip is her uncle's idea to cheer them up, to show them there are still places where people live neither under the tyranny of the English nor, on the French side, under such men as Jacques d'Arc. They have not exactly asked her father's permission to go; earlier in the day, she, along with her uncle, her dog, and her sister, simply climbed onto a cart and left. When they reach the fair, Joan rolls from her seat. Salaud leaps. Catherine descends like a princess, with a dainty jump. The dust of roads in August has powdered Joan from head to foot in a sandy yellow.

"Didn't I tell you not to sit in the front with Uncle?" Catherine says, fussing. "Look at you." She licks the inside of her hand, a feline movement too quick for Joan to dodge. With wetted palm, Catherine rubs her cheeks, chin, and forehead in small, expert circles. Then, as if remembering she is a sister and not a mother, she pinches Joan's nose.

Joan returns the favor. Using her thumb and index finger, she flicks a single spot of dust from the top of Catherine's arm and steps back, as if to inspect a finished painting. There. Now you are perfect again.

At first, Joan is shy; her head darts around, trying to see everything at once. When she hesitates, her sister takes her sweating palm. Out of the corner of her eye, she glimpses showers of red-hot sparks. She thinks of her friend the blacksmith and points, before wandering over. These men may also, like the blacksmith, treat her kindly. They may give her free nails. But when she reaches them, she sees what they are making is far more beautiful than candlesticks and horseshoes.

The helmet-makers notice Joan staring at the great helm they have put on display. It is not a style known for its beauty; there is a thin slit for the eyes and vents on one side for breathing. A section juts out, creating a protruding lip that closely resembles a frog's mouth. That has become its second name, the master helmet-maker tells her, making her laugh: frog-mouth. But in all other respects, it is a square of iron that one sticks, without rivets or straps, onto one's head. He lets her examine it, hold it, and weigh it in her hands. He tells her Henry, King of England, wore a great helm, and so did the Black Prince.

"But what do you want with a helmet?" he asks. "A girl has no use for such things. She wants everyone to see how beautiful she is." She knows he is laughing at her because she is not beautiful, because she has a head of burrs and a face as colorful as the merchants' cloths.

Then he lets her try the frog-mouth on, and she knows he does this because he feels sorry for making fun of her. In a moment, her head disappears. The helmet is too large; it wobbles. Her eyes don't line up with the opening, so she can't see anything, and she feels dizzy when she turns, as if her head is in a cage. The master knocks his fist a few times against her iron forehead, and she hears a dull clang somewhere above her.

When she takes off the frog-mouth, the air is sweet and fresh. Her face feels warm. She must look flushed, because the helmet-maker and his apprentices are chuckling at her. They cry, "Another! Another!," so the master shows her a bascinet, a helmet where the face is mostly exposed and a visor, separately commissioned and sold, may be attached to it. Without prompting, he sticks the bascinet onto her head. This one fits better, so she swivels around. They laugh again; she has an audience now. To amuse them, she throws the side of her armored skull against the wooden boards of the stall to test its effectiveness. Their laughter turns to howls, and a younger lad tumbles from his stool, nearly dropping his hammer on his foot.

Behind her, Durand, who is holding her barking dog, says, "Now, Joan . . ." while Catherine covers her mouth, trying not to laugh.

Joan takes off the helmet and passes it back to the master tenderly, like a newborn she is returning to its mother. She is tempted to kiss the helmet as she parts with it. She moves on.

The armorers, after observing her exchange with the helmet-makers, are already expecting her. They show Joan a completed mail shirt, long enough to reach a man's knees. They permit her to run her hand over the individual links, of which they say there are exactly forty thousand. "Exactly forty thousand?" she repeats, not quite believing them. Nothing snags. Nothing cuts. When they shake the shirt, it clinks cheerfully with a life and humor of its own, as if aware of being admired. "How is it done?" she asks them. "I can sew," she adds, thinking this is helpful for them to know.

"Sew?" She hasn't yet butted her head against a wall, and already they are slapping their thighs and shaking with laughter.

"This isn't done by sewing," they say, and the eldest of them, a grizzled man with a dense beard, explains the process from beginning to end. First, the blacksmith provides the armorer with wire, which is cut to form links, like rings. The links must be hammered, pounded until they are smooth and flat. A hole is added to each link, then connected to four more. In this way do they grow in number, and a shape begins to form after weeks of delicate labor. This shirt, the one she is still stroking, has taken no less than three months to finish and will go to a lord living in Vaucouleurs named Sir Robert de Baudricourt.

"Our work requires both strength and an artist's touch," the grizzled man says, showing her a finished breastplate. He seems to forget he is not actually speaking to a potential customer. She stares at his hands, glistening with sweat. He has blackened fingernails, like her father, but from the soot of fire, not of earth. The knuckle of each finger joint bulges beneath toughened skin.

"War is a good business," he adds, smiling. "And there is art in what we do. Consider a gauntlet, which, when made by artisans less skilled, simply takes on the form of a knight's fist. But a master will make you think the fist is already inside, snug and ready to split your enemy's jaw open." She wants to tell him, I wish you could be my grandfather. She wants to say, Tell me what you know, tell me about the cities you have been to for your trade. The biggest town I have ever visited is this one, and I've only been here for half an hour, no more.

The grizzled man is about to describe a street in Milan called the Via Spadari, but someone calls to him and he turns away. A group of well-dressed customers are waiting to be served; their leader's foot twitches, scuffing his fine boots, the toes pointed and long. Still, her host is courteous. He nods to Joan and excuses himself. The shirt of pounded iron slips away, and she stares after it. Is it possible to feel a loss for something one has never owned? If so, she thinks she feels it now.

The man with the anxious foot notices her lingering. He appears to be in his early twenties, handsome and strong; her sister, she thinks, would like him. He reminds her of a prince from a tale with castles, pots of gold, and cherry orchards. But when he sees her, he frowns, wrinkling his nose. Oh, is that how it is? She sticks her tongue out.

Salaud is at her feet, but her uncle is gone. She runs off in the direction of the jewelers' stalls to look for her sister. Catherine likes metalwork, too, just of a different kind.

◆

EVERYWHERE SHE TURNS, something is happening. In the distance, she sees a pair of acrobats nearly collide with a cart of vegetables. The cart owner shakes his fist at them, and the acrobats flip away to another clearing.

There are people, like the angry cart owner, selling surplus goods from their farms. There are people who have a single chicken to peddle. There are merchants bending over scales and rulers. There are prostitutes, the only vendors who don't congregate in one area. Business is better if they spread out, each woman to her own door, alley, or wall. Some are seasonal workers, available solely for the duration of the fair, others professionals, women who commit themselves to the art of love year-round. They hover mostly in windows, where they watch and wait, the more audacious blowing kisses at those below.

Joan thinks a prostitute has just waved at her—it's hard not to notice them, even if you aren't interested in what they're selling—when she realizes her sister isn't where she should be, nor her uncle. Only Salaud follows close, watching her expressions. He stops when she stops, his tail thumping the earth.

The moment panic makes her throat close is the moment she becomes aware of smoke and the smell of incense. A crowd is gathering, and a procession of monks heading her way. Joan sees a large wooden cross, wobbling slightly on the shoulder of its stooped bearer.

She steps back to let them pass and observes it is not really the monks the people are craning their necks to gawk at; it is the woman moving with them, in the center of their procession. A woman dressed in a nun's gown, limping, because she is walking barefoot. Her feet are raw, spotted with blisters. From her neck hangs a crucifix fashioned of crude iron. It can't be very heavy, yet she keeps her head bowed, her eyes shut. Her mouth moves; she is muttering a prayer. Prayer, however, doesn't give her a better sense of direction. When she veers off course, the monks at her elbows must nudge her gently back onto her path like mothers correcting the steps of a small child.

From the crowd, coins, which would have otherwise purchased a lovely bolt of rose-pink linen, a garnet pendant, or a carving of the Madonna, are falling into the outstretched palm of a monk who has missed his true calling as a butcher. Keep him away from the knife stall, Joan thinks; he looks ready to cleave anyone who doesn't give in two.

But now a gasp. A rustle through the crowd. Joan's eyes are still on the menacing Franciscan, so she doesn't notice that the woman has stopped, forcing the procession to stop with her. The woman has ceased her prayers, is looking with an expression of bafflement at her audience. A shout goes up from the crowd: "Someone is to be blessed—by her sainted hands!" Slowly, step by painful step, the woman is shuffling through the lines of her cowled protectors. *This isn't part of the procession,* they seem to say, holding up their hands to block her path. Yet she is pushing through their ranks with surprising vigor, heading with alarming speed in Joan's direction.

It feels like a scene from a nightmare one might have after hearing a story of spirits and the dead. Up close, the woman's eyes are a watery gray. Her face is skeletal, and her mouth is a line etched with a quill fast running out of ink. Joan is rarely afraid, but she is fearful of this woman who looks like she has just crawled out of a grave and who is covered with welts of her own making.

She feels a hand, as dry and hard as a plank of wood, lift her hand. Something cold drops into it. She does not look at the woman but keeps her gaze fixed on the ground, on Salaud, who, she notices, is trembling and undecided between running away to save himself and biting the woman's ankle to save his master.

She realizes that a space has been made around her, that a stranger not far away is talking loudly: "Ah, what an honor. To be blessed by Colette of Corbie herself. The girl must be an orphan—poor mite, her parents killed in the wars. Look at her hair. Englishmen or worms, do you think?" A giggle—malicious or kind, it is difficult to tell.

She does not want to be blessed. She does not want hands, if they are not the hands of Catherine or Durand, touching her.

She meets Salaud's eye, and a blink of understanding passes between them. She looks up just as the holy woman is about to bestow a kiss on her head, and pulls back, wriggling away before taking off. The holy woman is left staring, a corpse shocked into life. One of the men—she thinks it must be the butcher-monk—bellows after her, "Shame! Shame on you, child!"

As she runs, she passes a large circle drawn with chalk; inside it two roosters, hackles raised, peck and lunge with stabbing talons and beaks. She nearly brushes against the legs of a stilt walker stepping over a huddle of children, who scream, half from fear, half in delight. She runs so fast, looking over her shoulder, that she doesn't see she is heading straight for—

She is pulled back—only just—by a rough hand that grabs the collar of her dress. For a moment, the sensation is like flying backward. Then the hand drops her, and she lands with a grunt on her feet.

"You might have cracked your skull against that," a red-faced stranger with a nose as large as an onion says to her, pointing. He is staring at her wide-eyed.

Wherever she has run to, these are friendlier climes than before. Here, there is laughter, and she sees what she would have crashed against: a wooden pole set in the middle of a square. The pole is as tall as a giant, and at the top, something is squawking and writhing inside an open basket.

"That would be the goose," the same person explains. "Sitting on a bag of gold coins, or so we are led to believe."

"And we are waiting for the basket to fall?" she asks.

"No, no, look!" And again, an emphatic hand gestures in her face. "If you reach the top and take the basket, it is yours: the goose and the coins both. Courtesy of the Duke himself. Of course, he knows no one will reach the basket. It is impossible. The pole is greased with pig fat."

Inside her, a weight seems to shift. Before, she had been on the verge of crying. But there are no holy women here who remind her of corpses, no monks who look as if they might pick her up and shake her pockets clean. Now there is a greasy pole. There is a basket with a goose in it and money, too. From the top of the pole, she may be able to see where her sister and uncle are. This is a good enough reason for Joan to climb it. And a pole, she considers, is very much like a tree.

Someone steps forward. The fair must be small, for it is that well-dressed idiot from the armorer, the one with the restless shoe who believes calfskin boots are made for scuffing pebbles. She watches him remove his hat and hand it to an obliging servant, who bows upon taking it. Beneath a shirt of finely woven linen, his back muscles twitch. For several moments (too long, Joan thinks; now it is her turn to tap her foot with impatience), he paces around the pole; he drums a hand, ringed with shining stones, across its oily surface. Then one shapely ankle winds itself around the bottom; the second follows. He shifts upward, emitting animal grunts.

But he hasn't made it two feet before his pretty red sleeves begin slipping against the grease. He yelps, like a frightened dog, as he slides down.

Joan laughs. She laughs so hard, tears spill out of her eyes. For the first time in her life, she is crying with joy.

"Hush, child," a woman near her chides. "That is Sir Robert de Baudricourt."

And my name is Joan, she thinks. She is tempted to say this aloud. So, who cares?

When she recovers, she wipes her face and steps forward. At her feet, Salaud whines.

"What do you think you're doing?" the woman who hushed her says.

She doesn't answer. There are whispers when she enters the clearing and when she imitates the gestures of the young lord, sliding a finger to test the pole's surface. The whispers grow louder as she hikes up her skirts, exposing her bare ankles. She has to tilt back her head to see the basket. The pole seems even taller now. From where she stands, it seems less a pole than a column propping up a whole piece of sky. She swallows, takes a deep breath. She jumps.

Running, climbing—these things have always come naturally to her. She hugs the pole and emits the same animal grunts as the handsome idiot. She uses her knees to nudge herself up, inch by slow inch. Those in the crowd who had said such a thing was unheard of and who had wanted to stop her grow quiet. They are waiting for her to slip and fall.

Soon she is sweating, her arms and legs so tired, so sore, they have begun to shake. What's more, the squawks of the goose don't sound any closer. She sighs and rests her cheek against the grease, which smells of mold, excrement, and pigs. Her dress, she thinks, so recently washed, will be ruined again.

Below, the crowd laughs. But someone raises his voice in support, saying, "It is nothing to laugh about. She is nearly halfway there, the little monkey. Who does she belong to?"

She has never considered herself heavy, but her whole body, every limb, feels as dense as the blacksmith's anvil. A warm breeze touches her face, makes strands of hair tickle her chin, and she must fight the urge to scratch. When she shifts her weight, she hears a metallic sound coming from her dress. She frees one of her hands to reach inside the pocket even before she understands why.

"What is she doing?" someone from the crowd shouts. It is a stupid voice. Probably, she guesses, it is Sir Robert de Baudricourt.

In her pocket, a nail rolls into her hand. She cups it, hiding it from sight, then frees the other arm, reaches down, pulls out the second.

She grips the nails in her fists, allowing the points to protrude like single metal talons. She stabs them into the surface of the pole and climbs. At once the goose feels nearer, more possible.

But the nail heads rub against her skin. If she was ever in greater pain than this, she doesn't remember it. She hears nothing but feels everything. Her hands will be chafed raw, even if she fails.

In an unthinking moment, she slips, and the gasps of the crowd reach her from below. She tells herself it's over. She's almost relieved, but her body won't let her surrender so easily. As one hand falters, the other compensates, supporting her weight. She shudders and licks her lips, tasting her own salt. Her whole dress is damp. The warm breeze returns, though this time it is cool. It blows over her, rustling her skirts. The breeze is a gift, she thinks, sent by angels.

A few more feet, and something swats the side of her head. She turns and looks straight into a pair of dark, angry eyes very close together. A wing buffets her face, and she inhales the scent of feathers. The goose must also be in the service of the Duke, because it doesn't make things any easier. It lunges, so she has to dodge its snakelike neck and press herself even closer to the pole. She bats the head away long enough to release her hold on each nail. Slowly, taking her time, she inserts first the one and then the other into her pocket. She reaches up and unhooks the basket from the top of the pole, as below, there is a roar from the crowd like an explosion. They are cheering.

Sliding down is easy, her free arm hugging her reward. The grease that made her climb nearly impossible facilitates her fall, though she still needs to be careful. She doesn't want to crash and break her legs.

The instant her feet touch the ground, her body crumples, and her elbow is jerked sideways. Someone is gripping her arm and dragging her. She has no strength to resist, only enough to hold tight to the basket with the goose and the coins she hopes are under the goose, though she is ready to ward off any thieves with her fists.

She looks down. A fine pair of boots! She stomps on them, kicking like a horse being dragged to slaughter.

"Stop that!" a voice bellows into her ear. She can't believe she was ever called a little lordling by that farmer in Domrémy. She doesn't bear the slightest resemblance to this fool.

"Let me go!" she screams back.

She doesn't know where he is taking her, but they've reached their destination. He swings her toward what appears to be a large litter, a square vessel draped in swaths of brocaded cloth and hitched to two great horses.

Sir Robert goes up to the single window. The corner of a dark purple curtain is briefly lifted by the litter's occupant; a white finger protrudes, and for a moment, it looks like the idiot might kiss its finely manicured tip, though he doesn't. The shadow of a face murmurs instructions, then points at her.

Her escort returns to where she is standing, with her goose and her dog.

She speaks first. A single bark, worthy of Salaud: "Well?"

Sir Robert flinches. He looks as if he would like to slap a hand over her mouth and gag her.

"His Grace the Duke of Lorraine would like to know how you climbed the pole," he says irritably.

Oh, is that all? She glares at him and shoves a hand into her pocket. She sees no need to lie. But when she opens her fist, blisters already jumping beneath her skin, it isn't nails in her palm: It's something she has never seen before. A piece of tin on a loop of black string. A holy medal.

Sir Robert eyes the object with suspicion. "Where is this from?" he asks.

"From the hand of the holy woman who passed through here," she answers. Her tone is casual. You would think she spoke to fine ladies and lords every day. "Colette of Corbie."

The medal is snatched away and brought to the litter's window for examination. Behind the curtain, a hand emerges, and a slender finger curls at her to approach.

The corner of the window stirs. A head appears and hovers in the square like a living portrait, an angular face atop a collared neck mantled in dark silks.

The Duke of Lorraine leans forward; his eyes glow golden-brown. They flick over her with the readiness of an eagle observing a fidgeting rabbit in a field. He looks from her to the medal, and she sees him make the connection. A pole impossible to climb. An item given by a woman who many already say will be venerated as a saint after her death. And he, the Duke, not a young man anymore, who would like to live a little longer. Also, if the tin piece does not prolong his life, then it may still help with his joints, which at night give him such pain.

From his hand, a ring emerges, as if conjured from thin air. "This for your medal?" he offers her. The ring has a small stone the color of fire.

In a deal, one must be quick to decide. Joan nods. All that is missing is a shake of the hand, soft ducal flesh against rough peasant skin. She watches the ring pass from the palm of the Duke to Sir Robert to her own. There is nothing more to say, yet she thinks she sees the Duke smile, the eagle eyes shimmer as the curtain falls back into place over the window. She knows why. He believes he has come out of their trade with the more valuable article: a holy object purchased at bargain price. And maybe he has, though she wouldn't agree. Then the litter is carried away at an easy pace, the two horses snorting, and Sir Robert trailing behind it. He turns, seems about to stick his tongue out, except wouldn't this be beneath his dignity? So, he refrains.

But it isn't beneath her dignity. Her tongue wags at him. She makes the most grotesque face she can conjure, an expression worthy, she hopes, of a gargoyle.

He narrows his eyes. He flicks his face forward and stomps away.

◆

BEFORE THEY CAME TO THE FAIR, Durand had warned her, "Don't draw attention to yourself, Joan. Don't look anyone in the eye." Then added, as an afterthought: "And don't get into a fight or argument, either." I am like a hero from a tale, she thinks. Haven't I won my treasure? The pouch of coins, which she hasn't yet had the chance to count, are snug in her pocket, along with the Duke's ring. The goose is in its basket. But she isn't out of danger. A group of youths about her brother Jacquemin's age are trailing her. They watch for their chance to spring, like patient jackals, so she stays close to men and women who look as though they wouldn't condone thieves and child murderers. There is still no sight of her sister or her uncle, and now that the thrill of victory is over, and she has no sneering lordling to stomp on, she thinks she really is going to cry.

The goose has calmed itself. Its feet are tied, its wings are clipped, and it looks weary and sick and ready to be eaten. Joan sets the basket down beside a cart of penned chickens; rows of fresh white eggs are arrayed outside the cages, like a before-and-after pantomime. She slips her hands into her pockets to feel the shape of the ring, the bag of coins, and the two nails, now bent. She pretends not to notice the jackals lean against a nearby wall, waiting for the crowd around her to thin.

A hand falls heavy on her shoulder. She thinks it's Durand, but when she spins around, she stares into a face both strange and familiar.

"Come with me," the owner of the hand says. He has tucked a single chicken under his arm, which he has either bought or been unsuccessful in selling. "I have been watching you . . . and watching them." He juts his chin in the direction of the youths.

When she doesn't move, he shakes his head. "I have a daughter of my own. She is only two. I wouldn't hurt another man's child, not for a whole kingdom. Where is your father, girl? Your mother?"

He has misunderstood her hesitation. It isn't that she is wary of him, but she's finally remembered where she has seen him before. This is the man with drooping shoulders and swaying paunch from Maxey, the man who agreed to buy her father's pigs. She would know that threadbare shirt of his anywhere.

But she doesn't reveal what she knows. She just nods and entrusts her free hand to his. When she observes the jackals move on, scowling with disappointment, she sighs. Relief breaks over her head, like cold water poured from a bowl. Her knees buckle.

"Ah, don't cry, little one," he says, peering down at her. The dam has finally shattered. She is crying, in shameless heaves and hiccups, because she thinks she will never see her sister or her uncle or even, God help her, her father again. Because things are so bad she is actually holding hands with a Burgundian.

The man from Maxey is still placating her when she hears shouting. She looks up. It is Catherine.

He releases her so she can clasp her sister's waist. Around Catherine's thin arms, she catches sight of Durand, not far behind. He is loping up, flushed, his hair in disarrangement, a light sheen of sweat making his skin glitter.

Before they leave the fair, Joan offers the man from Maxey a lift in the cart as far as the edge of Domrémy. He declines. It seems he refuses everything. Cake. A cup of ale. A free ride.

She slips a finger into the pouch of coins and shakes one out, offering it to him. Surely you cannot refuse money? But when he sees the coin, he only laughs. He puts his immense bear paw over her hand and pushes the coin back to her.

"So, you are an heiress," he says, smiling, "and that is why those rascals were following you like hunting dogs on the scent."

"I will give you a coin for your chicken," she says, not giving up.

Again he laughs. "You won't be an heiress for long if that is what you would pay for a single chicken, sweetheart."

◆

SHE STANDS IN THE BACK of the cart as it rolls away, waving to the man from Maxey, who is still holding his hen, a good layer, he informed her. He still has hopes of selling it before the day is over. Her uncle pleads, "Will you sit down, Joan, before you suffer an accident? Before you roll off the cart and under it, your legs smashed to jelly? A cart is not a chariot. It's happened to others. I have seen it." But she doesn't listen to him.

She is remembering a scene from two months ago, in late June: Saint John's Eve. A great wheel was prepared, and every household in the village contributed an armful of straw. When the wheel was finished, it stood nearly as tall as her father. One of his friends even joked, "What, did the carpenter use your dimensions when he made it, Jacques?"

The idea is this: Covered in straw, the wheel is lit on fire and then rolled by the men and the boys down a hill to a nearby stream. The object is for the wheel to reach the water before the fire goes out, though, she is told, this has happened only once in thirty years. If the men succeed, the harvest will be plentiful, the village prosperous. If it doesn't, well, then everyone shall have to pray harder and listen more closely to the priest's sermons.

The wheel did not make it to the stream. The fire went out, and the crowd groaned. In the night air, there was the smell of smoke.

She thinks of the wheel's shape, how life, too, tends to move in circles: Her father is cruel to her, thrashes her; she runs away. She returns home, is beaten again. She sleeps and has nightmares about Guillaume.

But sometimes the circle breaks. There is a pause, a lull, and in that lull is when angels grant wishes, saints sign off on prayers, and God arches His ear, listens, and nods. When the pattern of daily life skips a beat, that is when a poor man may stumble upon a cave full of treasures, by luck, by accident, or a twist of fate. That is when the fever of an ailing child breaks or the force of an unstoppable army falters before it fails.

Today, for a few hours, the circle has paused its cycle of beatings, of misery. And into the lull she has had a taste of good fortune. At her feet is the goose, which now feels more like a pet, and each bump of the road makes the coins in her pocket jangle like the shirt of mail from the armorer's.

The Duke thinks he came away with the better deal, but Joan knows he is wrong. She is saving the best for last. When they reach Domrémy, she pulls the ring out of her pocket and offers it to Catherine. She wants to see her sister's face.

But Catherine shakes her head. She has been quiet the whole journey back. Joan does not have to ask, What is it, what ails you, tell me. She already knows. They do not have to speak to understand what pains the other, for pain has followed them, like a shadow sibling, their whole lives. She knows Catherine is ashamed for losing sight of her at the fair. She knows she is worth more to her sister than a whole kingdom full of jewels.

Durand once said to her, "When you so much as stub your toe, Joan, you kick the table leg or the root that tripped you and bellow at it. God gave you such a pair of lungs. The whole world must be made aware of the table leg's transgression. But Catherine is different. Do you think she suffers less because she doesn't complain? And which, if I asked you, is the harder to do? To bear one's anguish in silence or to shout?"

Catherine doesn't accept the ring, so Joan takes her sister's hand and slips it onto a finger. The ring is too large. The cart shudders, and the ring jumps back into Joan's palm. Now it is Joan's turn to look dismayed. But a smile flickers across Catherine's face; she tells Joan she may wear it on a piece of string around her neck, or if not around her neck, then she will keep it somewhere safe, as the most precious thing she owns.

"I am only its keeper for the time," Catherine says. "When you grow, the ring will fit you better."

"How do you know?" Joan asks.

"I just know." She lays a hand on her sister's head, the movement like a blessing. What need do we have for holy women, Joan wonders, when we have sisters like Catherine?

The saint for whom Catherine is named was a virgin of exceptional beauty, a scholar who spent the duration of her short, martyred life in the city of Alexandria, in the land of Egypt. But, Joan thinks, my sister must be more beautiful than even this saint, and I would climb the highest pole to heaven to dress her in the jewels she deserves, though my hands should be rubbed raw, though every finger of mine should bleed.

VII

◆ ◆ ◆

THE CIRCLE TURNS. And the wheel spins back, three days after the fair, to the fists of Jacques d'Arc. This time, Joan is limping not in the direction of Hauviette's cottage but toward the Bois Chenu. She cannot always seek sanctuary in the same places, and tonight she thinks her father's mood is foul enough to pursue her. Salaud doesn't follow at her heels; he is safe in her sister's arms.

Her prize money, which she has sewn in secret into the hem of her dress, is enough to buy two strong cart horses. She couldn't keep the goose in her skirts, too; otherwise she would have done. But her father has taken the bird to fatten it before it becomes his and her brothers' supper.

The woods at night do not frighten her; she has stepped through their darkness before, when she was younger. She staggers into them now, holding her ribs, where the pain is like the point of a spear jabbing from within. It makes her breathless. She feels along the edge of a tree; her legs give way, and she sinks against its solid bulk, resting her sweating forehead on a patch of moss.

Between trees, she sees a flicker of light: a torch. There is no time to give in to self-pity. She pulls herself to her feet and begins to limp away.

"Wait." A soft rustle. In the light of the fire, her uncle's face glows bright orange, like a talking star.

She hasn't yet forgiven him for losing her at the fair. But even she knows when a blessing has come her way, so she stops, returns to the tree, and drops to the ground.

He crouches next to her. "Have you broken something?" he asks.

Have *I* broken something? As if her father had nothing to do with her crashing into walls and doors and a table.

But she is too tired to argue. She says, "If I have, the bones will mend again. They always do."

Distractions help with pain, so she talks. "I've had an idea," she says. "Tell me if you think it is foolish. An idea for how I shall leave Domrémy and also make my living. I will build a stall for polishing swords and shields, and all I will need is a little space, a stool to sit on, and a sign over the shutters.

"I will hire someone to make the sign for me," she continues, "since I cannot write or hold a brush. And I shall have to find a painter who is trustworthy, else he may play a trick and write some obscenity that will get me into trouble with the authorities. I will work for cheap until word spreads. People shall hear of my business, and then all the knights, their pages and squires, will come to me, and I may be able to hire an assistant after a time, too. Well? What do you think?"

Durand listens. "Don't take a stool leg to my head, Joan," he says, knowing her temper, "but isn't that what pages and squires are for? To clean their master's armor and weapons?"

"I have thought of that," she replies. "And the answer is: I will clean them better."

"Because you are a girl?"

She thumps her uncle's arm with a fist.

"You are always hitting me," he complains.

She would thump him again, except guilt makes her uncurl her fist. With the hand that struck the blow, she rubs the sore spot on his arm. She does not say, though she is thinking it, Sometimes I worry I take after my father.

"I don't see you as a cleaner of armor—I am sorry to disappoint you. I see you as . . ." In torchlight, he frowns. "I don't know what I see you as, but when I picture you, it is always alone and standing apart, like a dragon in a cave guarding piles of treasure, somewhere far away, on a mountain protected by mist and fairies. Not in a crowd. Not with others."

She likes the idea of being a dragon in a cave. She likes even more the idea of guarding treasure on a mountain far, far away from the reach of Jacques d'Arc.

She sighs. Durand echoes her sigh. A question hangs between them, a question she has asked more times than she can count. Perhaps her father's latest beating will be worth something if it makes her uncle feel sorry for her.

So, she groans. She leans forward, as if to throw up. Her fingers tighten around her ribs.

"Joan?"

She smiles. Her back straightens. "Will you take me with you when you leave?" she asks.

A pause. Durand shifts the torch so the light moves away from him; he turns his head to better hide his face.

Every time he comes to Domrémy, she asks. And every time, he finds a different way to say no. He has told her, plainly, kindly, but with firmness: "I know it seems tempting, the life of one who drifts, sometimes here, sometimes there, like a small boat on the great sea, but you don't want to spend your days with a scoundrel. And I am a scoundrel, Joan. Your father, whatever his failings, is made of more solid stuff than me. And what of your sister? Will you have her come with us, because you can't bear to be parted from her, and ask her to sleep beneath an awning, when it is raining and there is thunder, and have cold water drip down the back of her beautiful white neck?"

But she must ask. She must hear her uncle refuse her wish to leave with him, to leave Domrémy, even if it brings her more pain.

She stares. "Well?"

By the time the torch returns to his face, he is faintly smiling; his eyes are mild. He says, "I heard this story once from a sailor. A knight and a lady fell in love with each other." (She groans again. This time the groan is real, but he tells her to be patient: the story will get better.) "They married. But their happiness did not last. One day, as the knight was on Crusade, he was defeated in battle, and though the Saracen king spared his life, he turned the good knight into a slave, for he wanted to make an example of him.

"His wife soon heard what happened. She disguised herself as a traveling musician, a troubadour, for she had a quick wit and could compose verses as easily as walk. She armed herself with only her lute and a little pouch of money. And she made her way alone, if you can believe it, from the heart of her own kingdom to the palace of the Saracen king, halfway across the world. There she played sweet music for him, which made the king, a famed warlord, weep like a child. He said before she left his court that he would grant her a wish, anything in the world so long as it was in his power. So, she stood on the palace's pavilion, which overlooked the fields where the slaves worked, pointed at her husband, and asked the king to free him, to give the prisoner a single chest of treasure, and send him back on the fastest ship to his own country. And the king obeyed her, though he was sad to part with the musician, whom he had begun to consider his friend.

"Of course, the knight knew nothing about this. He thought it a miracle that his enemy had had a sudden change of heart. He was put on a ship and returned to his château, where all of his servants were waiting to greet him. Everyone except his wife, who, his steward informed him, had disappeared shortly after hearing of his capture, and this, as you can imagine, made him angry. He thought, So this is how my love is repaid! How fickle the heart of woman is!

"Yet only a few days later, his wife, who had taken a much slower ship back home, appeared before her husband. And the knight did not recognize her. She was so changed. Her hair cut like yours, Joan, but in a slightly improved style and much cleaner, without lice or any fleas. She wore men's clothes, and even the manner in which she walked was different. She had become famous around the world for her verses and music. Every prince and king had invited her to court to play her lute and sing for them, but she had decided to come home. She missed her husband and had always been a good mistress to her servants."

Joan waits. You cannot end the story there, her expression says. That would be cruel.

"They parted," her uncle says with a shrug. "Before the first night was over, the noble lady was back on a ship. She continued to travel and returned to the Saracen king's court to serve, for a time, as a courtier to him. She wanted to mend his barbaric ways and to free the other captured slaves. The knight, I am told, fell into a life of dissipation. He abused his tenants, gambled away his money, and had affairs with his tenants' pretty wives, so the husbands soon rose up against him and tore him apart, like wild dogs on a carcass."

Joan nods. She likes stories with just endings. Then she thinks, considering the moral of the tale. "Are you saying you will be torn apart by angry husbands?" she asks.

He laughs. His hand finds her cheek in the dark and pats it. "Let them catch me first," he says.

She thinks she understands the purpose of the story. This must be what happens when you leave your home, travel, and see the world. Little by little, you begin to change, even if you are not aware of it. What was once alien becomes familiar: foreign tongues, the music of strange instruments, the vagaries of the sea. Slowly you alter until the very stars that spin in the heavens are as familiar to you as the lines of your own hand. But first you must step out your front door. You must leave behind what you know and possibly what you love. You must be willing to lose every inch of yourself, for the next time you look into a stream or a mirror, which may be weeks, years, or half a lifetime from now, you will not recognize your reflection. You must risk this much in order to gain what the world is ready to offer.

They stand, brush themselves, and begin the long walk back to the village. It is another way of saying, No, you can't come. Another way of telling her, You must make your own map of the world. Search out your own piece of sky and patch of earth, your own awning to sleep under when it is raining and it feels the sun may never shine again, for there will certainly be such days. No one can walk this path for you. You cannot simply follow in another's footsteps, as though life were a complicated dance, every turn and twist memorized and prepared for ahead of time. There are many things in the world one can inherit: money, land, power, a crown. But an adventure is not one of them; you must make your own journey.

◆

RAIN DRIPS, the slow warning patter before the angels dump their buckets over the heads of the living. The torch in her uncle's hand hisses. They are laughing because Joan is making different faces ("This is my mother's penitent look," she says), and the fire, casting shadows that tremble and waver, lends her expressions a demonic quality.

They are still snickering when shouts come from behind a patch of trees. In a clearing, an argument is taking place. Her uncle grabs her arm, pulls her back.

She wriggles away from him, creeps closer, bends. She is curious. Between the narrow space of two trunks, she sees men, their backs to her. Her father is here; next to him, Guillaume's father, and three other men from Domrémy who are Jacques d'Arc's closest friends. They are always with him.

She recognizes their shapes: Guillaume's father is reedy—a gust of wind might knock him down—while Jacques d'Arc is muscular and square. The others are lesser versions of the man they worship like acolytes. They make a half circle around another figure she can't see. She motions to her uncle for the torch, and he passes it to her, all the while beckoning her away. She keeps the torch low beside her so the men don't notice the light.

"Leave," she hears her father say. "Leave before we make trouble for you."

From behind the wall of bodies, a voice protests: "But we had an agreement. And you have taken my money. You cannot keep your pigs and also keep the money. Return one or the other, and I will say no more of this deception."

Joan recognizes the voice. It is the man from Maxey.

Then Guillaume's father speaks up: "What money are you talking about? I don't think any money was exchanged, do you, Jacques?"

She can just make out her father shaking his head. "I never received any money. We may have discussed the idea of selling certain pigs to you, but a price was never agreed upon."

"We are only taking what we're owed," Guillaume's father breaks in; his speech is rushed. "And what we have taken is far less in value than what was first stolen from us. From me. My son's life, or don't you remember?"

"I had no part in that," the man from Maxey replies after a pause. He is in earnest; his voice is shaking. He swallows so hard, it is like he has gulped down a whole egg. "I swear to you. My own sons are too young to play such games. They were not there. I was not there. And wasn't it an accident? I was told the boy fell and hit his head."

Now it is the voice of Guillaume's father that shakes: "It was not a game. It was not an accident."

Jacques laughs. "I knew, when I first came to Maxey demanding reparation, that you were the one to cheat. You have a fool's face."

She feels her uncle tug her sleeve. "Come, Joan," he whispers. "Come quickly."

But she pushes his hand away. There is a sudden roar of voices. The man from Maxey has lunged at one of them, perhaps in an attempt to break the circle and run. But Guillaume's father is ready. He has something in his hand, and she feels her stomach lurch at the sound of a muffled thud, followed by a moan and a whimper so small it could have come from a child.

It is like a bad dream, a dream where you don't feel your legs move, but you find yourself in another place. When she looks up, she is in the clearing, in front of these men. At her feet, the man from Maxey touches the side of his head. He is dazed, blood oozing through his hands.

For a moment, Jacques's friends are so stunned, their bodies jerk, like horses that have been spooked. Even her father's eyes are wide and aghast. Where has she come from? It is as though she has materialized from thin air.

He soon shrugs back to himself. "Leave us, Joan," he says. His voice is calm. He looks at her as if she were a beetle he could pick up and squeeze slowly between his fingers.

"You have no place here." It is Guillaume's father who speaks. His grip tightens on a rock, its edge shining with blood, and she thinks of the stones she picked up that day from the field. "This doesn't concern you."

She holds up the torch, as if to inspect each of their faces and memorize them. She is buying time. A decision must be made and made quickly. Her father will not leave, and because he will not leave, she knows his friends will also stand their ground. She looks over her shoulder. Perhaps Durand will come and save both of them? Would they really kill a man in front of not one but two witnesses? Yet from behind her, there is nothing, no sound but rainfall hitting the leaves.

The man from Maxey, still groaning, has slowly picked himself up. He is standing behind her, trying to conceal his giant body.

"You have what you came for," she says, though her eyes are on her father. "You have your money."

"Jacques, he may talk," Guillaume's father says. He is suddenly pale. He glances at the rock in his hand. "We had better finish what we have started, and soon."

Her gaze is still fixed on her father. This moment feels personal. It is like there is no one else in the clearing save the two of them. So, who will give way first?

When he speaks, his voice is strangely at ease. "Joan," he says, and the sound of her name lands like a dull blow to her skull. She almost steps back out of habit, though she hopes her face registers nothing. "You will regret this."

A pause. She feels her fingers loosen their hold on the torch. Her arm thrusts forward, and with it, the fire spins toward her father's chest. She hears him scream an oath and the other men cry out, as if they, too, had been burned, though this is impossible. She turns and runs. The man from Maxey bounds after her. He is close at her heels.

She doesn't remember when her legs give way and she falls, tripping over a root. She is never tired from chores, from running around the village and climbing trees. But she is tired now, her energy spent, as if the act of rebellion has drained her.

She feels arms close around her body, lift her up and up, and she is aware that she is moving again, though her legs are limp. The man from Maxey is carrying her. They move faster and more nimbly than she thought a man of his size would have been capable of. Around her, the dark flies past; she loses consciousness. For how long she doesn't know, but when she wakes, they have left the woods behind, and she can see the sky above them.

He sets her down, and his expression seems to say, *The world is small but not this small. How have we run into each other once more?* Then he peers at her with narrowed eyes. He catches the resemblance. "Ah, you are that man's child," he says finally.

They are in Maxey now, enemy land, but for him it is home, a dirty cottage with a low roof, three children, and a wife only a few inches taller than Joan and who stares, like an unblinking owl, when Joan appears on the threshold. The children, tawny owlets, blink, glance at one another, communicating in the unspoken language of siblings; they don't know what to make of their guest.

She watches the man lift the youngest of his children, his daughter, and kiss the crown of her head. She watches him pet the heads of his sons, though the whole side of his own head is bleeding and he hasn't had time to wipe the blood away. She thinks, Perhaps I am dead and don't know it. Or the Burgundians love their children more than the French do. His wife is still staring. Her eyes pass back and forth between Joan and her husband. She says, in a voice barely above a whisper, "What has happened? Thieves? Brigands? Where does the child come from?"

The man considers. He answers slowly, thinking through his pain, "Yes, it was thieves. We have lost some money." He glances at where Joan is standing and doesn't say any more.

After his head is bandaged, they give Joan a bowl of something warm and viscous to eat. It is worse-tasting than pottage, but she is starving and drinks the contents down. The wife takes Joan's empty bowl, refills it, then passes it to her again. They show her where she will sleep for the night, for she cannot go back home, not today, and she lies down. She watches the other children, and they watch her. They could have given her a pallet hard as a rock, and she would sleep soundly on it. How is she still alive, she wonders. How has Jacques not pursued them here and wrung both their necks? It is a warm night, but her body is shaking.

Morning comes. Her eyes open. She reaches up to rub an itch, and a spider falls from her cheek, skitters away. It is almost possible that the events of the previous night didn't happen, until she sees the siblings who are not her siblings sleeping next to her, and the parents who are not her parents and who, it is still astonishing to her, seem to love their children and have no wish to hurt them. Her gaze passes over their arms, their faces, their bare feet. Their breathing is regular and peaceful. They show no signs of beatings.

She sees the man has been waiting for her to wake. From the cottage they walk to the end of the lane that leads out of Maxey. When he is ready to turn back, he sticks a hand into the front of his tunic and removes a piece of cheese wrapped in damp leaves. He looks sorry for her. Whatever is waiting for her at home . . . he shuts his eyes, does not want to think about it. But he has suffered, too. Blood has seeped through the bandage on his head.

She takes a good look at him before she crouches, her fingers feeling the hem of her dress for hardness. Her hands tear out the stitches, and coins spill into her palm. She offers a few to the man, who considers their glinting surfaces as if money could make sense of what has happened to him. She watches his fingers close over the coins. This time he takes them.

"I'm sorry," she says, though she doesn't add *for your wound*, *for the money you have lost*, *for my father and his tricks.*

She hesitates. Even before she speaks, she feels sure this is something her father would try to do: to get as much value as possible out of the money one has already paid. "The boy who died . . . his name was Guillaume," she says. "He was only seven years old. I know you think it was an accident, but have you heard anything else in Maxey . . . You see, my village believes something different happened. We heard he was pushed."

They stare at each other, and his gaze goes flinty before he shakes his head and leaves her side. It is the first time he has been unkind to her. He will not betray his people, as she has done.

Joan turns in the direction of home. It is still early; the sun has opened only a single eye, and the air is mild, the land covered in a translucent yellow mist. Later, it will be hot, and dust from the roads will billow up in clouds whenever a cart or mule passes. But for now, each blade of grass is dressed in last night's rain, and dreams are still spinning out their threads behind the shuttered windows of cottages.

She is surprised to find her sister waiting for her at the door. She looks up. Catherine is crying.

At first, she thinks this is because she has been missing for a whole night. But these are not tears of relief. It is quiet, and she has grown used to the *tap-tap* of paws running out to meet her. Where is the shrill bark that can wake a whole village, the single howl that can raise the dead?

What comes out of Catherine's mouth is an incoherent blubber, but Joan thinks she hears a curse word somewhere. It takes her by surprise, her sister cursing, before she remembers. Her dog's name. "Salaud . . ."

And then it is Joan's turn to wail. Her throat strains from the effort of forming words in a pitch higher than usual. "Could no one protect him?" she asks, each word stretched thin, though she is not really asking. She is begging. She doesn't wait for an answer. She bows her head, and her chin sinks like a weight to her chest. She is aware her sister is trying to pull her into an embrace, but she slips through Catherine's hands, as easily as a minnow through a hole in a net. She moves away, tripping over her feet. She weeps.

She walks until she reaches the edge of the Bois Chenu. But why has she come here? It takes the time to wipe snot away with her sleeve for Joan to understand. Her presence here is a plea for a wish that can never be granted. If she returns to the place of last night's events, perhaps she can take everything back. She can keep walking and laughing with her uncle by the light of the torch, which will remain safely in his grip. And she can leave the man from Maxey to meet his fate, whatever that may be.

She stands without moving, her hands cupped under her chest to catch whatever may leak through her skin. Out of sight in a nearby tree, a lark sings; the note holds, a needle's point of sound in a silent, sleeping world. In that sound, her grief.

There are no words—no words for this.

◆

THEY HAVE STOOD HERE BEFORE, in this precise spot on the field now nearly stripped of its harvest. Her eyes are so waterlogged and sore, it is painful to blink. The sun is setting, and grief still seeps through. Her nose drips.

When she asks how, Durand shakes his head. "Spare yourself this much," he whispers, but she is adamant. "Tell me everything," she demands.

So he begins: "Your father returned alone, and he was pale with anger. The fire had only singed his shirt—he was not burned. But his hands were trembling. He kept on repeating, 'My daughter, my own daughter, a traitor.' It seems he knew what he planned, for he did not stop moving. He lit a fire. And we—Isabelle, myself, even Jacquemin—who were all trying to calm him, asked, 'A fire, Jacques? It is warm enough tonight without a fire. Surely none of us will catch cold. Come and sit, take some ale and a piece of bread. Or we can warm a bowl of pottage for you.' We were pleading with him, yet you could tell he didn't hear us. His gaze was distracted. He was still turning over the scene from the woods, and the flames he saw were not the ones in front of him, no. They were from the torch you threw at him, Joan. We watched him light his own torch with some straw, and go upstairs to where your sister was.

"I saw his intent, as soon as the torch was lit. I blocked his way, but you know your father's arm. It knocked me clean across the room. Your poor mother had to fetch me up from the ground. I did not see what happened, though I heard it. The cries. Catherine tried to flee downstairs, to shield . . . It was no use. He was torn from her. Lit, like the wheel on Saint John's Eve. He died in her arms, half his body burned, and your sister held him, though he was in agonies, and so was she for being unable to save him. All of us knew what he meant to you. I, who have sinned so much in my life, could still never have done such a thing. The smell alone . . . I went out of the house and was sick into a bush."

She thinks, Another person might not have gone into such detail. They would leave out the burning, the cries, say it was done with a single blow, as easy as twisting the neck of a sparrow. He died quickly, Joan, her uncle might have said. That is all.

But they are two soldiers, one old, one young, and this is a battle they have lost. It cannot be only victories. They cannot always escape unscathed.

With Catherine, he never talks about the war. It's always little jokes, how many hearts has she broken today and how many hearts does she plan to break by the time they sit down to supper tomorrow? It is always songs and stories of love, of pining, tales of lovelorn knights and princesses, and these princesses must all be sisters or twins, for they are identical in every tale, with straw-colored hair and gowns of silver brocade; they wear pointed slippers and walk through airy rooms in ancient palaces. The stories he tells her sister usually end well: in marriage to widowed kings or with the birth of healthy, pink-faced children who giggle as soon as they are born.

Not so with Joan. With her, it is news of the war that France is slowly but surely losing, even with the help of their faithful ally, the Scots. It is reports of sieges, of the market price of a cat when the citizenry is starving; it is accounts of recent battles, of bands of mercenaries burning whole strips of France, setting fire to everything—homes, churches, people, livestock—that they cannot take with them or sell for a cutthroat price. He tells her how a hanged man always pisses himself. "Always?" she asks. "Always," he replies, nodding, and he explains it must be a natural reflex, or perhaps just fear of death that causes a man to disgrace himself when his feet are kicking the air. Also, one who is burned at the stake will curl his hands into fists, as if he is trying to fight the flames. "How do you know that?" She is skeptical, full of questions; she thought those who were burned were tied, their arms and hands bound to a pole. But he shrugs. He says, "I have seen it. I have seen, in the course of my travels, such things I wish I could unsee. I thought, The older I get, the more I will forget. But that is not so. In fact, it is the opposite. You remember certain things more vividly."

She thinks, There must be something wrong with me, and not because I usually look as if I have just escaped from a battle with the English, some part of me swollen or cut open that brings to mind the war, the wounded, and the dying. Perhaps I am a child born under an evil star or a comet. Perhaps there is something inside me that is unlucky or ill-fated, which makes my father hate me, my mother pray for me, the priest shake his head, and my uncle tell me accounts of plague and famine after he bids me good morning.

The priest, who has heard her dog has died but not how, feels sorry for her. So, the next morning, he invites her to the church and lets her sit at a table with a slanting surface. He places a book in front of her and opens it gingerly, as if the pages were made of butterfly wings. It is the first book she has ever seen or touched, a compendium of the lives of the saints. He lets her turn the pages and look at the pictures, since she cannot read. She sees Sebastian, body pierced with arrows, a human porcupine, and recognizes Michael, stomping on the head of the serpent Satan. She sees a young woman with a face very like her sister's touch the spoke of a giant wheel, which cracks at her small feet, drawn in the shape of flower petals. The priest, stealing glances at Joan's swollen eyes, her wet nose rubbed raw, wants to show her suffering that is great and noble so she will forget her own misfortunes. But it doesn't work. There is no contest between her grief and the martyrdom of the saints, who take their pain mildly even as they are clubbed or beheaded. She tells the priest she likes the colors, the dark blues of skies and soldiers' cloaks and the stars and halos cut from gold leaf, and the priest closes the book, aware that he has failed. She leaves.

Later that day, when she is again with Durand, he turns to her. She is still crying. She thinks she will never stop crying.

He touches her shoulder. "You made a choice, Joan. They might have killed him or left him for dead, and then his wife would be a poor widow and their children without a father."

He says, "Here. I have a gift for you." She looks down and sees a small knife in his outstretched hand, the kind for paring fruit or cutting sticks.

She remembers the meeting of women in Guillaume's cottage, her mother's eyes shut tight as she muttered a prayer. She recalls the hunched bodies, like doves gathering against the winter cold. No one spoke if they could whisper. An old woman, the dead boy's grandmother, stirred a pot with a bony hand, and this was the loudest noise in the room. She remembers, too, the meeting of men in her father's house: the restlessness and pacing, the twitching of muscles beneath shirts, the fists that opened, then closed around throats of air. The men wanted vengeance. The women wanted deliverance. If I had to choose, she thinks, I would choose action over prayer. I would avenge, but I would also save. Is such a thing possible? If she could relive the past, she knows she would do nothing different. She would still step into the clearing and fill her father's eyes with the torch's fire to defend the man from Maxey, just as he had rescued her from thieves in Vaucouleurs.

She takes the present. She does not need to ask her uncle what she can use it for. In her pocket, she has two bent nails. Now she has a knife.

In the morning, she comes across Guillaume's cat in the road. The dead boy's family hasn't treated the animal well. The grandmother is always shooing it away with a broom, but the cat is sunning itself, its expression unconcerned, in a patch of wilted dandelions. She picks it up. She rubs her face, as its former master did, along its soft, curving spine, until her eyes itch with tears and cat fur. Around its neck, she ties a pouch, and in the pouch, she puts the remaining coins from her dress. She sets the cat at the door of the dead boy's cottage, and the next time she sees the animal, it is being stroked in the arms of Guillaume's sister and the pouch is no longer hanging around its neck. In the story making its way around the village, the cat went out one day and returned with treasure. The family thinks the cat is lucky and has given it a name: Matagot, after a spirit from Gascony. A matagot may be evil or it may be good, but it is known to take the form of a cat. Treat a matagot well, feed it, and it may bring you a gold coin. Soon the cat is plump as a fine lady's cushion and too contented, she hears, to be bothered to catch mice. When she passes Matagot, its gray-green eyes blink at her, watching.

She hears that Henry, King of England, is dead. Dysentery finished him, though this may be another rumor. But he has a brother, John, Duke of Bedford, who will serve as regent until his heir comes of age. She thought the war would end when Henry died, but it seems England will not leave France because their king is now a corpse. There are still towns and cities to take. There are other kings. She and her family may tomorrow, the next week, or the next month wake up and find themselves Englishmen.

So, the war goes on. So, the circle turns.

Part Two

‡

In August 1422, Henry V, King of England, dies. Two months later, in October, Charles VI passes away. Days after his father's death, the Dauphin, Charles VII, declares himself King of France at Mehun-sur-Yèvre but without any of the traditional accompaniments to this important ceremony, such as being anointed with the oil of the Holy Ampulla in the city of Reims (now occupied by the English).

The Dauphin's makeshift coronation does not hinder any of England's plans, however. The gaps left by Henry V's and Charles VI's deaths are quickly filled by Henry's younger brothers. While Humphrey, Duke of Gloucester, assumes his role as Lord Protector of England, John, Duke of Bedford, takes over as regent, a step vital to ensuring England's hold on France, as Henry's only son (Henry VI), still an infant, is too young to rule.

Thus there exist not one but two "kingdoms of France": the first comprises territories under English control (where a fine is imposed on any subject heard to acknowledge the Dauphin as the rightful king); the second, the "kingdom of Bourges," covers territories that remain loyal to the Dauphin. In 1423 and 1424, the French suffer two humiliating defeats, at the Battle of Cravant and the Battle of Verneuil. To make matters worse, there is also much infighting within the Dauphin's own court. Seeing a bad situation grow dire, in 1426, Yolande of Aragon, the Dauphin's mother-in-law, takes over his council, while English forces prepare to launch more campaigns.

Prospects for a glorious and triumphant reign look bleak for the Dauphin, who, with his court favorite, Georges de La Trémoille, now resides in the castle at Chinon. By October 1428, reports arrive that the city of Orléans is under siege. This is a calamitous development for the French. If Orléans, strategically placed on the Loire River, is taken, England's grip on France may soon become a stranglehold.

So, the Dauphin attends Mass daily. He prays for a miracle.

I

♦ ♦ ♦

DOMRÉMY, SUMMER 1428
SIX YEARS LATER

SAINT JOHN'S EVE. A bonfire burns. This year there is no wheel, and the fire takes on a ghostly human form, like a sacrifice.

The top of Durand Laxart's head just reaches Joan's shoulder. She has grown and grown and grown and now towers over everyone: the women, her brothers, even her father. How did this happen? No one knows, but this bodes ill for Jacques d'Arc. He can no longer raise a hand to her. Strike her with a stool leg, and it won't be Joan's arm that breaks.

Jehanne jokes, "Did your mother betray her husband with a giant, Joan? It would explain a lot if she did." Then Jehanne looks away, aware she has gone too far, but Joan takes her meaning. Time hasn't made her grow fonder of Jacques. They still hate each other. Only the odds have changed.

Her uncle nudges her arm. They are standing a distance from the bonfire; the sound of a stream floats under the crackle of flames.

"What are you thinking of?" he asks.

She is quiet. "Nothing." She glances at him. "Nothing," she repeats. This is his sixth visit in as many years.

When he arrived, she had news for him. "You will hear about it from my mother, so I want to tell you first," she declared as soon as she set eyes on him. "Earlier this month, to get rid of me, my churl of a father tried to marry me off. I refused. Then the fool, the man he had pledged me to, said I had promised him personally and broken my promise. We had to go to court. Me! In a breach-of-promise suit!"

"How did you get out of it?" Durand hesitated. "Or did you get out of it? Are you married, Joan, and I have missed the wedding?"

She shoved him, though she was smiling. "I made a speech worthy of Jacques d'Arc. It astounded everyone. My father looked like a ghost by the time I was finished."

This is the most exciting thing that has happened to her in six years. That and three years ago, a band of Burgundian and English marauders drove off some cattle. "Lucky it was only cattle," her uncle said at the time. "Lucky they left quickly" was her answer.

She doesn't like war. She doesn't like the stories she hears, the same ones she's heard all her life: convents desecrated, churches plundered, wheat days away from being harvested reduced to cinders, livestock that the attackers can't take with them slaughtered, blood and meat to feed the flies. It is bad enough that some years the crop is ruined by bad weather. Winter alone, she thinks, is sufficient to starve and to kill. We don't need the English and the Burgundians to aid winter. It isn't the work of the English that makes a calf stillborn or a child stop breathing in its cradle.

But she does like the idea of change. A world in flux is a world where something may happen, and for the better. Only it hasn't happened to her.

Sometimes in secret and under the cover of night, she cries. She cries because if you have churned butter once, you have done it a hundred times. After several years, the novelty of turning sheep's tallow into candles grows old. She did not expect that her body would grow and grow, that she would become a giantess among the men and women of Domrémy, but nothing else would change.

In church, she has stopped praying. What is the point? If you don't even know who you are praying to, then you may as well pray to a wall and expect the stonework to answer you. So, she uses the time to rest her eyes, and sometimes the priest catches her asleep, which makes him angry.

The flames of the bonfire are dying down, but she can't look away. Life is hard. The earth is not always fruitful. There are some parts of the kingdom where people would be glad to say, *All my days are the same; I have lived to see the sun rise and set again.* She knows she should be grateful.

But there is a pain in her heart as the fire dies out. All my days are the same, she thinks. It is like a prayer, spoken into the last of the flickering embers, then emptied into the bubbling stream. All my days are the same.

◆

IN THE MORNING SHE RISES. For some time, she has slept every night under her father's roof. No more days beneath the Faerie Tree for Joan. He can't kick her out anymore.

If once she carried two bags of grain under her arms to take to the miller's, now she carries six. Ox dead? Horse half-starved? She can lift the plow as easily as pick up a head of cabbage. There is Joan swinging a scythe; there is Joan threshing, with a flail. There is Joan crouching on a roof, thatching a hole, and chopping wood to build a new fence. And who can forget the time a neighbor's cart got stuck in the mud after days of heavy rain? He was an old man, though in good shape for his age. Hard as he pushed, it did no good. But Joan took up a corner of the cart. In her grip, the wood groaned before the cart jolted like a living thing and shuddered onto the road. She recrossed the lane and went back to her work.

This balmy morning in August, the sky is clear, the sun a washed-out yellow, and the air fragrant with fresh-cut hay. From the treetops: the hum of birdsong.

But by midday her body feels cold, and when she touches her arm, the skin is damp. On the stump of a tree that her uncle has transformed into a table, he is showing her brothers a trick with three cups; a pebble is concealed beneath one of them. Her brothers keep their eyes on the cups: a mistake. She turns, sees Catherine in the distance walking in the direction of the Virgin's shrine just outside of the village.

It is when she looks away from Catherine that she stumbles; her head spins. She had been tilling her mother's garden, and the ground moves, actually tips, beneath her feet. She is never sick, but her cheeks are feverishly warm. Her legs give out just as her uncle and brothers notice her. Panic closes up her throat, like a strangling hand, so she can't cry out.

Above her, church bells thunder, but the timing is wrong. It is too early for the bells to ring the hour of Nones. As she lies on the ground, she hears shouting. The shouting isn't coming just from her uncle and brothers. It is the whole village in uproar. Why, she wonders. Why is everyone making so much noise because I have fallen?

Then she hears: beneath all the shouts, the beating of horses' hooves. The sound is like a sudden storm, a torrent of summer rain pummeling the earth. She hears, from a distance, words she can't understand. The language is foreign to her, the speakers of this language even harsher than her father. As her brothers lift her arms, she catches sight of torches. Torches in daylight? She shakes her head. This makes no sense. She must be dreaming. Yet she watches as a man mounted on a horse, a man she doesn't recognize, tosses a torch as if it were a pebble into a pond, and the first cottage in the village goes up in flames. The people inside, a whole family, run out. She is aware that she is sweating. Her body, her very insides, shake.

The English are coming, she thinks. They have come to Domrémy at last. So, this is the fear the English inspire. She is ashamed that now the enemy is here, she is afraid.

◆

With the rest of the village, they flee to Neufchâteau, a neighboring town. The roads become a maze of jostling carts carrying poorly knotted sacks and people. Dresses and tunics have been turned into bundles, and already there are disputes over what belongs to whom. She, too, is a weight, carried into Neufchâteau. Noise and the swaying of the cart make her head hurt, and new beads of sweat drip into her eyes. She can only look up; her gaze is fixed on a cloudless blue sky, a too-bright sun. She hears her father say, as she is carried into the inn by her brothers, "Of course she would choose such a time to fall ill. What else would you expect? Any trouble she can give me. Any trouble."

She tries to speak, though nothing comes out. Later, she thinks. Later she will answer him with a few choice words.

Her body sinks onto a pallet not her own. Outside, there is a commotion. Men are already counting their losses, and mothers consoling weeping children sing them snatches of songs. She hears the creaking wheels of carts as more from Domrémy arrive.

On the landing, footsteps stamp up and down, and Jacquemin is swearing oaths. "I will kill them," he declares. His voice is high-pitched. He is practically squeaking. Yet something in it sounds hollow, even false, to her. "They are cowards, those English barbarians. What does it take to light a cottage on fire? Hm? Tell me what it takes. A woman can do it. So, is that what they are proud of? Slaying a few chickens! Leading some pigs away!" It reminds her of another moment in another year: a day as fine as this one. She thinks, before her world turns dark: When a boy was dying, you made the same oaths. You could do nothing then. You can do nothing now.

◆

WHEN JOAN WAKES, there is a new pain to contend with: hunger. The sky outside the single window is nearly dark, the last of the light slipping fast away.

She is still dizzy. The room teeters, as though balanced on a single sharp point. In the far corner by a low table, she thinks she sees the shape of her sister.

She is tired but wants to talk. She is in the mood for swapping stories. "Do you remember," Joan begins, "that time when I returned home, and as soon as our father saw me he threw a cloak over my head and told me to fix a hole in it."

"Do you need it now?" she'd asked in protest. Her voice then was small. She was young. Maybe seven or eight.

"Now," her father said.

It was night and too dark for sewing. But she took the stub of a candle and, crouching, lit it from the last few embers in the hearth. When she stood, she felt the cloak slip out of her hands. Above her, Catherine said, "Hold the candle while I sew for you, Joan," because Catherine saw she wanted sleep.

So she raised the candle close to where Catherine's needle moved, darting up and down like a silver fish, but not so close that she would set the cloak on fire, though she was tempted.

As she watched, she felt the candle wobble in her grip; her eyes closed, opened, closed again. She was falling asleep on her feet. Melted tallow dripped onto the cloth in a column of shining, pearly beads. "Careful," Catherine said.

It was so still, Joan could hear her sister's breathing. Neither of them spoke, until she saw that the flame was about to go out. Her pulse quickened. Before the last thread is cut, Joan thought, a wish must be made.

"Quick," she said, a whisper in the near darkness. "You must say what you want. What you want more than anything else in the world."

Her sister bowed her head, as if she were about to pray. She considered, then spoke quietly, unrushed though the flame was already dying. "I want to make a good marriage," Catherine said. "Healthy children. One boy, two girls."

It was a wish typical of Catherine: sweet-mannered husbands, rosy-cheeked babies, the peace of the hearth is the peace of the kingdom.

Then she turned to Joan. She said, "And you?"

In Joan's hand, the flame sputtered before dying. She saw nothing but smelled smoke.

"I want . . . I want too many things."

When the cloak was finished, she heard Catherine sigh. In the dark, her sister's arm was like a swan's neck. It wound itself around Joan's shoulders and brought her close. Joan felt the top of her head kissed twice. "Have only good dreams," Catherine said before she went upstairs to sleep.

The next morning, her father picked up the cloak and examined the place where the hole had been. He grunted.

"Soon you shall be a seamstress," he told Joan. And for a whole week, there were no beatings. A record for Jacques d'Arc. For her, a small miracle.

Her story finished, she waits for Catherine to speak, to confirm the facts of her memory or to laugh at her for remembering wrong. But there is no answer.

"Can you bring me some water?" she says after a pause. "And is there anything to eat?"

When she turns her head to look, the corner of the unfamiliar room is empty. Outside, the town has become still. The sun has set; the light of the day is gone. From behind the wall, in another room, she catches the sound, like a strange humming, of someone softly weeping.

II

◆ ◆ ◆

BY MORNING, discussions have begun, and meetings are being held at the inn. People talk about what has been lost. Gardens and their herbs. A spare linen shirt. A pot not three months used. A plow newly fixed by the blacksmith, now for nothing. Fresh batches of ale, made with hops only recently picked and dried. Grown men lament lost sows and sheep as if they were their children. Yet even now they must remember their blessings. To appease God's rage, they also talk about what has been saved. For as long as anyone can remember, ever since the English began to ravage the land with fire, the hems of women's dresses have been weighted with coins, a whole family's savings concealed on a single body.

But there are still things people won't speak of: the jump of the pulse as the tip of a knife presses against the skin; how there is strength in numbers, even when the person who faces you is a young woman unarmed; how as soon as the first blow is dealt, she falls, and the circling wolves close in, marveling at their own strength.

"There were three of them," Catherine says.

Joan listens. She listens as she sweats out her fever, a blanket over her shoulders. Outside, the day is warm. You can even smell the heat.

Catherine's arms are spotted, marked where fingers have pressed into her flesh. Next door, a friend of their father's, a brutish man, is lamenting the loss of a cow days away from giving birth. "What will happen to her now?" he asks. "What will they do to her, do you think?" His voice cracks.

But in this room, there are no tears. This is a place, Joan thinks, beyond tears. Catherine's eyes are swollen but dry. Across her jaw, Joan spots the outline of a purple shadow. A slap delivered backhanded to shut up her screams.

"What did they look like?" Joan asks. "Did they address each other by name? Did you catch a name?"

Catherine shakes her head. They both know it's a foolish question. Unless you put a whole country on trial, you will never find these men.

But Catherine replies so that Joan has something to hold on to: "One had a long scar on his arm. They didn't speak French."

Men who are cruel. Men who don't speak French. Men with scars.

The room is still. Her mother has gone to the cathedral in Neufchâteau, a larger and more impressive edifice than the small church in Domrémy, to pray. Her father and uncle are tending to other matters, including village disputes that have nearly come to blows. In the chaos of fleeing, a few chickens were crushed. Now the question is, Who will pay for them? There is another family making a lot of noise; they claim their neighbors sabotaged their cart by replacing a good wheel with a rotten one and taking the good wheel for themselves. The neighbors' defense: "How would we have known the English were coming? Are you calling us traitors?" On all sides, emotions run high. If you can't yell at the enemy, the next best thing is to shout at your friends instead. And this morning, supplies are discovered missing. Possibly thieves take no pity, not even on those who have lost their homes. There is the matter of how long they will remain in Neufchâteau, how they will pay their room and board at the inn, and where they can keep the livestock they have salvaged. None of these things are beyond the abilities of Jacques d'Arc, but who, Joan wonders, who will attend to what has happened to Catherine? To crimes beyond crushed chickens and sabotaged cart wheels? Who will find a solution to this?

She does not ask about the pain, only listens as Catherine explains that it was their uncle who found her after the men took what they wanted and left her behind. By then, the enemy had moved on; it was growing dark. But as they walked, a cart passed them on the road. Durand paid the man a few deniers to take them to Neufchâteau. When they reached the inn, she could no longer move; her legs had become numb, and he had to lift her down and carry her in. Joan had been asleep.

"How many people know?" Joan asks. She is surprised by how practical her questions are.

Catherine doesn't answer. She bows her head, wraps her knees close to her chest. So, everyone knows.

Her sister looks away. Their mother and Jehanne have washed her body, and she is wearing a dress borrowed from Hauviette. Her hair is damp. She stares at a spot on the floor where a spider is crawling.

Joan throws off the blanket, and it slips from her shoulders to the ground. She stands. Her legs are unsteady, but she moves, her hands feeling along the walls, to the single window to look out of it.

Catherine says, "I had not reached the shrine of the Virgin, but I thought of her."

It is all Joan can do not to shake her head. And how would she have helped you? How can compassion, temperance, mercy, which are all the features of the Virgin, serve you against such men as these? The answer is, they can't.

In her chest, she feels a hardness, like the tip of a knife has broken off and is left there to fester: a splinter of steel in her heart.

When she looks out the window, she doesn't see the roads, the sky, the market stalls of Neufchâteau, the steeple of the church where their mother is praying. She sees the path to the Virgin's shrine on the edge of Domrémy, the grass patterned with white patches of bishop's lace, the warm pools of sun Catherine would have stepped through, alternating with stretches of shade. She sees her sister bending to pick wildflowers to lay at the Virgin's altar. Yet in the distance, shadows wait. A huddle of wolves watch, jaws dripping.

She thinks of years of poor harvests. The nights they sat down to eat when food was scarce and Catherine said she wasn't hungry. She edged her half-filled bowl toward Joan and lived off scraps of crusts and water for more days than Joan could count. When asked why she starved, she said she fasted to show her devotion to the Virgin, yet it was Joan who ate all the offerings.

She thinks of men who are cruel. Men who don't speak French. Men with scars. I do not have to seek out these men. They are everywhere.

Behind her, Catherine rises to light a candle. Her movements are small and pained, but her face is like stone and gives nothing away. She will not pity herself.

Already, as Joan stands, half-leaning against the wall, she can feel her strength returning. By the day's end, her fever will have broken. Her limbs will be as they were before. The sweat on her body will have dried. She will no longer suffer from chills, and her sight will clear.

But too late. All too late.

She, Joan, is not beyond self-pity. As the candle flickers, she asks, the question directed to her God: Who else will You have me fail?

She thinks, Perhaps I should not have fallen asleep in church. Perhaps I should have prayed harder.

◆

Her father has struck a deal with the innkeeper, a burly, laughing woman named La Rousse because of her flame-colored hair. For reduced room and board, he offers the services of his two daughters. They will help with anything that needs doing around the inn.

Before Joan goes down to work, she seeks out Hauviette. Nothing has changed since she was a child of ten. Though Joan now stands a full two heads taller, as soon as they see her, Jehanne sweeps her into her arms.

She asks them to stay with Catherine. "As a favor to me," she says. "I have nothing to pay you with, but I will sneak what I can out of the kitchen when I have the chance."

"Payment!" Jehanne cries, as if the word has a bad taste. She shakes her head at Joan. "Not everything is resolved with money and bargaining, Joan. You are becoming as bad as Jacques."

When Joan goes downstairs, La Rousse is waiting with her father, who is tapping his foot. "Well? Where is the other girl, her sister?" the woman complains. Her face is as red as her hair. "Wasn't I promised two girls, not just the one?"

Joan gives the innkeeper a hard stare. "Look at me," she says, and she does not even try to keep the edge out of her voice. "I am two girls."

La Rousse stares back. "You needn't worry. I will work you as hard as two girls," she replies.

And she means it. First, Joan is given sacks of flour. "Weevils out," the cook says, jutting his thumb. So, she sits down on a low stool with a bowl by her feet, into which she drops wriggling beetles; some manage to crawl out of the bowl, and she stamps them dead. Next, she beats eggs, until the cook's hands fly to his ears and he shouts, "That's enough, woman. That's enough! Move on to something else!" She pounds dough, kneading it with her fists, until what is left is like a sad death mask.

With her uncle's knife she pares vegetables, and the small boys who are hired by the day to run errands or make deliveries gather at the table to watch her. "You are so quick," they say in awed voices. "Don't distract me," she replies seriously, "or my knife may cut you into strips of tender meat for a fresh pie." She smiles to show she is only teasing, and they smile back.

She plucks birds, slices eels, and scours pots until her callused palms are rubbed pink. She rinses brine-cured pork. And when she is done in the kitchen, she is sent out to serve with a pitcher of acrid-smelling ale in each hand. By the third day, she has developed an unnerving habit of appearing at customers' elbows when their cups are nearly empty. It becomes a kind of joke: guests will shout or jump in surprise when they see her standing over them, waiting to refill their cups. "Where have you come from?" they ask her kindly. She says, "I don't know. Ask that man over there," and points her chin at her father, who struts about the inn as if he, and not La Rousse, is the real owner.

One time, a guest complains about the ale. "What's in this?" he groans. "It is upsetting my stomach." So, she goes back to the kitchen, adds water to both pitchers, and returns. "This is from a new batch," she says without blinking and pours the man a fresh cup. She watches him drink it off. "Better?" she asks, and the man shrugs at her before nodding.

An old knight arrives at the inn. For three drinks, he will tell a story—a good price for half an hour's entertainment, don't you think? Before anyone can offer, she is there to hand him a clean cup and fill it, and fill it, and fill it again; she wants to hear all the stories he has to tell. Ale dribbles down his unwashed beard; his thirst is impossible to quench.

He says he knew the famous knight Bertrand du Guesclin. "Oh, did you," the crowd roars, not believing him. "How old are you really, Grandpère? A hundred?" But he insists and grows so angry, tears spring from his eyes. "I did, I did!" he shouts. As proof, he talks of past victories, his own name in the tournament lists, and how once he unhorsed a man and his lance pierced both armor and mail, entering the flesh below his opponent's left shoulder just short of the heart. He talks of the Battle of the Thirty. He wasn't there, of course, but he heard about it growing up. Thirty French chevaliers against thirty English men-at-arms. And oh, the French victory, sung and resung by the troubadours, recorded by all the chroniclers of the time. Ah, those were the days!

Mid-story, he loses his train of thought. Both wars and tournaments have taken their toll on him, and now he is poor, reduced to traveling from town to town, like a beggar, and performing tricks with his horse, the only possession of value he has left in the world. He can make his horse bow as if it were a person. He can make it kick, to ward off wolves and attackers. He can make it step in a perfect circle as if it were dancing.

Joan listens while moving around the room, filling cups that don't need to be filled, and taking the knight's cup from him to pour more ale into it so he won't stop talking. The more he drinks, the more stories he tells, though the more incoherent he becomes, too.

The next day when he limps out of the inn, shielding his eyes from the sting of daylight, he discovers that someone is sitting on his horse. He peers at this figure, and his eyes narrow. Wasn't she the girl always bobbing around him last night with her pitchers of ale? And it was terrible ale, he thinks. Worse than horse piss.

"Who are you? Get off my horse!"

"Didn't you promise you would teach me to ride?" she asks.

"I promised no such thing!" But she looks so serious, and she has not budged from her seat. "When was this, then?" he inquires, more civilly than before.

"Last night" is her reply.

"Was I drunk?"

"If you were, then you still kept drinking for hours after, Grand-père. And I gave you no less than three pitchers of La Rousse's finest ale for free. At least two others at the inn heard you make this promise. Shall I call them now to bear witness?" She is able to keep her face straight, though it is a bluff.

His wiry hands pat down his beard, as if a reply could be found inside the hairs.

"Don't shout at me!" He holds his head, cringing. "I am old. My bones ache. The scars on my body—if you only knew! An old wreck shouldn't teach anyone, and I've forgotten practically everything I have learned. Too much ale." For a moment, he looks genuinely sad.

"You look fine to me," she answers.

They make a deal. For food, preferably dishes of meat, he will give her lessons. If she falls off, she gets back on again. If she is maimed or has her teeth kicked out of her head by his horse: not his problem! When her attention wanders during their lessons, he raps the ground with a stick. Notice the horse's ears! Why are you slouching? Not too tight on the reins now—what, are you afraid you'll fall off? She gives him eel pies, slices of cheese, and, when she has nothing better, a fistful of raw carrots. For another lesson, she'll boil and mash them, since his teeth are bad. She learns and learns quickly. But after a week, the knight leaves, and the horse with him.

Each day is long, and sometimes it is nearly the hour of Matins, two in the morning, when Joan finishes her work.

"She has had another bad dream," Hauviette tells her, waking with a yawn, and Joan feels helpless. She can't beat off nightmares with a stool leg.

When her friend leaves, she sits next to Catherine. She strokes her sister's head, and the motion of her hand is quick and smooth; beneath her, Catherine sighs. No nightmares visit her when Joan is here. But sleep for Joan comes in fits; her body never relaxes. The slightest creak of a floorboard or the stir of the wind against the shutters, and her eyes fly open. She watches the door, daring whatever devil standing behind it to show himself, as her fingers creep toward the handle of the knife in her pocket.

In her mind's eye she imagines two men: one steps from a cloud, a rose-scented mist; he is a prince dressed in cloth spun from gold. The second emerges from shadow. She hears him before she can see him; he shouts, uttering words in a tongue that hurts her ears. He has a stubbled chin and a pockmarked face. He spits on the ground, licks his lips, beckons.

She recognizes these men. One is from Catherine's dreams; the other, from her nightmares. Every night for the month they spend in Neufchâteau, Joan faces these two men. She thinks, If I had the chance, I would knock not one but both of you down, for the princes of today seem about as useful in battle as cornered virgins in a convent. I would dig my heels into your thighs. I would break all your bones.

Her rage does not go out with the first light of dawn. What she sees, what she feels, is as clear to her as if it were a vision sent from God.

III

◆ ◆ ◆

When they return to Domrémy in late summer, a sad procession of hanging heads, she is surprised by how wrong she was. She had thought, What could the English take from a place like this? We have nothing. We are poor. A few tallow candles? The bowl called Joan's bowl? A woman's linen apron? We have no golden altarpieces, no statues with emerald eyes and ruby-stone lips, no secret treasury spilling over with coins. But these men, so gifted in destruction, have kicked up the herb gardens and set fire to heads of cabbage and tender bulbs of fennel; they have broken whole pieces off cottages and torched the thatched roofs; they have snatched up the chickens, whose feathers litter the ground, like a panicked trail, and entered people's homes, it seems, for the sole purpose of shattering cups and axing stools, disfiguring cupboards and battering cauldrons. They have decapitated the statue of Saint Margaret that stood outside the church and toppled it, so the woman who crawled out of the belly of Satan now lies on her stomach, her head thrown several feet away, facedown in the dirt. Whole fields have been burned, along with the meadows, which the livestock need for grazing. It isn't the longbow that is the secret weapon of the English, Joan thinks; it's fire.

But the church is intact. And like a testimony to his strength, his relentless nature: Jacques d'Arc's house of stone remains, too.

She tells her uncle when they are alone, "I hate this, this feeling of living as though I am waiting for another attack. What's to stop them from coming a second time? And then we shall all be flattened." Durand, who has an answer to everything, is silent.

Often she thinks of the three men. She pictures them: the dark grizzle of their chins, their lightless eyes, their giant fists. She has seen the bruises they left on Catherine's body and memorized their shape and breadth, created from them what these men's hands must look like. If it had been her and not Catherine, Joan wonders, would she have escaped?

"They wouldn't stand in the same room as you, Joan," her uncle says, trying to smile and failing. "You'd scoop them up and shake the teeth out of their heads. They'd take one look at you and run."

She doesn't think this is true. Anyone is fair game in war. So why not her? She clenches and unclenches a fist. It isn't beauty the enemy wants but power.

A month passes. One morning, Catherine comes to her, says nothing, but her face tells Joan everything. A cold sweat washes through her, like the day when she fell ill. She had asked Catherine to forget, but forgetting is no longer an option. When their father is told, he is speechless; he stumbles into a chair to sit and stare at his own feet. Their mother prays, weeps, prays again. Durand covers his face. Joan watches as his free hand floats to his chest, to the place where his heart is, and hovers there, senseless. She learns that the body cannot distinguish between a laughing tumble in a feather bed with what is taken by force. The result is the same.

She watches Catherine grow weaker and confine herself to their room. "Keep the shutters closed," Catherine says. Light pains her, and she wants to keep the sounds, the chatter and noise of the village, outside. And there are girls, Catherine's former friends, who gather beneath the window and think it funny to ask when the wedding feast will be. Joan's response: she collects a bucket of pig feces and empties it over their heads.

"I feel you are growing smaller," Joan says.

Catherine's mouth twitches. She looks as if she would like to tuck herself away into oblivion. "Will you take me to the shrine?" she asks in reply. The Virgin's shrine is on top of a hill, and the weather is growing cool. But Catherine wants to make an offering. Joan just stops herself from saying, "Still?"

"We will go when it is dark and take Jacquemin with us," Catherine says. She is ashamed.

"We will go when it is light," Joan answers. "And we will walk the roads as if we own them."

At the shrine, Catherine prays while Joan stands outside. The shrine is small, and confined spaces make Joan feel cornered. Someone must keep a lookout. Also, what is the point of prayers now? Her body is strong, but she is tired. She is also angry. These days, she is of a temper to put her shoulder into anyone who walks too close, just for the chance to exchange a scowl and a crude word.

But she also wants to tell her uncle, I know what you meant when you covered your face and your hand rested over your heart. There is a pain here, just here, in my chest. It is like someone is pushing down with a bar of iron, and I am waiting for the bone to cave in.

When Catherine steps out of the shrine, it appears she has taken a lesson from the Virgin. Her face is as hard and placid as the carved expressions of the saints.

Around them is the glory of autumn, leaves stained vermilion and gold, the sky a shifting dome of blue-gray. It is the kind of landscape that invites the eyes to linger and to rest, a waking dream that feels better than sleep.

Catherine rubs an eye; she looks so young, like a child rising from her bed. "I said a prayer for you," she tells Joan. But Joan doesn't answer, only slides a hand over her sister's belly.

"Your child will be loved," Joan says. "And you know, it will be pleasant to see our mother fall to her knees and pray to Saint Agnes when your baby is teething and won't stop crying. It will drive our father mad, too, and our brothers; they'll have to stuff wool into their ears. Won't that be a pretty sight? But our uncle will teach the child tricks, and I'll hold the baby on my knee and bounce it up and down to make it laugh and teach it, whether it is a boy or a girl, to climb trees and to run. We shall hear the sound of little feet in the house again. And though you will deny it and pretend to be modest, you are beautiful enough that one day, a prosperous farmer or a wealthy tradesman will catch your eye and want you for his wife. So, whatever happens, there is no way we can lose."

She feels lighter, having laid out all her plans, but Catherine does not look at her. She moves away, and Joan's hand slips off her stomach. "Wouldn't you have left?" Catherine asks quietly. "If it weren't for me?"

Joan shakes her head. That's just dreaming, she doesn't say. "Where could I possibly go?"

Catherine smiles. "The better question is, Where wouldn't you go? You have stayed here too long, and I know you stay because of me."

It seems the only things impervious to the destruction of the English are those that have an element of magic to them. The Faerie Tree is scarred—a brute has attempted to set fire to its roots and to cleave its bark—but it still stands, home to the invisible winged people who play tricks, bestow curses, or grant wishes. And another survivor, the spirit in the shape of a cat, is Matagot. Older, gray fur each year a lighter shade, the cat is often found these days in a tree, though never the same one twice. This spirit is not a creature of habit. If you look up and think something has just blinked at you, you would probably be right. Camouflaged in a covering of yellow foliage, Matagot watches over the village. Leaves stir. A spine stretches, and a paw, hanging casually off a branch, flexes claws sharp as any whetted knife.

◆

In the morning, Catherine wakes, and she is smiling. Perhaps the prayers, the visit to the Holy Virgin's shrine, the walk in brisk air have done her good? She blushes as she motions Joan to come closer. "I want to ask a favor. Will you do something for me? But I am a little shy to speak of it.

"You know how women with child are," her sister says, though she hasn't been so talkative in months, "how they get it into their heads they want something particular to eat? Well, I have heard of a dish, and I would like to taste it. I have no appetite for pottage or bread, not even for meat."

Joan bends, so that Catherine can whisper in her ear.

"I have never heard of this dish," Joan says. "What is it?"

"They make it in Vaucouleurs," Catherine replies, dipping her head. "It is a very special food. Our uncle told me about it."

"Vaucouleurs?" Joan repeats.

"Will you go? For me?"

There is no need to say more. Joan counts the money she has: six pennies. What worries her is that her father has taken the cart, so she must walk. The distance is nearly twelve miles. It will take her four hours to reach the town and four hours to come back.

She pockets her money and her knife, and she is ready.

"Don't tell Uncle," Catherine says. "Let it be our secret. Promise. I am afraid he will think you are indulging me or that I am being silly."

Once she promises, her sister closes her eyes, smiling. She relaxes; for the first time since they returned from Neufchâteau, Catherine appears content. She takes Joan's hand.

"It may be a long wait," Joan says.

"I will be waiting." Catherine hesitates before releasing her. "Now go, Joan."

◆

SHE FEELS LIKE A KNIGHT ON A QUEST: a prince given an impossible task, the princess waiting in the locked turret for his return. When she reaches Vaucouleurs, it is nearly noon. She stops passersby. "Pardon," she says to each person, "do you know where I can find this dish?" But most ignore her, and the rest shake their heads and claim they have never heard of it.

"It is a special dish," she explains patiently when they stare. "And it is made here, in Vaucouleurs."

"Well," one woman replies, "it must be special, if it doesn't exist."

Most would rest after walking such a distance on the doorstep of an inn or beg to catch their breath on a tradesman's board stool. But Joan hurries to the street of bakers' stalls. They have heard of the dish, yes, but they still treat her as if she is a simpleton. "Who is it for, did you say?" they ask. "You won't find that anywhere here."

"It's for my sister."

"Ah, well, your sister has been dining lately with the lords and ladies, I suppose?" And they shoo her away while laughter shakes their bodies from head to foot.

But this gives Joan an idea, and she waits outside one of the gates of the royal garrison. She sees, some distance away, a cart led by a slow mule, barrels and sacks swaying in the back. She times its progress, and when the moment comes she slips behind the cart. Her hands snatch two of the sacks, balancing them on her shoulders. At the gates, the guards assume she is another laborer carrying in extra bags of flour.

The flour still on her shoulders, she asks the driver of the cart where the kitchen is. He studies her with his one good eye, the other bleared a milky white.

"New, are you?" he asks.

She nods. "Now quickly," she says, her voice rising. "I need to get these delivered so I am paid on time."

The kitchen is busy, but she searches out the cook and manages to corner him. "This dish, have you heard of it, do you have it here?"

The cook shakes his head, chuckling. He looks her up and down. "Sick of black bread, are you?" he says. "Well, I suppose you must be if you have such high standards."

She wipes the sweat from her face with her palm. "It isn't for me. Please, I have already asked all over town."

A thick finger points at a pile of tablecloths in a corner. "Wash those," he says. "Get the stains out, hang them up to dry. I'll show you where. Then I will give you something if you do the work properly and don't dally."

So, she takes the tablecloths to a tub, which is already prepared with water and wood ash. She kneels, scrubbing, and then beats each long linen sheet. When she is done and the cloths hung up to dry, the cook returns. In his hands, he holds a small object wrapped in a napkin.

He checks the tablecloths, studying them as one would a finely woven tapestry. He turns to her with a smile. "Here," he says. "It is not what you wanted, but we can't afford to be choosy, not in these times, can we?"

She takes it, disappointed. She slips the object into her pocket beside the knife and six pennies.

The cook only laughs at her. There are few who are as tall or taller than she is, and he is one of them. He pats her cheek kindly. "You are a good worker," he says as he follows her out. "If you come back, there will be a position here waiting for you, and you won't just wash the towels and the tablecloths. If you are interested in good food, one day I'll teach you how to make the dish you wanted. That's a promise!"

She leaves, her prize swaying inside the pocket of her dress. It is already dark when she reaches the house of white stone. Before the door she stops to catch her breath.

The priest comes out as she slips in. She greets him, but he gives her a strange look; he does not speak, only glances away as if she has baffled him.

Her brothers are here, and her mother and father. In the gloom, she cannot make out their faces. At the top of the stairs, Durand emerges from the shadows and she goes up to him, more slowly than usual. The muscles of her legs are tight, and she is sore.

"Where were you?" he asks, though she barely hears him. His voice travels to her from somewhere far away.

She walks toward their room, a space now lit by candles. Surprisingly, her legs don't give out. She feels she will faint, but she doesn't. She is, despite herself, as solid as a wall.

There is a stool where her mother and father, the priest, her three brothers, and her uncle have already paid their respects. Now it is her turn.

From a distant place, her uncle's voice travels to her, like whispers through a crack in the wall. "It was about noon," he begins. "There was no one in the house but your sister and myself. Your father and brothers had gone to the market. Your mother was visiting Jehanne. She told me you had left for the Bois Chenu hours ago and had failed to return. She asked me to go and search for you; she was afraid you had met with some accident. So I left, and your sister was then alone in the house. When I returned, I found her at the bottom of the stairs. Where were you, Joan?"

She raises a hand without looking at him. Stop. Please.

She is too shocked, too tired to cry. She kneels, takes Catherine's hand, and presses it flat to the space over her heart.

If you die, she thinks, all of my goodness dies with you, and this, here, this heart will become as hard as stone. I am afraid of what I will become. You hold my heart in your hand.

She waits for a response: a stir of the palm, a twitch of the finger. For hours, she keeps her eyes on Catherine, whose face is restored by candlelight to an amber-shaded, flickering beauty. But soon the pull of sleep is too strong for her to resist. She has walked over twenty-four miles, more than eight hours in a single day. She has cleaned a month's worth of tablecloths. And she has still failed.

In the morning, the bells ring and she stirs. She looks down. Her sister's hand is clutched in hers, but it is already cold.

◆

IN DAYLIGHT, Joan steps out of the house. She heads for the burnt fields, ruined by Englishmen's fire.

This morning is only deceptively warm; the ravaged furrows are lit by a shining, white-colored sun that gives off no heat.

She thinks of Catherine's bed. After the first few hours, she had fallen asleep. But she thought—or was it her imagination?—she felt movement in her hand, and when she woke, that her sister's head was turned toward her. The shadows of the room, the flames of the candles made Catherine's eyes two points of light against a watery darkness, like twin stars. But when morning came, the position of the body was the same as when she had first entered the room. Her uncle said Catherine had never stirred, not once, before her breath gave out and she died. So, she thinks, it must have been a dream, and the memory of her own making.

She thinks, The priests don't teach you to pray, at least not like this. It is always kneeling, back bent, head bowed, hands pressed in supplication, a stifled voice aware of its own lowness. They don't instruct you to stand, feet apart, arms raised, human eye meeting the eye of heaven. They don't tell you to bargain with your God, like you are trying to whittle down the price of a piece of mackerel with a fishmonger, to command the angels as if they were kitchen boys, and to treat the saints like servants who have forgotten to empty their masters' chamber pots.

But she looks straight into the eye of her God. She spreads her arms and bares her new heart of stone.

Give me strength, she prays, and not just the strength to endure but more, the strength of ten, fifty, a hundred men. Give me such gifts as the heroes of old were given: the gifts of slaughter and of victory. Give me a courage that is wild and uninhibited, one that will make men's teeth rattle. Make my flesh, my heart, and my soul invulnerable to all pain.

She tells her God, Let me have my revenge on those who have hurt the one I loved most in the world. These are the people responsible. These are my enemies, who are France's enemies, for if the war were not here, if it had taken place somewhere else, in another kingdom and country, then none of this would have happened. Not to me. These are their names. Remember them.

John, Duke of Bedford, regent of England

Henry, sixth of his name, future King of England

Philip, Duke of Burgundy

She hesitates only a moment before adding the Dauphin. It was your weakness, she thinks, your inaction, and your fear that brought us to this point, that kept the door wide open so these wolves could enter my village.

She repeats the names, as if God were a slow pupil in need of reminding and the angels scrambling for styluses and wax tablets to jot them down. She tastes the names in her mouth, each word a bitter seed: John, Duke of Bedford, regent of England. Henry, sixth of his name, future King of England. Philip, Duke of Burgundy.

And who can forget: the three men who hurt Catherine, who drove her to despair. Men who look like wolves. Men who do not speak French. Men with scars on their arms. God, direct my path to these men; guide me with Your divine hand. Before their souls go down to hell, let my face be the last they see on this earth. Let their deaths be full of pain. Let them repent, though they will receive no mercy.

His Majesty the Dauphin, Charles, seventh of his name. King of France. You don't know my name. You don't even know I exist, but I am coming for you.

◆

THE NEXT DAY, before her uncle leaves, she asks him what blancmanger is. Is it real?

He used to work in kitchens. "Yes." He nods. "Yes, it is real, but it is not a simple dish. You need meat finely chopped, which can be fresh capon or fish, and sugar of high quality. All this must be cooked in rice and almond milk until it is thick as a custard. And anise or saffron may be added, too. So as you can see, it is no commoner's food."

"My sister sent me to Vaucouleurs to fetch a dish of blancmanger for her," she explains.

Her uncle lowers his eyes. He doesn't say, Then Catherine knew full well what she planned to do that day.

The priest is satisfied that what happened was an accident, and Joan has lied to his face. "Before I left the house," she told him, "I forgot to put a pitcher of water beside her bed. She was probably thirsty and took a fall."

But God, she thinks, sees everything.

She has forgotten about the prize in her pocket, what the cook in Vaucouleurs gave her, which remains wrapped in a clean napkin. When she unfolds the cloth, a golden wafer rests in her palm like a miniature sun.

Her uncle bends until the tip of his nose hovers just over its surface. He inhales, smiling. "It is an unmistakable scent," he says, "the smell of cinnamon." She folds the wafer back into the napkin and gives it to him. As he takes it, he looks about to cry. She knows they are both thinking the same thing: This was not meant for you.

He is leaving, and she is aware he won't come back. This is the longest he's ever stayed in Domrémy. How many days had he sat with Catherine, held her hand, and tried to make her forget? But for the first time in his life, he has run out of stories to tell. The princess with the straw-colored hair who wears a brocaded gown and pairs of silver slippers is now a figure both comical and ridiculous. She is still happily married, in a kingdom far, far away, a new child in her belly each year and infants sighing sweetly as they roll inside their gilded cradles; but Catherine, she is already dead.

Invasion, death. He has seen these things before, just not so close, and they have taken their toll on him. This village, too, will never be the same again. His wanderer's heart must move on.

When they reach the edge of Domrémy, Joan cries. She holds him to her, digging her chin into his shoulder. Her arms are like a death grip, and he is thinner than when he first came, wisps of white in his hair. She can feel every section of his spine. She holds him as if he were the cat Matagot.

He is patient. Only when her tears have run out, when her body shudders away from him and her arms fall to her sides, does he step back.

"We have known each other a long time, haven't we?" he says, and she nods.

She thinks, as he smears her tears and snot away (who else would do such a thing, touch her tears and snot?): We are soldiers on a campaign that has come to an end, and though we are both alive, we have lost almost everything.

He smiles at her, his eyes shining, and she can't tell what he feels: whether he is pleased to go or grieved. But his smile says, The world is large, yet it can also be small. Our paths may cross again. I am not worried about you, and you shouldn't worry about me.

He turns from her, chewing on the wafer. It is his last lesson to Joan: how you should approach life when its fists are pummeling you. Head up. Shoulders back. Your heart may be breaking, but you don't let it show, not on your face or in your eyes. You walk with a spring in your step toward a destination yet unknown. And your next warm meal may be hours or days away, your next bed in an inn or in a wet ditch, but in your mouth is the taste of cinnamon. The past is the past, and the dead, buried in their shrouds, must always be left behind.

IV

◆ ◆ ◆

SUPPER. A slip of the hand. The bowl that teeters before it breaks. And pottage, like the droppings of a large bird, spills across the floor. Without a word, her mother hands her a cloth. She doesn't meet Joan's eye, and Joan wants to tell her, If it were my child that was dead and less than a month gone, I wouldn't take it as quietly as you do. But at the edge of their vision, her father has already stood and is stamping in her direction.

If her shoulder flinches, it is because Jacques is jabbing it and bellowing oaths into her ear. The oaths, the curses have not changed since she was a girl of ten. He bawls, as from years ago: Why don't you go drown yourself? If only he could find a sack big enough to fit her. There might have been a sack big enough, she thinks, when she was ten. There isn't one now.

But then she stands. For a moment, his eyes flick over the whole of her, which takes a moment. She is a full head taller, and her shoulders are just as broad as his, her chest flat, her arms and legs longer. And she does not have a paunch like he does.

Between them is the spilled pottage. Her head is still swimming in grief—Catherine dead, her uncle gone—but she thinks she hears him instruct her to eat what is on the ground, what she has spilled, so that it does not go to waste.

There was a time when she would have done this. That time, however, has passed.

In the middle of swearing, he falters. His words skip and trip over themselves. She watches his face twist into a grimace and his hands fly to his chest as if he feels a sudden pain. She recognizes the motion, and her own heart softens. It is the first time she wants to throw her arms around him—and not to wrestle, to squeeze, or to wound.

She watches him blink back tears. He sniffs, and her brothers and her mother look away.

He says, in a barely coherent mumble, "The wrong daughter died."

She wants to say, I agree.

"See how I am left," he continues.

She wants to say, See how we are all left.

But the moment is over. He straightens, and he is again Jacques d'Arc. Indomitable. Unrelenting. The finger returns to her shoulder. The jabbing doesn't hurt. It's just irritating, and she wants it to stop. She takes her father's hand. She won't pretend it doesn't give her pleasure to hear him gasp. She shoves him away—gently.

It's as she reaches for the cloth on the table to clean up the mess that the blow lands: a backhanded slap across the mouth. A pause. Then the front of her father's tunic is in her hands, and he is wriggling like an eel. She hears her mother and brothers shouting, "Put him down, Joan, put him down!"

When she releases him, he staggers. His huge bulk does a drunken dance and trips into the opposite wall.

She throws the cloth onto the puddle on the floor. She doesn't have to say, Clean it up yourself.

Her arms are shaking as she leaves. In her grip, her father's feet dangled, and she didn't even have to try. She is thinking of her own strength. She is thinking, There is nothing here for me anymore.

◆

When she returns the next morning, she finds Jacques sitting at the table, tossing a pouch between his hands. On one side of his head is a small bump. Otherwise he appears himself: scowling and in bad temper. He has been waiting for her to come back.

They do not speak; they do not bid each other a halfhearted, embarrassed good morning. She watches as her father empties the pouch and coins drop out in a sharp, ringing clatter, the noise too loud in the silence between them. Ten in all.

He counts the money slowly, so she can see each coin and know he isn't playing a trick, not slipping one into his pocket or tucking two up his sleeve. When he has finished, he returns the money to the pouch, refastens the string, and pushes it toward her.

"My brothers? My mother?" Joan says. She tries to keep her voice steady, but her throat tightens.

"Working," her father replies.

He stands. Briefly they look at each other. "Catherine will be missed," he says. "You won't."

He leaves the room. The door swings shut behind him.

She takes the pouch, recounts the coins (in dealings with Jacques, it is better to be sure), and pockets the money.

A single road leads out of the village, and it is still early. She will miss Hauviette's wedding, only a few days away. Her friend is marrying a widower from another village who has bad teeth but many acres of good land and two small children who need a mother to watch over them. But Joan was never one for weddings or wedding feasts.

She is walking through the story of her life, past the stream into which she pushed boys, the tormenters of songbirds. The walls she fixed, the roofs. The Faerie Tree and, in the distance, the Bois Chenu. She sees, too, what her life could have been. There, six years from now, in the meadow: a child running and Joan in pursuit while Catherine stands a little apart, watching them. Her arms catch the child, swinging the small body off the ground from behind. "Careful!" her sister calls. And she thinks there is a little dog—some stray they found shivering in a ditch, wrapped up, and saved. Another Salaud, though they won't name it Salaud, because now there is a child in the house. She hears the dog bark, and the sound flies straight to her heart. She stops. It takes effort to hold back tears.

At her feet, something slides past. Fur brushes her ankle, and she nearly trips.

It is Matagot, slipped out of a tree and come to see her off. The cat, tail twitching, allows itself to be held one last time. As she strokes its fur, she hears Catherine's voice: "Now go, Joan."

She remembers how she picked up Saint Margaret's fallen head from the ground and studied it, tracing her fingers over eyebrows, eyes, cheekbones, nose, and chin. The book of saints will tell you Margaret's story. It will tell you where she came from, a place called Antioch, and what happened to her: that after being cast off by her father for her Christian faith, she watched sheep, received a marriage proposal from a Roman prefect, turned the proposal down, and was tortured. Among her many trials was being swallowed by Satan.

"How did she get out?" she had asked the priest.

"With a cross she kept close to her," he replied.

Joan thinks of this now, what it would be like to find oneself in the belly of Satan, one's only tool a wooden cross small enough to cup in one's hand. She has seen the insides of animals before: the entrails of a sheep, the bladder of a pig. So she wonders, How did Margaret find her way out? Through guts and blood. Through a labyrinth of intestine and pools of sulfurous bile. The book of saints doesn't go into details, how long it would take for a cross—perhaps Margaret had sharpened the ends on a piece of bone she found in Satan's stomach, remnants from a previous meal—to cut through skin and serpent scale.

But she imagines the moment when the saint emerged, crawling out, drenched from head to toe and sputtering. She imagines the first breath of air, how she, Margaret, would have filled her lungs with the scent of topsoil, how she would have looked at the sky, a single passing cloud, a common sparrow flitting to its next tree, in wonder.

Behind Joan, the village grows smaller, until the outlines of the cottages become a patch of muddy brown. She glances back only once; the slope of gray hills and pale-yellow fields have covered Domrémy. It no longer exists. She, Joan, takes a breath: a first breath in new air. She pauses to shake a stone out of her shoe. She walks.

V

◆ ◆ ◆

THE DAY SHE LEAVES DOMRÉMY is the day she finds her way back to the kitchen of Vaucouleurs's garrison.

"I am here," she announces to the cook, who remembers her. He gives her a friendly pet on the head and smiles.

"So, you still want to learn how to make blancmanger?" he asks.

She shrugs. She wants to be in Vaucouleurs not for blancmanger but because it's close to soldiers and armory. Because the English have tried to take Vaucouleurs and failed, so she thinks they may try and fail again, and if they fail, she wants to be there to see it happen, to see her enemies run and weep. And in case of invasion, she could help with . . . Well, she doesn't know, but she believes she can be useful. War is not only the half hour of fighting, the seven-month siege; it's provisioning supplies; it's driving mules and building and digging; mucking out stables, lending money, collecting taxes, cleaning up after the bloodshed is over, identifying and naming the noteworthy dead. If the English came to Vaucouleurs, she could boil water to fill up the cauldrons and dump them over enemy heads. She could carry buckets of hot oil up to the ramparts. Or, if there happened to be a gambeson and helmet left unattended in the middle of fighting, who would know if a girl from the kitchens had found her way inside them? A spit, a plate, a brine-cured leg of mutton can be a weapon. And there is always her childhood dream: the sword- and shield-polishing stall. French customers only, of course.

The kitchen work would make another throw up his arms and scream at the cook, "I quit and curse you for a slave driver!" But she is used to it. Her time at Neufchâteau under La Rousse was not for nothing. Quails are plucked, feathers flying, as if she is the fox who has slipped into the chicken coop. Fish skinned and filleted. Meat turned on a spit. Floors cleaned. Towels and tablecloths washed and beaten. Basins scrubbed.

And she learns. She learns how to tell the quality of eels by the size of the head, which must be small, the thickness of the body, and the sheen of the skin. She can tell whether a brace of partridges is fresh from a mere glance at the feathers.

In the middle of the day, with a manchet loaf that she kneaded and baked herself, she goes to watch the soldiers train; the knights and squires spar; the pages run to fetch their masters linen cloths and refreshment. She sees the destriers, the great warhorses, take their exercise, manes rippling like glossy flags. There are more crossbowmen than archers, who are few in number, but she watches them practice, waxing and stringing their bowstaves of yew; she counts how many arrows they can shoot in a single minute and thinks it is usually no more than ten or eleven. Their posture is imprinted in her memory. As she watches, she imitates their movements with a bow and arrow of air.

She will remain until she hears a bellow: the sound of her name. It is the cook. She is a good worker, he tells her, one of the best he has ever had, but she is never around when he needs her. He would bind her legs and tie her to a chair if it meant she would stay put. Again and again, he has found her standing like a sad orphan near the stables or the yard where soldiers train. "Do you have your eye on someone?" he asks her kindly. "These are young men of good family, so your chances of success are not high," he explains, "but you never know. Stranger things have happened in the course of history. If you continue to do your work, I will give you a plate of warm Parma tarts to take to your loved one, and he may love you back."

She groans and folds her arms. "I love no one," she declares, and she can tell the cook does not quite believe her. He has hit on the truth in a way. She is in love. Not with the men—the squires or the knights—but with their work, their weapons, their noise. She is in love with the smell of horses and horse sweat.

At night, Joan is assigned to guard the pantry; the cook complains of thieves who may be persons in his own employ, for there are always fresh eggs missing, a hare he meant to prepare for the captain of the garrison's dinner vanished (the captain is none other than Sir Robert de Baudricourt—when Joan hears this, she bursts out laughing), or even a whole goose and section of pike gone. Her pallet is placed before the door, and she sleeps deeply but not so deeply that a footstep or even the scratch of mice feet can't wake her. She sleeps, in fact, with a skillet tucked in one hand.

A week passes. Another week. Then a month. The pain in her chest is heavy but not as heavy as it once was. It lifts an inch, two inches, and some days, she feels she can breathe again without a weight inside her. In the hem of her dress, she has sewn the Duke of Lorraine's ring. It was her sister's. Now it belongs to her.

The cook sings as he works. He has taught her a song listing the names of meat dishes and cheeses. The song is part of a tale about a peasant who stumbles across a lord's feast and eats everything, though instead of punishing him, his host lets him go.

One day, Joan hears a second voice singing along. The voice, she is surprised to discover, is her own.

◆

BUT IT CANNOT LAST—the peace, the days all slipping and sliding into each other, one day not unlike the one that came before.

At the kitchen gate, there are beggars—among them, a child, the dirtiest, most unwashed child Joan has ever seen. He is so filthy, the other beggars make a small space for him and put on a show of holding their noses. Burned bread, bread that has not risen properly, or a mouse-nibbled loaf is doled out in pieces to the beggars in exchange for their prayers. She sees the child cannot reach the day's offerings and lets him in. A hag with a single jutting tooth hisses at Joan. She says, "Well, if I had known that I should roll in pig shit to be favored, I would have done."

It is late. The cook is dozing in his chair before the fire. She sets a plate before the boy, a dish of beef numbles covered in lamprey sauce. The food is steaming hot, but he eats with his fingers, swallowing pieces whole without pausing to chew, and when she gives him a napkin, he is shy to take it, so he wipes his hands on the front of his shirt instead.

Before he goes, she offers him a pear, washed and sliced. She watches as he sticks out his tongue, touches a crescent-shaped white piece to its tip, and bites down slowly, chews slowly, because now that he is full, he can taste; he can savor. He smiles at her and puts the rest in his pocket. Who knew the world could grow such sweet things?

But the door no sooner closes, the unused napkin folded and restored to its neat pile—another day's work finished—than she hears a cry.

Outside she follows the trail of dropped pear slices to a yard where a guard has pulled down the boy's trousers and is whipping him. The boy sobs, which makes the guard strike harder. "Thief!" he snarls. The boy's bottom is already scarlet. "Come out of the kitchens, have you? What else have you stolen? What else?"

But the guard's wrist is suddenly in her hand. And when he resists, thrashing like a caught fish, when he tries to strike her with his other arm, she squeezes until she hears the compression of sinew, of hard muscle against the threshold of bone underneath. She watches him writhe, shrinking closer and closer to the ground, until . . . *crack*. He shouts, a high-pitched yelp that echoes. Only then do her fingers unfurl; she lets him go, and he drops, nearly fainting.

The boy has pulled up his trousers. He is still crying as he runs away—though, not one to waste food, he retrieves the pear slices he dropped when the guard grabbed him, shoving each piece into his mouth.

She leaves the guard whimpering and nursing his broken wrist. Her fingers flex as she walks back to the kitchens, though she feels no pain. It doesn't bother her that she has just put one of the garrison's men out of commission, albeit temporarily. There is glory to be gained in whipping the enemies of France, none in making victims of those who are defenseless. Again she is reminded: It is not only the English who are cruel. Just think of her own father.

Her strength no longer surprises her. It is, she believes, the natural outcome of such a childhood. How else would she have survived if she didn't grow strong? All her life she has been fighting. The pages may begin their training as early as seven years old, but what do they know of pain? Fighting is as much about taking pain as doling it out. When she was five, she already knew what it was to be covered in welts. And she has always worked hard. Hard work, too, proved second nature to her. By the time she was ten, she had hands callused like a laborer's.

What does a page know about the twitch of muscle that precedes a punch? The cold gleam of a man's eye when he is about to strike? But she has grown up with these signs and would recognize them in anyone. At eight, she was held down by her older brothers while their friends laughed. They dunked her head in a stream, but she held her breath. She learned that day: When one man beats you, it invites others to try, too. People can smell out weakness. Only strength keeps them at bay.

She remembers the cart she lifted from the mud in Domrémy and the rotted stump of a tree in the church garden, which had to be dug out and moved. The priest had called for three strong men to help, but when he returned with them, it was Joan who stood in the garden, her arms wrapped around the stump, as if she had made a new friend and was hugging it. From the tangled roots, a cascade of dirt and pebbles fell. She said, looking at the open-mouthed priest, "Where should I put this?"

Others in the village have asked her, What is it with you and fighting, Joan? (For she always looks wary and ready for a scuffle.) Is it true what your uncle says, that at the fair at Vaucouleurs you made straight for the helmet-makers and armorers? Why do you treat stories of battle and sieges as though they were songs to be sung for children before they go to sleep?

When she thinks of these questions now, these are her answers: Because I've been beaten most of my life and beatings are not among those things in the world that improve with time; because I don't want what happened to Catherine to ever happen to me; because the chances of getting killed these days is high, and if I die, I want to say I didn't die with my back to the enemy, running; because I would like to think it is possible to be strong without also being cruel.

After her feat in the church garden, the priest showed her the book of saints again. He explained that there is the strength of one's body and the strength of one's faith, and of the two, only the latter is unbreakable. But Joan looked at the picture of Saint Catherine. She saw the severed head in a neat pool of blood, eyes still open. And she thought, Faith didn't save her life, and I would rather have the strength that keeps me alive to see a new morning.

The following night, three of the guard's friends come to pay her a visit. They think, because the hour is late, they will catch her asleep. Soon they cannot get out of the kitchens fast enough; they clutch their heads, scalps and cheeks popping fresh skillet-shaped welts. They run, seeing stars.

These men are too shamefaced to admit what happened to them. When asked, they grumble. "Walked into a door." "Was drunk and fell out of a chair." "Got into a scrap at the inn, just your typical brawl."

But walls have eyes, and a servant reports what he saw to the captain of the garrison, Sir Robert de Baudricourt. "It was a girl," he says. "She works in the kitchens. I saw her catch the guard's hand and crumple it as one would crumple a fresh flower. I couldn't believe my eyes, but it happened! I swear it!"

Joan is summoned from the kitchens. She remembers Sir Robert well, but Sir Robert doesn't remember her. She thinks the years have neither changed nor improved him, not at all. He is still very fit, very handsome, and as enamored with himself as on the day of the fair when he tried—and failed—to climb the greasy pole. He is even wearing, she sees, boots of a quality not dissimilar to the ones she stomped on when she was a child of ten. This makes her smile.

For a moment, Sir Robert forgets himself. His eyes widen briefly before narrowing. It is clear he thought she would be someone he could easily frighten with his own imposing stature. What threat does a girl of sixteen pose, after all? But as he looks her up and down, then up again, he seems less sure.

"Have I seen you before somewhere?" he asks, studying her face.

She shrugs. "I work in the kitchens."

He tells her why she is here. After the servant made his report, the first guard was questioned and finally revealed what had happened. Yes, it was her, that kitchen wench, who broke his wrist. And he'd no sooner confessed than his three friends came forward, showing where they had been thrashed by her skillet. But Sir Robert says to her, "I don't believe a word of it. I think the servant who told me about you is lying. They are all lying. It is impossible. You are a nobody, a woman. But what are they lying for? And to what end? That is what I want to know."

"You can believe what you like," she replies.

He ignores her and continues to talk while pacing the room. Charges must be brought against the beggar boy who stole from the kitchens. He will be fined, and if he cannot pay the fine, which is likely, then he will be whipped, his hand chopped off, or both. Sir Robert taps his chin thoughtfully. "Which would you prefer if you were in his place?" he asks.

"He is no thief," she replies, stepping forward. She thinks of the work she still has to do and all these years later her time wasted by the same well-dressed idiot in fine boots. God knows why their paths have crossed again. Her temper rises. "I gave him the food."

"Then you are a thief, too," he says, "for that was not your food to give."

A pause. She sees a change in his face.

He chuckles at her, grinning, and his grin is exuberant, that of a father holding for the first time his bawling male heir or a newly married bridegroom about to lie with his young wife. At any moment, he may actually begin to hug himself. He crosses the room to stand beside the windows that overlook the training grounds, but she thinks he has moved there only because he knows the light will show him off to better effect.

"I shall see if my guards and the servant are lying to me," he says. "And if you are, then I promise I will make fools of all of you. Also, it has been a dull few days. This will make for a fine afternoon's entertainment." He crosses his arms, stands at full height. He is a betting man. "Let us make this interesting. If you can do what I ask and prove that my men have not lied to me, I will drop the charges, against both you and the boy. You have my word."

She can tell he believes he will win. This, Joan thinks, is the problem with having a short memory. He has forgotten that she has bested him before. What is to say she won't do it again? But this time, if she wins, she will make sure he remembers it. "What must I do?" she asks.

She has answered so quickly, without hesitation, that it takes him by surprise. He tips his head, appears for a moment to search for his words.

Then he says, "That is for you to find out. We shall test your strength. See if you can really break a man's bones with your bare hands." He leans against the wall, laughing at whatever picture he has conjured in his mind (while he laughs, she stares and yawns loudly). When he has finished, he adds, his expression sneering, "But if you fail, I shall have you whipped in public before all of my men. And the boy, too."

He doesn't give her time to answer. "Follow me," he says and without ceremony leads her outside to where the archers practice. She realizes he has thought up this plan ahead of time. There is a space, and a single bow is already prepared: strung with a bow string of hemp, the yew oiled.

The draw weight of the string is a hundred pounds, maybe a little more, he tells her. This bow, a longbow, was taken from the hand of an English archer, who is dead. In that place, he goes on, even peasants can shoot. Their kings say all men who are of good health should take up the bow and practice, including on days of rest. So, this is what I propose: If an English peasant can wield this, why not you?

A crowd has gathered—a smattering of pages and squires who have received advance notice of this spectacle. She recognizes their faces as they nudge each other and laugh. "A giantess," she hears them say. "And probably as stupid as one."

"That is where you must shoot the arrow," Sir Robert announces, and he points at a small target, a light-colored speck, in the far-off distance. He speaks as if he is asking her to carry a dish across the room. Just that table, there, he might have said. "We will be patient and give you a little time."

"What about you?" she asks. She keeps her gaze fixed on the target. "Why don't you shoot first to show me how it is done?"

"Ah, not so sure of ourselves now, are we? Well, I shall not be unkind, not to a lady. I will call our best archer to aid you, and we can have a little contest. He is not French, but the bow was his plaything in childhood. And as he grew, the bow grew with him, until he became a master of it."

Sir Robert turns, glances over his shoulder at one standing in a line not far behind him, and nods.

From the crowd, a man strides forward and takes up the bow.

She watches him: the posture, the positioning of the legs, the angle at which he shoots, and the momentary strain that crosses his face as his fingers draw the tight string back.

The arrow flies. There are men waiting near but not too near the target, and a shout goes up. "A fine shot!" The crowd applauds, cheering.

Sir Robert cocks his head at her and smiles. *Your turn*, his expression says.

It is the first time she has ever held a bow, and the bow is nearly as tall as she is.

Afterward, she will try to describe the moment and fail. How, for a moment, just a moment, her eyes had wandered, and she had caught sight of the church near the fortress, the steeple with its thin cross reaching up to a clear sky. It was too late for prayers; there was no time to mutter even a short Ave, but she had noticed the cross, and when she'd looked away, when she had raised the bow and the arrow with it, the cross was still in her eye, seared into her vision, overlaid against the target of straw. The bow felt light in her hands. A gentle wind blew and moved a strand of hair across her ear.

She did not hear the gasp of the crowd when she pulled back the string as easily as an oar in a seasoned bargeman's hand. But she heard the arrow fly, its sound like a sharp inhalation of air. She felt an energy vibrate through her body, just over her heart, a sensation like a hardness unraveling.

A silence. The silence begins to lengthen.

Sir Robert grows impatient. His foot, tapping again, seems to do a little dance in the grass.

"Well?" he calls to his men in the distance.

No answer.

"Bring the target!" he shouts.

A puffing servant runs, carries the target closer for viewing. This is the first arrow, he reports truthfully. That the kitchen wench's.

The crowd had not been biased. When they'd cried out in support of their friend, none had lied. It was a fine shot, as good a shot as any, Sir Robert would later say, to console his men.

But hers—hers has plunged through the center of the innermost circle, the pupil of the iris of the eye. At the sight of it, Sir Robert gapes. He is sweating, and with a trembling hand, he touches his damp forehead, releases a sound like a sob. He crosses himself, and others in the audience follow his example.

Joan sets down the bow, sends to it her silent thanks, and looks at Sir Robert. She asks in a quiet voice, though she, too, is shocked by what has happened, "Do you remember me now, my lord? This is already our second meeting."

◆

THE STORY SPREADS by whispered words into covered ears, by rumor, growing and growing. It reaches the Duke of Lorraine, who has, it turns out, a far better memory than his servant. Sir Robert would have preferred to keep the incident quiet, but stories like this travel fast. For the Duke, six years is not such a long time. He remembers Joan. When he sees her, it is as if in the whole of Vaucouleurs, he alone is unsurprised. "The greasy pole, of course," he says languidly, having summoned her to him. His smile is one of secrets he keeps close. "So, it was not the holy woman's medal that helped you that day."

By this he means, *It was God.*

From the hem of her dress Joan has torn out his ring. She shows it to him. "Do you want it back?" she asks and means it. She explains, "I gave it to my sister, and she is dead. I have no use for it now."

He takes the ring and then her hand in his own ducal palms. A seasoned soldier, he has been in the Crusades. His skin, however, is as smooth as new parchment. Whatever scars and calluses he once had are long faded. When his hands slip away, she looks down. The ring was not made for her, but it is a perfect fit.

Letters are written without her knowledge. A royal messenger from the court of Yolande of Aragon, the Dauphin's mother-in-law, arrives in Vaucouleurs. No one tells Joan this; she finds out only because of the piquant sauces and bowls of sugared almonds specially prepared for his meals. She continues her work in the kitchens, though now when she goes to watch the sparring, the riding, and the shooting, the men look up at her like cows in the field at a new arrival. The archers lower their bows; the pages stare. The messenger has been in Vaucouleurs only two days before she is called up from the kitchens by Sir Robert. She thinks he is planning to make more trouble, but the royal messenger, a wiry, bouncing little man, says she is to go with a small group, comprising a knight, a squire, an archer, and himself, to Chinon. To the Dauphin. A king has many homes, and the castle at Chinon is one of them. It is a favored retreat of His Majesty's and finely situated. Outside, a river view, the gently flowing Vienne, and on all sides, one is surrounded by the quiet splendors of the Loire Valley, the messenger informs her sweetly as if she has won a prize.

In reality, the journey is over three hundred miles and dangerous, so she is given a man's outfit: a gray tunic and breeches, a black doublet, and a hat to shade her face. She cuts her hair to her ears, so that from a distance, she may be mistaken for a youth who has grown his hair long. The Duke gifts her a dark horse, a strong mare from his stables, to ride under cover of night. The well-dressed idiot Sir Robert, mouth turned down, offers her his second-best sword, though she still carries in her pocket her uncle's knife.

It is the first time she has held a real sword. He watches her, petulant, as she admires it. These last few weeks have been unforgettable for him, and not in a good way. He has insisted on testing and retesting her. "Give her a different bow. Restring it. Let me check that arrow and make sure it is sound." The result never varies. But, Sir Robert barks, desperate, can she ride? By this time he is sweating; dark patches appear across his surcoat and under his arms. It turns out she can.

Their last meeting: his sword is in her grip. She has grunted her thanks as though he were a stable boy tasked with saddling her horse. He is subdued but not so subdued that he doesn't mutter beneath his breath.

"What?" she says.

"Nothing," he replies quickly. His voice is small. He has prodded the first guard's broken wrist to check her handiwork. The man howled with pain, and Sir Robert doesn't want to push his luck, not with Joan. Every time her arrow found its mark, it felt personal, and he would look in bewilderment at the sky, as if the heavens were mocking him. One morning he heard angels chuckling and thought, I have finally gone mad; but it was his own men trying not to laugh at his expressions of despair. She isn't a knight from a tale, and things like this aren't supposed to happen. They are, in fact, unheard of.

"Good luck," he says to Joan. "You'll need it."

Before she leaves, she will find the boy who was whipped, crouching in a wet and dripping alley. In her men's clothes and with her hair cut short, he doesn't recognize her, not at first. She has to remind him how they know each other. Kitchens. Beef numbles with lamprey sauce. A sweet pear. He looks closer and makes certain she is the same person before folding his hand into hers. She takes him to the kitchens and, when he is shy and tries to hide behind her, nudges him before the cook.

"He does not look much," the cook says uncertainly.

"He has a fine taste in sauces," Joan replies. "And likes fresh pears. So, he appreciates good food."

"I never did teach you how to make blancmanger, did I," the cook says to her. He looks sad that she is leaving. He has heard the story of what she has done. (His reaction was indifferent: Joan is good at everything; if she can expertly slice apart a fish, why should she not be a natural at the bow?) His world is the kitchen. The goings-on of the rest of the garrison didn't concern him.

"No, but you can teach him, can't you?"

Then she leaves. If all goes smoothly, the journey will take no more than two weeks, much of it through enemy land. During the day, they sleep while two of their company keep watch. At night they ride. Each morning Joan dreams with sunlight in her eyes.

She had asked the Duke, "Why am I going to Chinon?"

"To meet His Majesty the Dauphin."

"Why am I going to meet His Majesty the Dauphin?"

"Because you may be useful to him."

"How may I be useful?"

He sighed. The saints give me strength, his expression said.

Later, during their journey, the royal messenger explains in his lilting manner, as if speaking to a child: "Sometimes a lord will present his king with a gift to remind him of his loyalty. Sometimes this gift is a beautiful book. Other times a chest of gold or a lion cub or a feather from a griffin's wing."

"I am none of those things," Joan says.

"Well, if you do not please, we can probably find you a job in the kitchens" is his answer. He sees from her face that she is still confused.

"I am being brought to Chinon to work in the kitchens?" she asks, and the messenger groans.

It is during these days, eleven in all, that the knight, Bertrand de Poulengy, and the squire, Jean de Metz, teach her to spar. They tell her the various parts of armor and the sections of a castle, describe to her strange weapons she has never heard of, weapons with names like holy water sprinkler and morning star. They show her how to properly hold a sword.

On day one, she is beaten by the two men training her. First the squire, and then the knight, knocks her to the ground. But if she is breathless, they are, too. It puzzles them. A whole lifetime's training against one who is new to fighting: Gaining the upper hand should be easier, so why isn't it? And she recovers quickly. She is hungry to learn more, even if it comes at the cost of pain. They tell her to use her shoulders and every part of the sword, even the hilt. They tell her to use her fists, if that will help her win a fight. And she does.

Days two through four, she is still beaten, but the task—she can see it on the faces of her instructors—has grown more difficult. It is a challenge to knock her off her feet.

Day five, she beats the squire for the first time.

Day six, she sends the knight reeling. Also, she seems to have an affinity with horses. When she whistles, not only her own horse but the horses of other men come running.

Days seven through eleven, she has bested both men more times than they can count. The archer, who has witnessed her skill with a bow, tests her. He ties a piece of black cloth to a far-off birch tree, intending this as a joke. There are other trees in her line of vision, but she sees—and her arrow sees—only its target. Later, the torn cloth is passed around the circle of men so that they can inspect it. They slide and wiggle their fingers through the hole, shaking their heads. They mutter beneath their breath, How is this possible? The two servants tasked with carrying and guarding the supplies think it may be witchcraft. But the knight and squire believe her gifts come from God.

A journey is a passage to a new place. It is a chance to forget. On the last day, Joan climbs a hill. The hour is dawn; the light casts a mist like a spell over the land, and she is quiet as she takes in the sight beneath her. For nearly two weeks she has lived like a bat, but now her eyes are opened to new things. Her body is the same, but also different.

Still, it is impossible to leave behind the past. On the hill, she feels someone's hand brush her arm, though when she looks there is no one. She hears a voice that seems to speak from the air: "Now go, Joan."

In the castle of Chinon, the royal messenger escorts her to a bare room with a single window. He invites her to take a seat.

Another Robert, not Sir Robert, a more important Robert, is standing near the window in a wash of azure light. This Robert is a courtier, a trusted advisor to His Majesty the Dauphin, and he tells her, by way of greeting with a brief nod, that he has been waiting for her arrival.

VI

◆ ◆ ◆

CHINON, MARCH 1429

THE CHAPEL IS SMALL, but there is an alcove on an upper floor where Joan stands with the courtier and former chancellor of France, Robert le Maçon. Eleven years ago, le Maçon was with the Dauphin when Paris was taken by the Burgundians. He gave the Dauphin his horse so that the prince, then a pimple-faced adolescent of fifteen, could flee with his life. He is no longer chancellor of France, but in the Dauphin's court, his word still carries weight.

The chapel is a chamber of white stone and stained glass. When the light is right, the bright red of Saint Jerome's robes and the cerulean blue of the Holy Virgin's cloak will fall on a distant panel of wall or a square block of floor and one can step inside a pool of color and pray in color, as though wrapped in the Virgin's own linen. At the altar, the Dauphin, swathed in dark velvet, kneels, waiting to receive the body of Christ.

At Joan's side: a whisper into her ear, and le Maçon murmurs, on tiptoe, "Regnault de Chartres, Archbishop of Reims, confidant of His Majesty." Then he grumbles, "Present chancellor of France." By which he means: the highest-ranking judicial officer in the kingdom. By which he means: it is not a hereditary office, so it can be bestowed and it can be taken away at the Dauphin's whim, and whoever occupies it is bound to be a favorite of the King.

She sees the Archbishop, a lean man weighted down in robes. Such men rarely smile. He bends and places the wafer on the tip of the Dauphin's tongue. A moment, and the body of Christ disappears into the body of the French King.

She half-expects a small puff of the chest, a surge of confidence, as Christ's spirit moves through royal limbs and is absorbed into royal blood. Instead, the Dauphin seems to deflate. Shoulders hunched, he prays, as though to be heard by God requires an act of concentrated will. One must focus as the prayer floats higher and higher through the strata of the heavens to His divine hand.

Prayer finished, he rises slowly to his feet. A nod to the Archbishop, a final genuflection to the altar, and then he turns. He is not alone. Courtiers emerge like black beetles from behind the chapel's columns. One stands out in particular, an especially large and bulbous beetle dressed in rich layers of purple, who trails close behind.

"Georges de La Trémoille," le Maçon says. She hears something else in his voice: bitterness, jealousy? "Court favorite." He coughs. "And the Archbishop's personal friend. Both are thorns in my side.

"Any moment now," he says. He is watching the Dauphin closely. "Any moment now His Majesty will look up. I informed him we would be here today, so be ready to kneel when I tell you to."

A long time ago, her uncle had told Joan a story about the Dauphin. She wonders if the Dauphin, too, thinks of it every time he steps through a door. How, seven years ago, His Majesty had entered the bishop's palace on a visit. All was at peace, the morning quiet; only the murmur of pleasant conversation could be heard, when a strange noise creaked down the length of the hall. The next moment, the floor wasn't where it was supposed to be. The Dauphin did not have time to stand, much less to run. He found himself dropping through the air into darkness, where just before, sunlight had splashed across the flagstones. Later, he told his courtiers, who told their wives, who whispered among themselves and were overheard by the servants, that it felt as though the devil had taken hold of his soul and was flying with him to the pits of hell. The sensation had been so clear, so vivid. He had seen the skirts of his robes flutter around his poulaines as he plunged through empty space, like a small animal in the maw of a great beast. He could smell sulfur and smoke. He heard the screams of men and women coming far above him and also, he believed, below him, the sick, splintering lurch of crumbling wood and shattered stone, the squelch of a marble pillar falling across heads and shins.

It is well known. Even the best palaces, the finest châteaus and towers can fall apart, and it is not always hurricanes, earthquakes, or Englishmen that are responsible. One day a room is a room, and the best builders will claim it is sound; the next, the ceiling collapses like a failed jelly. However, many considered the incident a miracle, as the Dauphin was one of only three who lived to tell the tale. So, like any survivor, His Majesty is still a little hesitant, as if he does not trust the floor to hold his weight, though he is a thin man, his clothes the heaviest part of him. He does not stride across the chamber but takes small shuffling steps. Because he walks slowly, his courtiers, too, are forced to pace themselves behind him, and Joan nearly laughs aloud to see the flashes of impatience on their faces, the measured intake of breath, the steady count to five, the gradual exhalation.

Suddenly, at her side: a hiss. The Dauphin has paused in his journey across the chapel and, with unexpected swiftness, as though he meant to surprise their plan, looked up at them. "Kneel, Joan, kneel!" le Maçon whispers. He nearly elbows her arm.

She drops to her knees. Her hands are flat on the cold stone. The chapel is silent. A moment passes, then another, and she peers through the balusters of the alcove, as if through the bars of a cage, to the Dauphin below.

He is still watching her, expressionless, like she is a part of the wall. The big beetle, the courtier named La Trémoille, leans forward to whisper into his ear, but the Dauphin raises a hand, flicks him away. From above she hears le Maçon chuckle.

The Dauphin scratches the side of his nose as another would scratch his head when trying to figure out a problem. He turns. A last glance over the royal shoulder and then he moves on. The doors of the chapel close with a rattle behind the last ambling courtier in his train.

Joan rises to her feet. Her eyes do not leave the space where the Dauphin stood. "What now?" she asks, dusting herself off.

Le Maçon smiles. He has known the Dauphin long enough to perceive when his master's interest is piqued. His expression says, *Did you see how he swatted away that purple beetle? That is a sign in our favor.*

He gives his beard a little scratch. "What else?" he says. "We wait until His Majesty summons you."

◆

Joan remembers her first meeting with this Robert. They were alone in another room of stone. It wasn't how she'd imagined a room in a castle would be, more like a prison cell with a chair for her to sit on, and he had paced, circling her, while he spoke. His speech was wandering—sometimes personal, other times as if he were practicing an oration for a lecture at the Sorbonne. He asked about her childhood; he wanted her to describe to him the village of Domrémy, her father and her mother, the church, the sermons of the priest, how often she prayed and confessed. He did not directly respond to anything she said but rambled about kings and what it means to be a king, about the reign of the great French kings, this Dauphin's grandfather, Charles, fifth of his name, known as the Wise; an earlier Charles, the greatest Charles, whose name was Charlemagne; Saint Louis, King Louis the ninth, who was canonized less than thirty years after his death. And as for the current one, the Dauphin . . . He trailed off, cleared his throat, and changed the subject. Well, we have our hopes, he concluded. Briefly, he touched on recent events: Only three weeks ago, a battle had taken place at Rouvray, and people are already calling it the Battle of the Herrings for the barrels of salted fish that were fought over. Another loss, though the French greatly outnumbered the English; another cut on the body of our kingdom, and because the wound is fresh, how it smarts.

"It is hard not to feel for the Dauphin," le Maçon said thoughtfully. "He is his father's true son and would have been seven years into a peaceful reign were it not for this war. You may have heard that the late King agreed to the terms of the Treaty of Troyes, but this is a falsehood. His Majesty's father was ill, and it was his mother who gave away her own son's inheritance. She saw what direction the wind was blowing and aligned herself with Henry, King of England, and the

Duke of Burgundy to remove him from the line of succession. Well, we who recognize His Majesty as sole heir to the throne, as ruler and overlord of the duchies of France, do not agree to the terms of that treaty. We refuse to call Henry's brat, a mere child in England, king. But our enemies take our towns and our cities. They have taken Paris, and it isn't uncommon now in this kingdom for a town to be French in the morning and, after a long day's fighting, to fall into the hands of England and Burgundy before the sun has set. This is the problem. After so many defeats, His Majesty has grown discouraged, and he has always been a sensitive young man. He feels that the world is working against him, that fate is conspiring to disgrace his name and strip him of his throne, and he has not had an easy life. He fears whatever he touches will turn out for the worse, and so he is afraid. He does not dare do anything that might tip the scales."

Then le Maçon stopped. He said, as though it had only just occurred to him, "Do you know why you are here, Joan? You are number four. The one who came before you was a boy who experienced stigmata in the manner of Saint Francis of Assisi, and claimed an angel appeared at his bed every night to whisper prophecies into his ear. It turned out the angel was no angel but his mother and sisters, telling him what to say. Number two was a monk, a disaster we won't begin to go into. Number one, the first to come to us, was a holy maid, a novice no more than twelve or thirteen. An abbess from Lyons brought her to our attention. She had never had a room to herself or taken a bath in hot water. She ate a lot and gave us vague answers to every question we put her way, until we realized she knew little beyond her Pater Noster and could offer us even less. We had to tell the abbess who recommended her: Being simple should not be confused with holiness.

"So," he concluded, "now that I have been transparent and laid these facts before you, I can say I do not hold out much hope for you. Why should you, as number four, be any different than the boy, the monk, or the holy maid? Yet we are desperate. We must try everything to shake the Dauphin out of . . . How does one even describe His Majesty's condition? His torpor? His melancholy? That would be putting it kindly. His mother-in-law, Yolande of Aragon, has tried and failed, and she is the greatest lady at court, the wisest of any of us. You know, I have kneeled with the flower of France's nobility beside me and begged him to save the city of Orléans, even if I have to take a sword in hand myself—I, who have just turned sixty-four years old. I have told His Majesty in every possible way—plainly, secretly, laughing through bitter tears—that if Orléans falls, then we are done for, are you aware of this, my lord? This cursed war is like a game of chess, and the Dauphin's forefathers have been playing it for ninety-two years. There were times when the game was stalemated and times, too, when England was steeped in its own troubles and it appeared we would win. But now we are losing. We are so close to losing everything."

Joan listened. What he said didn't surprise her. There are still places and people loyal to the Dauphin, but everyone in France—the prostitutes blowing kisses from their windows, the singing minstrels, the bakers, the tanners, the butchers, and the pig farmers—knows it isn't enough to turn the tide of the war.

"Though before we can even talk of winning," le Maçon continued, "we must turn our thoughts to Orléans. Without Orléans, all is lost, and the city has been under siege since October, with no access to the river, which means no supplies."

She was fast losing patience with the aged courtier. Why had she been brought to this place only to receive a lecture? "You think I do not know this," she said. "You would be amazed, you would find it incredible, how the names of royalty roll off our peasant tongues. In Domrémy, we do not confuse one Jean with another, one Charles or Philip or Louis with his forefathers or heirs. We have heard of the plight of Orléans and, before Orléans, of the losses at Verneuil, as terrible as Agincourt, a reminder of what it means to be humbled. We know all the great defeats: how Meaux fell, Rouen was starved out, a former King of France captured at Poitiers, and Calais besieged." Her mind is moving backward in time and ticking off battles, most of them French defeats: more stories from her uncle. "Shall I go on?"

She stood then, rising out of her chair to face him. "But what do you want from me? I am no prophet. I do not bleed from my hands and feet. I have never been visited by angels."

He took a step closer to her. The top of his head reached only to her chin, but he did not flinch. "There is a time to be humble, Joan, and this is not one of them. I have questioned the men who accompanied you here—the knight and squire, the royal messenger. I have heard the Duke of Lorraine sing his praises of you, and read a letter from the captain of the garrison in Vaucouleurs, Sir Robert de Baudricourt, a steady and trustworthy man, who asked that we should grant you an audience with His Majesty. Would you call these men liars for what they have reported about you? Would you say they are deceivers?"

In an almost tender voice, he added, "We are all afraid to fail, yet we must still try. There has never been more at stake. More to lose.

"For we are down to our last few pieces, some scattered pawns, some handful of knights, and the Dauphin—so terrified is he of being remembered as the king who surrendered the crown of France to her ancient enemy that now he does not move at all, not even the pieces he still has on the board. Three times a day, he goes to Mass; he makes devotions to his protector, Saint Michael, and spends most of his time praying, so a number of us thought, perhaps God can give him courage; perhaps God alone can imbue him with the strength he needs to fight and win this war. And how does God speak to us, save through those He favors, His appointed messengers? Thus the holy maid, the monk, the boy with bloody hands and feet." Le Maçon bowed his head. "And now: you."

VII

◆ ◆ ◆

THEY ARE IN A SMALL PRIVATE ROOM, brightly lit and warm. A strong fire burns. Beeswax candles flicker, illuminating, on the writing desk, a pair of dancing angels worked in gleaming silver. On the opposite wall: a tapestry of the Tree of Knowledge. Before Joan casts down her head and kneels, she glimpses Adam and Eve, huddling for shelter from the first storm cloud to visit Paradise. The tapestry hangs beside a door, and it is this door that leads into the chamber where the Dauphin sleeps each night with an obliging servant at the foot of his bed and a pair of armed guards outside.

But now she and the Dauphin are alone. Joan's vision lingers on a carpet, a swirl of indigo and vermilion dye, placed beneath the Dauphin's chair. In her blurred periphery, a figure detaches itself from the chair and rises. A swift, careless turn of the wrist indicates that she may stand. He has summoned her only hours after their initial meeting in the chapel. A good sign, according to le Maçon.

Her gaze shifts from plush carpet to royal person, wrapped, in spite of the heat, in heavy velvet robes dyed a deep blood-red, the collars and sleeves trimmed with black fur. He has changed his clothes since receiving Communion in the chapel. Self-consciously, he shuffles away from the tapestry, as if to say, *What happened there has nothing to do with me. I cannot account for all of mankind's troubles, only the troubles in its most Christian kingdom, and this, too, gives me such grief.* He moves to the pair of dancing angels, rests his hand across both of their heads, as if that is what they were made for: to be petted, to bear the weight of a prince's smooth and unscarred palm.

Le Maçon has warned her: Don't stare. The Dauphin doesn't like to feel that he is being watched, as who, unless he were a very vain individual, would? And His Majesty is sensitive about his looks, his appearance and his wardrobe, ever since circumstances forced him to make his home in Chinon. Yes, Chinon is a beautiful place. You may ask yourself, What else could a monarch possibly ask for? But you would be wrong. The Loire Valley boasts some of the finest lands in France. Its soil is rich; its vineyards are full. Heaven only knows the fresh air here surpasses any day that of Paris's stinking sewage and waste, both human and animal. But isn't even the absence of sewage a reminder that Chinon isn't Paris? This castle, grand though it is, isn't the Louvre. It isn't the Château de Fontainebleau, located some thirty miles south of the capital, another favorite of kings, though now out of His Majesty's reach.

The Dauphin doesn't speak, so Joan's gaze moves to the snake in the tapestry. Its forked tongue tickles Eve's white heel, like a single flame. But if the Dauphin doesn't address her, he still commands all attention to himself. So, he gently clears his throat. He rustles his sleeves and, turning sideways, offers Joan a profile to look at and to admire, the prominent Valois nose, which, some argue, is his best claim to the French throne and physical proof that he is, in fact, his father's son. He tilts his head and the glow of candlelight beams across his cheekbone, makes his skin shine a liquid, silken gold, as though all his features were in the process of being melted and sculpted to classic Romanesque handsomeness from scratch. The effect lasts for a heartbeat. The candle's flame shifts, and when she looks again, he is no longer glowing but dim, even slightly drooping beneath the collective weight of robes and black fur. He is tall, a slender young man twenty-six years of age, and his clothes, despite their opulence, have the impression of being passed down from a father or older brother. They are tailored for a person with fuller shoulders, a broader chest, someone with a healthy appetite and a rotund, protruding stomach, not one flat as a plank of wood. From a steeple of red cloth, the narrow gatepost of his body, his face juts like a pale moon.

Joan thinks, Perhaps the Dauphin does not look like a king because he was never made into one, not properly. Le Maçon had told her that when his father died, the Dauphin was named king by his own court in Mehun-sur-Yèvre with the first suitable crown the Archbishop could find. But the holy oil, which baptized the first Clovis nearly a millennium ago, was missing from the ceremony. As was Joyeuse, the sword of Charlemagne, and his crown. Still, she does not know if either would make the Dauphin droop less, if they would fill out his body so his robes do not sway so much like sheets drying in the wind.

She also thinks he looks tired, which is why he is yawning. A rumor has spread that he is considering a move to sunny Castile, just south of the kingdom's border. And Castile would welcome him with open arms, give him sanctuary for the term of his natural life. But don't bring that up, le Maçon warned her. We want him to stay where he is.

Again, the Dauphin sighs. He wavers, and she reads his thoughts as he glances back at the chair, the plump cushion. He is wondering whether he should remain on his feet or sit. The result is a compromise. He hovers closer to the chair but stands.

As soon as they left the chapel, le Maçon sat her down for another lecture: A king's mood can change faster than good weather to bad, so let him work out flares of temper or sudden fits of sorrow for himself. Don't cajole him. Don't coax him into a sweeter, sunnier frame of mind, unless he invites you to. If the interview seems to reach an impasse, be patient. A king may sigh. He may rub his eyes or dab a square of linen to his nose or to the corners of his mouth. He may suddenly take up a book, open it, and begin reading from a verse, as though he thought you had already left the room and he was alone. He may eat a grape and chew slowly and when you think he has finally surfaced from his reverie, when you see him leaning forward as if to return to affairs of state, he may instead reach out to pluck the strings of a harp and entertain you with a song: "The work of a single morning," he might say with pride. If the fire is low, he will expect you to build it. If a candle goes out, be prepared to light it for him, even if a dozen, nay, two dozen others are shining around the whole room. "You may consider this strange behavior," le Maçon explains with a shrug, "but it is strange only because you are not used to it, because you have grown up surrounded by sheep. You may believe it erratic, ill-mannered, or even cruel. But it is none of these. It is merely kingship."

So Joan both looks and doesn't look at the Dauphin. She thinks that le Maçon knows him well, for at the moment, what is His Majesty doing but nibbling at the corner of a small sugared tart taken from an arrangement on a gold platter? What is he doing but chewing slowly and staring out the room's one arched window, to blink at the fine nighttime view of torchlight and turrets as if she were invisible? When the pastry is eaten, he touches a clean napkin to his lips and to the tips of the fingers that handled the food. He picks up a thin folio from the desk, holds the book in one hand, as if it is a prop and he is about to be painted, puts it down again. He resumes his seat, taking his time to settle into cushioned and velvet-draped softness, and turns to his guest, as if to say: *Now, and only now, do we begin. You have my full attention.*

One thing you cannot say about the Dauphin: that he is among those lords of royal blood who have never known suffering or pain. God knows, the whole of Europe knows, he has had his share. Misfortune seems to follow him, closer to his person than his own shadow. Yet there may be something to a ruler who has been through so much. You can open a book of misery, turn to any page, point at a random word, and the Dauphin will probably say, Yes, I have been through this. Wretched childhood: yes. Mother who hates me: yes. Sister married to an enemy kingdom: yes. Infighting at court, my favorites cast out or murdered under my nose: yes. Receiving news of the very worst kind—that is, another battle lost to the English; finding out your father has died and you are banned from attending his funeral; being disinherited from your throne through a sham treaty and called by your enemies the greatest offender of God's law since Judas Iscariot sold Christ for thirty pieces of silver: yes, yes, and yes. This is a prince who knows what it means to run and to hide, to look out a window and see not the pleasant view below but everything lost. He has lived for years in the uncertainty of whether he will emerge from this war monarch or prisoner.

Joan's thoughts return to the present. She thinks this room too small for so large a fire; every surface is bathed in light, as though its occupant were afraid of the dark, each candle meant to scare away an imp loosed from hell. The Dauphin is a haunted man. One does not need to be a courtier, learned in manners, fluent in Latin, Roman quotations tripping like folk songs off the tongue, to see this is true.

How much time has passed since she first entered the room, she wonders. Five minutes? Ten? She feels she has been here whole years, that if she stuck her head out the window, a guard would shout back to tell her the war is officially over. They can all come out now, unlock their doors, fling open the shutters and casements, let fresh air in. As for her, she can return to Domrémy to help her parents on the land, or she can get married, bear several healthy children, whatever she would like to do. Except she can't. She can never go back.

Just as she thinks this, the Dauphin stirs.

"I have been informed of you," he says. His voice, when he speaks, croaks at first, like a person who has just risen from a nap. He does not wait for her to confirm or deny the statement but goes on: "There are those who support you at court; otherwise it is unlikely I would have granted you an interview. You have traveled some distance to come here."

Some distance. If over three hundred miles is some distance, then yes, His Majesty is correct. She nods.

"From Vaucouleurs," she says, looking up.

The Dauphin tilts his head. He is thinking, Vaucouleurs, Vaucouleurs, where in my formerly vast kingdom does this place lie? The answer comes to him. He seems to smile, or possibly it is the leap and glow of candlelight stretching the ends of his mouth.

"They have remained loyal to me," he says. So perhaps it was a smile she saw. "Sir Robert is an able captain. The English tried to take this town and failed. I remember the letters informing me of their attempt. You were born in Vaucouleurs, then?"

"No, I was born in a village called Domrémy. I doubt Your Majesty will have heard of it. I have lived there most of my life."

Again, the head tilts, this time in the other direction. The eyes blink, counting over duchies, cities, rivers, towns, as the map of France turns and turns.

"A little too close to my cousin Burgundy," he says at last.

"Domrémy is loyal to Your Majesty," she replies.

A pause, filled with the pop and crackle of fire. When he speaks next, it is a new beginning.

"What protection were you given for your journey from Vaucouleurs to Chinon?"

She names the men who were her guards: the knight, Bertrand de Poulengy; the squire, Jean de Metz; and Richard the archer. She names Colet de Vienne, the royal messenger in the employ of His Majesty's mother-in-law, and the two servants of de Poulengy and de Metz who accompanied them, tasked with guarding the supplies, though they all took their turn keeping watch.

"We traveled by night and kept off the main roads," she says. "In daylight, we took sanctuary in churches and abbeys, and if none were to be found, the trees and hedges protected us from discovery. It was the safest way."

"How long did your journey last?"

"Several days. Eleven in all."

It registers: the danger, the sleepless nights, the fear of betrayal. From the book of misery, the Dauphin nods, acknowledges the shared experience. So when he replies, "A quick journey, all considered," you know he is thinking back to a not-so-distant memory, eleven years into the past, his adolescent self on horseback, hair standing up on scrawny arms and neck. That night, no matter how hard he rode, the screams of Paris were never far enough behind him. Blood washed the streets when John the Fearless took the capital for his own.

The Dauphin sighs. He looks tired. What is a decade, a mere eleven years, when so little has changed?

She wonders, Is this why the Dauphin has memorized the shape and lines of France: its valleys, its rivers and lakes, its major cities, its rural clusters of wattle-and-daub cottages, its forests, meadows, and pastures, its marshes and swamps, its caves and nooks, its mountain passes? Imprinted in his mind is a map stuck with miniature flags, like a general's plan of battle. Red for England, my enemy. Blue for France, my friends. He has drawn, with a mental stick of charcoal, various escape routes. If this and this are blocked, then we can still flee to such-and-such a place, which has remained loyal to me and my ancient forefathers. And if the English are at our backs, we can escape along this tributary, which empties into this river. All other options exhausted, we can always jump into barrels and trust to the current.

"I am pleased God has favored your journey," he says, and does not say, Because goodness knows, He seems to favor little about France these days. "I am pleased that you and those who traveled with you have arrived safely in Chinon."

She senses a shift in the air. The courtesies are over, idle talk come to an end.

"We remain unclear, however, as to what services you may render for our benefit," he says with another sigh.

For a moment, she marvels at the smooth transition, the sleight-of-hand swap of pronouns, the personal "I" tossed aside for the royal "we." For a king, shedding his human skin is the equivalent of changing hats: the fashionable chaperon, with its liripipe, its tail of cloth, switched for the heavy crown. In an instant, the mortal body swells into something less definable: one part flesh-and-blood man, one part sovereign whose power derives from none less than the Divine.

"Do you claim to be a holy woman?" he asks when she hesitates.

She shakes her head. "No." The word falls like something heavy dropped.

A frown creases the Dauphin's forehead. His expression says, *Haven't I been informed I was to be served a dish of salmon tonight, which I was looking forward to, and now I do not even recognize what has been placed before me?*

"But you have enjoyed visions," he says, insisting. He leans slightly forward. "Have you not? Didn't my lord the Duke of Lorraine tell me so in a letter? Well, in several letters. He said you were standing in a field one morning and God spoke to you, that you have performed impossible feats—miracles."

It is like the old Duke to exaggerate, she thinks. "I believe I told His Grace that it was I who spoke to God."

"About?"

"I made a wish. Several wishes."

She remembers, Your Majesty was on my list of names. And if you were a better prince, king, whatever you call yourself, then we would all be living in a different world.

But something holds her back, and she feels, just out of sight, the touch of her sister's hand against her shoulder. *Do not be so hard, Joan.* It surprises her. There was no stirring of hatred when she first saw the Dauphin in the chapel. She recognized the uncertain step. The bowed head. The pause before he rose to his feet from prayer. This was a man afraid. She felt—and it bewildered her—pity for him. She realized: her list of enemies was also his. So, perhaps they could help each other. When she sees him now, all she can think is, You don't look much of anything. Aren't all lords and princes supposed to be lions among men? Yet here was just a person, a thin man, not handsome, with dark shadows under his eyes, probably, she guesses, from bad sleep and nightmares. A face such as his could be found selling cooking pots at a fair—and not doing a good job of it, either. With his luck, he would probably come away with less money in his pocket than what he started out with.

"And have they come true?" he asks, interrupting her thoughts.

"I do not know yet."

To her surprise, he doesn't push for details. He does not command her to speak up. She hears him shift in the chair. From the wide hollows of his sleeves, two hands emerge, thin as paper, and press together as if the moment calls for prayer. But he is not praying. He is looking at her and thinking.

"Then, if you are not gifted in prophecy, like certain holy women who have graced our company; if you are not an astrologer and do not possess the skill to read our kingdom's fortunes in the movement of the stars and heavenly bodies; if you are neither a scholar nor a philosopher nor an ambassador learned in statecraft and religion, then it is a mystery how you think you can be of service to our cause."

He speaks gently, like a person who is breaking bad news to someone unprepared for the blow. But he is growing bored. Briefly the Dauphin's eyes close, and he exhales. Another sigh.

"The Duke writes your gifts are such that they could originate from no other source but God," he continues, as if making excuses for her silence. "So, I ask again, what is it that you can do for us? There are councillors who were against the idea of my meeting you. I would not like to tell le Maçon, whom I trust, that they were right."

She wonders: Why is it so hard to say what I can do? Why, if I possess strength, must it also be bound up in holiness? The Duke has used these phrases to describe her: *Beloved of God; touched by the Divine; favored by our Lord, this simple maid*. Why can't they just say . . .

Somewhere at the base of her neck, she feels her blood jump. Her nerves skitter away from her. She has only this moment, this chance. If she is to go where her enemies are, she cannot do it alone; she will need help. Behind her back, the fingers of her right hand flex into a fist.

Now it is her turn to surprise the Dauphin. She steps forward to the edge of the carpet and returns to kneeling; her eyes take in a woolen rose, its thorns like tiny green fangs.

It was never decided what she would say if asked. Le Maçon had instructed, suddenly nervous before her meeting, Commit yourself to nothing! Be vague. Don't boast. Though you are not a woman in holy orders, wasn't our Lord, too, only a shepherd? And you said you sometimes watched sheep in Domrémy. So perhaps, though you should not say your prayers are more efficacious than ours, you can hint that this is so? Just for this first meeting? You understand, we have never handled someone quite like you before. We don't know what you *are* yet.

She doesn't listen to le Maçon. "Majesty," Joan says quietly, "I can fight."

Personal tribulations have instructed the Dauphin in patience, in the kingly art of forbearance. Le Maçon says these are his positive attributes. He is not the kind of prince who will strike a servant simply because he is angry or because he can. He will not rush to judgment. It was a hard lesson that taught him first to think, then to speak, and finally to act—that is, when he acts at all, which these days is rare enough. For if John the Fearless, father of the current Duke of Burgundy, were alive, how things might be different for him, for France . . . but it never does any good to dwell upon the sins of the past.

The Dauphin lets her words sink in. He exercises serenity worthy of a bishop. Except for the momentary disappearance of his bottom lip, his expression doesn't change.

But he must say it. He must say aloud, in order to further the conversation, what needs to be said, for if this hurdle cannot be surmounted, then there is no point in continuing.

"You are a woman." There. With a slight lilt at the end, as if it could be a question. But it is said, and, she notices, he is sitting a little higher in his chair.

She agrees with him. She nods. "I am—a woman."

Bidding her to stand, he looks her over.

"You are not a delicate flower. This I grant you." The Dauphin's eyes travel slowly over the length of her body, head to foot. He seems tempted to test her sturdiness by poking her in the arm, but there is no servant ready with a basin of rose water and a towel to wash peasant dirt and sweat from his hands.

"And you are tall, taller even than most men. It is clear you enjoy good health. I have heard it is sometimes the way with those who work the land, who are lowborn," he says easily. "But even a strong woman is not equal to a man. This is well known since the days of antiquity. Strength is not a natural attribute of womanhood. It is not in her body's composition. This trait is and has always been the provenance of men."

She is silent. She is tempted to say, Not with me. And to add, And not with you either, it would seem.

The Dauphin's hands disappear into his too-large sleeves. His expression is questioning, but at least he is not laughing at her. "Are you suggesting you have received training?"

"I have sparred with the knight and squire I traveled with. When I worked in the kitchens at Vaucouleurs, I watched the soldiers train." She doesn't add, I broke a man's wrist with one hand. I took out three strong men with a skillet.

He shakes his head. "That seems hardly enough. A knight begins his training when he is a boy."

"And before I made this journey, I sparred nearly every day with my father. He was famous in Domrémy for his fists and hated me worse than he hated the English and the Burgundians. I do not exaggerate when I say this: that if every soldier in your army was the equivalent of my father, a Jacques d'Arc, in height, weight, and temper, this war would have ended in your father's time and we would be living in an age of peace. He would have sent the late King of England running like a serving boy whipped for dropping the soup ladle."

She sees that the Dauphin cannot help himself. He smiles at the image.

But he tips a beringed finger at her, as if he has caught her out. "So, you were an unruly child then, if your father beat you."

She hesitates. "I do not think you have to be an unruly child to be hated by your parents."

The Dauphin looks down. The smile on his face vanishes. It is another entry from the book of misery that rings true for him. He nods.

"Before I was born, my father made a bet. He said I would be his third son and he lost the wager, along with a good sum of money. Ever since, he hasn't known what to do with me."

"And your mother?"

"My mother should have been a nun cloistered in an abbey. She lives in fear of my father and subsists off prayers instead of food and drink."

"Yet you are well built." It is not a description, she thinks, that would flatter most of her sex. "To be so tall, you must have been well nourished or, at the very least, well fed."

For a moment, a memory washes through her and she forgets herself, where she is, who she is speaking to.

“My uncle used to joke to strangers, ‘Joan must eat a whole heifer to sate her appetite.’ ”

“And did you?” The Dauphin’s expression is serious.

“No, I ate bowls of pottage and black bread, like everyone else. And when the harvest was bad, we would skip a meal and go hungry. I was no different.”

Another rumor: His Majesty cannot pay his butcher’s bill. No more credit will be extended to the castle at Chinon. Even the battles of the household, of the kitchen, are ones he cannot win these days.

The Dauphin settles his head on his fist; the glow of a ring, a bright ruby, makes it look like he has a boil on the point of his chin. He seems to contemplate what has been laid before him, as if a scribe had written on scraps of parchment her various attributes: tall; young; female; well built; claims she can fight.

So, it seems a continuation of his thoughts when he says, “Then tell me what you know of war.”

This is the question for which she has been waiting.

“Majesty,” she says, “I will tell you what I know.”

◆

SHE TELLS HIM ABOUT A ROOM. It is the room she and her sister slept in. She describes the slanted, low ceiling, the shuttered window, the air that is musty and old because no wind or light is permitted to enter. And next to her, Catherine’s shape in the darkness. The sounds of quiet weeping. She recalls the dust motes like fairies, lit by splinters of sun filtering through the shutters’ gaps, and the spider webs, which grow and widen with the hours and the days, spinning miniature gray curtains in the corners of the room.

“It will be no news to you,” she tells the Dauphin, “to hear the English burned our fields, which were ready for the harvest. It may be no special thing to you that I picked up the black stalks of ruined wheat, and under my fingertips I felt the grain crumble like ash. I saw a child’s straw poppet, which she had dropped, crushed in the center of an Englishman's boot print, and a woman enter her home not through the door but through one side of her cottage, for a whole wall had been battered down." Because she knows that His Majesty prays often, she tells him about a saint's statue: defiled.

And the misery doesn't end when you have righted your fences and rebuilt your pens or put Saint Margaret's head back on her shoulders. No, misery, too, must play out its cycle, in the fullness of the seasons. In autumn, food is scarce. But in winter, the meadows for grazing razed, the livestock starve. She has watched the spirits of horses and oxen break. She has witnessed the moment of collapse when they could take no more. Nothing could be wasted. Any beast that died was cut up for meat, though there was always little to salvage. She has pulled out a newborn calf, wet and shining with mucus and blood, only to hold its head in her lap as it died, because there was no milk to spare and its mother was already gone. She has wondered, What is the point of this? To bring new life into the world and then to extinguish its light so soon, a mere hour of consciousness on this earth? What lesson can be learned from this?

And without the horse and ox, the plow must be pulled by a man and his wife, though both are hungry and sick. Even the crows would be hard-pressed to make a meal of them.

She tells him: For war is not just battle plans. It isn't France's preeminent *chefs de guerre* gathered around a table, signing off on orders for provisions and discussing formations of attack. It isn't the various implements of war: the sword, the special dagger that finishes a felled knight, which she learned about from the men who trained her. It isn't the shifting borders of a kingdom, the towers and battlements that change names and hands and loyalties in the space of a few violent hours. To her, it isn't even the dead on a battlefield, the casualties, young, middle-aged, and old, who know that to be struck down is what happens when you choose to stand your ground against those who wish to take it from you by force.

And it's not about ancient rights, for she doesn't believe, not a whit, that the English really care about France or adding new subjects to its sad little population. It is an English king who uses the excuse of an ancient claim because he has gazed across the Narrow Sea, into the dim and murky offing, and seen a vision of himself as the richest, most powerful man in Christendom. In the end, it's about money, the accrual of wealth and land. It's about making English knights rich with French treasure so they can build more castles on their gray-green island, where, she hears, it never ceases to rain and even the woodland and meadows are as wet and putrid as swamps. For with wealth, you can buy comfort. You can buy prestige, and you can buy culture: carpets to walk on, books studded with sapphires, tapestries, statues, a second castle, a third castle, a smattering of country manors. You can eat peacock meat, swan meat, and fresh salmon every day for every meal. *Why not?* the English ask themselves upon waking, before they pillage, burn, and destroy. And, she tells the Dauphin, ever since Catherine died, she can almost hear it in her own ears, this question the English ask each morning: "Why not?"

To her, war has become something else, and here lies the problem. When kings have gone bankrupt from the expenditures of war, when they are unable to pay their troops, and soldiers go hungry and feel they have put their lives at stake for nothing, for less than nothing, looting happens. Murder happens. Rape happens.

"I believe God crafted the sound of a woman's scream," she says, "to pierce the heart and to test our humanity, whether we still have it or whether we have left it behind.

"But there are men for whom a woman's scream is as a fist that bounces off armor. I have thought to myself, *What choices does a woman have for vengeance, for justice?* For we cannot simply pray. I can't stomach my mother's prayers. We cannot afford to wait and be still. I won't live this way—not anymore. So when I spoke to God that morning, I decided, if I am to scream, let it be in battle. There is no chance for peace except at the point of a sword."

She stops to catch her breath. A silence settles between them. How will His Majesty take this lesson? And from someone like her?

But his face doesn't change. He clears his throat. He says, as calmly as before, "You talk well. This I grant you, too."

Without looking at her, he raises a jeweled hand and beckons. "Come," he says, and when she hesitates, he repeats himself: "Come closer."

She steps across the carpet of woolen roses. A distance of less than two feet now separates them. From here it is possible to see that they would stand shoulder to shoulder.

"You may know my elder sister's name is also Catherine," he says. "And though she is alive, she is as lost to me as your sister who is dead. She married Henry, the late King of England, and had a son by him. If the English and Burgundy win this war, then this boy, my nephew, will call himself King of both England and France. He will wear my crown. So, you see, there is no hope between us for reconciliation, given her loyalties and"—he pauses—"my unique position." It is like he is reciting from his own book of misery, and it has become a contest between them. Everything you have been through, I have known, and more. "If we are to speak of family—sisters, brothers, uncles, cousins, friends, my father—so many now are gone. I understand loss in its many forms."

The time for her to speak has ended. On the platter of sweets, there is a gap like a lost tooth where the consumed pastry once rested; he extracts a single golden wafer from a ring of comfits, tarts, and sugared flowers. He holds it beneath his nose and inhales. His eyes close in pleasure.

"Cinnamon," he says, and she feels her heart skip a beat. She thinks of cinnamon birds, of her uncle, and looks down.

"This wafer, the oublie, is no less than an art form," he tells her. "The Greeks made these as well, but not like we do. They could not hope to achieve such perfection. I have gone into the kitchens myself to watch the cooks and their helpers, though you can buy an oublie in any street of France. The ingredients are deceptively simple. Only some flour and water.

"But I think a truly fine oublie is the work of an artist. See here . . ." He points to the front of the wafer. "My cook has stamped a picture on this one because he knows I pay special honor to Saint Michael. It is Michael slaying Satan."

She steps closer. In the cake, she sees a clear outline of two bodies, one winged and gripping a sword, the other an enormous serpent wriggling on its stomach. The cook has given the angel a crown and wavy hair reaching to his shoulders. He has dressed him sparsely and in the Roman style, in a draped gown that reaches above his muscular knees. A sandaled foot rests upon the serpent's head, its mouth open, fangs bared.

He holds out the wafer to her. "For your troubles," he says as she takes it.

The Dauphin is watching her carefully. "This wafer, it reminds you of something? Or you have tasted it before?"

She doesn't answer. Around them the haze of candlelight blurs into memory. She is thinking of another wafer wrapped in a piece of clean linen cloth, of blancmanger, a dish as intangible as a dream.

"But you are like me," he continues, still watching her. "We no longer permit our tears to fall."

A pause. Then, as she leaves, the Dauphin's voice reaches her at the door: "The time of miracles that cannot be seen has passed. If you are truly blessed by God, it must be proved. You will be tested."

◆

Le Maçon has given her a room in Chinon, with a bed, a small table, a chair, and a window that looks out onto the starlit valley below. At night, the room is locked and guarded by two men in his own employ. "Why should I be a prisoner?" she asked him in protest, but he shook his head. "You are mistaken. It is for your protection, not for the protection of others." He is thinking of his rivals at court and the men who work for them: the current favorites of His Majesty, the men Joan saw that morning at the chapel.

"And do not say you don't need protection!" he snapped, anticipating her reply.

In bed, she inhales the scent of the wafer, holding it under her nose as the Dauphin had done. For a moment, it is as if she has stepped into the body of the French King. The fragrance is like nothing, no flower or herb or sap of a tree she has ever come across. She takes a bite, and her teeth graze the top of Saint Michael's wavy locks. The warmth travels across the surface of her tongue. She cannot help smiling.

The Dauphin had said, upon giving her this gift, "For your troubles." She thinks there may be some truth to this, however accidental the wisdom. Perhaps all she has been through feeds into the seconds it takes to finish a single oublie. Perhaps troubles eventually distill themselves into something else, as a few lines of the troubadour's poetry distill the pains and secrets of love.

On a cloudless night in another time, the moon like a perfect Eucharist wafer, she had dreamed of tasting, if only once, the spice of the cinnamon birds. Now she has.

VIII

◆ ◆ ◆

THE TESTS COME IN DIFFERENT FORMS, most of which feel less like tests in holiness than exercises in patience: How much will she, Joan, take before she goes back to her village?

"It is in the hands of the Archbishop and La Trémoille," le Maçon says grimly.

"Why?" she asks.

"They believe I am biased in this matter."

"And they aren't?"

She imagines they will throw her in a river (if so, she's not too worried; she can swim) or give her a holy text to read aloud (this would be a problem), but they don't. A boy brings her to the royal stables, addresses her respectfully. While she waits for the Dauphin and his councillors to deliberate on what to do with her, she can make herself useful. He hands her a shovel. And if she doesn't like the smell of horse manure, didn't she once work in the kitchens? She can put on an apron and clean the spits and cauldrons. The cook would be grateful for any extra help.

Her reply: I can help the cook after I am done here.

The boy who works for La Trémoille expects to find her idling. But by the time he returns, the stables are cleaned. The horses brushed. He finds Joan paring apple slices for a chestnut mare. She tells the wide-eyed messenger, "You had better close your mouth before you swallow a fly."

The next day, she is taken to the training grounds. Ah finally, she thinks. But no, the same messenger leads her to a stool placed in full view of the riding and sparring. Here is a breastplate. Here gauntlets, a pair of greaves and sabatons. And here, says the boy, is a brush, some sand and vinegar, and cloths.

She is tempted to tell the boy about her sword-polishing stall. She wants to say, You know, it was a dream of mine when I was a child of ten to do this; but she doesn't, because she is afraid he will change his mind if he sees this task gives her pleasure. At the end of the day a different man returns to inspect her work. She is given watery stew and a piece of dry bread for supper.

The following morning she is tasked with rolling barrels filled with sand to clean chain mail. And the day after: It's back to the stables and shoveling horse manure. Then cleaning out the kennels of the hunting dogs. Two men find her sitting on the straw-covered floor, hugging the Dauphin's greyhounds. Her face is wet with dog kisses; they love her as much as Salaud did. She says to the men, trying to keep the pleading out of her voice, "Can I come back here tomorrow?"

After a week, she asks one of La Trémoille's servants, "Am I getting paid for any of this?"

The boy's face brightens. "You want money, do you?" He thinks she is like the other pretenders—the first holy woman who came, the monk—and she wants to get rich. If so, a bribe can be negotiated so she will go away.

But she shakes her head. "I only meant, should I be paid what the dog boy or stable boy receive each day in wages?" She wouldn't mind a few pennies in her purse. "I am doing the same work as them."

They thought she had come to put up her feet and eat supper by a comfortable fire; that she would complain about working long hours and being fed little more than the beggars at the gate. This is something else they can't understand: We feed her almost nothing, the bare minimum, and give her the hardest work. So why doesn't she weaken or complain of a sore back, of aching limbs? Why does she never tire?

In the evenings, le Maçon visits her. He holds a perfumed square of cloth to his nose.

"You smell, Joan." But his face isn't without concern. Has she had enough?

Dog shit from the kennels. Horse shit from the stables. She gives him a look: What do you expect me to smell like? A garden of roses?

◆

THE HOUR IS LATE, but the door of her room flies open with a bang. Here are three men. Two of them are in La Trémoille's employ; the third she recognizes as the messenger who traveled with her from Vaucouleurs. They expect to find her asleep, but she was awake at the first sound of footsteps.

They escort her outside to where there are four horses and a boy watching them.

Before they mount, she asks, "Where are we going?" In her pocket: her uncle's knife. At her side: Sir Robert's second-best sword.

The men tell her, smiling and not blinking an eye, "We are going to kill a dragon in the woods." Only the royal messenger looks away when they say this.

She knows that to refuse would be to fail. The report would fly straight to the Dauphin's ear. But if they lay a hand on her, even by accident, she will kill them.

The whole journey La Trémoille's men talk about the dragon, which stirs only at night. It is over fifty feet long. No, a hundred, the other says. With scales hard as diamonds and teeth as large as a man's head. One of them glances back at her. A laundry maid went into the forest; it was said she was meeting her lover. Well, after some searching, she found him, all right: his body torn in strips by the dragon's claws, his face burned to a cinder.

"Then how did she know it was him?" Joan asks. She keeps her own face still, like a face of stone.

They ignore her and continue talking. The huntsmen have found deer ripped to pieces. "No work of a bear or a wolf," they say to her cheerfully as they reach the woods.

"Frightened?" one of them asks. "We can turn back if you are afraid. But then we would be compelled to inform our master."

She looks ahead. The lights of torches flash like demons' eyes in the dark. Now left, now right. Now they seem to be retracing their steps and moving in circles before plunging deeper.

She thinks she hears the royal messenger say to the others, in a low voice, "Not too far."

"We will decide how far," one of La Trémoille's men snaps back.

They have reached a stream. "Here. We will stop here." The same man hands her a leather flask. "Fetch us some more water. We are thirsty."

She looks from one to the other of her escorts, takes the flask, dismounts. She moves slowly. Under her feet, the ground is solid, but it is dark, the only light the shuddering flame of torches. The men's faces are solemn. They are like executioners, who must carry out their task.

As she kneels to reach the water, she hears a whistle from behind. She turns in time to see La Trémoille's men ride away, and they have taken her horse with them.

Only the royal messenger pauses. In torchlight their eyes meet. He looks frightened.

"Good luck, Joan," he whispers before fleeing.

She is alone, and she can see nothing, not even her own hands. The moon tonight is weak. She feels for the opening of the flask, fills it, and takes a drink of water to steady herself. There is a small pain in her chest where her heart beats quickly.

When she was a child of five, her father took her to the Bois Chenu. She has since forgotten her offense, but whatever she did, it was grave enough that he considered the usual punishments inadequate. In the village, the children had been taught to be afraid of the woods, and Joan was no exception. She remembered how she kept looking from her father's back to the sky. The sun was then slipping below the horizon. Soon it would be dark.

She thinks now, as she moves along the bank, if the men hoped to hear her scream, they will be disappointed.

Her father dragged her into the woods until they were far enough that she couldn't see where they had come from. He told her to sit and not to move from the clearing where they had stopped. If he had time in the morning, he might return to fetch her, or he might leave her there for good.

She remembers how fear turned her skin damp. When a fox cried from its hole, she wetted herself. Every skittering beetle, every tail or snake that rustled a bush, jolted her heart until it seemed to loosen from its place, to slip and slide all through her body, knocking against her ribs.

But then an hour passed. And another. And by the third or fourth hour, she had sweated out all of her fear. Her eyes grew heavy, and she made a pillow of the grassy floor.

She learned: Everything changes when you enter a forest. There is no conception of a past or future; there is no sense of time. Each moment carries with it the same urgency as the moment that came directly before. You cannot see beyond your next step, and sometimes, you cannot see even that much. Yet you feel alive, your body measuring its chances of survival not in days, weeks, or years but by the second.

As she moves, she can no longer hear the stream. She puts her trust in her body, the voice that tells her to turn left, move forward, and now right. Do you remember this clearing? Yes, yes, I remember. And here, her mind flicks back. We circled at this point, which means . . . It takes her only a moment to work through the labyrinth of steps and turn them backward into a sequence, like a dance.

But the journey is long. She traveled here on horse, and now she is on foot.

The dark is for reflection. She had told the Dauphin what she knew of the war. But she didn't tell His Majesty: since Catherine died and her uncle left, whole days have gone by where she has felt purposeless. She wonders if he feels that way, too. She hates the English, the Burgundians, any enemy of France, but her heart is tired. And she has asked herself since arriving at Chinon what she is doing, why she is even here. It's not the horse manure she minds. It's these games.

She stops to rest and to take another drink, holding the cold water in her mouth before swallowing. Her hands feel out a solid trunk, and she sinks to the ground.

The air is brisk. When she closes her eyes, it is only a little darker than when she keeps them open. Soon she falls asleep, her hand on the hilt of her sword. She dreams of Domrémy, that she has returned to her father's house, and there on the doorstep two women call her by her name. One has a face like her sister's; she has seen it before in a book. The other resembles the statue that stood in front of the church. They tell Joan to sit and offer her fresh water, a piece of bread. They move swiftly, and wherever they step, a light seems to follow them, making their bodies glow. Joan drinks the water. She wolfs down the bread, and she is surprised. A single piece makes her feel full. She asks if her father has sold the house, if her parents and brothers have moved away from the village, and they smile. How little she understands, their expressions say, and they tell her they have known her all her life, from even before she was born.

She wakes. It is not yet dawn; she has slept at most two hours, but the forest is already lighter. Her mind picks up where it left off, but now she can see better. The voice says, Watch out for that stump, Joan. Turn here. Do you remember this tree? Its trunk was twisted. You noticed it in torchlight, its strange shape. Yes, yes, I remember. And from the tree, she reads the path just as easily as if she were turning the pages of a book from back to front.

The first spear of sunlight falls at her feet. She looks up. Ahead: a narrow opening of pale light. Her exit.

This is a night of small miracles. As she leaves the forest, she hears a rustle over her shoulder. Her breath catches. When she looks back, she sees the clear outline of a stag, watching. The crowns of beasts are no less glorious than those of kings. The stag is framed in the gathering mist of morning, like a host come to see her off, and he does not move from his place until she is well on her way.

The guards at her door were bribed to leave their posts, le Maçon later explains. He has already dismissed them, but now La Trémoille has hired them, so what has that achieved?

"It was a cruel test," he says. "When did you return?"

Early. The bells had not yet rung for Prime. They—La Trémoille's two men, the royal messenger—heard snoring from her room as they passed her door. They found her in bed, her clothes scented with moss and oak. She stirred, sat up, and looked at them. They seemed more tired than she was, for reasons she couldn't fathom (after all, they had taken the horses). So she thinks they must have lost their way returning to the castle.

Le Maçon says, "My sources tell me the messenger, Colet de Vienne, accompanied La Trémoille's men only to ensure nothing . . . untoward happened."

If she could give her opponents at court some advice, she would tell them: Do your research. Though she supposes they can't, not unless they make a special trip to Domrémy and interrogate her father.

Because her father would tell them: Oh no, that's not how you trick Joan at all. I tried that when she was a child of five! Work my daughter like a plowhorse? That won't do it, either! She would outlast any ox or mule.

She is seventeen now. Twelve years ago: She slept in the woods as children are accustomed to sleep, deep and dreamless. At first light, she rose from her bed of moss and left the clearing behind. She walked through the Bois Chenu, and from the woods to the only house of stone in Domrémy below. The door swung open and her father stepped out. As he stared, eyeballs bulging, she yawned at him.

Now she thinks, smiling to herself: This is why when the men looked in on her this morning their expressions were so familiar. She had seen such faces before.

◆

It is Nones. Three in the afternoon. In a large courtyard: Straw targets in various states of disturbance. Some beheaded. Others disemboweled. The ground is strewn with straw blood, and stable boys have been called in to clean up the mess.

Le Maçon shakes his head, which, unlike those of the targets, still rests firmly on his shoulders. His Majesty came to witness the display. He watched each spear strike home, each arrow hit its mark. And he watched her ride.

It was the first time the Dauphin saw what others—the Duke of Lorraine, Sir Robert de Baudricourt—meant by feats. By miracles.

Le Maçon thought the Dauphin would be pleased. Here, for the first time, is no pretender. But in Joan's room he is pacing. "I heard His Majesty was upset," he said. There is a tremor in his voice. "I heard he said to the Duke of Alençon, his cousin, So? So she can throw a spear! And shoot better than most men. How does that help me?"

Joan scratches her head. More lice? She hopes not. And she would like to offer His Majesty a small correction: *All* men. She shoots better than *all* men.

She thinks perhaps he could not believe what he saw, as she herself sometimes cannot believe it.

She says to le Maçon, "Give His Majesty time."

But le Maçon answers her quickly: "Orléans has been under siege almost six months. We are running out of time."

IX

◆ ◆ ◆

WHEN COLET DE VIENNE NEXT SEES JOAN, he smiles. A sheepish smile. And he looks a little afraid, as if Joan might pick him up and throw him across the room like a pile of sackcloth. "Just through here," he says quickly, bouncing across the antechamber.

She is led to a scene straight out of her uncle's princess stories. A woman dressed in kingfisher-blue silks sits in a chair like a throne, a dark-colored garment in her lap. As if enacted for the moment, her hand is poised with a single needle, the thread dangling. Encircling her, resembling a merchant's display of finery, four ladies-in-waiting attired in rich greens and sumptuous yellows, sleeves trailing, headpieces glittering with pearls and studded with garnets large as ox eyes, sit on cushions. Two sift through an iron chest, laying out jewels on a platter. One bends over a headdress as large as a swan; another sews.

For a moment, Joan is breathless. The knights may have breastplates of steel and shirts of chain mail, but these women cover their hearts with ruby-studded brooches and star-shaped diamond pins. The knights have their helmets, but these women are horned. From their heads jut hennins like towers, and from each tower streams a flag of victory, a translucent, shimmering veil so fine one's hand might pass through it like air.

Faced with such a gathering, Joan feels shy. She is still wearing the same outfit as when she left Vaucouleurs. Only now she notices an unsightly smudge on her gray tunic. It may be a grass stain, or the remnants of hound or horse excrement. And as le Maçon said, she smells. After she bows, she takes a step back; she doesn't know what to do with her hands or her feet, which now feel unseemly and large. And she hopes the women won't start screaming, that they won't mistake her for a lumbering ogre.

The women seem to know what she is thinking. They look at her with a subtle raise of their plucked brows and smile discreetly.

But then: a flash of color. A sudden sweep of a kingfisher sleeve like an outstretched wing, and the ladies-in-waiting rise in silence from their cushions and shuffle out.

"Well!" Yolande of Aragon says, dropping the garment to the floor and rising. Le Maçon has told her, The woman you will meet is a lady of many titles. The Dauphin's mother-in-law. Queen of Four Kingdoms: Aragon, Sicily, Jerusalem, and Cyprus. She is also Duchess of Anjou and Countess of Provence, though at one time she was regent of that fine place.

A single finger, a dark red stone jutting from it like a swollen knuckle, curls at her. "Let me have a closer look at you," she says.

Joan steps forward. If the Dauphin had any reservations about catching a disease or lice from her, his mother-in-law has none. Soft hands reach out and pat Joan across her shoulders. "What shoulders!" Yolande cries. She raises her face to beam at Joan. It is a beautiful face: the eyes a shining green, the mouth coy and small like a child's, and the forehead smooth as a dome of marble. "What a jawline!" she adds a moment later.

"Raise your hand for me," Yolande says, and Joan obeys. She places her own palm against Joan's, as if they might begin a dance. A moment is spent studying the difference in size and hardness, in calluses and scars, of which, naturally, the older woman has none. Joan holds her breath. Then Yolande says, "These are such fine hands."

Joan feels herself blush.

"Ah, you are still a young girl to blush so deeply." A deep-throated chortle follows. "You are, of course, the talk of the court. I hear that the training grounds are crowded with onlookers every day, and the pages no longer obey their masters because by dawn they must reserve their place to stand by the barriers to watch you. How many arrows can you shoot in a minute? Has anyone timed you?"

She is ready with the answer: "Twelve, Your Highness." Sometimes a few more, she doesn't add. And I never miss.

"Twelve," Yolande repeats, clasping her own hands in delight. "It is . . . wonderful. Poor girl, she is blushing again. If my compliments make you blush, I wonder how you will feel when you meet the Duke of Alençon. My maids of honor swoon whenever he comes into the room, and I have to give them a little kick to make them sit up again. He is also a good man, brave and faithful. You have met His Majesty?"

She nods.

"And what do you think of him?"

She hesitates, bows deeply.

Yolande laughs. Another happy chortle. "That bad, is it?"

"I . . ."

But her host raises a hand to stop her. "You cannot fool me, child, so do not try. Though you must understand, His Majesty is as dear to me as if he were my son and I, not Isabeau, had given him life. You do not know him. He is a person difficult to fathom even after a lifetime's acquaintance."

Yolande moves away, bending to pick up the dropped garment. She tosses it carelessly across the chair. "Isabeau never cared for him. She treated all her children like chess pieces, each to be played at a different time and discarded if they were useless. She only ever loved herself. A shameful woman. To her, being a mother is not so different from being a queen. When one sits at a great height, it is easy to enjoy many favors. One can live one's whole life never knowing what it means to give, to sacrifice. And she still does not know.

"From an early age," Yolande continues, "I took an interest in Charles. I saw how he was neglected. No one cared for him; no one minded if he was in a room or if he was missing. I once asked him, when he was a boy only so high—he was very small as a child: How long has it been since your mother took you in her arms and kissed you? Since she called you her special darling and said she wanted to gobble you up like a dish of stewed apples with spoonfuls of white sugar? We were on a barge traveling to the south of the kingdom. It was the first time he saw such green and beautiful country. He said, without taking his eyes off the land, which he did not know at the time would one day be his, 'It has been three months since my mother held me.' And my heart, it broke for him. I folded my arms over his thin body. I told him, From this moment on, Charles, you have two mothers: your natural mother and me, Yolande. You have my children to be as close or closer to you than your own siblings. And after that day, he always called me his 'good mother' and became like another brother to my second son, René. They would read poetry together and draw. I took what he made, what he wrote, and I made a point of showing his work to all the drawing masters and the famous poets who would visit the court. The attention frightened him at first. This was to be expected. But later he learned to laugh. And he learned to be at ease with his true friends. Who knew then he would become King of France? Two of his elder brothers were not infants when they died; they were already men. But illness took them, God rest their souls, and then it was my own sweet son who became Dauphin."

Yolande sighs. She needs no prompting. She says, meeting Joan's gaze, "How do you think a mother feels when she sees her child suffering? My heart breaks every day. For we are all waiting, from me, his good mother, to the lowest servant of the castle. We are waiting to see what king he will become, and I harbor no illusions. My Charles may be a great king, like his grandfather, or merely a good king, though let us hope he will not be like his father, who was mad, or a horrible king, like England's Richard, not the first, but the second, to whom, believe it or not, I was once almost engaged. But in order to become any of those things, he must first take up the mantle passed down to him. He must *act* to show his people and the world what king he will be."

Joan watches Yolande glide back to her in a vision of blue. How do the dyers manage to capture such a color, Joan wants to know. When she looks down, she stares at her own rough boots, scuffed, one buckle already broken. She feels her hands squeezed. "I can tell what you are thinking," Yolande says. "You see all of this, you see me, and you think, Ah, what can a woman know of the court, of kings, beyond her wifely duties and childbearing? You have, if I am not mistaken, spent more time in the company of men growing up. So, you see me in this fine room with my sewing and my ladies-in-waiting, and you think I asked you here only to marvel at your size and your strength, and to tell you how much I love His Majesty. You think, because I am a woman, I am capable of appealing only to your heart, to your feelings. See? I am right! You are blushing again, Joan!

"But I would inform you, if le Maçon has not told you already, that I married not at thirteen or fourteen, which is the custom for a woman of my standing. At nineteen, I wed my Louis. He was a man I did not think I could love, though I did love him. After seventeen happy years of marriage, he left me a widow, and this will be my twelfth year without him at my side. But my mother-in-law, Marie of Blois, taught me everything I needed to know. When Louis was fighting wars in Naples for his kingship, I ran Anjou, and I ran Provence. I collected the rents, rebuked lords when they bickered like children, and saved my income. I had my eye on all the figures from ships and trade in the region, and I knew the names of all my household, along with what came in and what went out, down to the basket of the last greengrocer. Would you believe that when the castle in Angers was under attack from the English, I traveled there in my capacity as Duchess? I raised an army of six thousand men, and I am pleased to tell you the English failed to take what was mine. And now . . . my work is still far from done."

She sweeps her arm over the scene behind her, the cushions where her women had sat with their needles and thread.

"You think my ladies were sewing, that they were simply admiring my jewelry?" She picks up a silver plate next to one of the pillows. Rolling across it: a smattering of seed pearls, a large winking emerald. "Well, you would be wrong. We are making an inventory of what I possess and taking apart anything of value." With her foot, she nudges the headdress, now only half-shining; the other half is bare. "I have pawned my stones before, for my husband's sake, and I will do so again for my children. At the very least, the Dauphin's butcher must be paid, don't you think?"

Joan is silent. The cushions, the room itself have taken on a different aspect. The headpiece resembles an emptied coffer. Has it really come to this?

Yolande goes on: "And I have given Charles money from my own treasury for his war because I want to see him crowned king, not with a crown snatched from a cupboard, not in any royal chapel, but in the cathedral at Reims, like all the French kings who came before him. I want to see my daughter Marie, his wife, made queen. So now we arrive at this point, this moment on which the fates of so many depend . . ."

She moves to a desk, on top of which lies a sheaf of papers. She gathers the pile and returns to stand before Joan.

"You will learn that I make my decisions swiftly." She takes a page and passes it to Joan.

"I give you supplies: grain and livestock and salted fish to feed the people of the city of Orléans . . ."

She takes another page.

"I give you weapons: barrels of arrows, bow strings, battering rams, crossbows, war hammers . . ."

The final page.

"And I give you an army . . ."

"What?" Joan nearly drops the pages.

"You are an instrument of God," Yolande says, laying a hand on Joan's cheek. She has to lean forward to reach. "The moment I heard of you from the Duke of Lorraine, I sent my messenger to seek you out. I know now I was right to do so. I believe that God shows Himself not only in holy words, prayers, and sermons, but in . . . genius. I have been told that after the pages watch you fight, they are silent as if they have just been read a lesson. And when a servant of mine asked a boy no more than seven or eight years old why he was so quiet, the boy said he did not know such things were possible, and he was sorry you had spent so much time polishing armor and working in the stables. He had felt ashamed."

Yolande's hand falls away; the crush of rose petals recedes.

"I am no one," Joan says. She offers the pages back to Yolande. "No one will listen to me. You forget I am nobody."

Her host considers. "Yes . . . yes, you are no one, and no one will listen to a peasant, it is true. A poor, unlearned woman who has run away from home with no family to protect her. What is she? Nothing! But everyone will listen to an instrument of God."

Joan looks down at the pages. For all she knows, these could be love letters.

She thinks back, back to Domrémy. She thinks, My biggest wish used to be that I would grow large enough to pummel my father. In church, I closed my eyes not to pray but to rest. It was the only place my father held his temper, so I slept during sermons. When I think of my mother, I feel only disdain . . . impatience. She wore her piety like a new dress, and she was vain about her devotion to God. But piety didn't save her eldest daughter, and God must have missed my mother's prayers. Just think, a whole lifetime's work: wasted.

To her, it doesn't make sense. Holiness is for the people in the priest's book of saints. It is for the women who rub ashes into their wounds, for monks who pray until their voices grow hoarse, for nuns who fast and grow so weak from hunger, they see angels. It is for people who suffer and suffer quietly.

She had always thought, My gifts come from myself. They were beaten into me. That is all. For if it was God who gave me this strength and these gifts, then it is the same God who is also helping the English to win and the Burgundians to gain more and more towns. It is the same God who let Catherine die.

And she would rather put the blame on men, not on spirits of air. So, call her simple, but she believes this war has nothing to do with God. It's about money. It's about land. These men who came to France, whether kings or common soldiers, they chose to become thieves and murderers. They are the work of their own hand. And I—I am no different. I, too, am the work of my own hand.

And yet . . . the fact that she is here, standing before a queen. How did this happen? How is this possible?

Yolande says, "I do not profess to be a holy woman, but I have had a vision of what you will become. I picture . . ." She raises her arms. "A banner of white painted with gold fleurs-de-lis. Possibly angels. Saint Michael or the image of our Lord. Perhaps both. We shall see if there is enough room. I picture a famous sword. And a suit of white armor, polished to a shine. You will become a holy warrior."

There is a pause where Joan makes a face. She nearly shakes her head, except this wouldn't be appropriate before her host. It feels excessive, she wants to say. A waste of money.

"I have a sword already," she says instead. "And the Duke of Lorraine gave me a horse."

"Ah, I thought you would be quicker than this!" Her host makes a sound: a small grunt of impatience. "You are still a woman, as I am a woman. Do you think the captains of France will rally behind a peasant, a mere girl? Your abilities, your talents and gifts, are not enough. You have no status, no titles. You are not even the daughter of a free man.

"Consider what people will think when they hear this: A woman on a battlefield. A woman fighting in an army. A woman sent to free a city from siege. It is laughable, no? And there are many at court laughing already. At you, at me, at poor le Maçon, despite all the arguments he has made in your favor. They laugh, too, at the Dauphin for even meeting with you. But I will tell you something I have learned in my forty-eight years. Either a woman must be raised high, higher than the heads of men, or she will be crushed beneath their feet. So, we must raise you high. We must raise you to the height of the heavens themselves. We must dress you in the very mantle of God. Do you understand, Joan? Or must I summon le Maçon to explain?"

If you don't know what to say, just bow, so Joan bows.

"There is only one small thing left," Yolande says, smiling. She is satisfied. "Now you must convince His Majesty, my fine son, to give you permission to go and raise the siege at Orléans. I will take care of the rest."

Oh, is that all? Joan thinks.

Turning from her, Yolande removes the garment she had been sewing from her chair. She shakes it out. It is a man's doublet worked in dark purple velvet.

"Try it," Yolande says. "Go on."

Joan slides her arms into the satin-lined sleeves. The fabric is so smooth, it seems to ripple across her arms. Yolande brushes down the front. She helps Joan fasten the buttons, as a mother would for a child, and takes a step back for a better look.

"It is a little tight," she says, frowning, the first crease of that perfect forehead. "Alas, Louis, my eldest, does not have such shoulders. So much the worse for him. This was his, but we shall have the size adjusted. I will send the doublet to you as soon as it is finished. I thought you would be in want of new clothes, and see again, I was right. Look at that filthy tunic! Oh!" Yolande waves her hand in front of her nose.

Then, looking up, she smiles. "I am sorry to say it. We could put you in the finest gown in Christendom, and it wouldn't do anything for you. But this . . . this suits you. So, you see, one must wear the clothes for which one is built. And soon you must put on the mantle of God."

At the door, the messenger pops in his head. He is here to escort her out.

"This may be the only time we meet," Yolande says, her voice soft. "Unless you save Orléans and return the victor, it is unlikely we shall ever see each other again. And so, I hope that God will bless your endeavors. I hope the thousand saints and angels of this most Christian kingdom will stand behind you and watch and guide you in all things. I will pray for you in my capacity as a queen, as a noblewoman of the kingdom of France, but also as a former wife, a mother who loves her children, a humble servant of the Holy Virgin. A woman."

As Joan goes out, the four ladies-in-waiting shuffle back to their places. They settle on their cushions and resume their work.

Behind her, Joan hears the rattle of pearls being loosed and counted. She hears the clunk of stones that will pay for the cost of war.

X

◆ ◆ ◆

It is the hour of sunset, and the Dauphin is waiting by the river Vienne, the water shining like a basin of melted gold, the sky a ceiling vaulted with pink and blue clouds.

They are alone, or as alone as a king can be in an open space. The ring of guards make a clearing for them. The men avert their eyes and feign indifference while picking the hilts of their swords.

The Dauphin touches the side of his large silk hat. Mid-kneel, Joan thinks, Just as the finest gown in Christendom can do nothing for me, the best hat does nothing for you. He doesn't turn, only glances (less, it seems, with his eyes than his prominent nose) at where she is kneeling before motioning her to come closer.

They stand nearly side by side, but she remains a little behind him. An interval of silence. His Majesty appears to be reminiscing. When he speaks, he stares at the water.

"My father once stood here." He brings his furred sleeves together, draping them across his thin body to hug warmth to him. "The people who speak only ill of him are wrong. There were days when his mind was clear, and he was himself again. He wanted to follow the example my grandfather set for him. He tried. But no one knew when he would lapse into his madness, and what might happen if one of his children was near when he suffered a fit. And so none of us, not my brothers or sisters, ever saw much of him. But we were allowed visits, and one such visit took place here—at Chinon."

The Dauphin motions to the golden river, with its gentle tide.

"It was this place, this season and time of day. I was a child, but I remember the cold, the wind like a whip against my face. I was frightened, for I had met my father only a few times before. And my elder brothers, they had said to me, Our father hides daggers on his person and possesses the strength of Heracles, so beware! It was le Maçon who brought me to him. He held my hand and said, Go to your father. Be gentle with him. I, a mere boy, told to be gentle with the King. But I was afraid. I saw the river and feared he would throw me in. He stood with his back to me, and I remember praying, Please, do not let my father throw me into the water, for I cannot swim, and I do not want to drown."

That was a problem I never had, Joan thinks. Thank you, Uncle.

"We stood as you and I do now. For a long time, we did not speak or acknowledge each other, though I shivered. If people passed at that moment and did not know us, they might have thought we were strangers admiring the sunset. But then my father turned to me, just so."

As if reenacting the scene, the Dauphin faces Joan. "He looked at me, and all my fear, whatever reservations I had, fell away. I felt calm. I knew then my brothers had deceived me, for I saw that this man would no more throw me into the water than Yolande or le Maçon would think of harming me. And when he asked me who I was and what I was doing here, I realized he was more frightened of me than I was of him. I told him that I was his son and he my father. And he did not speak but searched my face for signs that I was telling the truth, that I was, in fact, his child. At last he must have settled on something, because he placed a hand on my arm and drew me close to him.

"He kneeled so that he could be on a level with my height and kissed the top of my head. He embraced and held me. And he said, 'How blessed I am to have a son, and such a fine son as you. Why did no one tell me that the throne of France already had its son and heir? Why did they keep you a secret?' He had forgotten his other children, that I was not the heir, that I had then not one but two elder brothers. And though I was young, I had an answer ready. I told him it was because he had enough cares at court, and the Queen, my mother, and the rest of his councillors did not want to trouble him until France was finally at peace. 'And is France at peace now?' my father asked, still holding me.

'It is,' I told him, though it was a lie, 'because you are king and have made it so.' 'Those accursed men,' he said, 'the English. They are all gone, my child?' And I said, 'Yes, do you not remember how you rode into battle clad in full armor, flashing your sword? It was only a matter of hours and the sea was crowded with Englishmen's ships, setting sail for home.' He believed me, and I recall he stood again to full height, as though renewed with faith in himself. He took my hand in his and held it, and we remained like this without speaking. Together we watched the setting of the sun until it became dark, and le Maçon returned and took me away from him. It was the last time my father and I shared such a moment. It was the last time he acknowledged that I was his."

The Dauphin blinks slowly. With the toe of her boot, Joan nudges away a pebble. In her chest: a subtle ache.

"My father has been dead seven years. Is it strange? I possess almost no memories of him, yet I miss him."

Joan wants to say, I miss my sister. I miss my dog. "We cannot bring the dead back, Your Majesty. If we could, God knows I would do it."

He looks at her. His eyes, she observes, are small and watery. His nose, rubbed red, drips from the cold. A thread of snot hangs from the tip, quivering. She would offer him a cloth to dry it with, but she has none. She thinks, The Dauphin is just a man who misses his father. He is a son and a brother, as I am a daughter and a sister. So, why should he remain my enemy when we have both been wronged and by the same people? Royal blood aside, it is possible we are more alike than different, and to get what we want, we need each other. She looks away. From her list of names, she strikes out the Dauphin. She exhales, and the ache lightens.

"My son will turn six this year," he continues. "Not three days ago, his nurse brought him out to where I was walking in the garden. It was early. I wanted to be alone, to think and to plan for the future. But my son approached me and bowed. I did not take him in my arms, as I should have done. I did not comfort him. How do you tell your child, who is also your heir, It is possible that one day soon we must run from our home and leave this behind? How could I say, I may lose what is your birthright, and we may never in our lifetimes return to this kingdom again? So, I left him standing, and I heard his cries even when I was already far away."

What is it about our early years, Joan thinks, that leaves its indelible mark? A slap, a punch, a violent shake stays in a child's memory like kernels planted in new earth, and from these seeds spring sometimes bitterness, sometimes violence, other times fear. For what is put in a child's heart will never grow there of its own accord. So, we must be careful. We must, if we can, be tender.

"I knew another boy," Joan says when there is a lull. "He was a year older than your son. He had a father and mother who loved him. An elder sister and a grandmother who doted on him. He liked animals and had a cat he would feed from his own meals." She tells him the story of Guillaume, the season summer, and how the air was filled with birdsong; how he died in her arms of a head wound, the front of her dress soaked with blood.

"My brother had said to me before the fight, 'Look for sharp rocks, Joan. Ones that fit snugly in the hand.' I gave the sharpest to this boy. As he bled, he returned the rocks to me. He had not thrown them to save his life.

"He died for Your Majesty just as any of your soldiers on the battlefield." She thinks, My sister, too, died for you. She lowers her head as she remembers Salaud. Why are the good always the ones to be sacrificed?

The river is so bright it looks like it has been set ablaze, rippling with fire. The sun hits the Dauphin just so. He stands half in light, half in shadow, one shoulder lit up in gold, the other in darkness. In his veins flows the blood of the old kings, of Charlemagne and Saint Louis, of his grandfather Charles the Wise. She thinks of Yolande's words, how we are all waiting to see when and how this lineage will show itself, waiting with bated breath for him to pass from the anteroom of princedom into the chamber of the anointed kings of France, to take his kingship in hand as one takes the orb and the scepter on the throne. What kind of king will he become? A great king, a good king, or a horrible king, for he must decide, and soon.

She pauses, hesitating. She is no courtier. How does one convince any man, much less a prince, to act against his nature, to act at all? But she must speak.

"I, too, am afraid," she begins, and though she keeps her face forward, she sees the Dauphin glance at her. "I am fearful of many things. When I was young, I was afraid of my father and of pain. I was afraid I would always remain in the same village, that I would only ever see one piece of sky and land forever. And I am still afraid. I am afraid that what happened to my sister may one day happen to me. I am afraid that if I am strong, I will become the same brute as Jacques d'Arc. I am afraid of disappointing those who have put their trust in me: le Maçon, the Duke of Lorraine, your good mother. I am afraid of dying." She looks down. She does not say, I am afraid that if my strength comes from God, He may take it away, that I will lose my strength as I did the day the English attacked Domrémy and I fell ill. This frightens me most of all. For I do not know how my arrow always finds its mark, only that the bow, the sword, the spear feel right in my hand. I do not know why a horse will grow calm as soon as I approach, when just seconds ago it had bolted its rider. I do not know how I can break a grown man's wrist with one hand merely by gripping it. Or how I can find my way in darkness without seeing where it is I step. I can't explain any of these things.

She has tried being soft, but now she must be hard. "Melun," she says, and the blood drains from the Dauphin's face. "Your Majesty was seventeen, the same age I am now. You had an army and your cousin the Count of Vertus to defend the city, under attack from the English. But your cousin fell ill and died, and you took it as an omen—"

The Dauphin's eyes flash with anger. His right hand clenches into a fist. "You dare—"

She keeps talking: "How many suits of armor did you commission, in preparation for battle? I heard it was two, the finest work from the best armorer gold coin could buy. You had your chance to step into the breach, to lead your men. Instead you disbanded your army. Fifteen thousand men scattered. Your Majesty escaped to safety, and Melun surrendered, though hundreds had already died and most because they had starved."

She holds his gaze as she would hold the eye of a nervous horse. His hands, she notices, are trembling, and not from the cold.

"I wish you could avoid the fate of the boy from my village, the boy whose name was Guillaume. Your Majesty has stones, and perhaps they are better stones than the ones England and Burgundy have ready in their pockets. So you must use them."

She says: "Send me to Orléans."

He shakes his head. "If Orléans falls, I shall lose everything."

"And if Your Majesty does not act, you shall lose everything." She steps closer to him. "How can we know our fates? I think of the day you were forced to flee Paris. You did not know, you could not know as you were riding through darkness, fear striking your heart, that you were also riding toward your destiny. For you are here and I am here. Against all odds, fate has brought us together. You, who are your kingdom's future, and I, who am no one." She looks across the river. "Yet we cannot stand always on this shore, shivering in the cold. We must step into the water and cross it, and it is possible we will reach a better place and live in a better clime than where we are now. There is a chance. I beg Your Majesty to take it."

"You forget I cannot swim," he says without looking at her. He attempts to smile.

"You will not have to. Send me across first, to Orléans, and I will deliver a barge to carry you in comfort to everything that is yours: your birthright, your crown."

"And if you fail? What then?"

"If I fail, I won't come back. I will be dead. Your Majesty will never see me again."

He glares at her. "And what good would that be to me? I will still have failed. If Orléans is taken, I will have all but lost my birthright, my honor, and my dignity."

The words fall out before she has time to think: "Is this dignified now? Is this what Your Majesty calls honor?"

His eyes fly to hers. His fist, which he had clenched, unfolds, and he smooths the front of his robes, as if to pacify his own temper.

He steps away to put distance between them. When he speaks, it is on a different subject. He is no longer pale, and his expression is wistful. "Do you know the history of this place?" he asks. They raise their heads to look together. The castle is like a sleeping dragon resting on a cliff, supine and beautiful. One can almost see the towers that form its arched back rise and fall with each silent breath.

Joan listens as he tells her Chinon's history. It was an English king who built much of the castle—yes, English, not French; his name was Henry Plantagenet, and he was the second husband of the beauteous Eleanor of Aquitaine. Chinon was one of his favorite homes. This Henry Plantagenet was also Duke of Normandy and Count of Anjou and Maine. And he had nearly all to rule. So though he possessed no shortage of castles, Chinon was always closest to his heart. Then his youngest son, a bad English king named John Lackland, lost it to the French.

But a castle is not just a pleasant place, Joan thinks. It is not simply a home.

A castle is also its towers and baileys, its drawbridges, its walls, its meurtrières, or murder holes, where archers can take aim or keep secret watch on the enemy's movements. A castle is its machicolations for spilling vats of boiling tar and scalding water on enemy heads. It is a place of tricks and traps, doors that open only from within—a stronghold of siege instruments with which to fling great stones and piles of filth on those camped outside. This is what a castle is. Not halls hung with finery and portable art, but gates so hardy they can withstand the shock of the battering ram.

"You can see why he favored Chinon," the Dauphin says, breaking her thoughts. "This is an easy place to love."

"But one must fight for what one loves," she replies. "Or else it will not be hard for others to take it from you." She thinks, I have learned this the hard way.

"If the English came tomorrow and took Chinon," she continues, "they would not raze it to the ground. It would be too precious for them to destroy. They would live in it, as others have also lived in it. And a different tongue would fill the halls, the harsh language of the English, though much else would stay the same. The musicians would play their instruments for the noblemen. Performers would pass through and entertain at feasts. There would still be fine ladies working at their embroidery, knights to woo them, and banquets every evening: plates of swan and salmon and venison. And servants to swill out the privies, to scatter fresh rushes on the floor. New stable boys to watch the horses. New huntsmen to organize the hunt.

"But Your Majesty knows it would not be the same. In your heart, you know it would be different. What would happen to our songs? Our ballads? *The Song of Roland* would become the song of the defeated." She pauses. "What would happen to the oublie, Your Majesty's first gift to me? Would the English know how to capture the taste of heaven in a wafer? Would they care for what has taken years, decades, even centuries to perfect?"

"You forget your place," he says. "You who are no one dare to read me a lesson as if I were a child called to stand before his tutor."

"I would dare much more," Joan says, and she does not add, *for my revenge, my hatred of my enemies, those who have hurt me in a way I can never forgive.*

The Dauphin shuts his eyes. He inhales and holds his breath; he seems to be counting in his head.

She sees the moment slipping away from her. In her ears, she hears the words of Yolande. Her heart quickens. She must try again.

"Remember the night you flew from Paris," she says. It is as though a voice is whispering into her ear, dictating her speech. She does not have to think; the words flow from her mouth like water. "In a single night, how many were cut down? The Burgundians had seized everything. Yet you escaped. Your Majesty lived. Remember the day the floor of the bishop's palace gave way under your feet. Out of all the courtiers and servants who accompanied you, you were one of a few who survived, your body unmarred. And now . . ."

She feels as if she is talking to La Rousse in Neufchâteau. Look at me, I am two girls. Your Majesty, look at me: I am an instrument of God.

"Now that defeat is so close, now there is so much to lose, I am sent here by God to aid you. I am the stone you must cast at your enemy. I ask you again: Send me to Orléans. Give me your burdens, your nightmares, your fears. Give me, too, your hopes as you would put them in your prayers to God alone. I will shoulder them all."

It is like coaxing a small child to be happy again. He cannot help himself. At the corner of his lips, a smile tugs. He likes the idea of wishes, of prayers being granted. "And what shoulders you have," the Dauphin says softly. He turns to bestow upon her the royal gaze. "What gifts you have been given. These are impossible to deny. The boy you mentioned, I am sorry for his death. And for your sister."

A moment of silence, perhaps it is to remember the dead. Then: "Go." The command is a whisper, spoken like a secret. "Go with our blessing, and we shall see if you are truly as you say: an instrument of God. Go and free Orléans. Though God help you, Joan, if you fail."

It is the first time he says her name. She bows her head, kneels.

What you see and how you see it can change your life. A sleight of hand. A shift of perspective, and one can suddenly become an instrument of the Divine.

Three weeks ago she had come to this place. As she rode into Chinon, the church bells had rung the hour of Prime. But there are some today—and both at court and in town, they are a growing number—who would say the bells had rung for her.

Part Three

‡

For nearly two weeks, Joan is tested by clergymen in Poitiers. At the end of these sessions, they agree that the outcome of Orléans—victory or otherwise—will be taken as a sign of whether she was truly sent by God.

Joan then travels to Orléans by way of Tours and Blois, in order to collect men and supplies. At the end of April, she enters the city with an army and provisions, including cattle and grain. Song accompanies her arrival; a procession of priests sing "Veni Creator Spiritus."

Now the heart of the conflict has moved to Orléans, which has been under siege for almost seven months. It will be no simple task to liberate the city and drive out the well-entrenched English forces.

I

◆ ◆ ◆

ORLÉANS, EARLY MAY 1429

THIS MORNING IS MILD, the light gentle. The shutters of Joan's room are flung open to let in fresh air and a warm wind. It does not feel like a morning when men should die.

Two women are dressing her from foot to head. Around her ankles, they lace greaves, the armor that will protect her shins, and tie together the leather thongs that will secure the plates to her legs.

At her shoulder, she hears a throat clear. One of the women motions her to raise her arms. They must strap on her breastplate. Soon every part of her will be encased in steel.

The other woman holds up a gauntlet, and Joan slides her hand into the glove. She watches her hand of flesh disappear, her palm become stiff leather and metal.

A suit of armor costing one hundred livres tournois has been crafted to her precise dimensions. A banner has been painted, which one among her company will hold. On the banner: A white field gilded with lilies and two angels. An image of the King of Heaven presiding over the world.

Scholars, too, have been hired to locate prophecies in ancient manuscripts. One prophecy is this: that France will be brought low by a whore and saved by a virgin. The whore is thought to be Isabeau, the Dauphin's mother; the virgin is Joan. They have found something they can use from the wizard Merlin: "a virgin who ascends the backs of archers." Another, from the Venerable Bede, describes only "a maid carrying banners." Like most successful prophecies, they are vague. They can be taken to mean both everything and nothing.

Joan's retinue comprises these members: two pages, both seven years old, named Louis and Raymond; a squire, Jean d'Aulon; a chaplain to hear her confessions; and three servants to wait on her—though, as they soon discover, they are rarely required to do anything, for she is used to looking after herself. So, they idle. They call her the best mistress they ever had.

◆

WHEN JOAN ARRIVED IN ORLÉANS, she saw Yolande had done her work. The people believed she was a holy woman appointed by God. They thought her presence alone would save them.

She quickly realized: There was no army called Joan's army to report to her, and she had no title. Her status was as amorphous as Merlin's prophecy. Her pages, her squire, every person assigned to her—she wonders, Did they draw lots?—shrugged and scratched their heads when she asked them what she should do. She was given a room in the city treasurer's house, where she would be waited upon by the women. The other captains of France were also staying here, but no one cared what she did with her time. Joan could stay in her room and sleep. If the mood struck her, she could pray. She was commander of nothing, but no one commanded her, either.

The *chefs de guerre*, the leaders of France's army, thought she was a bad joke. Jean de Dunois, the illegitimate brother of the Duke of Orléans, refused to look at her. When she came into the room, he faced the other way. La Hire, the famous brigand turned captain, did look at her and a ball of phlegm rose in his throat; his spit landed not far from her feet.

At her door, someone left a pile of unwashed and soiled laundry. Her response: in full view of the men, she kicked the sorry heap down the stairs.

The foot soldiers, too, would be happier if she were replaced by a sighing mule and a cart of supplies. A mule and supplies would be practical, at least. Most couldn't help staring, though some went further: they shook their heads when she passed them. They thought her presence here was wrong, even insulting. Why was her hair shaved and trimmed in the bowl-shaped cut fashionable among noblemen? Why did she wear a man's doublet? She could never be a knight, so why should she have a squire and pages and servants?

But they didn't know her. They didn't know that the more they stared, the more she would carry herself as if it were she and not Yolande, Queen of Four Kingdoms, who doled out the soldiers' pay.

She didn't mind being ignored; she could take the sour looks, the shakes of the head quietly, but La Hire went a step further. Soon after they arrived in Orléans, he sauntered up to her, picking his teeth in a way that reminded her of her father. She wanted to tell him anything that reminded her of Jacques d'Arc made her temper rise.

He looked her up and down. "You have no place here," he said. "You, a woman? A farm wench, a shepherdess who knows little more than how to squeeze the tits of cows and goats for milk, who crawled out of some hole, some ditch in the kingdom, and now calls herself a virgin warrior? My God, woman, you won't last five minutes on the field. I don't care how big you are. Our prince, king, whatever he is, has gone mad like his father, and you think I wouldn't say this to his face, but I would bark it into his ears if I thought he would listen. I could stand the little boy with bleeding hands and feet, even that lecherous monk. Let them claim to be prophets. Let them sleep until noon and eat meat and pies. What harm could they do? But this?" He beat his chest, wincing at the force of his own fist. "The sight of you offends me as it would any true soldier here. Now grow out your hair and put on a dress!"

He stood a few inches shorter than Joan, so she stared down at him. She took a step closer, covering him with her shadow.

"And I know you, La Hire," she replied. "Oh yes, I have heard of your reputation. You are a cheat and a liar, a mercenary of the very worst kind. I have heard that years ago, you were the honored guest of a duke, and what did you do when your visit came to an end? You locked your host in his own dungeon and demanded that he pay you ransom for his release. If you weren't on the side of His Majesty, I would knock your head off your shoulders right now."

The fact that she talked back seemed to take him by surprise.

"I would like to see you try," he growled.

"Try?" she repeated. "I wouldn't have to try."

They were nearly nose to nose. He scoffed, "Oh, I have heard what you are able to do in training. But the battlefield isn't a closed pen, sweetheart. It isn't an empty yard with one straw target for an opponent."

Dunois stepped between them. "Leave her be," he said, facing La Hire and ignoring her. "She will soon find out the difference for herself, though she may not live to tell anyone about it, and then the Dauphin will see the error of his judgment."

"My lord Dunois," Joan said. It was the first time she had ever addressed him. "How is your wound healing?"

His lip curled at her. "What wound?"

"Your wound from Rouvray, the Battle of the Herrings," she replied. "The French, as I recall, lost that fight, though they outnumbered the English. And you were forced, I think, to run for your life. So, how is that wound healing, my lord?"

"You unnatural bitch," La Hire said before Dunois could answer. "I would not lie with you if you were the last whore in the last brothel of the kingdom."

Joan smiled. She was already rolling up her sleeves. Let me only make an example of this one, and then they will see, she thought. "If you tried to lie with me," she said cheerfully, "you would be dead before your breeches fell to the floor. This I can promise you."

Dunois gave his friend a shove and a look, and Joan and La Hire backed away from each other, like two snarling dogs postponing a fight.

The women of the house, the treasurer's wife and her daughter, had witnessed the scene. From the staircase, they gaped. Joan was only a little regretful. This was probably not how a holy woman, an instrument of God, should behave. But faced with such fools, what choice did she have? She raised her eyes to the ceiling. God give me patience!

◆

A POLITE COUGH shakes Joan out of her thoughts. One of the women is offering her something: a helmet. She refuses it. She wants the men—English, French, she doesn't care which side—to see her face. She wants them to remember it.

"You are trembling, Joan," the same woman tells her.

She does not speak. She is afraid that if she speaks, her voice will tremble, too.

Even today, a fine morning in May, no one woke her. No one informed her that the captains of France were going to fight at the fortress of Saint Loup, one of the gates of the city, that this was the day of their first battle. But she has swallowed the insult.

The women step back to look at her. Their task finished, they lower their eyes and whisper a prayer before this figure of steel they have prepared for battle. Normally the squire would have dressed her, but the women of the household wanted the honor. It is as if Joan already belongs to them: the mothers, daughters, wives, and sisters of the city who look to her to lift the siege. The men will free the men, but you will free us.

A servant opens the front door, and she walks into sunlight. Her squire is here with her horse. He helps her mount. Her pages run up with her sword.

A week ago, a sword was taken from the cathedral at Sainte-Catherine-de-Fierbois, a relic said to have been wielded by the great Prince of the Franks, Charles Martel. But that sword, seven hundred years old, could not be used; the monks discovered the case held only a piece of rusted iron. So a precise copy was made with a decoration of five crosses on the blade. The monks, too, bless them, had thought it would look very pretty, very dashing, for Joan to carry a scabbard made of cloth of gold to battle. Cloth of gold for a scabbard? And what if the sword should cut through the thread? She had nearly laughed. So, a new scabbard was made, in plain but hardy leather.

As she takes the weapon, everyone is quiet. Her squire will ride after her with her banner. Her pages will remain behind. Her hand, which is now the hand of a metal giant, makes the sign of the cross across her steel chest, over her plate-protected heart.

The treasurer's wife is looking at her as if Joan were her own daughter. Even with this armor, this sword, they don't think she will return alive. They don't believe it is enough against men who are also monsters.

One more moment. One last prayer. Joan shuts her eyes, though it isn't a prayer that comes to her but a memory, like a feather floating from a dove's wing. It is a scene of peace in the house of white stone, her sister still alive and mending a shirt. Her uncle stood over Catherine, watching her quick hands. He said something that made Catherine laugh. At their feet, Salaud ran in circles. But when Joan entered the room, they looked up. Salaud rolled out his tongue, ears crooked. "I can't stay," Joan told them. "I promised to mend the priest's gate."

"That man should pay you," her uncle said. "But I suppose all his debts are paid by God."

"Our Joan," Catherine said, as the needle dipped and rose through the cloth of the shirt. "She is always coming and going. She can never keep still. We never know where she is or where she will be, whether she may be found in the woods or in some neighbor's field. One time, when I called out her name, her voice came from above my head. She was in a tree eating an apple."

Durand raised his hands in pretend helplessness. "What can we do about it?" he asked.

Catherine looked at her thoughtfully. Turning back to the cloth, she shook her head. She was always the picture of loveliness, her sister. "Nothing. Nothing can be done, and why should she change? She is our Joan."

When Joan opens her eyes again, she is greeted by the world as it is.

Her heart is the drumbeat that accompanies her to war. Over her shoulders, she hears the flutter of the banner that will signal her arrival in battle. A light wind cools the sweat running down the sides of her face.

As she passes the cathedral of Orléans, she mutters a prayer, a final word to God, but a figure catches her eye. Beside one of the doors, on a pedestal—is it her imagination?—she sees a statue, its hand poised above a wheel. She has seen this face before, first in a book and then in a dream, and its eyes are watching her. Even when she looks over her shoulder, the eyes seem still to be watching.

As she rides closer to the fighting, men are already running from the battle. They hold their wounds, leaving bloody trails as they stagger. Their faces are frozen in pain like masks.

Her last thoughts are these: The people who once stood in that room, in her memory, are all gone. There is nothing left to her but this.

◆

She feels she is moving through time. Overlying this battle: a clearing. Men are replaced with boys. Swords and poleaxes replaced with stones. At the edge of sight and hearing: a boy screams and falls. What is the difference? Grown men make more noise. There is more blood.

Someone is throwing himself against her horse. *Thump. Thump.* Joan looks down; it is the first time she sees an Englishman up close. Dark eyes meet hers. A face full of hate; a long white scar along the jaw.

Men with scars. Men who are cruel. Men who don't speak French. Was it you? she wants to ask. Do you remember Catherine's face?

But her hand moves before her mouth can form the words, and she barely registers the flash of steel. When she lifts her sword, she sees the edge is coated with blood.

She has no time to think about what she has done. There, a few feet away, two men are wrestling as her brother wrestled the redheaded captain from Maxey. But in place of Jacquemin stands the burly La Hire. And Joan isn't running with a stick anymore, clutched like a club; she is riding toward them with a sword.

A moment. When the Englishman's head comes off, it flies in a perfect arc through the air. La Hire shakes off the body, now lifeless.

He looks up, recognizes her. He rubs a cut on his chin and narrows his eyes. "I didn't need your help," he says, though it seems he is trying not to smile, not to laugh at how events have turned. Then he spins on his feet and punches another soldier in the face.

How long does a battle last? She doesn't know. In her head, a voice interrogates every man she cuts down: Was it you? When her sword pierces an opening in armor: Was it you? When her blade plunges through gambeson and her ears fill with the sound of tearing flesh: Was it you? The replies she receives: screams, groans, silence. Yet what she wants is a confession, even if there will be no forgiveness.

Here, too, is another scene she knows she has lived before. She is kneeling. Her gauntleted hand touches the side of a man's bleeding head, his face for a moment masked by another face much younger than his own: that of a boy of seven. Though, she thinks, he is still young, too. Sixteen? Seventeen? Perhaps he is an elder Guillaume. She remembers him: this man she has named Guillaume. When she passed the camps, the groups of soldiers standing to gawk at her, he was among them. She'd given him a hard stare. What are you looking at? And he had cast his eyes down, as if ashamed. The moment felt like a victory, however small. This battle, too, has been a victory. But he has lost both times. She notices: The elder Guillaume hasn't died with any weapon in his grip, so what had he been fighting with? His fists?

She feels someone touch her armored back. Even through steel, her shoulder flinches. It is La Hire. "The boy is dead," he says. His voice is even. The sight of death is nothing to him, a seasoned soldier. But even La Hire has called him a boy. He sees how young he was. "Leave him, Joan."

She does. The dead stay dead.

◆

She is fetching her supper to bring to her room and eat alone when a throat clears from behind.

They are all here. At the head of the table: Jean de Dunois, Bastard of Orléans. To his left, sitting on one side: Gilles de Rais, Jean Poton de Xaintrailles, and Raoul de Gaucourt. On the other: La Hire, Ambroise de Loré, and Jean de la Brosse. The captains of the French army gathered together.

Joan is about to walk past them with her bowl of stew when La Hire coughs in her direction. What? More insults?

At the corner of the table, the jutting end awkward to sit at, someone has set an extra chair.

"Yours," Dunois says, addressing the word to the ceiling. He gestures at the chair as if swatting away a fly. "Why don't you take a seat?"

The men are silent, but no one stands in her way or sticks his boot out to trip her. She sits, the table corner poking into her stomach. She breaks off a piece of bread and dips it in a cup of diluted wine, which La Hire has poured for her. When she raises the cup, she checks it first. No beetles. No dead mouse. She drinks.

La Hire, who is watching her, makes a clicking sound with his tongue. "You trust no one," he says.

"No, not no one," she replies. "Just not you." Yet their voices are bantering.

It is quiet but for the sound of eating. Everyone seems suddenly shy, like children left together to exchange names and become friends. Joan keeps her head down. A plate of ham edges closer to her bowl. She chews, pretending not to notice. But the ham keeps moving closer, as if it has grown legs. When she looks up, she sees the hand of Dunois nudging the plate. He is studying her.

"Where did you learn . . ." he begins. He cannot quite finish the sentence. He takes a breath. "Where did you learn to fight like that?"

She could be coy. She could say, "Like what?" But Joan knows the moment he is thinking of. She had been unhorsed. Panic made her limbs grow stiff, her sweat turn cold. From the ground, she saw an English knight charging down at her on his horse. Over his head, he waved a mace; the weapon's sharpened point flashed, catching the light. He was only a short distance away, but she stood her ground. He might have thought that she stood stunned, unable to move from fear, though he would have been wrong. As the knight thundered closer, her ears filled with the sound of hooves, their earth-shattering rhythm. All other noises, the shouts and fighting around her, had diminished to a whisper. She readied her blade. A breath. Another breath. When the horse was nearly on top of her, the knight's mace already swinging toward her head, she moved swiftly, crouching low. Her sword slit the underside of the beast's belly. She inhaled the steam of the animal, the dust it kicked up, and felt, inches away, the shudder of muscle; it had been that close. She stood, splattered in horse blood, her face wet and warm, the odor of fresh slaughter tickling her nose. She moved to where the knight landed before he had even risen to his knees. Her hand had only to turn and the point of her sword found him. As the dust settled, she looked around. She saw some men had stopped fighting. They had seen what she'd done: horse and man brought down together. And not long afterward, the battle had ended.

"It is a long story" is her reply. Then: "I am sorry I mocked your wound."

He nods, accepting her apology. He smiles and she smiles, too.

"What will happen to the dead? Will they be given burial?" she asks.

At this, the men raise their heads and peer at her. Only La Hire answers: "There would not be enough gravediggers, my little shepherdess."

Most of the ham is gone by the time she speaks again. She has another question: "What next?"

Word has arrived by messenger: English reinforcements are on their way to Orléans, led by Sir John Fastolf, the captain who bested the French at the Battle of the Herrings. The rumor: his army is well supplied and several thousand strong.

"We should wait for reinforcements," Dunois says, "before we fight again."

"Why?" she asks. She has been at this table no more than a quarter of an hour, and already she is talking as if these men were her brothers. Brothers can be pushed; they can be shouted at. "Why wait? We should go where the English are thickest."

She moves the plate of ham and the pitcher, setting them side by side. Meat and water are transfigured into crenellated towers: the two main fortresses of the city, Les Augustins and Les Tourelles. "Take these and take back Orléans," she says.

"I have seen the maps," Joan adds.

"What? When?" La Hire barks.

"When you left them out for anyone to look at," she bellows back.

Dunois touches his shoulder, his wound from Rouvray. He looks from the ham to the pitcher to her. Under the table, he taps the foot pierced by an arrow at Verneuil.

"I told you, Dunois," La Hire says. "Didn't I say we shouldn't have set a place for her? In a few days, she will be wanting your seat as well." But he is no longer spitting at Joan. He is smiling.

◆

A LONG, LONG NIGHT LIES AHEAD. Her pages, Louis and Raymond, are full of questions, and her squire, Jean, is composing a letter by candlelight, a message to le Maçon, which, since it contains good news, will find its way to Yolande's perfumed hand. For the first time in what feels like eternity, the result is *victoire*. Victory. La Hire is sitting before the fire, yawning. He followed Joan to her room after supper, kicking his boots off and making himself at home. How a battle can change a man. It is as if they have always been the best of friends.

She must be honest. War is horrible, she tells her pages, and means it. The noise, for one. The screams of the dying, both man and beast. Broken bones. The sickening thud of bodies colliding, of horse skull against horse skull. Steel against steel. You cannot look down; you don't even dare. What you see on the ground will turn your stomach inside out, so perhaps better not to eat beforehand. Your nerves will keep you on your feet anyway. La Hire is right about one thing: training is different from battle.

She describes the space: as wide and large as a courtyard, yet the dead are strewn like rushes across the ground. Some look like they're fast asleep. Others appear frozen, their muscles tense, as if they could still spring to their feet any moment. A few appear shocked. Death took these men by surprise. Most die with their eyes open, though she thought one corpse blinked at her. Sometimes you cannot tell those on your side from the other. They are just men.

Beneath her feet, the ground squelched, but not with rain or mud. When the fighting was over, she stopped and pressed a hand to her metal belly. She vomited straight into a pool of blood.

She tells her young pages, When you complain about your exercises or feel sore from running, just think what it means to fight three hours without rest, without break, the smell of sweat and dust in your mouth. You can't remember the moment of victory, but you remember all the other moments, little things, like how blood isn't at all like water or even like wine, but congealed droplets that stick to your armor; you remember the crooked line of teeth that scatter like dried peas over the back of your gauntleted hand when you strike a man across the face; the strange way some men die as if they are trying to heal themselves, to hold together a split-open chest, a cracked skull.

She takes her pages by the hand. She asks them, her expression serious, "Are you sure the two of you wouldn't like to enter the priesthood instead?" And they look at each other uncertainly. From his desk, her squire hides a smile.

"But?" La Hire shouts from his chair.

"But it is also a feeling like no other," she says. "You are never more alive than when you are in battle. Once you have felt every vein of your body thrum, like the taut string of a bow, energy brimming to the very tips of your fingers—"

"The need to take a piss forgotten seconds into a charge," La Hire adds.

"Once you have experienced all of that . . ." Joan trails off. She smiles. Such a smile would normally be bestowed on a newborn babe or a blooming garden in springtime. She shows them her hands. "My sword was no longer just a sword. I did not sense either the weight or the heft of it, for it was as though I were holding my own soul."

La Hire leans forward from his chair. "Well, lads?" he asks the pages, who are both grinning. "What do you think of the priesthood now?"

◆

THEY COULDN'T JUST PUT JOAN in a suit of armor and bring her to Orléans.

After her last meeting with the Dauphin, she was taken to a different city: Poitiers. There, eighteen clerics gathered by the Archbishop of Reims and vetted by Yolande interrogated her. It was not only the Dauphin who had lost his home. These men, too, had been displaced by the war. After Paris was taken, they lost their great university, they lost their sees and their sources of income, their comfortable and lucrative official roles. These servants of God were angry men. With their homes, they had also lost their sense of humor.

In a room too small for so illustrious a gathering, these men faced her, thin-lipped and grim, like rows of gray-faced toads, some skeletal and narrow, in the manner of the ascetics, others overfed, with chins that sagged to the bottom of their necks. One bishop came riding in on a mule; another, his good friend, from a neighboring city, swayed dangerously on a warhorse. Surely, she thought, the warhorse could be put to better use than as a mount for an overweight bishop.

Yet it was also a balding, liver-spotted reunion for them, these celebrated doctors of theology, who spent their days contemplating Thomas Aquinas's five proofs of God's existence. And now they had been asked to contemplate her.

Together they put to her questions, sometimes talking over one another, other times tripping over their own long-winded speech, so she could not hear and they had to repeat themselves. How many times a day did she pray? What prayers had she been taught? When was the last time she confessed, took Communion, fasted? Was she a good child? And if she obeyed her father and her mother—they didn't like that her answer on this point and other points felt ambivalent—why had she left home without anyone to accompany her? Why did she travel alone? And for what reason did she mention her uncle, by all accounts an unscrupulous individual, more than any other member of her family?

She knew their aim: to uncover the stubs of the devil's horns in her hair; to find the skin of serpent's scales beneath her tunic and hose, the pointed tail they imagined she kept coiled and hidden between her thighs.

But le Maçon told her not to worry. The conclusion of these proceedings was already decided. She would pass. So, what was the point then? "I thought there was no time to waste," she said, and le Maçon flushed. The proper order of things still had to be followed, he explained. Near the end of the sessions, she took to scratching shapes and patterns on the desk with her uncle's knife. A cloud. A triangle. A unicorn's horn. This made the priests angry, though none of them dared to take the knife away, because they had heard what she could do with a weapon, any weapon. "She is a proud woman, more arrogant than a prince," a bishop said. She couldn't remember which bishop; by that point, their faces had all blurred. But she would have told him, if she could, that it wasn't anything personal. She was just bored. When the interrogations concluded, they drew up a document and circulated it. The determination: She, Joan, is a good girl who knows her prayers. We can find neither sin nor any form of demonic influence in her.

The examination by the women followed soon after. Yolande had appointed these women, and they asked her to lie down on a bed and part her legs. The oldest among them touched her knees and peered between them, squinting, until something she saw there at last seemed to content her. A young woman replaced her, also staring, and then a third, a solemn-faced matron, who audibly sighed with relief between Joan's legs, which made her squirm. By the time they were finished, she had begun to miss the bishops; she stared at a spot on the ceiling and drummed her flat stomach with her fingers. With a restless nail, she picked at a scab on her left wrist. The faces of the women appeared over her head. They peered down at her and nodded. "You are chaste," the oldest announced gravely. "A true virgin."

Really? she almost said. I didn't know.

After each session in Poitiers, she went straight to the stables and the training yard. The knights kept well away, but the pages, the young boys between seven and twelve years old, couldn't hide their curiosity as they watched her stuff straw back inside the targets she'd impaled. At first, they pretended not to notice her. They whistled and kicked the hay at their feet while stealing glances in her direction. Then they crept closer, huddling together in a group. They blinked at her, and she looked back at them: the future of the realm, the young sons of the nobility, though they didn't seem to her all that different from the kitchen boys who had watched her pare vegetables in Neufchâteau. She smiled at them, and they smiled back.

From then on they watched her shoot, faces peering between the gateposts. They watched her mount her horse and ride and took turns touching and lifting her sword. They shaved and trimmed her hair to the bowl-shaped cut and washed it, many small hands on her head, as if to collectively baptize her. In the way of children, they each kept a lock of her hair for good luck and because they believed it would give them strength.

After Poitiers, she traveled to Orléans, stopping at Tours and Blois for supplies. She thought there would be fighting as soon as she reached Orléans, but her squire informed her that while the English numbers were strong, they hadn't enough men to cover every gate in the city. So, through the Saint-Aignan gate, she arrived with her small household. A train of supplies followed. It was already dark, yet the city, lit with torches, was as bright as morning. Some people held candles, the last stubs from their cupboards, to light her way. Fathers lifted their children, bleary-eyed with sleep, to watch her. She saw a man mouth the word "angel" into his daughter's ear. She saw they were hungry, that some were ill, and they were tired of living under siege with the English at their backs. They wanted something to believe in and were ready to believe in anything, even ancient prophecies from the wizard Merlin and the Venerable Bede. She saw they were ready to believe in her.

II

◆ ◆ ◆

NEWS OF THE VICTORY at Saint Loup spreads, and the next morning a crowd of men gather to hear Joan speak. They are not soldiers but citizens of Orléans: bakers and blacksmiths, tailors and goldsmiths, cobblers, lawyers, tanners, butchers and their apprentices. She faces them, suited in her armor, which her pages have polished so that the white steel plates reflect the sun, and she is as bright as a flaming star.

She is on eye level with these men. No dais. No stage. No horse. She moves through them as she talks. She touches their bony shoulders, clasps their skeletal arms, and looks into their hollow eyes. Orléans is a city of over thirty thousand. The supplies and livestock she had brought nearly a week ago are far from enough.

"You are men of the city of Orléans," she says. "A great city. One of the finest cities of this kingdom. And I know you are hungry. I know you are ill and sick with worry for your families, your friends, your neighbors. I, too, have felt hunger. On the day the English invaded my village, I was in the throes of a fever. I was near death. And I could do nothing to defend my home. When my family fled the village, I could not even walk. I had become a burden to the ones I loved."

She stops to look around her, to meet each man's gaze. She has learned, a speech made for a king can be adapted for a commoner and lose none of its effectiveness. She continues, "Should the English break through the walls of Orléans, they may spare your lives. They may take possession of your goods, burn a few homes, and shame you. But when the city is opened and the water mills rebuilt, you will regain your strength. You will wake in the early hours of the morning and there will be no siege outside of the gates. No more soldiers. No arrows shot over the city walls. Your wife and children will kiss you good morning, and you will be much as you were before. Laboring. Plying your trade in the marketplace. Sitting down each evening to a hearty supper. Praying before every meal and before sleep. You may one day smile again and laugh. And yet . . ."

She pauses. Her voice echoes over their heads; it rises from deep within her. "Yet I tell you now it will be different. A door, though you can still open it; a window, though you may look out of it; the very air you breathe will not be the same, though you may be alive. I do not know this city as you do. I do not know the sermons preached to you and your families in your great cathedral. I do not know the rooms where your fathers held you when you were children, and where you as fathers hold your own children. I do not know the streets where good men, men with skilled hands and skilled minds, make beautiful things and take pride in their work. I do not know the night skies that cover this city, the view of the Loire at the hours of sunrise and sunset. Only you, the people of Orléans, know these things.

"But what I know is this: though your life and the lives of your family may be spared, though you may resume your work and trade, it will be as if an invisible yoke had been placed around your neck. You will feel a heaviness you cannot explain to any physician or apothecary. And you will not be able to shake off this burden when you die, but it will pass from you to your sons and daughters, until it grows so light your children and your children's children will come to wear it with ease. A generation, two generations, and they will not even feel it, for by then it will be a common thing to name their children after the rulers of England, to bow not to their own king but to a king across the sea. And so, your grandsons' names will be Henry and Richard, not Charles, Philip, or Louis."

She rests a hand on the shoulder of an elderly man. "Already you have lost your duke, Charles of Orléans. At Agincourt, fourteen years ago, he was taken by the English and is still held prisoner today in a tower in their city of London. So I ask, what good will it do if we pay this ransom, if we raise funds and treasure for his release and do not free Orléans itself? What has your lord to come back to if he sees the flags of Saint George flying from the towers and battlements and not the bishop-saints of his own city, Aignan and Euverte, and the gold fleurs-de-lis of this kingdom?"

She stops. She shows off her armor, her steel-plated body. "If even a backwater village, a patch of cottages in the middle of nowhere, a village that no one may remember or love a hundred years from now can produce one such as myself, what may Orléans make of its tens of thousands of citizenry? What heroes may it find among its own men? So I ask you to fight beside the lords and captains of France. I ask you to fight beside *me*."

She does not have to reach out. They are stretching toward her, hundreds of fingertips grazing armor and steel as she passes them. The cheers are deafening. Next time she makes a speech she thinks she will stuff a little wool into her ears.

But someone catches her arm. It is the old man on whose shoulder Joan had earlier rested.

He bends until he is nearly bowing. "I confess I did not believe it before," he says. "I thought it was nonsense, this talk of sending holy maids and virgins to save us. But I believe it now. I see the prophecies about you—they are all true."

That evening, Joan fires an arrow into the enemy camp. The arrow carries a simple message, written in her squire's elegant hand.

"Abandon your posts. Retreat. Last chance." It is the fifth of May, Ascension Day, when Christ rose to heaven, and therefore a day of rest. But if fighting is not permitted, one can still recruit strong men. Only yesterday she had fought at Saint Loup. Tomorrow—she recalls the plate of ham, the pitcher of water she had placed side by side on the supper table—will be another battle.

◆

"Les Tourelles," her squire says. Jean speaks like a child learning new words, slowly. "A battle that will be remembered. Yet how can I describe what happened in a way that will make you understand?" He addresses the pages, the servants, the women of the household. Candles are lit in the cramped room. It is two nights later. The seventh of May, and tears stand in his eyes.

"At first light, the fighting began. She, Joan, was like a cliff in an ocean, and the English who had witnessed what she was capable of at Saint Loup, her first battle, came upon her in waves. They knew if she was defeated, our spirit would die with her. So they broke against her body, her armor. Each time they bounced off and scattered like seafoam at her feet; then another wave of men would gather, only to break again. Her body was like a wall of stone, and she cut through the English as a jutting cliff through water, parting each attack. One sweep of her arm: *boom*. A dead Englishman falls into the man behind him, then he the man behind him, until an entire line is downed by the resonance of her fist. That is how it was."

His hand grazes the space over his heart. He shuts his eyes and continues: "Hours passed of heavy fighting. I had just helped put up a scaling ladder. And as Joan climbed, our luck turned. An arrow struck her—here." He touches the base of his neck, shows his horrified audience the tender white skin, the pulsing blue vein inches away from the throat. "From below, I saw her head whip back like someone had dealt her a blow, and on the ladder, her body wavered before she fell. The crash was terrible. At least . . ." He pauses dramatically. "A twenty-foot fall.

"I did not need to call for help. If a thousand men, not soldiers but the common people of Orléans, had answered her call to arms, then at least a hundred defended her body. No Englishman dared come near her. No second arrow from the sky could finish her off without striking one of us first. But a cheer went up among the enemy, and we felt the chill of doom close at our backs.

"I remember I took her feet, La Hire her arms, and all the while she bled. Her great strength bled out of her, and she struggled for air. She was choking on her own blood. We carried her to the periphery of the fighting, and my lord Dunois rode up. He asked, 'What has happened?' Then he saw who we were standing over. 'Is she dead?' he questioned. And no one answered, not even La Hire, who is never silent on any occasion. Then La Hire said, 'With the English, it is always arrows. They do not possess the courage to face a man, so they must kill him from afar.' I had never heard that old soldier speak so tenderly, as though each word gave him pain to utter aloud.

"We removed most of her armor and her shirt of mail to see what damage had been done. The arrow had penetrated six inches deep. My lord Dunois left his horse and held her hand. As he prayed, someone ran off to find a priest. When she saw who was crouching next to her, she strained to lift her head and said in a whisper to him, 'Dark hair, shoulder-length, older than you.'" Jean imitates the rasping voice, clasping his throat. "We turned to one another, bewildered. We didn't understand what she meant, so she added, 'I think I saw the fool celebrating with his friends.' Then she closed her eyes. La Hire squeezed my shoulder and said to me, 'Sometimes it is like this. Not all soldiers live to a ripe old age.' His words were practical, yet his voice shook. I think the old brute had grown fond of her.

"I looked away. I stared at her twitching hand until it no longer moved. And though the sound of battle was still near, we leaned forward. We listened together for her death rattle."

Jean sighs, and for all of three seconds, it is as if he, too, has passed into the next world. "But her last breath did not come, and suddenly I heard my lord Dunois cry out. I felt my head spin as I saw the same hand that had fallen limp creep up to the shaft of the arrow at the base of her neck and pull. We heard the sound of flesh tearing. Her eyes were wild. I could see how her face trembled with pain. She bit down, gritting her teeth, and with one last twist, one agonizing wrench, the arrow came free. She threw it aside and gasped for air before sitting up, one hand over her wound. I saw she was as pale as the dead, that her shirt was stained with blood and the grass she lay on soaked through like a dyer's vat. She called my name, and I nearly fainted. It was only Dunois who kept his head and applied pig fat to the wound to slow the bleeding. But when she rose to her feet, we felt our insides turn. Her first few steps, she stumbled. You could see she was still light-headed, yet she made straight for Dunois's horse, which was guarded by his squire. When the man did not shift from his post—he, too, was stunned—she shoved him aside. I ran to her with her sword, and she took it. She did not hear La Hire's protests or Dunois's shouts. 'She will bleed to death if she goes back,' La Hire cried. 'That is my horse!' Dunois complained. But she mounted his destrier, and she did not have to call for me to follow. I was already riding behind her on another charger, and I held her banner over my head. No words passed between us as we returned to the fighting."

Jean sighs again. He keeps his hand over his heart. "The setting of the sun never waits for the conclusion of battles, and it was already growing dark. Did you know, after her first fight at Saint Loup, Joan told me that she could lift a whole cart out of the mud with no men to assist her. Now at Les Tourelles she ran down a line of men, foot soldiers and citizenry both. They had been pushing a battering ram toward the door of a fortress when two of the wheels broke. It was no trickery, just bad luck and bad timing. For hours they had been fighting, digging, shouting at the top of their lungs. These men were tired, and news had traveled quickly. They had heard that an Englishman's arrow had struck her, that it had pierced her neck. So, they thought she was dying, if not already dead. They thought all of their efforts had been in vain. And so, when the wheels of the battering ram gave out just short of the fortress door, they believed God would not let them win. Not today.

"As we ran to aid these men, I passed her banner to another soldier and said, 'Spread the news. Tell everyone she is alive and well,' before I followed her. She acted swiftly, gripping a corner of the battering ram and directing others to their place. They said, 'It is impossible. Two of the wheels are broken. We will not be able to reach the door, and there are far from enough of us.' She only replied, 'There are enough.' And when they still balked, she said, 'I have come back from the dead in order to aid you. So do not let me down.' And you could tell from their faces that they weren't looking at her but staring at the wound, the hole in her neck still trickling with fresh blood.

"She pushed, and it made the hair stand on my arms, my neck, to see the siege engine move forward by whole inches. Yes, whole inches. I would swear this in the cathedral of Orléans before the altar. These men, too, could not believe it. They stared as the contraption shifted in their grip, moved away from them while they stood idling. 'Stop staring,' she yelled. 'Help me push!' The men listened, and the several faces around her strained. Everyone's skin flushed a ghoulish shade. Their eyes bulged until we heard the first rumbles of thunder, and the battering ram creaked forward, closer and closer to the door. And even when, by some miracle, we reached the door, the door shook but did not give. 'Again!' her voice bellowed. Her voice was its own kind of thunder. 'Again!'

"The door shook a second time, but still it did not break. 'I do not care if it takes until dawn to beat down this door,' she shouted, looking each man in the face. 'Will you give up at the last? Will you let me down?' With this—one last heave—the door broke, it toppled with a crash like an explosion of cannon-shot. My heart leapt into my mouth, I thought again that my knees would give out, but I, too, released a war cry, second only to hers.

"I saw Joan climb walls. I saw her shake the English over the crenellations and throw them down to the French, soldiers and citizenry both, who waited below with their swords, pikes, spits, and hammers for what fell at their feet. I saw her move faster, for she was lighter without her armor, and yet no blade or arrow could catch her though she was already wounded.

"You could smell the fear in the air, my friends. Fear, too, has a distinct smell. Before her, the English crumpled. They tripped over themselves. They quaked, for they saw that her wound was real: the arrow hole, the remnants of blood still drying on the front of her shirt. She ripped their precious bows of yew from their hands. She halved them over her thigh. *Crack*. It was like rolling a siege engine through a flock of sheep. The sheep don't stand a chance. They fled. She had struck fear into their souls. 'Retreat, retreat!' they screamed.

"Still she did not rest. When the fighting was over, she tended to the wounded, though she must have been in pain. By then her banner had been returned to me, and I watched her reach for the cloth. I said, 'No, Joan, stop! We will find something else to use!' But she took the banner and tore long strips from it to bind the wounds of the men who were still alive. And that is why the banner is torn—not from any English hand, but because the pieces are scattered among the injured soldiers and citizenry of this city. Here, a painted angel's wing to stanch the bleeding of a man's gashed leg. There, a gold lily wrapped around a cut temple."

The women of the household are smiling, the pages and servants silent. Everyone makes the sign of the cross, whispers a prayer. And she, Joan, listens from across the room. She is standing at the door in partial view of the speaker and his audience. They thought she was resting, but she would never miss the chance to hear a good story.

Her squire has exaggerated, as is bound to happen with the telling of any tale—but not by much. What he has left out: After the battle, she sought out La Hire and Dunois. She fell exhausted into their arms, and they held her, supporting her weight. They embraced her as they would a man—not gently or with consideration of where she had been hurt. They squeezed her shoulders and compressed her spine until her bones cracked. And she left on them the imprint of her arrow wound, like a bloody handprint, which they touched as if she had just given them a holy medal.

Jean stood apart, holding her torn banner. He was patient. He waited until his betters released her from their grip, and then he came up to her like a supplicant. He whispered in her ear: "You alone are the savior of this city, and there is no man who has seen what you have done here today who would not also be willing to follow you to the ends of the earth, to death."

What her squire could not know: she believes she died. As she lay on the ground, arrow jutting out of her neck, there was a moment when all had grown dark and the world became still. Her breathing, already ragged, ceased. But her soul did not leave her body. It neither ascended to heaven nor descended to some other place. There was no burst of light. Death was a deep, senseless sleep. And when she woke, it felt like sitting up from a long rest, though only a short time had passed, no more than a quarter of an hour. But she was refreshed. She wanted to move, to finish what she had set out to do. She wanted to win.

Before anyone can take notice, Joan returns upstairs. Outside the window of her room: the bells of the city are ringing. Jubilation. Her pages bring her supper to eat in bed, a steaming plate of beef liver, and they watch as she finishes her food. With watery eyes, trying not to cry but still crying, they watch her dip fresh-baked bread in the sauce and eat portions large enough for two men. The women who dressed her for Saint Loup come in to kiss her hands, to talk. She breathes and breathes easily.

◆

EARLY THE NEXT MORNING, she gazes at the lines of English across a wide field. From Les Tourelles, the enemy retreated, yet they haven't left. Instead they are eager for a final rally, a final fight.

She had slept well, and the sheet beneath her was clean when she woke. The bleeding had stopped. But her neck still swelled. She couldn't put on her armor, so the women helped her slip on a doublet, the castoff of Yolande's eldest son, and they left the buttons unfastened at the collar when they saw she was in pain. This is how one dresses for a night of merrymaking, for a pleasant supper with friends, not for a battle, but what can you do?

She arrives a little late, sword at her side, and on her best charger. The captains nod their welcome. The fact that she is not wearing any armor doesn't surprise them. Wasn't it just last night that she had ridden into the thick of battle in a blood-soaked tunic?

In the distance, the English are small as ants, and Joan covers the line of the horizon with one hand. The width of her palm and her fingers block out half the English force from sight, from existence.

Her squire is behind her, torn banner held high.

She lowers her hand, and it is like a child who has just drawn a picture in the dirt with his fingers. Where her thumb was, the ant line of the English wavers, as though it had been smudged. And then—it breaks.

"They are turning." She hears Dunois at her side. His voice is amazed. "They are retreating without even fighting."

"If only all battles could be so easy," La Hire sighs. "But then we would be out of a job."

No one says, The line broke only when you arrived, Joan; they were ready to fight until you appeared, though she knows they are thinking it. She is quiet. This moment is one to be savored. She learns: It's not always armies that win a battle. Sometimes it's fear. Fear can stop a battle before it is even fought. Fear can turn an enemy back before they have unsheathed a single sword.

"This is a beautiful morning," Joan says to no one.

She looks up at the sky. She is stepping through memories as one steps into puddles of light in a shaded wood. Seven years ago, when she returned from a night spent in Maxey, the morning was not unlike this one: warm, gold-tinted. Her dog was dead, yet the sun still shone; a lark sang a high note from a tree. The sky is the same, she thinks, but what a difference from that morning. What a difference from that weeping child on a hill. She was master of nothing then. She could control nothing. Now men run at the sight of her.

♦

AFTERWARD IN JOAN'S ROOM, La Hire ambles up to her. "By the way . . ." His voice becomes shy. "Dunois and I have a wager. He says there are people in the world, rare but in existence, who are, in fact, born both as men and as women. They have breasts, but they have cocks as well."

Joan glances at him, keeps her face straight. "Here I was thinking you and my lord Dunois were spending your time wisely, planning battles, organizing France's army, being the preeminent captains of this side of the war."

"Oh, we did that in the first five minutes of our talk."

"It shows," she replies.

"You are a woman, are you not?" he asks. He is almost blushing. "It is just, I want my five livres if you are. But if you aren't, then we will keep it a secret between us, since I have spent all my money."

"Lose another wager?" she asks.

"You avoid the question," he says, smiling at her. "So, you imply that you may or may not have a cock. Well, I shall tell Dunois that there is every possibility he is right, then."

"Don't let the question keep you up at night, my friend."

"Only when my bed is empty," he replies, "which is a rare occasion these days. Everyone likes a winner." He adds, after a pause, he is serious, "But it is your name the people call out. It is 'Joan' that is on their lips, not 'La Hire.' You are like the warrior Yde, the lady who fled from her father and became a knight. Do you know the story? Every tournament was hers to win until an angel turned her into a man because a princess had fallen in love with her."

There is no resemblance between La Hire and Durand Laxart. One is built like an angry cannon; the other, a reed that nods to every passing breeze. Yet she feels it could be her uncle standing next to her, ready with another tale to tell. And she wonders what he, Durand, is doing now. What tricks he is up to. For a moment, she feels a small panic. She hopes he has a pallet to sleep on, a roof over his head. She hopes he isn't going hungry. Then she remembers, he is a better survivor than she will ever be. If he goes one day without dinner and a bed, then tomorrow he will be patting his full belly and whistling a song. He will be admiring a new pair of boots, fit for a lord.

And she is not like Yde, for she would rather keep her womanhood. Yde was already a great knight before the angel transformed her, so why did she change?

"What would I gain by being a man?" she says. "A cock, a deeper voice, hair across my chest. I would not become stronger. I am already strong."

And, she thinks, I would inherit the several weaknesses of man's nature: his lust, his boundless aggression, his desire to tame all that he touches—the beasts of the field, the earth, women. For a man cannot see anything in the world without wishing to wear it like a trophy on his back, to call himself master over it. To her, this is what it means to be a man.

She vows she will not be this way. If she will flatten, then she will also nurture. She will kill, but she will heal. She will shout at her men in battle and shame them so they can find their strength and do better, but she will sit by the beds of the sick and the dying to tell those too ill to stand that their city has been liberated. Their souls will journey to the land of Purgatory as free men of the kingdom of France.

"Ah, so you don't have a cock?" La Hire asks, brightening. "Then I have won my five livres, and Dunois had better pay up."

"Give me half?" Now she is talking like her father.

"Not a chance," he says. "Make your own wager."

A chuckle, then: "I once had the tip of a sword cut me here." He shows Joan the scarred flesh at the bottom of his eye. "I thought I was a dead man. 'It is over, La Hire,' I told myself. 'You have had a good career, not the best, though it has been long and occasionally worth your while. But you are done for and your soul is the devil's to claim.' Yet I lived, and now when I have nothing to do, when I find myself sitting in a chair and dangling a boot from my toes by the fire, I say, 'La Hire, it is time to find a war again.' And I go off running. I ask my neighbors, the ale brewers, the serving wenches who for some reason can never keep their hands off me, 'Where is there a war happening? For I must go there.'

"You have started on this road, Joan, and you should know it is a path without an end. War is like a box. Once you open it, there is no way to close it again, to unsee what you have seen. Other people will sometimes show you what they have done while you have been on campaign. 'Look, I have carved a statue; it is the best statue in the world,' they might say, or 'I have painted the finest portrait of the king, and he has awarded me with a chest of coins.' And you smile at them as if they are children who have made a circle of pebbles or a chain of daisies. You answer, 'But I have been to war. I have fought at such-and-such a place in this part of the kingdom or in a kingdom far away. I saw a thousand men die. And I killed some, too.' And then they blink at you. They are speechless, for they know you have lived through something they have never experienced in their little rooms and comfortable hovels and probably never will. You have skirted death, run circles around that king of kings. You have taken a man's life, felt it trembling at the tip of your blade or perhaps in your own hands. What is this to a statue, a painting, or a book? You have teetered on the edge of graves—your own and those of other men—and you are never the same again after you have returned from that place. You would be surprised. When you are an old soldier, winning matters less than you may think. Victory is just a prize. Winning is survival. Winning is to keep breathing until the next battle begins."

Joan lets a moment pass. She turns from the window to La Hire. "I am looking for three men. They came to my village last summer."

"You will not find them." He answers her quickly. "I heard from Dunois, who heard from le Maçon what happened in your village. By now everyone at court knows your story, but your search would be for nothing. These men, whoever they are, could already be dead. They could be anywhere, anyone."

"Then I will go everywhere," she replies, "and I will kill every Englishman I come across."

He raises an eyebrow. That will take some doing, he seems to say.

"This morning was the first time I went on my knees and prayed," he says. "I had not prayed for years. What was the point? The angels never seemed to heed the prayers of France. England is now God's favorite daughter. But I said to myself, This time God warrants La Hire's thanks, for He has seen fit to grant us a miracle. And that miracle is you. May you never stop fighting, little maid. May there always be battles so long as you draw breath."

"I will stop fighting when the English leave France. And when Burgundy kneels to the King."

La Hire grins. "Oh, but I don't think you will. There will always be battles: battles for land, for power, for the glory of God. The soul knows its own destiny. You were born for this, little maid. I hear that is what everyone is calling you now. *Pucelle.* A maiden. Purest of the pure."

Joan sticks out her tongue, gags.

He moves to the window of her room; below, a crowd has gathered. He cracks open the shutters. A shout goes up. He closes the shutters; the cheers stop. He opens them again. More shouts, more deafening cheers. He closes the shutters. The noise stops, replaced with groans of disappointment.

Joan's mouth twists before the room shakes with their laughter.

The people of Orléans have invited her into their homes to pray with them, meet their children, and share the little food they have in their cupboards. They give her their babies to hold and to bless with a kiss. She is named godmother to any child newborn, and any girl newborn is named after her. She hears that a boy whose arm she had bound in a strip of cloth from her banner has been going around the city telling people how he was raised from the dead by her hand. She does not dispute the rumor, only explains to those who are interested in hearing her side of the story that perhaps he was not as near death as he thinks.

Solitude and silence are rare. In the streets, "Te Deum Laudamus" is sung all hours of the day, and these same crowds follow her whenever she goes out. At her approach, men slip off their caps. Women bow their heads and bob to her, as if she were a great lady. She never ignores them but bows back, which sends the people into raptures.

It is possible La Hire is right, that once you lift a sword, it is hard to put down again. She recalls the arrow that struck her neck. She thinks, When I returned to battle I had forgotten her, my sister. In my mind was only what still needed to be done. In my mind was only the thought, the desire to win. And when next morning, the English lines broke with not a single drop of blood shed, she hadn't thought of Catherine, either. It wasn't vengeance that was on her mind but *la gloire* she basked in. Glory.

◆

IN THE CATHEDRAL AT TOURS, the Dauphin is waiting. On either side of him are courtiers, some faces familiar and smiling, others hard as stone. To his right: le Maçon and Yolande's messenger. To his left: the Archbishop of Reims and La Trémoille, who look as if they would like to give Joan a big kick down the steps.

The Dauphin is wearing a new set of robes in the colors of the royal House of Orléans, a plush velvet-pile green threaded with crimson, and a big hat with green and scarlet tassels. His fingers are ringed: a red cabochon as large as a tiger's eye, a gleaming emerald flashing like a mischievous demon practicing its magic. *Now you see me, now you don't.*

He is supposed to wait, to remain perfectly still as she approaches, but his patience fails him. He walks up to her, closing the distance, which makes the courtiers' mouths fall open, some in pleasure, others in dismay. When she kneels, he bends—actually bends—to raise her. He keeps his hands on her shoulders and leans forward to kiss her: a peck on each cheek.

She hears La Trémoille gasp and sees that the Archbishop is not looking; he is playing instead with the stones on his fingers. Le Maçon is beaming at her, as proud as if he were her father. Except that if he were her father, he would probably be drawing up a contract with several witnesses. You want to use my daughter for your battles? Of course this is possible, we can work something out, but how much are you willing to pay for the honor?

The Dauphin, she thinks, smells of books and of inks. He smells of sweet things, almond milk and anise comfits. And cinnamon.

"Now we shall spend some time in prayer," he announces. A smattering of applause. Weak on the right, enthusiastic on the left.

In the chapel, she kneels beside the Dauphin; the rest of the courtiers are expected to give their thanks to God from a distance. But His Majesty does not seem to have prayer in mind. Another definition of prayer, it seems, is conversation.

"Five days," he says, as soon as their knees touch the cushions prepared for them. "Five days to free Orléans." He turns to face her. "I could hardly believe it when le Maçon told me the news. I prayed for you—the captains, all my people. I attended Mass no less than three times a day as soon as word of your arrival in the city reached me. I must have said a hundred prayers, if not more." He pauses: Now, Joan, it is your turn to say something pleasant.

"Your Majesty's prayers reached Orléans," she says. This morning, she had received another lecture from le Maçon before meeting the Dauphin: In the company of princes, it is wise to be humble. Don't take all or perhaps any of the credit. Let them reach their own conclusion as to how well they are served.

He brightens. His hand floats over hers. There is no servant with a bowl of rose water nearby, but this time he will allow his hand to settle, covering her tough skin like a piece of unblemished parchment.

"I see now I was wrong to take offense the last time we spoke. For that and my hesitation I rebuke myself. But I did not think I would see you again." It is as polite a way as possible to say, I thought you were a fake. I thought you would be dead.

She bows her head. "I am glad to see Your Majesty."

He nods. "You see how . . ." Smiling, he shows her the green-and-red-striped hat with tassels. "I prepared this outfit especially for your arrival. It is my first time wearing it. I thought it appropriate as a celebration of our victory."

Joan glances over her shoulder. She sees no one is actually praying. With narrowed eyes, La Trémoille is watching her, and le Maçon, two courtiers away, is watching him.

"Do you like it?" the Dauphin asks.

She reddens. She wants to say, I like a suit of armor better. Instead she says, without thinking, "It is not clothes that make a king."

The Dauphin frowns: Try again.

She improvises: "I only meant . . . Your Majesty could wear a beggar's cloak and no one would spare you a single coin. They would see at a glance that you were a prince of royal blood born to wear a crown." Better?

He nods. Better. His hand floats back to hers.

His eyes flit to the altar as if it were an afterthought for prayer. "I have made mistakes. There are nights when I have gone to sleep and felt cursed by the hand of God. He alone knows how I have been tested. I have asked in my prayers, 'Why must I endure so much? When will my heart be light again?' and received no answer."

He strokes the tassels of his hat. Despite the celebratory mood, he wants a moment for self-pity. "You do not know what it is like for the world to hate you. Not only the English. Not only my cousin Burgundy, who wants to see my head on a pike. My own people despise me. They see how I am reduced and laugh behind my back. How can a king rule when his sovereignty extends only as far as the place he has run to for sanctuary? This is why they call me King of Bourges. But I would tell them I have plans, and they are not only plans to take back my throne and my kingdom. I should like to build . . ." His voice falters. He sighs.

"This story is not over," she says. "It is possible that one day the people will talk about the King of France who ended this war. Many were against him. On all sides was he surrounded by his enemies, but in the end, he defeated those who stood in his way and emerged victorious. He unified his kingdom. Then your meatless dinners will be something glorious to look back on. The days when you went without, when you could not afford a new shirt and the tailor refused to attend you because you had not paid your debts—you may reflect on these days and they will be the stones that make your crown shine brighter than any of your forefathers'."

"That is only a dream."

"Everything begins with a dream. What is a prayer but a wish? Your Majesty is fortunate. You are served by those who, like weavers, will take the fabric of your dreams, your prayers, and spin them into existence. It is true. There are many who desire to see you fail, but you also have friends like le Maçon and Dunois. You have God on your side. You have me."

He smiles. The smile flickers. He looks at her seriously. "I have heard of your feats in Orléans. You have killed men. Tell me, do you feel any guilt for the lives you took?"

They are in a house of God. She glances at the altar, returns his gaze. A brief pause. "No."

The Dauphin waits.

"I am a soldier," she says. "I have done what I must do. And Your Majesty is a king. A king must always do what he needs to rule."

Her answer satisfies him, and he moves on. "How else will you serve us?"

She pretends to think, though she already has an answer prepared. "Jargeau. Meung. Beaugency. These towns were seized by the English in the days before the siege at Orléans. If we take them back as we have taken Orléans, we shall free the whole of the Loire Valley."

"More battles?" A sigh rattles out of him.

"Your Majesty asked how I could serve you."

"And then?"

"Allow me to deliver you the places I have named first. Then we will talk again."

The Dauphin's back straightens. He dips his head, bestows the royal assent. "Restore the Loire Valley to us, Joan, and you shall have everything it is within our power to give. There will be no honor you would not deserve. I promise you this."

She looks to the altar. So, the man she once named her enemy is now her ally.

"Your Majesty's support is gift enough." It is the kind of phrase le Maçon has taught her: the language of courtiers.

"Friendship, Joan. Whoever God sends to aid me is my friend."

As he rises from his cushion, she rises with him. "Majesty, if I may give you some advice? The next time you pray, make demands. Bargain. Raise your voice to God and His angels. Tell Him what you desire most in your heart. You are the King of France, God's appointed. Tell Him what you are owed: the throne that is your birthright. Say the debt must be paid, and He will listen."

"Only you would dare speak so," he says, though he is smiling again. From the folds of his robes, he produces a small object, a figurine. He holds it out to her. "This was a gift from my mother. Not Yolande. My other mother."

The object passes from his hand to hers. "You see it is the image of my father. A gift from her when he was alive. He is praying. It is how I like to picture him still: in prayer, but his eyes are open as if he expects to see angels, to see God. So you must take this with you. It is a piece of me, just as my father is a part of me. You must take it for luck, and it will be as if I am with you and the rest of my army in spirit. And then . . ." Two spots of pink color his cheeks. "You will have to return, for I shall want it back."

It does not seem to occur to the Dauphin that one does not bring to a battle delicate and breakable pieces of art. But our King is a scholar, a poet, a musician. His heart is soft. She will keep the figurine somewhere safe. And he has called her his friend. It is a warm feeling, like stepping in out of the cold: to know one has friends again, that there are people who want you alive, who would like to see you do well, grow rich, be better than you were before. My squire. My pages. Le Maçon. Yolande. La Hire. Dunois. Now His Majesty. These are my friends.

She tells him: The book of misery and its many chapters, they bind us in the same way the future is bound to the past, in the way a subject is bound to her king, in the way a king is bound to his God. It is a chain of sacred links; it is unbreakable.

Majesty, you have me, Joan, on your side. So put fear out of your heart.

III

◆ ◆ ◆

LOIRE VALLEY, JUNE 1429
ONE MONTH LATER

At Jargeau, the English made Joan an offer. We will leave, they promised; no need for blood, no lives lost on either side. But give us a little time before we go.

She laughed, but stopped when she realized the messenger sent to bargain wasn't joking.

"It is a ploy," she said to Dunois, to La Hire. "Our enemy must think we are simpletons. They are playing for time because they know reinforcements are coming: an army led by the Englishman Fastolf. Surely that is as obvious to you as it is to me?"

The offer was rejected. Between the crenellations she saw heads peeping at her, but the sight of these heads, cowering and small, inspired no mercy. Now that you are on the defensive, she thought, now that I have driven you out of Orléans and you no longer have the upper hand, you are afraid. But your fear comes too late.

At Jargeau, the battle lasted four hours. But these are days when she knows that victory is hers for the taking, even before the first crossbolt is loosed.

She used to think every child who was beaten, who had not been coddled and loved, would grow up to be like her: as strong and unafraid, as tolerant of physical pain. She had thought it was the war and never knowing a single year's peace that made her this way: quick with a retort, wary of others, hand curled into a fist and ready for a fight if an argument couldn't be settled with words. But she was wrong. She is unique. Dunois says she has two fathers. The first is Jacques d'Arc.

The second is God. If Jacques d'Arc has given her nothing, then God has given her everything. He shows His infinite love for you, Joan, through gifts that are of no human making.

He explains, seeing she is skeptical, "I know what I am talking about, for are there not some in the world who have only to look at a lute before they are able to pluck its strings and make music? And as for the poets, I have heard their best work comes to them in sleep and in dreaming, as though a voice speaks directly into their ear, or that whole verses will materialize out of thin air in a flash of understanding. It cannot be explained, so do not try. It is simply genius."

Give her any weapon, and she will know how to use it. After an hour, she will make short work of the masters of the poleax, the mace, the crossbow, weapons she has never picked up before. Now she understands that even a grown man who has trained since he was a small boy cannot catch up to her. It isn't really fair, but who ever said that life was fair? Different words are used to describe her condition. She is gifted, special, remarkable, a nonpareil fighter; Dunois says there will never be one like her again—at least not for another age. Joan is blessed.

"When did you learn to fight?" La Hire asked.

Hard to say.

But she thought—back, back, to a day of good weather, mild, with open skies. She was thirteen. After church, a boy, one of Jacquemin's friends, had bounced around her. He was among those who'd laughed while her brothers held her under the water, who made a show of waving his nose whenever she passed. When she looked straight at him, he liked to shield his eyes: to protect himself, he said, from her great ugliness. But that day, she was in no humor to be taunted. "Joan, Joan," he sang, and he said how no man would ever want her. *Fine,* she thought. *Good.* How it seemed impossible that she should have come from the same womb as her sister. This she agreed with, too. But then he'd gone further. He said he'd had dreams of Catherine. Dreams of creeping into her room as she slept, of stroking her beautiful hair and neck, of kissing her—*thwack!* Before she knew what she had done, her fist had hooked his chin. The blow swept him off his feet, made him seem as light as a cushion, and he fell, like an acrobat executing a perfect backflip. With a crash, he landed, his jaw and nose at an odd angle to the rest of him, and it took not only his brothers but also the priest to pull him up again.

Behind her, she had heard a chuckle, which made her turn. Catherine? No, her sister was frowning, upset at what she'd done. And there was no one behind her, only the statue of Saint Margaret that stood in front of the church. Yet she could have sworn she heard the chuckle again as she walked away, one hand rubbing the knuckles of the other.

She instructs her pages, knowing it is her responsibility to oversee their training. "Sometimes a battle is won before it has even begun," she tells them. "It is an attitude." She explains this to their wondering faces. In their laps are plates of armor waiting to be polished, which they have forgotten about. "When you are old enough to fight battles, I want you to look across the distance at the obstacles in your way—the towers, the bridges, the gatehouse, the walls—and I want you to picture how you will topple them. The vision must always arrive before the event, and when it comes, you will know what you have to do. You will know as soon as you set a sabaton on the field that the day is yours."

After Jargeau, they moved on, taking a bridge at Meung, and left soldiers there to defend it before traveling to Beaugency. When that, too, fell, what remained of the English army fled in the direction of Patay.

Patay was the battle of Joan's dreams. An open field under a blue dome of sky. The ground firm enough for riding, covered with plush grass and wildflowers. And the air so still no breeze could threaten an arrow's flight path. It was in Patay the fleeing English were joined by Fastolf's long-awaited army. Together, they were several thousand strong, and most of the men Fastolf had brought were skilled archers equipped with longbows. Hundreds of these archers settled in the woods. Under cover of the trees they hid while waiting for the French to come upon them. It could easily have been another Agincourt, a second Verneuil, but something went wrong. The archers frightened a stag, and this stag leapt among the men until all was in tumult; shouts went up, and the army became disordered and gave away their position.

From the vanguard, Joan saw the stag leap out unharmed. But when she looked again, it was gone.

Within the first half hour, the English were scattered. It was less a battle than a massacre, the cumulative vengeance of past losses still fresh in French memory. As she rode, she no longer felt the weight of her armor. She no longer felt her limbs, her heartbeat, the rise and fall of her chest. She was transfigured. She had become a spirit and her horse a winged creature. The glint of her sword reflected the light, a golden sunbeam clutched in her metal fist.

Dunois said later that it was more usual for battles to be like Jargeau or Saint Loup in Orléans. Hours of push and shove. Hard on the body. Rarely, if ever, did you get a fight like this one. If all battles were like Patay, then every man would sign up to be a soldier. We wouldn't even need to recruit. The early estimate: two thousand English dead. This is what happens when a battle turns into a rout.

"I want you to understand so you are prepared," she tells her pages after Patay. "War is an unpredictable business." At Jargeau, a large soldier knocked her off the scaling ladder by throwing a rock over the wall. The rock broke against her helmet; she saw stars, lost her balance, and fell. The impact was so great that when she hit the ground, clouds of dust billowed up around her. She heard the deafening cheers of the English, which didn't last long. By the time the dust had settled, she was already back on her feet and climbing up the ladder again, though her legs wobbled like pudding beneath her.

Perhaps it is luck. Perhaps it is just the liveliness of youth coupled with good armor. Or perhaps it is God's grace.

But there is also what you can control. She instructs them: When you are hurt, there is a moment in which you must make a decision about what to do with the pain. For once it hits, you will want nothing more than to curl up into a ball. So you have to be faster than your own pain. You have to strike or turn your mind to the next goal before the wound holds you back or makes you cautious of losing your life, for that is the instinct of the body: to preserve, not necessarily to be brave. Whatever you have broken, whatever your body has taken in terms of damage, you can reconcile it afterward. Always after, never during. With every battle comes the backwash of excitement in the hours following, when your limbs and muscles jump, and even your pulse, as irregular as your heartbeat, leaps and bolts. So, you stay up through the night and watch the sun rise from the top of a fortress or the roof of an inn. And you think to yourself, I have earned this morning as I will earn every morning after this. The glories of the next day will always be greater, and what is suffered today will return to me a hundredfold in blessings sometime in the future. You must have faith this will be so. You must remember your body, the pains of your heart will heal.

She takes the two pages into her arms and plants a kiss on the tops of their heads. Love, tenderness. These are the things a child should have, but they don't protect him.

She doesn't tell them about the boy she met at Patay after the battle was over. From a distance, she spotted the restless twitching of a hand, like a rabbit leg jerking in a poacher's trap.

Walking up, she saw he was English. Her own hand shifted by instinct to her sword. She stepped closer. He was young, about her age: seventeen.

When he noticed her approaching, he startled and his eyes widened. He hiccuped. And then he calmed himself. He was already dying. There was nothing she could do to him that wouldn't happen in another few moments.

For some time she stood over his body, just watching. Clear drops of sweat gleamed on his forehead. He knew who she was and perhaps was willing himself to die at a faster rate.

"It is you." Bad French reached her ears, and she blinked.

"Who is 'you'?" she asked, but her voice was softer than she expected it to be.

"We have many names for you," he said.

She tried to keep her face still. "I think I have heard some of the names," she replied easily, "though I try to ignore them." A breeze rustled her short hair, and her hand left her sword to brush a few strands out of her eyes.

He seemed to attempt a smile. Instead he grimaced. "If I were you, I think I would do the same."

The field was quiet but for the sound of buzzing insects. Overhead: the occasional flap of black wings. His senses weren't yet lost to him. He heard the buzzing, the flapping. A panicked look. His mouth opened.

"My body . . . I do not want . . ." Her language didn't come easily to him, so he relied on gestures instead. With a finger, he pointed in the direction of the circling birds.

She watched them, as her hand drifted back to her sword. Her face was placid; if she left, he would die anyway, but she wanted to finish him. The grip on her hilt tightened. All it would take was one stroke . . . and what he wanted and didn't want, what were these things to her? When another deserving of mercy wished to be spared, who heeded her voice? Yet in her chest, she felt the chains of steel shake. She felt a small lock open, and out of it slipped . . . a question.

"What is your name?" she asked.

"William."

Guillaume. William. He might have thought she was frowning at him, but she was trying not to cry. They were not tears for him but for herself. She had asked God for a heart of stone, so what was this? How could she avenge if she could still feel for the enemy?

But she kneeled, giving in to a part of herself she thought was long dead. She lifted the boy's head from the ground, and her steel arm became a pillow against which he could rest.

She saw where and how he had been wounded. A stab to the chest a few inches from the heart. Blood was still leaking from the cut. Perhaps if he had been tended to at once he could have been saved, but now it was too late. She realized with surprise that her hand was applying pressure to slow the bleeding, that English blood was slipping through her gauntleted fingers.

"Did I . . . ?" She couldn't finish the question but stared at the gash. Her memory was good, yet there were so many faces in a battle. She couldn't remember them all.

"No." His reply was cold, even a little proud. "It was another. One of your captains.

"I did not want to come here," he said without prompting. "I did not want to fight. And now . . ."

He looked down at his own blood. His jaw tightened.

"Please . . ." He pointed again to the sky. "My body . . ."

She wondered, if she were not a woman, would he have dared expect such mercy? Would he have pleaded for burial if it were La Hire's face or her squire's staring down at him?

She nodded, and in her arms, she felt relief shake through him.

He grew quiet as he focused on dying. She looked away only a moment, but when her gaze returned to the boy's face, she felt her heart contract. His eyes were dim. Her hand passed over his lids to close them. To herself, she counted: two thousand and one dead.

She doesn't tell her pages how, seven years later, everything has changed and still nothing has changed. A small field is replaced with a bigger field. A boy is replaced with a man. Yet the ending of this story is identical. Sometimes with the conclusion of battles comes a clarity. One's heart races, but color—the blue of a surcoat, the red of a trampled flag—becomes more vivid. One has, for the space of a few hours, a falcon's eye, every sense pared to a sharp point. But when she left Patay, she felt a dullness, as if she had betrayed herself.

She didn't tell anyone when she returned to the field to dig a single grave, to whittle from two pieces of wood a makeshift cross tied together with string to serve as a simple headstone. But La Hire saw her hands, sore and pink from digging. Tomorrow blisters would come up, and her palms would sting when she gripped the hilt of her sword. She knew her body well. You couldn't live your whole life covered in hurt without understanding how the parts would eventually heal.

"You have a soft heart, little maid," he told her. "Be careful of it."

She wants to ask someone she trusts, her squire or Dunois, What do

I look like when I am fighting? What do I look like after a battle is over? Angel or gargoyle? I want to know. When I am splattered with blood and the water that washes my face turns red in the bowl, does my appearance frighten you? Does it frighten Raymond and Louis? If so, perhaps I should wash myself before seeing them. And are we sure, completely certain, that my gifts come from God and not somewhere else?

She can understand how God would inspire poets and artists. She can picture angels breathing sweet music into the ears of the dozing troubadour. But does a talent for slaughter count as a heavenly gift, too?

She confides this to Dunois, who replies, "You were not at Agincourt or at Verneuil, where the opposite of Patay happened. You have only known victory in battle. But if you had been witness to our defeats, our many losses, you would understand how the field at Patay was blessed. The tide is turning, and finally it is in our favor.

"It was a stag that warned us of where the English hid in the woods," he continues. "A majestic creature often linked with Christ. Why not a fox? Or a boar? I believe God sent this stag for you, Joan. I see now He will not suffer you to fail. If He deigns to love the kingdom of France, then we are blessed with His love through you alone."

◆

JARGEAU. MEUNG. BEAUGENCY. PATAY. When news of victory arrives, the Dauphin begins . . . decorating. At Chinon, he sets aside rooms for Joan. Overruling the suggestions of his courtiers, La Trémoille among them, he collects three of the castle's finest tapestries. He ignores the protests of these same courtiers, who are afraid he will hurt himself, and lifts a statuette of an angel, placing it in a corner of what in a few days will become Joan's bedroom. He says, holding up his hands, as if to frame the moment eternally, The light will hit her wings just so as the sun comes up, and from this angle Joan will see the statue each morning upon waking. Can't you picture it? I can. He laughs. The art of assembling a pleasant room numbers one of his many talents, and if Joan's arena is the battlefield, then his is here.

He hires an army of painters, masters and their smocked apprentices, to decorate the walls. Under his direction, they sketch rolling hills, a sun with a smiling face, forests bountiful with skipping deer, castles fit to occupy giants, for the ladies and lords on their mounts are nearly as tall as the towers. He looks over their shoulders as the apprentices mix their paints; they dab a shade of green on the wall and look into his face for a sign of approval, but he shakes his head. No, no, the green must be darker, much darker. Where is the light coming from? See, the sun is here! Therefore, the shadows must be going this way! Finally, he takes a brush from one of the masters—he is full of surprises, this king—and applies a dot of azure blue to one of the castle's flags. He steps back to appraise his work. La Trémoille grumbles. He mutters, "This is a complete waste of time. Is there a war going on or not?" But le Maçon applauds. The old courtier calls out, "What talent! Your Majesty is a natural artist."

The Dauphin directs where chairs should be put, and when cushions are brought in by a servant, he pokes one, selected at random, with a finger to test how plush it is. "I think not," he says, his expression grave, and sends the boy away to find better cushions, even if they already belong to someone else.

And when, at the end of a long day, the painters, exhausted, are packing up their supplies—they have worked tirelessly, knowing that they may not be paid on time or even at all—His Majesty has another idea. He wants the whole ceiling adorned with stars.

"And angels, too?" La Trémoille asks sweetly, though he looks as if he is about to choke.

"And angels, too," the Dauphin says.

When he sees Joan, he is as giddy as a boy who has been fed a bowl of powdered sugar. He leads her into her new rooms, watching her face carefully for astonishment, for gratitude. The tour is extensive. Every few steps they stop to admire a new detail.

"And here a pair of candlesticks," the Dauphin says, "of enameled silver."

"Thank you, Your Majesty," she replies. To her right, le Maçon nods at her. She picks up the candlesticks and makes a show of observing them carefully. "They are truly wonderful candlesticks."

"God! Are we going to go through every item in these cursed rooms?" La Trémoille hisses as le Maçon bursts out laughing.

But the Dauphin bristles, scowling. "Georges, if you do not like it, then you may leave. No one is keeping you here, and your company is hardly necessary to us at this time and place. Also, do not blaspheme."

Joan spins through the anteroom to the chamber beyond. She sits on the feather bed and smiles at her king, who looks for a moment as if he would like to curl up on the bed beside her and listen to her tell stories.

Over the next week, gifts arrive from the Dauphin's supporters. From the Count of Provence, Yolande's eldest son, Joan receives a chalice of gold, the base engraved with saints: Martin with his cloak, Paul with a sword, Hubertus dressed for the hunt.

Her pages are charged with a new duty: the sorting of presents. What courier comes from whom and with what message. The Dauphine, Yolande's daughter, sends a sapphire ring, the silver band adorned with jeweled crosses. The ring isn't new and was not commissioned for Joan, but was pulled from her own finger when she heard of Joan's victories at Orléans. The stone brings good luck, Her Majesty promises, for she wore it in the months that she was pregnant with her son, and he is a healthy, intelligent boy who has above all things inherited his father's famous nose.

Yolande's second son, René, also sends a gift. It arrives in a plain leather case, lifted by two of his liveried servants. One of them informs her it would do their lord great honor if she opened the case herself, for they are meant to inform their master of her reaction. So, she lifts the cover and peers inside, remembering to gasp as she pulls away the satin sleeve. It is a smaller model, they explain, of the famous Reliquary Shrine, once bought by Elizabeth of Poland, a queen. The box is fashioned like a miniature cathedral. Open it and you are greeted with the centerpiece, the altar where the Virgin sits in a dress of gold, holding the Christ child. The wings of the box are covered in panels, and each panel, painted to imitate stained glass, is unique.

She has received relics in jeweled boxes. Here, courtesy of the Count of Vendôme, a piece of the True Cross reported to have belonged to Saint Louis himself. And a clip of hair from Bridget of Sweden, less unlikely than the previous, Jean points out, as that saintly woman died only about sixty years ago, compared to Saint Louis's one hundred and sixty. Joan opens a miniature case worked in silver. A hard object, discolored and yellow, with a sharp edge, falls into her hand.

Raymond picks up the corresponding letter. "That is a claw from the lion Saint Jerome tamed when he healed the beast's paw."

She drops the claw back into its case. "I have never seen a lion," she says.

"If you want one, we could probably write His Majesty and ask," Jean suggests.

The Count of Clermont has sent her a brooch of a swan with a gilded beak; the swan was carved from ivory, each snowy pinion etched as if with the tip of a fine needle. The brooch, he writes, belonged to his mother. His only request: that she do him the honor of fastening it to her cloak the next time she rides into battle for France.

These are Joan's favorite gifts: a pair of blue lambskin gloves from the Archbishop of Embrun; a blanket woven by the hands of the prioress of Poissy; a pair of destriers, both ink black, from the Duke of Alençon. Dunois has gifted her a dagger with a curved blade, which he bought from a knight who had been in the Crusades. The hilt is carved with large roses in full flower; the guard of the hilt is a wriggling green snake.

La Hire, always practical, kicks off his own boots and passes them to her during his next visit. "We are about the same size," he says kindly. "And you will find more use for boots than holy relics."

The Archbishop sends a book of hours, small enough to keep in a pocket; or she could fix it, he suggests, to her belt, so then she could read from the volume at any hour and pray. Ah, but she cannot read, can she? What a pity! Le Maçon offers a Psalter with gilded pages and an enameled cover studded with carbuncles. His message: One day, she must learn her letters. He is not worried. She is a fast learner.

From La Trémoille she receives a purse of coins, an embroidered cushion, and a sack of malmsey wine, which he has imported specially from the region called Friuli Venezia Giulia. Does she know of Friuli Venezia Giulia, the messenger he sends is tasked with asking her. Perhaps she has tasted this wine before when she sat down to supper in her small village. Domrémy, was it? "Please inform your master we drank this all the time in Domrémy," she tells the messenger with a straight face.

A tray of oublies generously sprinkled with cinnamon and cardamom arrives from Yolande. Each oublie is stamped with the Valois coat of arms: a shield of fleurs-de-lis flanked by two angels holding between them a long chain of gold. Above the shield rests a great crown. Her pages squeal when the sweets arrive in the arms of Yolande's ladies-in-waiting, who glide into the room, a single creamy body of pale satin and silk veils.

Three clerks on loan from le Maçon compose flowery replies of thanks to the givers of these gifts. In these letters, promises are made of prayers for various maladies and ailments. Yes, Joan will have a word with God. A personal word. In her rooms, these clerks are given desks and stools. Their quills fly across the page. They are always running out of ink, so assistants must be hired to prepare ink for them and to fetch manchet loaves when they are tired and their wrists are sore.

The Dauphin now visits every day. Something in their relationship has changed, a shift so subtle it is barely felt. She no longer has to kneel when he approaches. If she is sitting, then simply standing will do; if standing, a bow will suffice. One morning, as she is in the middle of splashing her face with rose water and the Dauphin is already in the next room tasting oublies, it dawns on her. She is at ease with her king. They are allies who have helped each other. They are friends. And friendship, she finds, does not eat away at one's heart like anger, like vengeance. It does not weigh the soul down but lightens it.

The Dauphin inspects the gifts while chewing. He flips through the Archbishop's book of hours. He weighs La Trémoille's purse in his hands and is tempted to count the coins inside. Only his dignity stops him.

He frowns when he sees the model of the Reliquary Shrine. "I wanted this from René years ago," he tells her, stroking the gilded roof as if it were a cat's head. "The miser refused to give it to me, not even for a wedding present. I received a book instead."

"Then Your Majesty must have it now," she says.

The Dauphin blinks, smiles slowly. He pretends something has flown into his eye and turns away to rub it. She has had a hand in this, too: His Majesty's new happiness.

"I have lived so long with this weight that I am unused to this sudden lightness." His fingers, the tips sticky from eating sweets, hover over his heart. "When le Maçon first brought me the news of Orléans, the guards saw me sway on my feet. They were forced to hold me up so that I could hear the rest of his report. And then when he had finished, I called for my queen. I told her to bring me Louis. I kissed my wife. I held my son in my arms. You have made such things possible again, Joan."

◆

Opening presents. Going to bed late and rising well after the sun has risen. The week after Patay are days when the hours of light are long and the air is sweet. Joan is walking through a garden. The castoff of Yolande's eldest son has again been cast off, this time onto her squire's shoulders. Now she wears no one's castoffs. She is dressed in a shirt of gleaming yellow silk. Over this, a cream doublet with slashed sleeves, the lining the pink of a kitten's tongue and the buttons silver, each engraved with a lion's head. She wears hose that are parti-colored, one leg red, the other white, and calfskin boots not yet broken in. She has no mirror in which to admire herself, but she thinks the boots suit her better than they ever did that well-dressed idiot from Vaucouleurs, Sir Robert.

The world is smiling at her, the sun bright though not blinding. La Hire, Dunois, and Jean walk ahead, and laughter floats back to her on the air. From a distance, La Hire and her squire appear to be hugging each other; in fact, they are tussling to see who is the stronger, except they are giggling too much to exert any real strength. It just looks like they are both drunk and dancing.

They would never do the same with her: the wrestling, the shoves that end with one's feet sticking out of a hedge. Off the battlefield, away from corpses and puddles of blood, they keep their distance. It isn't that they aren't friendly with her—they are—but she is their brother-in-arms only when she is in harness. They see her clearest when she is covered in grime and guts, when her movements are accompanied by the sound of steel, and embrace her at the end of battles hard-won. Here in this space fragrant with the smell of sun and flowers, the world is different. One does not like to think of death in such a place. Dressed in silks or no, the memory of what she can do is inseparable from her. You can tease Joan. You can amuse her and tell her jokes. But would you go up and poke a giantess in the eye? Would you dare to grapple her in a headlock and test her patience? So, they are smiling yet wary. They feel safest in her company when the English are charging down at them.

Bobbing in the periphery of her vision is the Dauphin, who is prodding each rose bloom with the royal nose. When he turns, they see a butterfly has settled on his immense chaperon, today a checkered black and gold with a liripipe placed artistically over his shoulder.

"Your Majesty is as fragrant as a flower," La Hire observes.

Joan leans forward, waves the butterfly away from the Dauphin's hat.

"Oh, Joan, you have killed it," La Hire says. He gestures dramatically at the air. "Look how it is dazed and reeling, with only one wing left. Put it out of its misery, and quickly."

It may be the warmth of the day or the feeling of silk against her skin, which she is still unused to, but Joan laughs. Together they walk through a shaded grove, each bough a heavy blossom-laden garland, each leaf a waxy emerald green, as if the servants had climbed up on ladders to polish them. As she looks around at her company, shadows flicker over their faces; every man's expression appears to be in the process of changing into something else.

The Dauphin picks a white rose, twirls it like a quill between his fingers. He stops to choose another rose and offers it to her.

"Don't I get one?" La Hire says.

"Not until you win more battles" is the Dauphin's reply.

A servant brings wine, and Joan picks up her cup with heavy fingers. They glitter with rings: the Dauphine's sapphire, the Bishop of Poitiers's pink-red ruby, a diamond from a countess whose name she has for the moment forgotten. Ah, but the day is too fine to be spent remembering names, even if they belong to countesses!

La Hire blinks at the stones. "Christ, Joan," he says, forgetting himself. "What a pity you were not born with a dozen fingers on each hand, for then you could wear the treasures of the whole kingdom on your person. Here, let me look at that lovely blue jewel, I want to admire it . . ."

He takes her hand. "Very nice. But I wouldn't recommend wearing these into battle."

"And they say you should not drink before a battle either," she replies, "but . . ." She looks down. "Give me back the ruby. You thought I wouldn't notice you slipping the ring off, La Hire?"

The other men snicker. They are like boys playing tricks on their sister.

Her own household has expanded. She has clerks, and her clerks have assistants. She has two overly contented pages growing chubby on sweets, and a smug squire who walks among the other squires like he is head rooster. She has five servants, some of whom do her laundry, others who fetch water for her basin and sweep the floors of her rooms, and light-footed youths who send and receive messages, run errands at all hours of the day and night, and look after her horses, of which she has no less than four.

Wine finished, they play a game of bowls—the rules are simple enough, and she learns quickly. The Dauphin wins because, La Hire whispers into her ear, he has been practicing while they have been fighting his war for him. Another servant brings clean towels and a plate of sliced apricots and plums, and they set aside most of the apricots, His Majesty's favorite fruit, for the Dauphin. Then they walk, the sweetness still in their mouths, to supper. La Hire capers around them. He sneaks up behind Jean and spooks him.

But soon he and Dunois are back to swapping crude jokes.

"Know any others?" Joan asks. "I have heard these before. In Orléans. And all across the Loire Valley."

"Dunois, La Hire," the Dauphin says. He clears his throat and puffs out his chest. "What displeases Joan's ears displeases mine."

"Oooh!" La Hire says with delight.

For supper, they eat beef pastry and roasted lampreys in a brown sauce with cloves and galingale. They savor almond-milk flans garnished with saffron. But when the dish called blancmanger is brought to the table, a shadow passes over her face.

"Joan, you look at your food as if you want to kill it," La Hire says. "If you have no appetite, the rest of us will assist you."

One tries to leave the past behind and fails. From her grave, Catherine's cold hand touches the back of Joan's neck. She stops eating.

Now she knows why she prefers battles to candlelit suppers. In war, there is no time to think about your own dead. The noise alone is enough to drown out their cries from Purgatory.

Each man is sated and patting his stomach, and she wants to tell them a story. When she was no older than her pages and living off her uncle's stories of war, she had told her brother Jacquemin she would prefer to be a soldier, to march with an army, rather than live on the land. It was just idle chatter, but Jacquemin reported to her father what she'd said. Her father thought by soldier, she meant camp follower and prostitute. He said to Jacquemin and her brothers, "Drown this one if she ever disgraces us."

She wants to ask them, though she stops herself, What do you, any of you, know about earning your place in the world? You have had everything given to you. You were born into what you are today: a prince, a lord, a captain. With these titles, you thought the rest would come easily, so no wonder we are losing the war. Victory in battle doesn't take into consideration pedigree. When royal blood is spilled, it is the same as any foot soldier's. I know now there will always be this divide between us. Even if I fight beside you, I will never be the same as you.

"And now, Joan, you look as if you want to kill us," La Hire says. He scratches his chin.

"Tomorrow," she says, "there is work to be done."

The faces around the table appear baffled. Why bring up work when we are about to enjoy sweets? When we have just savored a walk through the garden and His Majesty has shown us his skills at bowls? But she is impatient to leave and return to her rooms.

In her company, talk is restrained. She can see it on the faces of La Hire, Dunois, even the Dauphin. They want to discuss—what else?—women, the gossip at court, which always means who is sleeping with whom, but they can't, not in front of her. So, she excuses herself. Back in her rooms, she ignores the table of offerings. There is a long list of nobility to pray for: So-and-so has gout; another lord believes he is dying from heartbreak. She shakes off her doublet, her shirt of silk, and puts on a clean tunic of white linen. She can sleep in anything. In the days when they traveled to Orléans from Blois, she slept on the ground in armor. When she rose, her limbs clanged with the sound of steel.

A servant emerges like a shadow detaching itself from the wall and creeps up to her with a message. The note is from Yolande. She is about to call for Jean, since she cannot read, but when she opens it, there are no words. Trust Yolande to think of everything.

The window Joan stands next to is edged in moonlight. On the page, like a child's scribble, is a drawing of a crown. It is Yolande's way of saying to her, "This is your next mission: to crown a king."

IV

◆ ◆ ◆

WHEN SHE VISITS YOLANDE, someone else is already with her. As Joan enters, she spots the princess from stories come to life. Here to the last detail is the straw-colored hair and the gown of silver brocade, the small waist, the arms destined to enfold the shoulders of a king. You aren't just my uncle's invention, Joan thinks. You really exist.

But the princess is no longer a princess. She is, or should be, the Queen of France. She is Marie, eldest daughter of her many-titled mother and wife to the Dauphin. She lifts her green-flecked eyes to look up at her guest and relaxes her rosebud mouth into a smile at the sight of the blue jewel on Joan's finger, worn so prominently. It is a smile that could melt steel.

The Dauphine balances a large book with pictures on her lap. At her feet, there is the rustle of cloth: movement. A small child dressed in a salmon-colored gown stares up at Joan.

"My daughter," the Dauphine says by way of introduction. "Her name is Radegonde."

Joan isn't certain how one should greet an infant princess, so she bows. The child opens and closes her mouth, continues staring.

Yolande rises from her chair. She waves a hand at Joan, and her own beringed fingers catch the light.

"How much you have changed! The last time we met—I did not wish to hurt your feelings—you looked like a sad minstrel who had been kicked out of a feast with your lute strings snapped and your lute bowl broken. Oh, that tunic was filthy. And you smelled, too. But now it is all silks. No more coarse wool for you! And you smell, well, you smell like you are one of us!" She chuckles, reaching out a thumb to feel the lining of Joan's green overtunic.

"It is from His Grace the Duke of Orléans," Joan says. "He commissioned a tailor and sent the material."

Yolande bobs a nod of approval. "If a servant came upon you from behind, he would kneel and say, 'My lord,' and realize his mistake only when you turned around. You could pass for . . . Well, I suppose some things are better left unsaid." Yolande steps back to survey her, tapping her chin. "It seems you cannot help winning these days. I heard the number of English dead at Patay was no less than two thousand! A fine number. Is that not a goodly number, Marie?"

"Would it were more," the Dauphine says simply, as she sets aside her book and picks up her daughter to join them. "Were it six thousand English dead. That would please us very much."

Yolande chortles. "See, that is my daughter. Do not be deceived by her sweet looks. Only one side of her heart is soft as a feather pillow. The other is sharper than any dagger. She is also marvelous with an account book. Give her any ledger, from any business in the kingdom, and she will make sense of it. Is that not true?"

The Dauphine smiles. It is true.

"You are the new favorite of His Majesty," Yolande says to Joan, who glances at the Dauphine. How will she respond to this? But the Dauphine's face does not change. Her expression is as serene as it is inscrutable. "You can do no wrong. The whole of the kingdom is beholden to you. Did you know, the Italians are already writing about you? A miraculous shepherdess they call you! Oh, don't look so horrified. I know you did not handle sheep in Domrémy. It is only because they know you are from a small village, and when people imagine villages, I suppose they think of woolly creatures." Yolande shrugs, as if to say, *What difference does it make?* "There are some who have heard so many different accounts of you that they have written to me for clarification. And from dear John of Castile, who just months ago thought Charles's best chances were to leave France behind for good, I quote from his letter: 'It looks as if you can stay put in your lovely castle in Chinon, and when you move again, it may be back to the Louvre, in Paris. We all wish God could send angels to preserve our thrones.' It is certainly something to wonder at: how many friends France has now that things are going well! From Charles's lips, I hear only, 'Joan, my miraculous Joan!' You are all he talks about these days. And is it any wonder? We had forgotten how sweet victory tastes that now we are all drunk on this wine."

A pause: to clear her throat, to take a sip from a jeweled cup. "Yet there is more work to be done. Reims," Yolande says, as if proposing a new stitching for embroidery. There is no chance to interrupt her. "Charles was never crowned there, and he needs to be made king. Officially. In the cathedral of that city and anointed with the holy oil, for how can one be king and not be anointed? And Marie must be made queen. My daughter has already given France a fine son and heir, as well as a little princess. Marie must be made queen. Officially."

"His Majesty did not come to Orléans," Joan says. "Why would you believe he will risk his life to travel an even greater distance to Reims in order to be crowned?"

"Oh, but he will listen to you." The Dauphine's voice takes them both by surprise, like hearing birds break into song in the branches over one's head. It is airy and musical. She shifts her child's weight in her arms and dips her nose to breathe in her daughter's hair. "I am not thinking of myself, you understand, but of my children. I want France restored by the time my son is named king. *He* will not go without. I shall have no one, no prince or duke of England or any other place, laugh at my children and question their titles. My son shall learn from his father's mistakes."

"Marie, let Joan hold Radegonde," Yolande says.

"Are you good with children?" the Dauphine asks Joan.

"Of course she is. Joan is good at everything."

But the Dauphine does not move. Only when Joan nods and smiles does she pass the child slowly, carefully, into her arms. At face level, the princess touches Joan's chin. She gapes, her tiny mouth open.

"Look, even your daughter cannot believe there are no whiskers," Yolande says, chuckling.

The women walk her out. As she is about to leave, she feels a hand settle on her arm, holding her back.

"It cannot be helped," Yolande says. "For a coronation, one needs the body of a king to be present. He cannot be there only in spirit, as at Orléans.

"You have replaced even La Trémoille in my son's affections, something I never thought would be possible," she continues. "But he won't go quietly, none of Charles's favorites do, and some of the bloodiest wars are fought not in the field but in the court. So, guard yourself. Watch what you say, your every gesture and action. Watch your thoughts. When you think a room is empty, know you are never alone. Against every door or wall an ear may be pressed, listening carefully for your first mistake. Trust no one. It is not always possible to see your enemy running at you from a distance, for at court we are masters of sleight of hand. Here, it is all shadows and cunning, a few poisonous words dripped into an open ear. La Trémoille's dislike of you is well known. He has made his position clear, but I would give you this advice: Do not trust even his friend who holds high office. It is, I hope, unnecessary to be explicit as to this person's identity."

Joan nods. The Archbishop of Reims. "I am not interested in court politics," she replies, "and as long as my lord La Trémoille does not get in my way on the battlefield, I shall have no reason to call him my enemy."

"What a simple view of war you have, child," Yolande says. She clasps her hands. "It is not just 'us' and 'them.' You do not comprehend how war is governed by bloodlines, which reach back hundreds of years; how a marriage arranged over a single supper may spare five thousand lives. A single gift, a jeweled book or a prized gelding, may stay the hand of an enraged prince bent on vengeance over some petty grudge. You do not know, as I do, how sometimes the birth of a healthy prince is celebrated on one side of the sea, only to be grieved on the opposite shore. The scales are changing every moment, every hour."

"I know who my friends are," Joan says.

Yolande bends her head. She considers a moment before speaking. "Yes, you have your supporters at court. And these supporters—I include myself among them—will remain your friends and allies, but in one kind of weather only: when the climate is good, the sun shines with your victories, and the gentle breeze blows through the fields and valleys of France. We will remain your most loyal friends for as long as you continue to win."

"And you shall win. You are the best at what you do," the Dauphine says. Her tone is final. She has taken Radegonde back in her arms. "Next time you kill an Englishman, Joan, I want you to think of me. Think of my son, who will one day take his father's place and wear his father's crown. Think of my daughter, whom you have held in your arms."

A pause. Not hesitation but to sanctify the moment. Then: "I will."

◆

Le Maçon takes her to a room she has never been to before. The chamber is large, with several desks and chairs such as scribes might sit at to copy out their manuscripts. At present, the desks and chairs are empty, all the quills and inkwells tucked away. Against the walls, she sees shelves built from a dark-colored wood. Each shelf, le Maçon informs her, contains nearly fifty books, so there are almost one hundred and fifty volumes in this room alone. He shows her how each book is chained in place, an iron ring fixed to the cover's front edge. Because she can't read, he tells her what some of the books are: French poems by Christine de Pizan, chronicles by the Roman historian Livy, including the *Ab Urbe Condita Libri*, and a personal Bible that once belonged to the Dauphin's grandfather, a gift from His Holiness, the Pope.

She is shy of these volumes. At first, she touches only the chains attached to the books, as if she were inspecting pieces of jewelry. "Which one interests you most?" he asks. "Because to hold a book, even to open it, is an experience in itself. If I showed you a beautiful tapestry, such as the ones that hang in your rooms, wouldn't you want to run your fingers up and down the cloth? Wouldn't you marvel at the level of detail, the head of a deer peeping out over a hedge, each hound's tooth perfectly threaded? It is no different with books. They are works of art."

She hesitates, so he chooses for her. He produces a key and unlocks the Bible, and she offers her hands to receive the volume as she did Radegonde. It is large and heavy as an anvil of iron. Like a supplicant, she carries the book to a desk and opens it. The frontispiece, a sky of stars, greets her. The sky is the blue of crushed lapis lazuli. The stars are gold leaf.

Le Maçon tells her it was another Charles, the Dauphin's grandfather, who built a library in a tower that had once housed falcons in the Louvre in Paris. Those who forget what he did for the war say it is his greatest legacy. The library contained nearly a thousand manuscripts, including the works of Aristotle, his *Ethics, Politics,* and *Economics.* Saint Louis's Bible was housed in that same library and the French translations of the work of the Italian scholar Giovanni Boccaccio and *Le Roman de la Rose.* Across the tower's three floors, there were books on every subject one could think of, all impeccably ordered and categorized. The significance of this library wasn't only the number of manuscripts it contained; it was that it featured so many works in French, not Latin or Greek. The King had ordered these translations and tasked the finest scholars in the realm with executing them.

But that library is no more, he says. We can no longer call it ours.

"The English have burned it?" Joan asks. But he shakes his head. It was sold to John, Duke of Bedford. The contents of that library now rest in Rouen, capital of Normandy, deep in English territory. The Duke of Bedford bought it for a price that would be disgraceful to tell, and it will be years before we see another collection of its kind, if ever again, in this kingdom.

They are silent. She closes the Bible and gives it to le Maçon, who chains the book to its place on the shelf tenderly, like a father putting a child to bed. His face is hidden from her, but she knows without having to look that he is crying. She wants to rest a hand on his arm, to say to him in a soft voice, "When the war is over, perhaps we can get the library back, too." But what consolation would that be?

"The Dauphin will be made king," she says instead. "Between Chinon and Reims, there are many towns and cities. We will retake them with His Majesty's army." With *my* army.

"And after?"

"Paris." The word drops out of her mouth, almost without thinking. Take back the capital; take the whole kingdom.

In the fields that day in Domrémy, she thinks, I made a bargain with my God. The rich food I eat, the sweets and spices now so familiar to me, have not made these names any less bitter on my tongue. John, Duke of Bedford, regent of England. Philip, Duke of Burgundy. Henry, sixth of his name, future King of England. These are my enemies and the Dauphin's enemies. The journey to Reims will only bring us closer.

I, Joan, am coming for you.

◆

THE HOUR IS NONES, and the Dauphin is in his garden with La Trémoille and the Archbishop. He says to his friends, having just plucked a fresh bloom, "I will go to the chapel now and pray."

But when the doors open for him, his hand flies to his mouth, and the flower drifts like a feather to the ground. He jumps back and nearly collides with La Trémoille's protruding stomach. In the narrow space of the chapel, he sees row upon row of his subjects kneeling, a great assembly of the nobility, the captains of the army. Dunois is beside La Hire, who is kneeling next to le Maçon. In the first row, the Dauphin spots his cousin the Duke of Alençon, and next to him, at the head of all these faces, wearing a cloak of purple pinned with a jeweled brooch, is Joan.

At his arrival, three others emerge from a side entrance: Yolande, the Dauphine holding their daughter, followed by their son.

There is no time for either La Trémoille or the Archbishop to ask what is happening. A flash of Yolande's eyes and a scowl from the infant princess silence them. Joan rises. She does not speak as she passes an object into the Dauphin's hand.

He looks down. A gift? His Majesty enjoys surprises. But it is something he has forgotten about in the happy weeks since Patay. In his palm is the enameled figurine of his father. Only there is a small difference. Someone has made for the late king a miniature crown of gold painted with brightly colored jewels; the detail is so fine it must have been done with a brush of a single hair.

The Dauphin looks from Joan to the kneeling nobility, his courtiers and friends, who since her victory at Patay have all at one point or another applied for an audience with her. They have sent her gifts of wine, platters of swan and salmon, treasured spices. They have removed rings from their own fingers, taken pouches of gold from their chests and presented them to her as offerings. They have heard her speak, and they call themselves her followers.

It is said the war began with a scene not so different from this one. In the English court, Edward, third of his name, was conflicted about the decision to fight for the French crown. He was a man easily angered but also rational. He knew the cost of starting a war, both in lives and money. And he knew France's strength, its long history of greatness on the battlefield. None could match its cavalry, the force and crush of its mounted attacks. But at his own table a heckler and troublemaker named Robert d'Artois served him a plate of heron meat, a bird symbolizing cowardice, and this gesture so mortified him that he agreed to go to war. The year was 1337, ninety-two years ago, and it is the same war we are fighting today.

But here are no hecklers. Joan says, "We entreat Your Majesty to listen to those who love you. It is time for the rightful king of France to receive his crown."

He scans the lines of the assembly and watches as the Dauphine approaches with Louis, a round-faced boy rubbing his jutting nose with a pink fist. A nursemaid carries Radegonde, who is not looking at her father but staring at Joan. They stand only a small distance away.

From behind, Yolande raises her voice: "I am not kneeling, Charles. I haven't brought a cushion with me, and my feet are already sore from waiting so long for you."

Joan thinks of the day they spent in the garden. In the shade, she saw the Dauphin's face change, passing between shadow and sunlight as the wind stirred the leaves. And it is changing now, first pale, then pink with embarrassment. But slowly the color drains from his face. His eyes settle on Joan, and she doesn't look away. They are of the same height. The corner of His Majesty's mouth twitches.

"To Reims then," he says. His voice is quiet as he addresses her. "God Himself paved the road that brought you to Chinon and to me. Now I understand, in the way only those who look back on the past can discern with clarity the pattern of events, their sequence and true meaning. Our paths moved together as parallel lines across the void of our despair. Like lost children, we traveled many miles off the road that leads out of the dark woods. But God sees all. And He sees you, Joan, with His great and depthless eye, His divine and perfect vision, which no one, not even the angels of heaven, shares. At the hour your king and France most needed you, His wisdom brought us together."

Here is another moment. As Joan turns to follow the Dauphin, the rows of courtiers are still kneeling. There is a moment—brief and fleeting—when it feels as if they are kneeling to her.

V

◆ ◆ ◆

In the weeks leading up to their departure from Chinon, a story spreads through the court. It begins, as many stories do, in the kitchens. A boy runs an errand. He sees for the first time the Dauphin. Oh, His Majesty was dressed very fine, the boy announces, feeling his own importance, and describes what he saw to his master. The days being hot, he wore a light doublet in bright yellow and matching hose.

"What was His Majesty doing?" his master asks him.

"Rallying his men, readying his army" is the boy's reply.

The boy is forgiven for dallying on his errand. He makes a full report of what he witnessed: His Majesty spoke with soldiers of high and low rank. He slapped the backs of his men, eating and praying with them. While a great crowd watched, his royal hands made up a poultice for a lowly foot soldier, wounded at Patay, whose shoulder keeps him awake at night with pain. He behaved with no airs, which took everyone by surprise.

Where the boy leaves off, the story is picked up by another servant's report. By two o'clock, His Majesty had convened a meeting of some thirty or forty soldiers and asked them for ideas about what could be improved. These men shared with the Dauphin their grievances: they are never paid on time; the food is bad, the meat rancid and vegetables scarce; they are expected to march on empty stomachs; there is no organization, and they do not always respect those in charge because their superiors are cruel, incompetent, or both. Three clerks accompanied the Dauphin to take detailed notes on the conditions of equipment, everything from the halberds and cannonballs to the sturdiness of the carts carrying them, and the Dauphin himself checked all the barrels and the wheels, crouching low to the ground when the moment called for an inspection. His royal hand picked up a crossbolt and he said to the masses trailing him, as he felt the sharpened tip, "This will soon find an Englishman's heart," and the crowds cheered in his wake.

But something is wrong with this report. The Dauphin has been in his rooms all day. His personal servants, who have also heard the story and are rarely absent from his side, laugh behind their hands. His Majesty? Walking among his own army? Are you mad or still drunk from yesterday's wine?

From one ear to another, a story flies so that identities become confused. Woman becomes man, a peasant body becomes a prince. It is an amusing story, a joke. Some misunderstandings are so ridiculous, so inconceivable, they become funny, le Maçon explains to Joan when she returns with her clerks, their arms full of notes. He chuckles as she brushes dust off the front of her yellow doublet. But she sees he is also uneasy. If such a story manages to reach the ears of the Dauphin, which he doesn't doubt it will, will His Majesty laugh, too? Perhaps he should be there to mitigate any damage? Le Maçon leaves Joan's side. He suddenly looks worried.

Though it hasn't been a year since she left home, her past already feels a lifetime ago. In this enchanted place, lords and their servants nod to her. The more reverent sweep off their hats. Noblewomen and their ladies-in-waiting step quickly to catch a glimpse, towering hennins wobbling on their plucked and hairless foreheads. She has no titles. She is technically still no one. Yet they are too shy to look her in the face. They believe she is something more than human.

While she practices shooting, her clerks read her letters aloud. They compile lists of her expenses, which are carefully reviewed before being passed on to her benefactors. The costs of her household are divided chiefly between Yolande and le Maçon, though it is not uncommon for those who have pledged themselves as her supporters and sent her gifts to also receive a bill, compliments of the Duchess of Anjou. In a separate note, Yolande explains to Joan's most ardent followers: Think of it as an investment, high-risk but with the potential for enormous return. When France is liberated, the men of England will slink back to their island kingdom, physically and financially crippled by the war. And then I will remember your kindness in this difficult time. I will put a good word into the ear of His Majesty, who is, as you already know, the most openhanded king in Christendom.

Joan's clerks have taught her how to properly hold a pen, and she is learning how to read and write. In a sheaf of papers bound together with string, she has written and rewritten her name and the names and titles of the Dauphin and Dauphine. The clerks gently point out her errors. They praise her steady progress and patiently watch as, tongue curled over her upper lip, she copies new words. "Soon you will be able to compose poetry," they tell her, smiling. She is as diligent with a stylus and tablet as with a sword.

Each day, hundreds arrive in Chinon to join the army, though no efforts are made to find these men. One no longer has to knock on doors to locate men who wish to be called soldiers. They have heard of the miracles performed at Orléans and during the Loire campaign. Now the story is *five* thousand English, not two thousand, were killed at Patay. They call their journey a pilgrimage, and they have come not to pay their respects to the Holy Virgin but to offer their services to the virgin warrior of France.

Joan visits the new recruits: the blacksmiths, the glaziers, the carpenters, the butchers, the weavers, the cobblers, and the grocers who have left their positions or closed up their businesses to fight behind her. She asks them their names and sits with them. She gives them the choice to turn back, for once they have set off for Reims she does not want them to desert. "You are skilled men," she tells them, "and soldiering is hard business." It isn't rare for even a strong man to faint from exhaustion on the battlefield. She has seen it happen. She shows these new recruits her sword, which, she explains, is not the actual sword of Charles Martel, just a copy. Why should she deceive them? She tells them the story of the Battle of Tours, which the Prince of the Franks led against the Saracen army, and they listen as she explains how it is not always numbers that matter but the mettle of one's spirit and, of course, good strategy. "My father said"—and every time she makes this speech, which is now at least two times a day, she can't believe she is repeating anything that has come out of the mouth of Jacques d'Arc—"that though we shouldn't compare ourselves with those of true greatness, like the Prince of the Franks, Charlemagne, or Saint Louis, it is possible we are walking on the same patch of the kingdom as they did hundreds of years before us. This kingdom called France." And these men nod. They look to each other; they think, There is some sense in this. None of them wish to become subjects of an English king, and she tells them to be proud of their land, that God loves the humblest among them more than any English pretender to the throne, that He is ashamed of the power-hungry Duke of Burgundy, however full his coffers are with gold.

She doesn't forget the soldiers who have already served, those men who have been with her since Orléans. She asks Jean to make arrangements for her to have daily meals with them, so that she is always on their minds and they know how she honors them. Though she is dressed in the silks of a nobleman, in doublet and hose, it is important they see her eating heartily from a bowl of pottage and sharing pieces of salted herring, spitting out the bones as roughly as they do. She is godmother to several of these men's newborn children, and small gifts of money are disbursed in her name. They are a different group every day, but she addresses each man by name and remembers his occupation. She remembers, too, the names of their wives and children and where they are from. Her memory, the men inform her, is wonderful. After the meal, she takes off her doublet and passes it to a boy to hold, though his palms are caked with dirt, while she helps to load a cart. She gives out gambesons and has the sappers try them on, along with kettle helms. She doles out knives, though first she tests them against her thumb, and if the blade is dull, there is no time like the present for sharpening it against a whetstone. Giant baskets are brought from the Dauphin's own orchards and apples distributed. The fruit, Joan says, is His Majesty's gift to any man who will raise a sword for his true king.

She tells them, reaching to clasp a dyer's blue-stained hand, "You are the heart of the French army. Do not let anyone say otherwise. If any person belittles you or treats you badly, you must take down his name and make a report and tell me directly who has shamed you. I won't abide cruelty, not among our own."

Another day's work done, she returns to her rooms. It is nearly the hour for supper: time to wash and change. In the half hour before food is served, she gives Jean commissions to execute. She has had a vision. And no, not a vision where an angel has appeared in order to whisper prophecies into her ear. She has seen no white light, not the archangel Michael, with his flaming sword, or the Holy Virgin. But a vision has come to her of a new and victorious France.

She tells him: We need better maps, so find the mapmakers. How does it serve us if we don't know what our own kingdom looks like? Also, scout out among the artillerymen and siege engineers those who are skilled at blowing things up and knocking them down. If you want new ideas, you have only to look. Talent isn't rare in this kingdom, and ability can be found in the most unexpected places. Is she herself not proof of this? Her squire is already halfway out the door, but she calls him back. Also, will you make an appointment for me to meet with the royal treasurer? She wants to know what everything costs, how quickly armorers can work, the price of a gambeson, a mule, a barrel of arrows, a shirt of mail, a helmet, a cut of beef, the value of this season's grain. And she wants lists made. She wants to know the name of every sergeant-at-arms and understand who is in charge of what, which carts hold the Dauphin's portable ovens, his wardrobe, which bear the pole-axes and the pavises, the large wooden boards crossbowmen take shelter behind as they are reloading their weapons, and which wagons carry the barrels of salted fish and meat. Oh, and the royal treasurer, whoever he is, can come here to me.

She eats supper with her guests and her guests' guests. To accommodate the growing number, two tables must be pushed together. Trenchers are set out for the usual personages: Dunois, La Hire, le Maçon, and, very often, the Dauphin will wander from his own better-stocked table and arrive around the hour of supper like a vagrant following the scent of fresh bread. The only two noblemen who never visit are La Trémoille and the Archbishop of Reims.

At Joan's table, the talk is always business. If the Dauphin does not come, discussion revolves around supplies and methods for raising funds. She will share new ideas and stories the soldiers have told her: accounts of mistreatment among the ranks, of going hungry.

"I would like changes to be made," she says.

"What changes?" La Hire asks, his mouth full.

It isn't holiness she is concerned with but what will sustain an army moving across hundreds of miles, what will keep a soldier's instincts sharp and his mind on the alert when he enters the fray. A blacksmith wouldn't light a fire while drunk, so why should a soldier stumble on his feet after a night's revelry on the morning of battle? "I want to ban gambling. I want to ban prostitutes and drunkenness. And I want every man properly equipped. No more men showing up with billhooks and cleaving knives from their local blacksmith. I want them to know why they are here, what their mission is. Reports issued out with regularity, no one kept in the dark, every man valued. I want more confessors, priests to say Mass to the soldiers, absolving them of their sins and listening to them. It will help with morale, believe me. These men need an audience, a sympathetic ear. They have suffered so much already. They want to talk. If I had my way, every other town of France would have an armory and, with it, a garrison." *I want*, *I want*, *I want* . . .

"And where will you find the money for all this, little maid?" he asks.

She looks at Dunois, at the members of the nobility around the table. Some are newcomers. She thinks of Yolande and her chests of jewelry. How much does a diamond brooch fetch, she wonders. "You?" she suggests.

But if the Dauphin comes, then talk shifts to His Majesty's day, how it was spent, how he slept, his digestion, whether good or bad. Is he in a fine mood or is he in despair (again)? For if the latter, then he must be consoled—which, depending on how the discussion goes, may take hours. Sometimes, His Majesty will arrive with a servant who brings his lute, and the Dauphin will play a song. La Hire or Dunois will sing.

The Dauphin may invite Joan to go hunting with him, but she always declines. Her reply: "I have come to the aid of Your Majesty to kill the beast called the English, not the stag or the boar."

Before she goes to sleep, Joan will remember the hill on which she and her sister once stood, the beauty of autumn spread below them like a tapestry. "You have stayed here too long," Catherine said, "and I know you stay because of me."

Across the room, she hears the sound of a door opening, and a servant stepping quietly to remove the basin of used rose water she had washed her hands and face in.

Whole days now pass when she thinks of neither her sister nor her uncle, and ideas grow in her mind like fruit on a ripe vine. Her eyes are full of the future: what is possible, what she must do by tomorrow, or in a week. Her memory stores lists of items that must be checked and rechecked. She imagines herself at the head of a long chain, a chain where she is the originator of thoughts and her clerks, her squire, le Maçon, those in her inner circle, make up the links. The space she occupies is one bustling with life, with change—and, she believes, change for the better. There is no room anymore for the dead.

◆

SHE HAS DRIFTED into a light sleep when the rustle of fabric makes her ear twitch. A servant? But the hour is late, and all the servants have already gone to bed. So, her eyes open. The room is too dark even for shadows. As she lies on her side, her back to the door, she can smell, and she can listen. And she knows she is not alone.

On the bed, her body remains still, but the hand beneath her pillow slides slowly from one end to the other, to the handle of the weapon she keeps concealed. It is the knife Dunois gifted her, and her fingers touch the jeweled hilt. They graze the head of the wriggling snake with glowing carbuncle eyes.

She inhales deeply. She smells . . . food. Ale, meat, and, she thinks, a faint scent of sour cheese, drifting closer. Beneath her left eye, a small pulse has begun to beat. She counts each tiny throb. The smell, like an approaching dish of leftovers, grows stronger.

A strand of hair falls over her ear. Her neck tenses. She holds her breath to listen, to gauge distance, position, and movement. She catches another rustle of fabric, this time mere inches away, directly behind her head.

Her body rolls. A blur of motion. She hears the tearing of fabric—the coverlet of her bed, as a weapon is plunged into its center. She hears a scream, though the cry doesn't come from her throat. Her hand, the knife clutched in it, has slashed upward; its tip has drawn blood, and she feels warm droplets spatter across her bare wrist. A weapon is dropped, and the sound is like a bell, echoing through the whole chamber. In the dark, her own breathing fills her ears, and her eyes catch dim movement. Panicked footsteps stumble toward her door, which is flung open, and the blue glow of an open window falls on the figure's hand. Bloody knuckles. The gleam of a gold signet ring worn on the little finger. The body is large and cloaked, the head concealed beneath a drooping hood. But in an instant, it is over, and her assailant is gone.

She doesn't need to call for help. Two servants have already come running. Her squire is on their heels, followed by her pages. Candles are lit. A hand offers her a cup of warm mulled wine.

She looks down at her bed. Where she had been asleep, there is a long gash in the satin coverlet. In the place of blood, a spray of goose feathers.

Jean picks up the weapon, and his mouth tightens as he passes it to her. "A misericorde," he says, though he does not need to name the blade. She has used the weapon herself. It is a dagger crafted long and thin to pierce the breathing holes of helmets, to slip through the cracks of armor and finish a knight who is already wounded and dying.

What had Yolande said? "It is not always possible to see your enemy running at you from a distance, for at court we are masters of sleight of hand. Here, it is all shadows and cunning." Her heart is beating so fast, she wonders the others in the room can't hear it. Or maybe they can, but they do not want to shame her.

It is the eve of their departure for Reims.

⬥

JOAN'S PRAYERS ARE LESS APPEALS to God than updates on the latest news. "Someone tried to kill me last night. I think it was one of La Trémoille's men," she says, kneeling in the chapel. "Luckily, I am a light sleeper.

"Do not worry," she tells God. "I can look after myself."

God is silent, which she interprets as agreement.

She tells Him, These are my concerns: I am worried about bad weather, which will slow down the journey to Reims and take up supplies, for the army is much bigger than we can sustain. I am worried about the towns we must pass through, some of which are English, others Burgundian. If they fail to open their gates to us, then we will have to settle in for a siege, and sieges take both time and resources. I am worried about money. No, not money for myself, she clarifies, but money to pay for everything I want done, money to pay the soldiers, to keep their spirits up. You know what unpaid soldiers do? she asks God, as if He doesn't know. They turn on their own people. It's not just English and Burgundians setting fire to French villages. It's discontented men, masterless men from any kingdom, including France. I'm worried that with the first cold supper, the first pang of stomachache, His Majesty will complain and wish he hadn't come. And sometimes I am worried that my worries are beginning to sound like a courtier's worries, like le Maçon's.

Behind her, she hears a small movement, another rustle of fabric. She rises quickly. When she turns, she finds herself face-to-face with a pale visage, long and narrow. A pair of lightless eyes blink at her. It is the Archbishop of Reims.

He seems to take no notice of her reaction, only nods, moves closer to her. "We have seen each other before on several occasions, but never spoken," he says. "I will join you this morning in prayer. It is an important day."

"I prefer to pray alone."

Briefly, two spots of red enter his cheeks before draining away. "You are a difficult person to find," he says with a shrug. "I tried three different places before I found you here, in the Dauphin's private chapel." He counts them off on his beringed fingers. She notes his hands: smooth and unscarred. So, the Archbishop does not go creeping around in bedrooms at night, trying to murder people, though perhaps he simply asks others to make his prayers come true. "Your rooms. The stables. The dog kennel."

"There is some advantage, I think, in being difficult to find," she says.

Their eyes meet. He exhales a small sigh. "I suppose you are right." His voice is bored, as if she has simply stated a fact.

"What were you praying for just now?" he asks.

"That is between God and myself."

"Ah, if that were true, I should soon find myself out of a job."

He smiles and walks past her, nearer to the altar. "My position does not deceive me as to the nature of men . . . and women," he says. "Praying . . . is just wanting, isn't it? We both know this. And what do men want but the usual things? Power. Money. Love. To be freed from illness. To be excused from death. To ascend to heaven without actually dying." He laughs. It is a crackling laugh, like a heel stepping on the delicate shell of a snail. "We always want something from God. Even if it is something noble. Scholars desire enlightenment, poets a better turn of phrase, physicians a cure for plague. I confess I am prone to the same greed. In my heart, I have many hopes. I pray every day for the Dauphin's good health, my own good health, and *your* good health, too. I hope the English will disappear in a giant puff of smoke, and they will send large chests of money to make restitution for all the evils they have inflicted upon us. In a way, we live nearly every moment in prayer. The laundry maid, who is just waking this very hour—you can probably imagine her very well, perhaps you have been one in the past?—hurries down a flight of stairs and hopes she will not trip and break her neck in her haste. The housewife slicing vegetables for her husband's dinner resolves to keep the knife in her hand steady, so she won't cut off a finger. Before we drink from any cup, we live, for a moment, in the expectation that what we are about to imbibe will nourish and give pleasure, not poison us and make us fall ill and die."

"Your Excellency is able to conjure such lovely images," she says. She does not smile.

"Oh, but a prayer tells so much about a man. So much may be learned: his strengths, his failings. A tradesman who cheats his customers and abuses his workers may still be a loving father to his children and a faithful husband to his wife. He may found a chantry in honor of his mother. It would surprise you, the conflicting natures of men's hearts. Vanity with tenderness. Ambition and arrogance with openhandedness and charity. Since you first arrived at Chinon, I have watched you carefully. And I have wondered, since that morning I saw you peering down at the rest of us with le Maçon, what it is you want: in here." He points to his heart. "Power? Money?" He hesitates, tries again: "His Majesty's love?"

If this conversation were with La Hire or Jean, she would pull a face: stick her tongue out and make choking noises. For a moment, they stare at each other, but this is a contest he will lose. He looks away, tilts his head. He brings his hands together as if to pray. "Ah, but of course," he says. "I forget you are God's appointed. A holy warrior. A chaste maid. A tried and tested virgin. That is why they call you *La Pucelle*. 'Death by Eve, life by Mary.' Isn't that one of the extracts the Duchess of Anjou dug up for you before you went to Orléans? So, I suppose not love then. No man in the world is able to tempt you. But what of power? And what of the money that usually accompanies power? What of gold and precious stones?"

"I will tell you, though I do not expect someone like you to understand," she says. "In truth, I pray for purpose. When you are no one, as I am, and beholden to nobody, you can only be yourself."

"And how easily you have stepped into your divine role."

"Well, if those in divine office cannot please . . ."

She has struck a nerve. He shudders, collects himself. "I heard a story about you once," he says. "Perhaps you will be so kind as to confirm whether or not it is true, so that my curiosity may be satisfied. I heard you were singled out by the holy woman Colette of Corbie when you were a child and that she tried to bless you with her own hands but you ran away. Yet before you made your escape, she managed to slip you a medal, which you later sold to the Duke of Lorraine, in exchange for a pretty bauble: a ring."

She shows him her left hand and points to her third finger. "This one."

"So, it is true then. You rejected a blessing from a woman as near to a saint as any we possess in this world, to feed your own vanity."

She grunts. "You were not there. I saw no holy woman, only a woman half-starved with bloodied feet because she refused to wear shoes. We don't need saints like that, not anymore. Saints who scourge and wear hair shirts, who believe that the will of God is only to punish, that His mercy and love are granted solely by the doling out of pain: who suffers most is blessed, who suffers least must live in sin. This is not God punishing us. It is just men punishing each other. What is there to learn from such lessons?"

"But I suppose we need you?" he says. He is still unruffled. "I suppose you believe . . . France needs you?"

She is silent.

"Do you think there can be two of God's appointed in one kingdom? By this, I do not refer to you and the holy woman Colette. But you and the Dauphin. A king is also chosen by God, or did you not know?"

Joan stares at him.

"It isn't a trick question," he says. "I am curious as to what you think."

"The Dauphin and I understand each other. We are friends."

He opens his mouth, as if to let the word slip fully into it before chewing. He seems to taste it, to roll it around on his tongue, as one would a new and surprising wine. "Friends," he repeats. "Well, it must be so. His Majesty has raised you so high. And why not, the court asks itself? It has never been done before, but neither have the miracles you have performed and which we have witnessed. And there is still more joy awaiting us in Reims. You must get us there, and I must anoint the Dauphin with the oil of the Holy Ampulla, which has anointed nearly all His Majesty's great forefathers."

"I will get us there, if Your Excellency does not drop the bottle."

She has already begun to walk away when his voice reaches her. "Oh, I would not think there is any danger of *that*. Though I may be an old man to you, my hand is steady enough. But I will have to be a little careful. If I anoint the wrong person, well, that would be an unforgivable mistake."

She turns. She does not even have to speak for him to know they are now even.

"Unless my sources have been lying," he says, "it would not be the first time you were mistaken for the Dauphin. I thought, when I initially heard the story, His Majesty outside loading carts? Opening barrels? Testing crossbows? It does not sound like him. No, not His Majesty. Not this young man."

"An easy enough mistake, since I put on a man's clothes," she replies. "And I am the same height. That is all. There are many who have never had the honor of seeing the Dauphin before."

"Another thing," he continues. "Does His Majesty know that you are learning to read and write? That you have made a book and filled it with your name written beside the Dauphin's name and titles? Now, why would you do that? It is a natural question. Why would you, Joan, write your name beside His Majesty's?"

She looks away. She doesn't answer.

"And does the Dauphin, your good friend, know that le Maçon was seen taking you to his private library, where you opened a Bible belonging to his royal grandfather, a gift of His Holiness, the Pope? By the way, I wonder where that book of yours is now. I hope you have not mislaid it. You should be careful. Some would find such stories about you . . . concerning."

He doesn't wait for her reply. Instead, he paces. "So, God's appointed is learning to read and write. And one day, she may even be able to understand Aristotle. She may master Latin and Greek, and what world will we wake up to, do you think, when she is able to quote the philosophers and poets as readily as she can fire a crossbow or draw a knife? For she is already by reputation the greatest warrior in Christendom. She is famous in every duchy, ditch, and fox hole of Europe. Soon she will have the might of both the sword and the pen on her side. And though it is inconceivable, though it should be impossible, an abomination, she is also a natural leader of men. So, I ask you, Joan, what world will France wake up to when you have everything and everyone lined up under your giant thumb?"

A better one, she doesn't say. She turns her back to him. She walks away, but the door to the chapel flies open. La Trémoille steps through, flanked by two men.

"Ah, Georges," the Archbishop says. "I was just discussing the coronation of the Dauphin with our friend."

La Trémoille sighs. "A ceremony seven years delayed," he says, addressing the air somewhere far above her head.

As he waddles past, ignoring her, she catches the eye—hard and angry—of one of his followers, and her gaze drops to his hand. It is bandaged. Through layers of white linen, she spots the first flush of blood: an innocent pink bloom.

Part Four

The journey to Reims takes approximately nineteen days, from late June to mid-July 1429. Having heard of the feats Joan performed at Orléans, many towns surrender and open their gates to the Dauphin without resistance. However, the city of Troyes refuses to capitulate, and the French army is forced to halt its progress and settle in for a siege. This is potentially disastrous, as supplies are quickly running out. Soon the men will starve.

Some may call it luck. Others a miracle. But well before Joan's arrival, a friar had predicted to the people of the city that the end times were nigh and encouraged them to plant beans in order to prepare. These same beans ripen in time for this siege and end up feeding the French army. After only four days, Troyes surrenders.

The rest of the journey goes smoothly. On 16 July 1429, two towns not far from Reims, Châlons and Sept-Saulx, open their gates, and the same day, the Dauphin safely reaches his destination.

Around this time, the leaders of France's enemies, the Duke of Bedford and the Duke of Burgundy, meet in Paris to further cement their alliance.

I

◆ ◆ ◆

REIMS, 16 JULY 1429
THE DAY BEFORE THE CORONATION

"What is France?" le Maçon asks. He stands in the great cathedral of Reims. He spreads his arms, permitting himself a rare moment of indulgence, and Joan, too, breathes in the scent of stone. She closes her eyes, wants to take a nap. In this vast space, they are alone. "It is a fertile land, its vine blessed, its wine sweet."

This is the seat of the Most Christian King. Therefore, its people are the best people, its knights the most gallant, its poets the most inspired.

And our language is the best language, for it turns the cogs of the civilized world. A merchant may be Dutch, Portuguese, or Italian, but he will always conduct his business in French. When the Venetian explorer Marco Polo shared the accounts of his travels with his friend Rustichello da Pisa, it was in French that he spoke of the grandeur of China and its capital, Peking, of the magnificence of the court of Kublai Khan. Our language is the language of song, of the chansons de geste. Our greatest troubadour, Arnault Daniel, no less a master of his craft than Dante.

How could life be the same without the entremet, a dish made up of no particular set of ingredients. It can take any form; its purpose is simply to dazzle and to please. Only we possess the ingenuity to redress a cooked peacock in its former strutting splendor, to carve Grecian maids and nymphs bearing urns from roasted capons, to build a miniature palace out of the carcasses of game, each tower and courtyard sprinkled with a snowfall of saffron.

France is its famous warriors: Roland, Charles Martel, Bertrand du

Guesclin. You. On this nineteen-day journey, how many towns opened their gates and surrendered as soon as the people heard your name? They knew any show of resistance would be fruitless. In your hands, only victory is possible.

And France is its rulers. The kingdom is not an island unto itself, like the sad, miserable home of our ancient enemy, its weather so poor that its people must sail to other shores for better climes. France is made up of fiefs, some of which have grown accustomed to independence and self-rule. But the best kings are able to tame these proud lords, and in our history, we have had no shortage of great leaders of men.

Le Maçon stops. The Dauphin has just entered the cathedral, followed closely by the Archbishop of Reims and La Trémoille. Joan looks up, to the vaulted ceilings. One can't start a brawl in this place. And as this is the Archbishop's see, she supposes she can't kick him back out.

"Watch your step, Majesty," La Trémoille says, offering his hand. "There is a stair just here, easy to miss."

The Dauphin's face is shiny with tears and disbelief. He sniffs, accepts the hand, and sighs, nodding, as she and le Maçon bow in his direction. He passes on.

"Our king is a feeling king," Joan says.

"Yes."

They have been in Reims only a day, but tomorrow the coronation will take place. Though the city is theirs again, who knows what might still happen? The English may already be on the road to attack, so preparations are underway. The Dauphine has remained behind; the journey was considered too dangerous. For now, the Dauphin alone will be crowned.

"It is an emotional moment for His Majesty," she says. But also, he has not stopped complaining since they left Chinon. He had nearly wept when the portable ovens he brought stopped working and his suppers were served to him cold. Though now he is tired, like a child who has had his fill of tears and exhausted himself.

"That is only natural," le Maçon replies. "It has been a long journey." In more ways than one, he means.

They are silent. Some things would be better forgotten, but it is hard to shut out the Dauphin's crumpled face struggling to master itself over a plate of lukewarm mutton. She had been tempted to show him how to eat the dish. She had fought the urge to spoon-feed His Majesty a bowl of mashed beans when food was running low and he had fallen to his knees to pray. She had nearly said out loud to him, her own stomach gurgling with hunger, "Christ, that won't help. Please, just eat the beans!"

Before the gates of towns, shouts went up at her arrival. Joan heard them from afar. "The Maid of Orléans!" the guards called. "She is here with her army!" Not long after, the gates opened. Everywhere she goes, a wall of sound follows. Arms reach to touch her horse. Fathers lift their children so their small hands can graze her armored body, and so she can bless their round heads with her giant metal palm.

◆

As soon as she leaves the cathedral, she is caught in a thunderstorm. It is one of those storms where the sun is shining but the rain is beating down as if the heavens have opened up and the saints are bawling their eyes out from above. The crowds that have gathered outside to catch sight of her run for cover, but she looks around at this new world, transformed in a mere blink into one of water and sunlight and mist, steam rising from the flagstones at her feet. She reaches out to catch rainwater in her palms and laughs at the empty streets. It is good sometimes to be alone, and overhead, a deep-throated chuckle of thunder booms across the sky in answer. As she walks on, water slips into her collar and across the ridged scar at the base of her neck, which is still sore on days of bad weather, a pulse beating where the arrow pierced her.

She ducks into a church, a small space of clean stone, to dry herself off. At the altar, several women have gathered. They notice her at the same moment she sees them, and a cry goes up when they recognize who she is. She hears them whisper. They fold into a tighter huddle, until one of the women detaches herself from the group and approaches.

The woman is old. She has been crying; her eyes are pink, but she also smiles at Joan.

"We know who you are," she says. "Since you are here, will you do us a favor and bless my grandchild by holding her? She was born just two days ago."

Joan follows the woman to the altar. Now that she has come closer, the family resemblance is clear. Here are aunts, sisters, cousins, and, in their center, the mother with her newborn swaddled in linen. The mother does not move, but her child is taken from her and passed carefully down a chain of hands until it reaches the arms of the grandmother, who turns to Joan and offers the bundle.

Joan takes the child. As she looks down, her heart seizes. The child is dead.

At her elbow, the grandmother explains: "She died suddenly, though she was born healthy and strong. But her breathing stopped, and nothing we did could save her. Also . . ." She bows her head. "My granddaughter died unbaptized, so we are afraid for her soul. The priest has told us there are no exceptions. God will not welcome her. Her soul will never enter Paradise."

Joan holds the child to her chest. The body is still soft and pink and light in her arms, as if all the weight were in the linen alone. It has always amazed her how something so small can hold so much power. She cannot bear to look away.

She thinks, If tragedy had not visited Catherine, I would have spent my years living with her and her husband and looking after her many sons and daughters. I would never have set foot in any of the cities of France. I wouldn't be here.

Her hand passes over the child's face, the mouth frozen in a delicate pout. She strokes the tufts of fine spider-thread hair.

"It is no accident that brought you here today," the grandmother says. "We have heard of you, as the world has heard of you. You are a worker of miracles. And we wonder, now that you have seen her, my grandchild, can you make an appeal on our behalf for God's mercy? Can you tell us where she is? If she is in pain or in a dark place, all alone?"

Why, Joan wonders, is the human imagination so morbid? Her fingers touch the linen. She smooths a wrinkle in the cloth.

No one talks about this: how a girl is born into the world, knowing nothing of its evils or what dangers lie in wait for her as she grows. When she is young, she is taught to keep still, to hold her tongue, to be good. She is chided if her voice is too loud, if she is too forward with her opinions. If she swings her legs under the table at dinner, or is found daydreaming instead of working hard at her chores, her mother and godmothers will take her by the arm and shake her. "Wake up!" they will say. "Wake up, recite your prayers, and work hard. Obey!" Yet her body is free. She delights in beauty; she skips down hills and runs through open fields. When she is older, she learns practical tasks: the patching of tunics, the baking of bread, the tending of gardens. She is taught the various uses of the sheep she is sometimes called upon to watch. She laughs easily, makes friends, enjoys good company, says her prayers, and into her prayers, she whispers the secret wishes of her heart. In the hours of her deep and untroubled sleep, she dreams of love, of her unformed destiny. Yet nothing in her upbringing prepares her for the world as it is. Nothing trains her for sudden death, war, hunger, the burning of homes, the pillaging of towns. She does not know until disaster strikes how ill-equipped she is to face danger; the watching of sheep won't help her now. If she has never felt pain, then she can't understand the desire others have to inflict it upon her, how her body, its very shape, form, and beauty, is a target for enemies she has never met and cannot name or even describe. It isn't every girl who has a father like Jacques d'Arc to acquaint her early on with violence and with pain. By the time Joan was ten, her skin was tough as leather. In a better world, she thinks, you wouldn't need a Jacques d'Arc. But we don't live in a better world. At least, not yet.

"She isn't in a dark place," Joan says to the grandmother. "When one dies, the moment of death is very brief. One instantly wakes again, as if roused from a light sleep, and the soul is transported between heartbeats to another world. This child will find herself in a meadow, a place unlike any other. On every wildflower, a butterfly. In every tree, a songbird. The sun never shines too bright, for the hands of the angels moderate its rays, and from their mouths, they blow cooling breezes so the climate is eternally spring. It is a place God reserves for only His most loved, the innocent souls He has called back to Him. In this place, she is no longer an infant but fully grown, yet none will ever covet her beauty or seek to tempt and destroy her. She will never want for anything, but it will be given, before she can even anticipate her desire. She will not feel hunger or pain; her heavenly body will move across the space of this great meadow and spin through orchards resplendent with fruit, of a kind we are unable to cultivate in this world, much less taste. But all the boughs of heaven's gardens will hang heavy for her, and she will drink from the streams of Paradise, whose water is as pure as it is sweet."

"Yet she will be alone," one of the women says, "without those who love her as much as we do."

"She will have better company than she could ever find in this world," Joan replies. "The saints themselves will visit her, and she will walk in the footsteps of Margaret of Antioch and Catherine of Alexandria. The angels will play their celestial music, so there is always heavenly song in her ears."

Some of the women are weeping as she returns the child and turns to leave. The grandmother catches her hand and presses it to her mouth to kiss one of her rings.

"Then you have seen heaven?" she asks.

Joan hesitates only a moment before answering. "Yes, I have seen it."

She doesn't say, as she leaves the church, But it is only my version of heaven. The one I created for Catherine, my sister, to console myself in my grief.

She pushes open the doors. Outside, the storm has cleared, and the sun is strong again, the air rain-scented.

Someone must have seen her enter the church and spread the word, because as soon as she steps out, a huge crowd greets her. They think she has just come from prayer, so they doff their hats; they bow. The children offer her bunches of flowers, drooping from the earlier downpour, water dripping from each stem.

She gathers the flowers in her hands, careful not to drop a single one. She walks on.

◆

THAT EVENING, she receives a summons from le Maçon. Most of his servants are familiar to her, but the boy who has come to fetch her, flushed and out of breath, is new.

Those in the Dauphin's private party, of which she is one, are staying in the Palace of Tau, the home of the Archbishop of Reims before he was displaced from his see. This is where the coronation feast will take place, a pleasant walk from the cathedral next door.

At the boy's request, Joan hesitates. She doesn't recognize him, and the memory of her last night in Chinon is still fresh. "Please," the boy begs. "I have just entered his service. If I fail to bring you back, my lord will dismiss me."

She relents, though not before slipping a dagger into her sleeve, and he leads the way. The corridor is lit only by the flickering torch carried in the boy's hand; a laughing orange shadow passes over the tapestries.

"Through here," the boy says, and he steps back to permit her to enter the room first. "My lord is waiting for you inside."

"Where is le Maçon?" She turns, but the door slams shut. A key clicks in the lock outside; she hears the boy run away.

She is alone and the room dark. Only a window is open, letting in the light from a fast-fading sunset. But an object catches her eye, a faint glimmer.

In the center of the room, someone has placed a pedestal. On the pedestal: a plush cushion of velvet. And on the cushion: a crown.

For a moment, Joan stops breathing. She takes a step, another step, and her vision fills with gold, a blue-red haze of sapphires and rubies, the brilliance of square-cut diamonds. She sees each point of the crown is shaped to form a fleur-de-lis, like stars that have been plucked from the night sky.

From her side, her hand floats upward. It reaches out to touch. The tips of her fingers, she notices, are trembling.

"Go ahead." A voice comes suddenly from behind. Her hand stiffens, just short of the crown. She doesn't need to think. A moment, and the hilt of her dagger is already in her palm.

"We will keep this a secret," the voice continues easily. "What is touching, after all? It means nothing."

The voice moves to her side, along with the giant bulk of La Trémoille. His eyes gleam at her.

"Go ahead," he says, raising his own satin sleeve. "Why don't you try it on? See how it fits? There is no need to be shy."

He picks up the crown, turns it over, and puts it down again. "I paid for this, you know." He pulls out a large purse, shaking it, so the room echoes with the jangling of coins. His fingers open the pouch, and he slips first one gold coin onto the cushion, then another. "Gold to buy gold, you could say. That is all a crown is. But a crown does not really make a king, does it? What is your opinion on the matter?"

"I was tricked into coming here," she says. "Kindly call your boy to let me leave."

"The door is locked."

"Doors can be broken down."

He scoffs. "I do not doubt it. You know what they say about rough persons and their manners. Those who are lowborn cannot be expected to change their ways. But in a short while, that boy who brought you here will return and open the door for both of us. So why waste your energy and ruin a perfectly good door, too? This is my friend's home. You are his honored guest and should behave like one."

"A gracious host usually does not wish to see his guest dead," she replies.

La Trémoille laughs. "Would you have met with me if I had been honest and asked to see you? Come now, Joan. Calm yourself. I promise I will make this conversation worth your time. We are alone here. We can speak freely. And are you not even a little curious? We know all about each other, yet somehow—well, I blame myself if we have never spoken at length, though you have nothing to be afraid of. If it should come to blows, who do you think would win between the two of us? I never carry any blade on my person, though I am sure you do." He glances down at her hands.

"*You* don't need to, my lord," she replies. "Others do it for you."

He chuckles and shrugs, as if to concede the point. "I was talking to my friend, our host, earlier today. He is one of the few people in the world I trust completely. I often confide in him. We were dining together, celebrating our safe arrival in Reims, and I said quite suddenly—I even surprised myself—'If I did not love the Dauphin so much, if I did not wholeheartedly support his reign, his royal bloodline, and consider him my dearest friend, I would think something was terribly wrong.' And the Archbishop failed to understand me at first. 'What do you mean, Georges?' he asked. 'What are you talking about? This is a time for celebration.' And I nodded. I was in earnest. I said, 'I agree wholeheartedly, yet how much of France's recent good fortune can be attributed to the Dauphin? Now come, Regnault, we must give credit where credit is due, no matter how lowly its source. Ask yourself these questions. Was His Majesty the one to free Orléans? No. Did His Majesty take any of the towns of the Loire Valley? Even one? Was he at Patay? No. Did His Majesty pick himself up and ride into Reims? Well, he is here now, but how he complained and howled when he realized a servant had forgotten to pack his favorite shirt!' And I leaned closer to Regnault, for you never know who is listening at doors. I whispered, 'We both know who is responsible for our sitting here, enjoying this excellent food and wine in your former palace. Now you have your see back, and I am glad for you. Truly. But it wasn't the Dauphin who returned these things to you, Regnault. No, it was quite another. Admit that this is so!' "

He holds up a hand to stop her from interrupting. "For those of us who have studied the past, we understand that these . . . these deviations . . . will occasionally happen. Dynasties move in cycles. Rulers change, particularly in times of uncertainty and turbulence. The son of a king will not always rise to the occasion. He will not always live to sit on the throne, even if it is his birthright. It is not uncommon, possibly it is even natural, for a dynasty to exhaust itself, even after only a handful of generations. And then a new age—a new world—must begin. So, I say this to you. I put it to you as . . . merely an idea. Perhaps we have reached that moment in time now. A new age with a new leader to guide us. A new appointed of God. What do you think? I ask only your opinion. We are simply exchanging ideas, you understand."

"I understand very well, and what you say is treason," she replies.

"Do you know the story of Childeric and his wife, Basina?" La Trémoille asks, ignoring her. "Childeric was the King of the Franks, father of the great Clovis. On his wedding night with Basina, they were awoken three times by sounds coming from outside the palace. Each time, Childeric told Basina what he saw. The first time—what a sight to behold! He reported only great creatures, beasts of strength: a lion and a unicorn. The second time, he heard howls. He crept to the window and saw a pack of wolves. The third and last time, he witnessed a scene that frightened him: wild dogs gnashing their teeth and salivating at the gate. Basina understood what her husband's visions meant. 'It is the degeneration of our dynasty,' she said. 'Each king will be weaker than the last until we are no more, and a fresh dynasty will begin anew.' These days, I often find myself thinking of this story, and I wonder. Where are we now? Are we past even the wild dogs? So, is it not time we brought in a lion? Well, Joan?"

She considers what he has said before replying with a story of her own: "There was a miller in Domrémy who cheated nearly every villager of what they were owed in flour. He had an ill look and a smooth tongue like yours. When he talked, he would utter such sweet nonsense that people would return home happy even if they went away with only half of what they were due. He was a fat man, this miller. Well fed. But I saw through him. When I brought him sacks of grain, I watched his every move. No trick he pulled went beyond my notice, and he would turn pale as soon as I showed my face. I think you should be careful, my lord. I think if you sing the wrong song into a lion's ear, there is every possibility you may lose something important to you."

An arm, a head. Your life.

La Trémoille's face tightens. He doesn't answer.

"I am ready to leave," she says, looking toward the door, "whether your boy comes or not."

"In some ways, it is a pity that your talents should count for so little. If only you were a cousin of the Dauphin, even the bastard son of a duke, there might be some hope. But for all your fancy dress, you are not one of us. You are a peasant. And you are a woman, which counts against you most of all."

He turns back to the cushion, and his fingers scoop up the two gold coins he had laid out. He drops them into the purse, refastens it, and throws the pouch at her feet.

"This is my offer. I will make it only once," he says. "Take the money. Leave court. With what is in that purse, any man, respectable or otherwise, will crawl on his knees and beg to call you his wife. Marry. Have children. Buy some land. Settle. I do not wish you ill. Only, I would be glad to see you far, far away and myself restored to the right hand of my good friend the Dauphin. I wish you every happiness as the wife of some prosperous farmer, some benevolent nobody, and in this role, I hope you bear many children and live a long, contented life. But stay, and you will not find me sitting patiently in your shadow. I will do everything in my power to remove you. Alive or dead, it does not matter much to me, as you already know."

Her hands tighten into fists, and for a moment, he looks less sure of himself. *Don't think I won't use them*, her expression says.

"I have heard that after the Dauphin is crowned, you intend to take Paris back from the English." He puts some distance between them, shuffling behind the pedestal. "Is that true?"

"Why? Will you join me in battle, my lord?"

"I can see it is true, even if you refuse to answer. Well, it pleases me to inform you that you will fail. I am in the middle of talks with my lord Burgundy, who is with the Duke of Bedford in Paris now. You are surprised only because you forget the Duke is still His Majesty's cousin. Burgundy has proposed a peace treaty, one I believe the Dauphin will accept."

This is the first time she has heard any talk of a treaty. "His Majesty will take Paris. You come too late with your empty peace treaties, La Trémoille. Accept the truth, however painful it is for your pride. You no longer hold the influence you once had over the Dauphin. You talk about a new age, a new world, and I agree with you. He is a new man. France's recent victories have emboldened him. He knows who in the court serves him best, and he finds those he formerly raised wanting."

"Would you like to make a wager?" he asks. "On Paris, that is?"

"I would hate to take your money from you." Actually, she thinks, I'd savor the opportunity. She looks down at the pouch of coins between them.

"That?" La Trémoille laughs, clutching his belly to keep it from shaking. "Oh, that is a paltry sum compared to what I would want, if I should win."

"What then?"

He stares at her. His voice is tempered, courteous even. "I know my own appetite, and I would not be content with anything less than your life, your head, your sword arm. And also, I want to see my rival le Maçon go down, banished forever from court, or worse. I want things to be as they were before he picked you, like a lost puppy, out of whatever hole he found you in."

"Then take my life. If you can."

Behind them, there is a knock at the door, the turn of a key in a lock. "You have tried once already and failed," she says. "I could smell your man from across the room. But let him make another attempt, and even if I should spare his life, he will have to live without his hands."

"Ah, that . . . that was a mistake." He frowns, and the expression seems genuine. "Stupid and, in truth, unnecessary. For I have since discovered, in the course of this journey to Reims, that I do not have to lift even my little finger in order to destroy you. If you were a fraud, it would take more effort. I would have to find some way to expose you, as we exposed those who came before you: the holy maid, the monk, the little boy. But you are no fraud. I confess I had not expected this. Here, come and listen. Come."

He leads her to the window, now dark. "Do you see those lights?

Those people in the streets?" he asks. "I had a servant inquire what they were doing. Do you hear them, Joan?"

"They are . . . singing," she says.

"Yes, good, Joan. Good. My servant said each man, woman, and child holds a small candle cupped in their hands. Like this." He imitates the gesture. "They are singing the 'Te Deum.' And when he asked a stranger why, was it in honor of the Dauphin who will be crowned tomorrow morning, the woman said no. Why should it be for him? What has he done to deserve our voices? It is for *her*, who will end this war and all its misery. They hoped that if you heard their singing, it would bring you out of your rooms and they could see you again."

Her eyes close, and she listens. "It is the sound of love. But how could I expect you to understand?"

La Trémoille brushes past her on his way out. "We will agree it is a sound."

◆

AT SUPPER, the Dauphin is quiet. He does not pick at the roasted capon on his plate but fingers a thread unraveling from his sleeve.

La Hire, breaking the silence, holds up a well-polished chicken leg. "One forgets that a man, too, is made of bones. Has your blade ever plunged into a body and gotten stuck? It takes more effort to pull it out again than it did to finish him in the first place."

"You must be doing it wrong," Dunois says. "I have never had such a problem.

"Perhaps Joan could give you a lesson one day," he adds.

She hides a smile.

They hear, from the head of the table, the scraping of a chair as it is pushed back. The Dauphin has risen to his feet. With his thin hands, he is rubbing his temples.

There is some awkward shuffling of boots and chairs, as the rest of the table stands with him.

"The chicken isn't to your liking, Majesty?" La Hire says.

"It is nothing. I am not hungry."

"I didn't ruin your appetite with talk of bodies and killing?" A slender bone juts from the corner of La Hire's mouth. He sucks on it. "This is much better than the beans we had at Troyes."

The color drains from the Dauphin's face. He narrows his eyes and aims his long Valois nose at La Hire, as if it were a knife. "You dare speak to me as if I have not also seen death and the horrors of war, as much as any of you standing here." From his right temple, a palm flies down, slamming the top of the table and making the trenchers flop. "Yes, just as much as any of you! And I have suffered more! Much more than you can ever imagine. When I was fifteen . . ."

He stops, folding into himself like a wilting flower. "Finish your suppers." He moves toward the door, but not before casting another glare at La Hire. "I must save my strength for tomorrow. Joan . . ." He tips his head. "Walk with me, and bring a torch with you."

"Oooh!" La Hire says in a whisper, grinning at her. "He loves you best, little maid."

She lights the Dauphin's way as they step into a courtyard, a square of clear night sky above them. His breath, still angry, rattles out of him.

"The weather will be fine tomorrow," she says, looking up. "For Your Majesty's coronation."

Beside her, the Dauphin exhales. "It has been a long journey." When she turns in his direction, he seems to have wilted further. He has covered his eyes with his hands. "All that I have had to endure to reach this point . . ."

She is almost tempted to say as a joke, Well, we shall remember to pack your favorite shirt on our next adventure. And perhaps there will be better portable ovens, too. Ones that won't break down.

"But tomorrow I will be king. And all that I have suffered before now, humiliation upon humiliation, like a long rope around my neck, will have been for this moment. My patience will receive at last its great reward. I shall be vindicated. No one will ever doubt again that I am my father's son and this my kingdom."

She has to catch herself. She wants to say, A kingdom isn't earned by the giving of a crown, by a ceremony held in a cathedral. Holy oil or no, Paris remains in the hands of our enemies, and now that we are so close, I want to see the Duke of Bedford's head detached from his body. And if he will not submit, Burgundy's, too. I want them made examples of. I want the child king of England to know my name and feel fear strike his heart at the sound of it, even as he grows and grows, so that no invader will ever set foot on this land again. There is still so much to do.

She wants to talk about the war. "The first time we spoke, Majesty, you asked if I had visions. I have since had a vision, and it is of France. The mounted knight no longer reigns supreme in battles. War is changing, and to save and preserve your throne, we must not only change with it but also stay a little ahead. My squire tells me he has heard of two brothers. Their names are Jean and Gaspard Bureau. They believe, as I do, in the untapped power of artillery, of cannonry and gunpowder. And what is more astonishing, Jean Bureau is not even a soldier by profession but a lawyer. So, you see, I am not unique. There is no scarcity of talent and resourcefulness in your kingdom, if only you seek it out."

She continues, "I have seen, in my mind, how a battle can be won, not with hundreds dead on both sides after four long hours or more of hard fighting, but in half the time. The English pride themselves on their mastery of the longbow, the Swiss on their skill with a pike. But we will be better than both. We will become experts at cannonry, at guns. For this, you need calm and disciplined men. Men who will keep their heads and know how to work together when they are attacked or doing the attacking. They must train to become accustomed to the sights and smells of battle. Do you know, in Orléans, I saw few such men. I have seen men falter and die where they stand."

"Cowards," the Dauphin says.

She shakes her head. "No, not cowards. They are good men: husbands, fathers, grandfathers, young men hoping to see a little more of the world than the narrow corner they were born into. But they are not soldiers. I envision a day when we can leave the chandler to his candle-making, the tailor to his cutting and sewing. And the farmer can remain on his land to tend the fields and bring in the harvest, for what good will it do, if whole villages and towns starve because the grain is ruined?"

She could talk for hours on this subject: the need for a standing army, how future victories in battle will be attained not through cavalry attacks but through artillery.

"The best days are yet to come," she says. "When we take Paris back."

A space has opened between them. A long pause.

She stares into the Dauphin's face, the light of the torch dancing over it, every eyelash and hair of his brow illuminated in the glow of the fire. The flame plays tricks. For a moment, his features blur, then grow vividly clear.

"But would that be your glory or mine, Joan?" he asks. His voice is cold as he meets her eye.

"It would be the glory of the kingdom," she replies calmly. "And therefore Your Majesty's glory."

The light shifts his expression, melting the hard edges. Slowly, he gives in. He hesitates only a moment before stepping closer. His hand settles over her wrist, and she feels the dampness of his palm.

"I see how I have come to rely not only on your sword but also your counsel. Tonight I shall leave you here. I need some time to be alone, to think on the future and to pray."

He turns. She hears his footsteps recede, though he is still talking. "I have decided. Tomorrow, you will stand on the dais with me when I am crowned, with your sword and banner. No one who attends my coronation shall say I am an ungenerous king who keeps all to himself. You have earned this honor."

She bows. Joy makes her heart beat fast. But when she looks up again, the Dauphin is already gone.

II

◆ ◆ ◆

A SLEEPLESS NIGHT. The Dauphin has been awake for hours, and Joan has remained at his side. At three o'clock, they attend a vigil. At nine, the ceremony of his coronation begins.

Certain items, normally requisite to the crowning of a king of France, are still missing. Among them: Joyeuse, the famed sword of Charlemagne, and his crown.

But these are only small obstacles. In the place of Joyeuse, another sword. And a new and shinier crown, courtesy of La Trémoille, has been presented as a worthy substitute for Charlemagne's. What matters is that the Holy Ampulla is here, intact, the miraculous vial dropped from a dove's beak into Saint Remigius's own hand. Some say this is the sacred oil that baptized Clovis, King of the Franks, and his three thousand followers nearly a millennia ago. It is a self-filling vessel; its contents have never had to be replenished by mortal means—so the story goes.

This day, Joan is outfitted as if for battle. She has other suits of armor—in total, four—but she is wearing her finest, the white-plated suit crafted by the Dauphin's personal armorer. None among her household has slept even an hour; her pages have wrung out their arms and hands polishing, but their efforts are far from wasted. On the blue-and-gold dais of the altar, her body glows. She wears, too, a new present from the Dauphin, one his household carried in secret from Chinon. A gift to be given only on the occasion of his coronation, it is a cloak of gold-and-crimson brocade. This morning, his own hands had swept the garment across her shoulders.

Among the nobility, she occupies the most honored space. Only the Archbishop stands beside her—and this because he is vital to the ceremony. No craning of the neck for her; no jostling of elbows and murmurs of "Pardon" for a good view. From here, she can see every detail, follow every step of the procession, and she watches the Dauphin approach. Except for the occasional shuffling of feet and clearing of throats, the cathedral is silent. All eyes are on the future king, dressed in a plain white shift. He seems to be counting his steps. There is, she perceives, a kind of doddering rhythm to his walk. When he reaches the foot of the altar, he lowers himself slowly and spreads his arms. He prostrates his body, until the Archbishop bends to raise him to his knees.

The Dauphin appears to be sweating; his skin shines with small, wet beads, glittering like crushed diamonds. A slight tremor has entered his hands, though his expression gives nothing away. It is as solid as the very stonework of the cathedral.

The sacred oil touches different parts of the royal body: head, hollow breast, bony shoulders, jutting elbows, thin wrists. A prayer is uttered.

During this sacred moment, she, too, closes her eyes. She thinks, This cathedral began as a rudimentary construction, a simple building, square and plain. But look at it today, and you would never consider it was anything but what it is now. This happened not in a day but over hundreds of years. A long line of archbishops added to the structure. A new façade here, some gilding there, certain parts demolished and other spaces opened. As with any worthwhile enterprise, there were setbacks: fires, which reduced most of the cathedral to rubble, and a disagreement between the officials and the people of Reims, which halted work, until the Pope himself was forced to intervene so that building could begin again.

All beautiful things take time. The masons of the cathedral understood this. In the nave, they built a labyrinth across a large section of the floor and put images of themselves wielding their tools in the four corners. The labyrinth is used by pilgrims, who follow the lines on their knees. The lesson: You must have faith the journey you started on was always the journey you were meant to take. Whatever has happened before, you must trust in the future.

Now Joan prays no longer for the Dauphin but for the King. A king, anointed by holy oil, is also made. He is born into the world a prince in title only. He must be molded by experience, by the instruction of tutors, by the wisdom of his elders and forebears. His royal person is added to over time, chipped away, added to again, until at the moment of his crowning, a ruler emerges from a prince, a man from the boy he was.

The King is dressed by the Archbishop in robes of blue trimmed with white fur. Once more he kneels. The crown is placed on his head. She sees it is a good fit.

As soon as crown touches head, the cathedral comes alive with roars of "*Noël!*" and "Long live the King!"

Joan holds her breath. The King has risen to his feet. He touches the sides of the crown. His head wobbles; the crown is heavy, and he has to grow used to its weight. But the sweat on his face has dried. His skin is now smooth as marble.

He turns in her direction. For a moment, all solemnity vanishes, and he smiles at her. He nods, and his eyes are bright with tears. She thinks, This king will be a gentle monarch, compassionate to his people, as wise as he is merciful. Where is the fifteen-year-old boy who fled from Paris eleven years ago, in fear for his life? The answer: he is gone. Pain is like this. You endure it, and if you live through it, eventually it becomes something else. Today, he has turned his fear into triumph.

The ceremony is over, and now the celebrations begin. Joan bows, melting away into the wall of nobility behind her. She hands her banner to Jean.

"Fresh air!" she yells into his ear over the noise. She is pushing her way through the crowd when she feels a hand on her armored shoulder. To her left, Dunois. To her right, La Hire. She waves at le Maçon, who is weeping into his sleeve. Let him enjoy this moment, she thinks, as Dunois nods toward the doors.

Together, they step out of the cathedral. Since dawn, the crowds have been gathering, singing hymns to God, to keep up the good weather. And they have been chanting her name in between songs to coax her to show herself.

When she appears, their screams are like a giant's fist, knocking the three of them back, so they must regain their balance. There are women tossing white petals, which slide over the plates of her shining armor.

A path strewn with flowers appears before them, and La Hire, though a part of her cannot believe it, is crying like a baby. "Are those tears, my friend?" Dunois asks, leaning forward to take a better look at him. But Joan laughs and blocks his view. She says, "Who wouldn't shed a few tears on such a morning? This is a day I do not think we will forget for as long as we live."

And she is right. In the space just ahead, there is an unexpected silence, an atmosphere of uncertainty. She sees a clearing ringed with guards, and from between the guards' shoulders, a head emerges, leering in her direction. It is someone she had never thought she would see again. She nearly groans aloud. Jacques d'Arc! What is he doing here?

She stops a short distance away, crosses her arms. They stare, each taking the enemy in from head to foot. No greeting. No shake of the hand, not even for show. She is first to speak. "What do you want?" Her words come out like a roar.

"Wasn't my idea," he spits back. It's as though she has never left home and they have simply picked up the thread of an argument where one of them last dropped it. "I was asked to come and given money to pay for travel and lodging. How could I have refused such an offer?"

"Oh, you could have refused," she says.

To her right, Dunois coughs. "To be fair, this was His Majesty's idea. A surprise. He thought your father would be proud of you."

"Why should I care about that?" She is suddenly petulant. She thinks, Any other gift would have been better than this. Even another holy relic.

"Are you going to introduce me to your friends?" Jacques looks at the men standing beside her, who gaze indifferently back at him. "They aren't your lovers, are they?"

At her shoulder, La Hire giggles. "No on both counts," she replies, nudging La Hire in the arm. "Well, we have seen each other," she says to Jacques, shoving past him. "You can go back to Domrémy now."

"What?" He is nearly spitting; his face is a mottled red. "Is this how you treat your father? Like a beggar seeking alms? Not even a meeting? I want to talk to you, you stu—"

"I can see the family resemblance," La Hire says pleasantly.

She turns. Perhaps they do need to speak, if only to say, We have nothing in common anymore, so next time fate brings us together, let's pass as two strangers on the road.

"Where are you staying?" Next to her, La Hire and Dunois flinch. This is how she shouts at her men on the field. Her voice is like a marching order.

"An inn."

"Which one?"

"The Striped Ass," he replies.

She blinks. It is hard to keep from laughing, and her companions don't try. Like drunkards, they bellow in the street, howling, and Joan follows them. She glances back only once. On his own, her father looks older. She could almost feel sorry for him, standing there alone and without any friends to make him bold, but she doesn't. When she visits him, *if* she visits him, she tells herself, it will take all her strength not to knock him down. From the crowds cheering after her, she thinks she hears, beneath the shouts, the sound of a single bark. Her eyes grow heavy. It is never easy—perhaps it is impossible—to forget the past.

◆

THE KING HAS TAKEN OFF HIS CROWN and put on a new outfit: white satin with gold trimming. And La Hire has gifted him a cloak, which has become His Majesty's new toy. The cloak is a deep, plush crimson and decorated with row upon row of tiny bells. When the King moves, he rings. And like a child, he is so amused by the sound that he walks with a jaunty air. *Ring, ring, ring.*

"How does Your Majesty feel?" she asks. She is curious. Does being anointed change a person?

He considers a moment before answering. They are outside, in a courtyard of the Archbishop's palace.

"Whole," he replies. "There are good days ahead. Your surprise, Joan. Were you pleased to see your father again?"

She can't even stop herself. She groans, as if someone has just stuck a knife in her and twisted the blade, and he laughs. "Can we send him back again, Majesty?" She is not really joking.

"This . . ." He touches the base of his neck to indicate where she was wounded at Orléans. "Does it still give you pain?"

She shakes her head. "I heal quickly."

"I have been thinking," he announces, as if this were something novel. He runs a hand along his sleeve, sewn with fleurs-de-lis. "As your friend, I deserve to be chastised. I have driven you too hard. In March, you arrived in Chinon, and we met for the first time. By May, you had raised the siege at Orléans. And now it is July. The summer is not yet over, and yet from Chinon to Reims, we have retaken all the towns in between. I feel you should rest, Joan."

"I am not tired."

Now that he is King, his smile seems to take on a new serenity. "That is because you are selfless. You think only of what more you can do to please me, but it is for your own good. I should not"—he searches for the right word—"use you so, as if you were a beast of burden, taking on more than you can carry because you wish to serve me well. You *have* served me well. And your plans, they are very fine plans, fine ideas, but, you know, one does not simply clap one's hands and make these things happen."

"Why not?" is her reply.

They stop walking. "All your ideas—improving our artillery, the two brothers you have found . . . What were their names again?"

"The Bureaus."

"One day they may yet prove useful to us, these brothers. But for now, we will spend some time here. This triumph should be celebrated, and then we will journey together back to Chinon in great splendor. You at my side. You will always remain at my side, Joan." He beams at her.

"What of Paris?"

His hands move to stroke his cloak. *Ring. Ring.* "Ah, Paris," he says, as if it were an afterthought. "There has been a development in that regard. My cousin Burgundy has promised to give up the city in fifteen days. Fifteen days, and the capital will be restored to us. Without any bloodshed. It is the best of outcomes, Joan. Better than any of us could have hoped."

For the space of a breath, she feels this must be some bad dream. She half-expects to see a winged horse descend or an imp dance on the King's shoulder. "And you believe him?" She can't help the edge in her voice, the incredulity as if His Majesty has just purchased at a fair a potion promising to make him beautiful. "You believe Burgundy will make good on his promise? I have heard the reports from le Maçon. Bedford is also in Paris, and he has more than two thousand archers and nearly three hundred men-at-arms. Does this sound to you like he will give up the city?"

There is a long silence. "Did Your Majesty not know?" she finally asks.

"For reasons that are beyond your understanding, I would like to make peace with my cousin Burgundy."

"The whole world knows your reasons. It is because of . . ." She hesitates. How does one say, diplomatically, Because you killed the Duke's father, who was your own father's cousin? And to this day, it remains a point of contention, whether or not you dealt the fatal blow as he lay bleeding and half-conscious at your feet. "But there are no favors granted in war. You cannot give way."

He stares at her. "Sometimes I think you forget your place."

"I have not forgotten my place. I have always remembered it, which is why I can only speak the truth. If we have come all the way to Reims and do not attempt to take Paris, if we give up this chance because we decide to believe, like innocent babes, the false promises of your sly and power-hungry cousin, then the world may laugh at us. They may laugh at you, and I would not be able to stop them. I would not stop them."

He turns a little away, does not quite look at her. "Tell me, do you love war so much that you refuse to accept peace even when it is offered? Would you kill innocents, men whose lives can be spared, simply to satisfy your love of victory?"

"Peace, like respect, like love, is won. I envision a day of peace for

France. But that is a day when we will no longer need to fight because all the kings of Europe will know that to try to defeat us would be to fail. Because we will have armories in every city and town of this kingdom. A standing army always ready to march. That is how we will secure peace, not through empty promises, not through false treaties that are a ploy to waste time while we grow content and idle."

She takes a step closer to him. She thinks, Doesn't the book of misery still bind us? All that we have suffered in our separate lives and that no one else understands . . .

But he does not meet her eye. He touches his collar, smoothing it. "I heard at Jargeau you were climbing a ladder when an Englishman took up a large rock and threw it at your head. Is it true? There are so many stories about you now, when I hear one, I hardly know what to believe."

"It is true."

"Then I would ask you to be careful. Life, like war, like what happens on a battlefield, can also be unpredictable. You would not wish to fall from a great height again."

The King looks up. A sound has caught his attention. He listens. There is the hum of insects. There is the rustle of a pleasant summer wind making the tiny bells of his cloak jangle. There is, amassed outside the gate of the Archbishop's palace, a group of no less than a hundred men and women, calling to her.

"It appears you are needed elsewhere . . ." He hesitates, frowning. He cannot bring himself to say her name.

◆

THE CORONATION FEAST takes place that night, but she isn't invited. The Archbishop's excuse: She is not a prince, a duke, a lord. She has no royal blood. And it is his palace, after all. His party. Can't he leave out who he likes?

"What does it matter?" She shrugs. "Now I can go to bed early."

"It is an insult," Jean says. His face is flushed red with anger. "Why does His Majesty not insist on your behalf? Why does he remain silent?"

She thinks back to their earlier conversation.

"The King and I may have had a small disagreement," she says, and the faces of her squire, her pages blanch.

"It is still a good day. The best day." She pets the heads of Raymond and Louis. "Neither the Archbishop nor his friend La Trémoille have any love for me, as you already know.

"But . . ." And she bends to speak on the same level as them. "We will have our own party tonight. Jean, go to the kitchens. The cooks and their assistants will be busy preparing for the feast, so no one will pay much attention as to who enters or leaves. And possibly they will not notice if a tray or two of pies go missing, some fresh fruit, a whole fish . . ."

Her pages watch as she pushes the central table against the wall. She lifts the chairs, stacking one on top of another.

"Now then . . ." She faces Raymond and Louis in the center of the room, transformed into an open space. "Show me what you have learned. And if you make me fall, I will give each of you a surprise. A present, and I promise it will be better than any tasty duckling or pig."

Her pages look at each other. She beckons. "Come. Do not hold back. Pretend I am an English giant and you are two brave knights on a quest for your king."

Their faces light up. They charge together, lunging at her ankles. Their fingers dig in, though it is like trying to claw your way into a mountain. Above their heads, she laughs.

"Are you tickling me or trying to fell me? Is this how I have taught you to fight? By tickling?"

They don't give up. If she has taught them anything, it is to persevere when the odds are against you, and she has just given them an idea. They release her ankles. They jump on her, one in front, the other behind. They tickle her arms, her neck, her sides, and tug gently at her short hair, so she crumples, giggling, to her knees.

When Jean returns, he finds the three of them lying side by side on the floor.

"What is this?" he asks. "Have the English or Burgundians been here while I was gone? Or my lord La Trémoille sent another man to cut your throat?"

"You were not really trying," Raymond complains. He sits up. "You wanted us to win."

"I do not think you would want me to try," she says mildly.

"It would be like snapping the necks of two very small birds," Louis says, and he shows them with his boyish hands what he means.

Servants from the kitchen are here. They carry in large platters and trays, which Jean directs them to set on the table, pushed back to the center of the room, along with the chairs.

"I have done better than steal a loaf of bread like a common thief," he says, puffing out his chest. "The head cook feels as I do. He is enraged you were not invited to the feast, so he has sent these up to you, with his compliments. The Archbishop will be wondering why his own table is so bare."

Her pages jump to their feet first. They run to smell the sauces, the steaming beef and duck and veal pies, the tray of stuffed mutton, and the platters of sugared wafers.

They eat hungrily, and she gives out the prizes she promised them, gifts she received before they set out for Reims. For Raymond, a silver brooch with a large purple stone. For Louis, a small knife in a jeweled sheath.

"What have they done to warrant these?" Jean asks. He looks at her, faintly hopeful, as if to say, *Do I get one, too, for bringing so much delicious food?*

"We were wrestling," she explains. "I said if they knocked me down, they would receive a prize. And they did."

Jean laughs. "Yes, and I would sooner believe His Majesty bested you than either of these children." He scoffs. "The Dau . . . I mean the King has one talent. He can eat and eat and eat and never add a sliver of flesh to his own person. The very opposite, of course, is true of my lord La Trémoille. Now, La Trémoille has only to look at a partridge, and before he has taken even a single bite, he will fatten himself up."

She covers her mouth, but laughter still escapes.

"His Majesty is like this . . ." Raymond arranges the small bones on his plate into the shape of a person. "Here, his legs, and these are his arms. It is all clothes that make him big. Like feathers on a chicken, but once you pluck the bird, it is . . ." He imitates the crowing of a rooster. "He does not have the figure of a king."

"Be quiet," she says, though her mouth twists. "Do not say such things."

"Let him talk," Jean says. "We are alone, and what he says is true enough. Lord strike me if I tell a lie, but I nearly broke into a sweat for His Majesty when he was making his way to the altar this morning. Everyone thought he would trip himself. You could see it on their faces. Our knees were shaking for him, and I am certain he, too, was shaking. Did you see anything? You were closest to him, Joan."

"No," she lies. "I noticed nothing."

Louis takes the bowl of sugared almonds and empties it. He reaches to place it upside down on her head.

"This is your crown," he says. "There. Now you, too, are a ruler of France."

"Ah, no, you have forgotten her mantle, Louis." Raymond runs into the next room; he returns with the bright blue coverlet from her bed. He drags it across the floor, and together, they sweep the cloth over her shoulders.

She stands, balancing the bowl on her head, and crosses the room. Her hand sweeps the coverlet. To make the others laugh, she gives it a little flourish. She thinks of the King's cloak of tiny bells, jangling sweet music. "How do I look?"

"Better," Jean says. "Much better!" He applauds.

Raymond dips his fingers into her cup. "Now kneel, and I, the horrible Archbishop, will anoint you with this foul-smelling oil nearly a thousand years old."

She obeys, smiling, while keeping a hand on the bowl to stop it from rolling off. He touches her forehead and cheeks with the wine, which drips down the sides of her nose and onto her lips. She sticks out a tongue to taste its sweetness. She laughs.

"And now what happens, Your Excellency?" She hears more giggling.

"Shall I get up?" she asks when there is no answer.

"And now, Raymond?" she repeats. "Am I made king yet?" She rubs away the wine, sticky on her palm and sliding down the bottom of her chin. She looks up.

But Raymond is gone. He is cowering in a corner of the room, trying to make himself invisible, and in the doorway, a new guest has arrived. It is the King, and he is alone.

The bowl crashes from her head. It shatters across the floor, and the sound flies, like arrows freshly loosed, straight to her heart.

She stands, and the coverlet falls from her shoulders in a heap. Now she knows what some men feel on the battlefield. They freeze, as she is frozen.

The King is holding a box, which he sets down carefully on the nearest table. The movement is quiet and his expression calm. He betrays no emotion, neither surprise nor disappointment. But as he turns to leave, she catches a flash of the eye, a flickering brightness. No one moves.

The room is silent, as they listen to his receding footsteps.

"What is in the box?" she asks. Her voice is strangled. She cannot take her eyes off the doorway, now dark and empty.

Jean passes it to her. "This is the King's gift," he says. "Only you should open it."

She feels along the edges of the wooden box, and her fingers find the clasp.

The scent floats up to her before she is able to look down. It is a warm fragrance, a fragrance now commonplace, though once it was exceptional. She shuts her eyes, afraid to look. When she opens them again, she sees the box is lined with golden-brown oublies, and each one bears the image of Saint Michael defeating the serpent Satan. The box comes with a note, written in the King's own hand. She passes the note to Jean, and he reads with a bowed head, the words heavy on his lips.

Do you remember our first meeting? See how far we have come, Joan.

III

◆ ◆ ◆

IN THE SHRINE of Saint Marcouf in Corbeny, the King sits in a large chair, elevated on a cushion. Here is another dais covered with cloth of gold and fleurs-de-lis. But at his feet, a boy no more than ten shivers from fever. Open lesions garland his neck, like red blooms. This is the disease known as scrofula, or the king's evil, which an anointed monarch can cure by royal touch alone.

It is not how she would treat a leaking, infected wound, but she has been invited this morning only to watch.

So, from behind two rows of courtiers, she stares, with le Maçon next to her. The Archbishop and La Trémoille are in front, and there are liveried servants keeping the line of those still waiting their turn quiet and humble.

The King takes his time. He places his hands carefully on the boy's shoulders and frowns with concentration. A moment, and he removes his hands. He nods. The boy rises, is ushered down from the dais by another servant, and the next in line pushed up as the King yawns.

She yawns, too, and le Maçon elbows her, glaring. She glares back. *What? I hardly slept last night.* Since dawn her mind has dwelled on . . . cannons, specifically a large cannon known as the bombard, which can fire a ball of stone weighing well over three hundred pounds into a wall. As a general rule, walls are built tall but not thick. So, she imagines rows and rows of these bombards replacing the wooden catapult and trebuchet outside the walls of Paris. Though the cathedral is silent, she hears an explosion; it is as sweet to her as the music of angels.

Her body may be in the cathedral, but her soul is floating elsewhere: on a field. On one side, thick woodland. She places archers there, hidden behind trees, tucked away in shadow. But the rest of the land is open. She sees lines and lines of cannonry, and an English army moving fast in the distance toward them. Timing is everything. You have to understand how far cannon-shot will travel. You have to account for fumbling hands, powder that is spilled and wasted, for a man's uneven breathing as he inserts a slow match into the hole of a hand culverin. How to cure men of shaky breath and shaky fingers? There is only one way. Practice.

On the way to Reims, she had spoken with artillerymen, who told her, There is an art to knowing how much gunpowder to pack in—too much can be disastrous—and to studying the land. Walls, fields, or a hill makes a difference, and the placement of artillery is vital. Her answer: "I think we can do better than men charging across a field and being slaughtered by arrows." She wonders why it has taken so long to change tactics. If you are singed once by fire, you know to avoid the flames. So, why has the lesson not been learned since Agincourt? She tells these men, "I believe the future of the army lies with you."

And there should be a better way to cast these cannons, so they don't explode and end up killing our own, which is still a common enough occurrence, both tragic and embarrassing. As a sauce can be made more piquant, gunpowder, too, can be improved, so let us adjust the amounts of saltpeter, charcoal, and sulfur until we find what works best. She is asking herself, Where is there a plain? Some arid land of no use to anyone where we can conduct trials, test newly cast cannons, and train artillerymen.

But before she can find out, she has to visit her father. She had sent a servant to check at the inn. She thought he might have left, but after the coronation he had remained. "Eating and drinking like a lord" was the report she received.

Le Maçon nudges her again. "Joan!" he hisses. "You are muttering to yourself!"

The King has finished. Now he sits back on the throne and bestows the royal touch upon his own forehead, as La Trémoille brings him a cup of spiced wine and a napkin. She watches him drain the cup, sigh, dab his lips. Healing is hard work.

"There were not many today," le Maçon whispers; he has to stand on his toes to reach her ear. "After a coronation, there are usually hundreds. And subjects from other places, like Italy, who come as if on pilgrimage."

"Perhaps the war has prevented them from coming," she says.

The King rises, and the rest of the court kneels. He extends a hand to the Archbishop, who helps him off the dais, and he descends one step at a time, always looking to see where his feet will land.

Outside the shrine, Joan gulps fresh air. She stretches her limbs and steps into a puddle of sunlight. She shakes her foot, which has fallen asleep, and yawns loudly, so that people's heads turn in her direction.

Le Maçon taps her shoulder. "Joan," he says. "Look."

In the distance, a servant is running up to the King. He falls to his knees and begins talking rapidly, but the report he makes is too far away for her to hear. Something, a small object, is passed from the servant's hand, first to the Archbishop, then to La Trémoille, and finally to the King.

She watches as the King stares at what he has been given, and he sways. There is a moment, shorter than the intake of a breath, when none of them can believe what is happening, when the willpower of the whole group, servants and courtiers alike, strives to keep a single man on his feet. But it isn't enough. His Majesty stumbles; his arms flail, in a strange and almost fluid motion, like a dancer. He falls.

It always surprises her how few people are able to keep their heads in a crisis. By the time Joan reaches the King, La Trémoille is fanning him with his thick hands. The Archbishop is praying; his mouth moves but his eyes are dazed. As if either of those will help, she thinks.

She shoves both men aside and lifts the King up, puts him over her shoulder like a sack of looted treasure. It makes people gasp. At her strength? Or at how light the King is in her arms?

"Can she do that?" someone says out loud. But she carries him all the way back to his room in the abbey, with le Maçon leading the way and courtiers following close behind. She sets him on his bed and calls for water to be brought—quickly!

"His Majesty has been too much in the sun," le Maçon says to the onlookers. "He has overtired himself."

On the bed, the King's hand stirs. He seems to know she is here. His fingers find her wrist, and something warm and solid is pressed into her palm. But when she tries to hold his hand, to comfort him, he shrinks away from her, like a cringing spider.

"What has His Majesty given you?" le Maçon asks.

She looks down. It is the second time a holy medal has been passed to her this way, slipped like a dark secret, a whisper between flesh. But footsteps interrupt them. A servant enters with a basin and a fresh towel. She gives the medal to le Maçon, who brings it closer to the window, into the light.

Joan pulls up her sleeves, dips the cloth in the water, and presses it to the King's forehead. His eyes flutter open, close again. His lips move without speaking. His hand floats to the space over his heart, and she recognizes the gesture. The pain is here, just here. This is what he wants to say to her.

For a time, they are alone. Le Maçon has left, and she hears whispering in the hall. When he returns, she knows to follow him. He takes her out of the hearing of the servants and the other courtiers. He shows her the medal again: a piece of cheap pewter with a hole bored through it, on a loop of fraying string.

"I don't understand," she says.

He is sweating and pale. He explains, slowly, that such medals are sometimes given out at the end of a pilgrimage, as proof the journey has been made. This morning, at precisely the time the King was in the abbey, hundreds of these medals were distributed. Not only in Corbeny but in Reims.

"Joan . . ." His voice is strained; he sounds as if he, too, is in danger of fainting. "There were thousands in the streets clamoring for these medals. So many the medals ran out, and now they are being sold for profit."

He looks like he is about to cry. "I will try to find out who commissioned these. But we can both guess. Who else would have the funds to pull off such a trick?"

Her thumb moves over the pewter, the profile and name crudely stamped. Now that she has had a closer look, the resemblance is clear enough.

Here is her face. Here is her name.

"We must convince the King this is not our work," she says. She, too, feels unsteady on her feet and needs to lean against the wall. "We will find out who ordered them and inform His Majesty."

There are times, like at Orléans and at Patay, when she feels she can control the outcome of any event, when it is as if a voice has whispered into her ear the future, and she is afraid of nothing. But what has just happened feels beyond her power. In her mind, she is keeping a tally of her enemies' hits. This isn't a fight where weapons can be seen, and only now does she realize she has been cut.

"It would be no use," le Maçon answers. "The damage is already done."

◆

HOURS LATER, she is summoned. The King, recovered from his fainting, shows her a book tied crudely together with string. A courtier, a good friend, had thought it wise, in light of recent events, to bring it to his attention.

"You have written your name next to mine," he says. "And, on some pages, *above* mine."

"Yes," she says. "I was practicing my letters."

"For the future?"

"For the purposes of practicing my letters," she answers.

He tosses another medal onto the table between them. "Explain this."

"I cannot explain," she replies. "Though perhaps Your Majesty should ask those in his company if they have any ideas. Their answer might surprise you."

"I do not need to ask. I have only to trust my own eyes and ears, what I have seen and heard since arriving in Reims. This medal alone, these pages. Either would be enough to condemn you. And we have not even discussed what is unspeakable, how when you were with your household, you made a mockery of my kingship, thinking I would not find out."

She looks down. She supposes the moment calls for her to kneel, that she should grovel and beg, but she doesn't want to. She is angry.

"I am guiltless," she says.

"These proofs do not support your innocence."

On the tip of her tongue, Then you are a fool to be so easily tricked.

She expects him to keep barking at her, like an angry dog, but the King sighs, slumping back in his chair. All his energy seems to have left him. "I do not want this, Joan."

Her reply: "Nor do I."

"This rift between us, it must be healed."

She bows. "I agree."

"Return with me to Chinon, and all will be forgotten. We have completed our mission, what we have set out to do."

A pause. "But I want Paris." Her voice is small for so great a demand.

"Paris! Paris!" The King stands, and because he stands quickly, the desk in front of him teeters on its legs. He is angry; his right hand shakes, and he has to press his palm against his robes to still the trembling.

"I am sick of hearing about Paris. It is as if you are deaf to everything I have told you. My cousin has promised to turn over the city. But I would not expect you, a commoner, a woman, to understand one nobleman's pledge to another. No, and why should you? You have grown up listening to the lowing of cows, the bleating of sheep. You do not know anything about statecraft."

She has to bite down to keep from talking. What difference does that make, she wonders. Your Majesty does not know a thing about war!

"I have raised and raised you," he continues. "I alone have elevated you to heights unheard of at court, defying tradition, and letting others laugh because I saw in you a worthy and true servant of God. You said my cousin Burgundy was hungry for power, yet how are you any different than him? You, too, have had a taste of power and find you want more. Your appetite for it will never be sated. I see now that La Trémoille was right."

"It is not power I want," she says. Her voice fills the room. "I have power. I have within me the power to end this war. So, let me. Why do you hold me back?"

The hour is Vespers. Outside, the crowd has begun to sing again—for her. Bad timing, she wants to tell them.

"I have overlooked your errors, your arrogance, and said nothing because I favored you." He trails off, as his gaze moves to the window. "But now you must choose. Will you feed your ambition? Will you pursue this quest for control, believing you can indulge your folly without my protection as your king? Or is my favor, the loyalty you owe to me as a subject, and what remains of our friendship more important to you than your love of war and bloodshed? You must choose, Joan. Choose between them"—he points out the window—"and me."

She only appears as if she is staring at the ground, head hung in defeat. But she doesn't tell the King, When the Archbishop placed a crown on your head, in that sacred space where strength and holiness collect, I received a crown, too, and this crown came from the invisible hands of angels. The light of God shone on me and was absorbed by my armor, and I felt such power surge through my body. I feel this energy wherever I go—in the cries of the men and women who reach out to touch me, who ask me to deliver them from the war. When I see you now, it is as if a cloth of very fine material has fallen away from a painting, and I find the picture is a little dull, a little frayed around the edges, in need of some restoration work. I see a king but I also see a man. I see that oil, however holy, however ancient, is just oil. I see a person of the same height—yet somehow smaller than before.

A helmet is also a kind of crown, and she will bestow on every soldier of France such a crown. She will make every solder a king of the plot of ground he must defend: the land beneath his feet.

And what would you, Your Majesty, do with a helmet-crown, she thinks. If you put on a helmet, a bascinet, would you be able to endure that confined and narrow space, as the world you are familiar with—the perfumed rooms, the warm halls filled with delicate music—collapses into darkness? Into stale air that soon turns into the smell of blood, either your own or someone else's? A suit of armor weighs no less than fifty pounds, and I would tell you that my own skin is as welded to my armor as if I were born with a covering of steel. Would your kingly body be able to bear such a weight? If we entered the crowded place of battle together, what would happen? In battle, you may find yourself in a ditch, a man wriggling at your feet like a worm that tosses and turns in earth, while another is screaming, dying with his body pressed against your back. Sometimes there is no space, so one has to make a space, to carve it out in order to keep alive. And it is the same rule with life. If there is no space for you, then you must create it. So, I ask myself, what is a king but a leader of men? And if he is not a leader of men, then is he still a king?

She wonders, too, At the end of this imaginary battle, would I find you standing? Or would you be sitting far, far away in your tent, wearing armor that is very polished and beautiful, and sipping a goblet of mulled wine? If we swapped clothes now, mine for your finer robes, would others know the difference?

The silence has stretched too long to be saved, and the King is staring at her as if he has guessed her thoughts. She opens her mouth, closes it. He does not try to stop her as she leaves. From the hall, she can still hear faint voices raised in song.

You must choose, Joan, he had said. Choose between them and me.

Her answer she keeps to herself. But if she had spoken, her reply would have been this: A throne, a crown is nothing without the people. There are those in the kingdom who possess so little, yet their lives are fuller than that of any nobleman or lady at court. These men and women labor the whole year long. They have never tasted the entremet or swan, but they will wrap a piece of cheese for you to take home and pour you a cup of fresh milk if you are thirsty. They will slip you a penny, money you did not ask for, if you patch a hole in their cottage or help weed their garden. They will break their bread and give you half, though it is winter and their own children have little enough to eat. Your throne, your crown would be empty without them. And as king, you are not only a servant of God, but a servant of them. If I choose them, I choose the kingdom, which includes Your Majesty. But if I choose you, I forsake them. I forsake myself. Everything I have set out to do.

◆

AT NIGHT, she visits the inn of the Striped Ass. She has put off seeing her father. What is the point? They will just argue. But curiosity gets the better of her. She makes the trip alone, dressed in her finest doublet, and carrying her sword. She isn't afraid of him, but a part of her still flinches when he opens the door, swinging it like he wants to break down the wall.

The first thing she does is throw a purse of money on the table, like a dagger at a target.

"This is what you came for," she says. Her reasoning: If they end up arguing, she wants it to be on her terms.

But he pretends not to see the purse. "You took your time coming here," he says.

"I'm a busy person," she replies.

"I can see that." He sucks something out from between his teeth and spits in the space between them. "Too good for us now. I suppose you tell people you grew out of the earth, like a tree, or came out of a stone or an egg, hatched from a bird. No mother, no father to speak of."

"I tell people about you."

He flushes, but he seems pleased. He stamps to the table and pours out two cups of ale. So, he had been expecting her to come.

"This is all they have. None of the fancy wine you must be used to." His hand picks up the purse. She watches as he turns his back to her, and she hears the light jangling of coins and a grunt, like a pig that has just been fed.

"How are my brothers?" she asks. "My mother?"

"What do you care?"

"Hauviette?" she asks, trying again.

"Unhappy marriage. Comes running back to the village a lot. Is about to give birth to her first brat. Won't be her last."

As far as she is concerned, the meeting is over. She sniffs the cup before draining it. She begins to leave, but he steps in her way.

"I have ordered up some supper. For the last three nights, thanks to you, I have been eating for two."

Supper with Jacques d'Arc? She could almost laugh, except she remembers scraping pottage off the floor with her hands, and she wonders if the hard edge of the bowl she swallowed out of fear is still somewhere inside her. "How sad for you," she says. If she were a child of ten, she would have gotten a slap in the mouth for that, but his eye falls on her sword and the knife at her waist. He looks across the expanse of her chest and shoulders, which, even under the fine silk of her doublet, are as solid as the limbs of a full-grown oak.

She has reached the door when a thought occurs to her. "Have you heard"—she doesn't know why she hesitates—"anything from my uncle?"

A second grunt, a shake of the head. "Nothing."

His voice pulls her back from the door. "You have always worshipped Durand Laxart, but he doesn't deserve your love. You have never been able to see that man as he is."

Same old Jacques d'Arc. She looks at him over her shoulder. "And you do?" she says.

"Your uncle was a coward."

She turns to face him. Before she has even taken a step, her finger is already in his chest, jabbing him backward. She does not need to speak. *Careful.*

"I never told you." His voice is quiet as he moves away from her. He rubs the sore spot on his chest. "The day when the English came to our village and Catherine . . ." He refills his cup, drinks it off. He takes a seat at the table. "Do you remember how Durand went to find her? He found her, not after, as he claimed, but just as she was taken. He was there. He saw all of it happen and did nothing. He confessed to me when she was already dead and buried and asked me to keep it a secret from you. 'What could I do?' he said. His whole body was shaking. 'Three against one. They were armed and would have killed me! Tortured me even!' I took him by the neck; I nearly strangled him with my bare hands. I spit straight into his eye and said, 'That is not the point. You watched it happen, and you did nothing! You call yourself a man? You are a disgrace!' He never returned to Domrémy again. And not long after he went away, you left, too."

She stares, but his face is smooth. "You are a liar," she says, though she feels cold. "I know you are lying, and you tell me this now when he is not here to defend himself."

"Why would I lie? When it concerns my own daughter?"

"Because you are jealous." The words come out hollow. "You have always been jealous of Durand. He is a free soul, a wanderer. He has seen everything. Done everything, while you strut around your sad corner of the world, pretending you are a lord."

It seems he is considering what she has just said. When he next speaks, his voice is thoughtful. "I was cruel to you. How could I deny this? I would have continued to beat you had you not grown too large for my fists. I had no love for you, though you were my child. But if any Englishman or Burgundian had tried to hurt you, I would have struck his head off. I would have chopped his liver under my heel and smashed his skull in."

Her heart is beating fast. For the second time, she turns to go, but he crosses the room, barring her path with his thick arm.

"Get out of my way before I make you regret it," she says.

He doesn't listen. He takes her wrist and drops the purse back into her hand. She expects it to be empty, but it isn't. There are coins inside.

"What does this mean?"

"You have given me too much. Do you want me to be robbed on the roads back to Domrémy? Well, knowing you, I suppose you might."

She weighs the purse.

"Half," he says, answering the question she doesn't ask. "Don't be a fool and give away all you have. You may be what you are now, but who can say what will happen tomorrow? Whether it will be for or against you. One minute, Fortune is blowing kisses into your ear. The next, she is pelting you with stones. Save your money, and don't think you know everything, because you don't."

He opens the door for her, and his hand flicks toward the hall. *Now you may get out.*

She had not intended to look at him before she left. But at the last moment, she turns. "Next time the King issues an invitation, don't bother. I never want to see you again." She drops the purse at his feet. "Keep it."

IV

◆ ◆ ◆

PARIS, SEPTEMBER 1429

Before Joan: the walls of Paris. Behind her: an army of three thousand.

After meeting her father, she was angry. Everything he'd said about Durand somehow fit. What she found endearing—his simpering nature, his ability to wriggle out of any difficulty, his tricks—these things now repulsed her. What she would never have believed possible: that if her father and her uncle were standing in front of her, it would be Durand she knocked against the wall and Jacques she left alone.

When she returned from the inn, she headed straight for le Maçon's rooms. She pushed past his servants. In front of the aged councillor, she fell to her knees.

"I need your help," she said, looking up.

He was alarmed.

"Appeal to the King for me," she said. "Tell His Majesty to give me an army to take Paris."

He shook his head. "You know I cannot do this, not even for you. It can't be done."

"It can. He trusts you."

She stayed on her knees until he gave in.

The next day, as she waited, restless and pacing in her rooms, le Maçon came to her. His face was gray; he looked ill. "The King will give you an army," he said.

She sighed with relief.

"Three thousand men."

For a moment, she forgot to breathe. "Three thousand men," she repeated slowly, "to take Paris."

"Or give up the enterprise," he said. "I have done all that I can. I asked for ten thousand men. The King smiled. Five hundred, he offered. It went back and forth like that until I dropped to my knees and begged. I reminded him of your victories at Orléans and in the Loire Valley. I said, 'Have we not seen with our own eyes the gates of Auxerre and Châlons open to us on our journey to Reims without a single life lost?' To this, His Majesty said, 'Then three thousand. No more, or I shall have to consider your place at court, too, le Maçon.' La Trémoille was with him. And the Archbishop. They never leave his side now. So, you understand, they watched me beg. And as I left, the King said, in my hearing, '*La Pucelle* must perform another miracle. Let us see if she can.' And they laughed."

She went to him, gripping his shoulder, as if to pass on courage. "We may be able to take a smaller gate at Paris with three thousand men. It is possible. Believe it."

"This is the most I can do for you. I can do no more than this, so, please, do not ask. You have put yourself in a dangerous place with the King."

She nods. "There is still much we can do with three thousand men. Have faith."

So, here they are, before Paris.

La Hire is here. He would not miss a fight, though Dunois has excused himself. He has said to her, regret in his voice, I cannot go against His Majesty's wishes. But a surprise: one of the King's own cousins, the Duke of Alençon, has joined her.

"My God," La Hire says when he hears Dunois will not come. "You know what this has turned into, Joan. It's not about taking back the capital anymore. It is about you and the King. Who is on whose side."

But all she feels is anger, and it is not even anger at His Majesty. Her meeting with Jacques is still fresh on her mind. Those who do nothing, who stand by and watch as chaos unravels, who feel that as long as they are alive and in good health, it does not matter what else is happening in front of them, why should they be innocent? They are guilty, too.

When she rallies her men, a pulse in her forehead throbs. The King would like everything both ways: his peace treaty with Burgundy kept intact, though if Joan can take Paris with an army of three thousand, then all the better for France's negotiations with her enemies.

It is the eighth of September, the feast day of the Nativity of the Virgin. One should not fight on holy days, but there are so many saints in Christendom.

"The walls of Paris may be tall, they may be well fortified," she tells her men. "But our strength is greater. Our courage is greater. And do not forget: I will be with you."

La Hire squeezes her arm, tugs her back. "These are bad odds," he says. "It is still not too late." She sees he has been rehearsing this speech in his head. "Your men, they will understand if you decide to give up the battle today, if you choose to fight another morning. None of them will think any less of you, I will make sure of it. And this may be a blessing. There will be other opportunities, perhaps ones more fortuitous than this. Other chances to take Paris, and with more men than what we have now when you regain the King's support." He stops to see if his words have had any effect. They haven't. "Friends are like this," he continues. "Good friends, the best of friends. Sometimes, they hate each other because of some perceived slight. And then they come together and wonder what it was they were fighting about. They return to a state of perfect amity and are able to laugh at past events."

But Joan shakes him off. She gives him a shove. "If you wish to leave, La Hire, I will not stop you. You remember Les Tourelles at Orléans. Dunois wanted to sound the retreat. It was already dark; the sun had set. If our men weren't wounded, they were fainting from exhaustion. But we held on, and that is what a battle is. Whoever holds on wins. Numbers don't matter. It is the spirit of the men who fight."

Energy pulses through her. Her sword is light in her hand.

"And not everything is about pleasing His Majesty," Joan adds.

Before she rides into battle, she thinks of her uncle. The walls of Paris loom ahead. He might be there now, cheating a widow, pretending to be a bricklayer or a muleteer. Still tricking his way through life.

Though for a moment, just a moment, her heart softens. Childhood still feels close, like a small person waiting in the next room. She does not have to think hard to remember the many times he held her, visited her in her corner to mutter soothing words into her hair while she rubbed her swollen mouth and picked at scabs. There are wounds in this world not inflicted by poleax or morning star—hurts that seep through the crevices of even the best-made armor and weaken the limbs, turning the bones as soft as water. Yet you must stay ahead of the pain. There will be opportunities enough after a battle is over to salve your cuts, to wonder at your bruises and cry. And if you cannot cry, if you cannot mourn, that can mean only one thing: you are dead.

Before her: the walls of Paris. Behind her: an army of three thousand. Her heart is full of rage.

So, let us go.

◆

The miracle is when a crossbolt rips through her thigh, she doesn't fall. She keeps moving. But slower and slower, until behind her is a long trail of blood and she is forced to kneel.

Her hand grips the bolt. She grits her teeth, pulls. From above, the archers see their chance; they take aim, their bows clustered together. They have only one target, and it is her. Though a distance separates them, she can almost hear the strain of bow strings being drawn taut, the smooth, expert release from chalked hands. It is a sound unlike any other: the broadhead tips cutting through air, the feathers slicing through a passing breeze.

A shadow approaches, just as the crossbolt is out of her leg and in her fist. She tries to stand, fails. Two shadows are racing to reach her. One from the sky: a dark blanket of arrows. The other belongs to a body, to solid arms outstretched, blocking her view of the sky and the sun, and waiting to receive the missiles already on their way down.

She hears the impact, one after another, in rapid succession, and a soft moan from above. The body staggers, wearing no steel, no shirt of chain mail. The man drops his shovel. He is a sapper, a soldier tasked with digging. His gaze meet hers, briefly, before he collapses: dead. A cloud of dust rises between them, obscuring her sight of the fallen body, just as arms grab hold of her from behind. It is La Hire, sweat dripping from his hair into her face. His eyes are wild.

"Retreat, Joan," he says. "We must retreat."

She struggles, though it is no use. Each plate of her left leg is dyed red from the thigh down.

As she is dragged, she passes corpses. Horse and human carcasses. She was too busy fighting and rallying her army to take notice of the field, but now she sees it is covered with her men. The sun shines, catching bright red pools, crimson oases so fresh even the flies have not had a chance to gather. Some wounds are still in the process of leaking. A twitching hand grazes her hand, stroking her thumb and forefinger. She peers up, and the sky is filled with other sounds: birds biding their time, waiting their turn to feast.

A lump rises in her throat, though she holds back her tears. She will let no one see her cry.

Later, a soldier comes up to her as her leg is being bound. He has barreled his way past her guards, past even La Hire.

Without introduction, he hits her across the face so she rolls to the ground from her stool. A solid punch. No one has punched her like this since the days of Jacques d'Arc. As she wipes blood-spit from her mouth, as he is restrained and pulled away from her, he screams, his voice high-pitched and broken up with sobs, "My brother is dead. You sent him to his death, yet you promised we would win. Witch!"

From La Hire she hears the final numbers: "You had three thousand men, Joan. One thousand and five hundred of these men are dead."

Before Paris, she had known only victory. This is her first defeat.

That night, praying, she talks to God. She asks Him questions, tries to explain herself. "Was I wrong to fight? Was it pride that blinded me? My own anger? I had believed we could take the gate. Not the whole city, but at least we would have had a point of entry into the capital. And then . . . and then I had hoped the King would send me more men."

She is rambling. From her thigh, blood drips, yet she barely registers the pain. Tomorrow, they will return to Chinon, though news of her defeat will travel ahead of them. Bad news, as well as good, moves swiftly.

She does not wait for an answer to her prayers. God is always silent. And she will not shirk her responsibility. At Patay, two thousand English died. But at Paris, she has lost half of her entire army. She does not blame God. Nor does she believe, like some, that this is divine retribution for fighting on a feast day. This is not God's doing. This is not God's work. It is hers.

V

◆ ◆ ◆

CHINON, OCTOBER 1429

Her rooms are bare, the tapestries of hunting scenes gone, the statuette of the angel flown away, and the window purposefully left open to let in a cold wind. There is no trace of her clerks' desks and chairs, nor the table where she had formerly dined with her household. Someone has defaced the artwork on the walls and taken a brush of black paint to the giant castles, the plump clouds, the woodland in shades of light and dark green, and the smiling face in the sun. On the stone floor, there are traces of a fire; they have burned the wax tablet where she practiced her letters; they have snapped her stylus in thirds and torched her clerks' quills so there are the remnants of feathers. Her letters, her lists and expenses, her communications to armories and foundries, the draft of her proposal to hire the experts in gunpowder and cannonry—all of these things have been confiscated. Who knows where they are now?

Le Maçon walks in as she is standing in the center of her bedchamber, empty save for a single feather bed. It was the King's own men, he informs her. They carried in sacks and nets and empty trunks, as if they had been tasked with catching feral cats. They took away anything of value, burning or tearing up the rest. He had watched them pour black ink from the clerks' desks into the fire, so that the flames hissed and sputtered. And an unpleasant boy went through all the rooms to gather up the cushions, as if he were sweeping out the rushes after a feast. It was all le Maçon could do to persuade him to leave the pillow on her bed, though even this turned into an argument. Did a pillow count as a cushion? The boy had express instructions from his masters. In the end, he'd had to be bribed.

"Children these days," le Maçon says, his lip curling.

Part of her baggage has gone missing. Most of her tunics, the smooth silks and satins in pale yellow, green, and purple; the doublets with silver and jeweled buttons; the parti-colored hose in red and white have not followed her back from Paris. She can't find the swan brooch or the silver case that held the claw of Saint Jerome's lion. The only rings she has left are the ones on her fingers.

But she still has her sword and a single suit of armor. She has a bed, though the blue coverlet is gone, and a desk where she can take her meals, a low stool placed in front of it. One leg, it seems, has been cut intentionally short, so the stool wobbles dangerously when she sits. She listens as le Maçon explains how meals will be sent up to her twice a day: an eleven o'clock dinner and a smaller supper. She will dine alone, though she is permitted to keep a servant for her laundry.

"What laundry?" she says. "I hardly have any clothes left."

In the next room, her pages are crying, and though her squire is not crying, he is cursing through the wall in language that makes le Maçon blush like a virgin.

She looks down at the dirty stone floor, the bare walls. No more tapestries. No more oublies. That is something she will miss, she thinks: the taste and smell of cinnamon.

"I want to see the King," she says.

"That is not possible," he replies. "I . . ." He is staring at the floor. "You should know I am here for a purpose." His gaze falls on her rings.

She removes the Queen's sapphire, the Bishop of Poitiers's ruby, a countess's diamond, and drops the rings into his hand. Her fingers flex from the sudden lightness.

"What about . . ." He looks at the one ring she is still wearing, which belonged to Catherine and before Catherine to the Duke of Lorraine.

"I had this before I came to Chinon. Even if you ask, I would not part with it. You will have to wrench it from my hand."

He relents and begins to move toward the door.

"I'm sorry," he says. His words come out crackling and dry. "I would never have expected things to end this way."

Her heart is too hard for her to shed any more tears. She shakes her head. "You don't understand."

For to understand, she thinks, you would have had to grow up with me in Domrémy. You would have had to endure everything I have endured. What is a doublet with slashed sleeves? What is a brooch, even if it should be made of gold? I have lived off bowls of watery pottage and still had the strength to lift a cart out of the mud. For more nights than I can count, I have slept in the shade of trees, my pillow a bed of moss, nothing but fallen leaves to cover my body, while nursing welts that would have turned your stomach to look at. If you took away this feather bed, I could sleep just as well on a straw pallet. If you took away the straw pallet, I would dream the same dreams on the stone floor. And if you took away these rooms, I would sleep as soundly in the stables with the horses. I still know how to cut a straight furrow, to mend a gate or thatch a roof, to skin and fillet a lamprey, to prepare a sauce that would make your mouth water. And I know how to make an Englishman cry from fear or from pain, for I was born to handle those weapons men invented to destroy one another, and can wield them better than any person living. Though I am not cruel, I am the daughter of Jacques d'Arc, and if you aren't acquainted with my father, then you don't know the seed from which I come. He is a man who, in peace, in war, in prosperity, in hardship, won't give away an inch of himself, and I am the same. Put him in a labyrinth, in the middle of a forest, or in a rowboat in the sea with only half an oar, and he will never give in to despair; he is always face forward, his head on straight, calculating what tricks he has left up his sleeve to play.

And do you know? Though I was defeated before the walls of Paris, I feel it in my bones, in my soul: I am still the greatest warrior alive.

She gives le Maçon a hard look. She is about to spit harsh words, but she stops when she sees he is in pain. She turns away. "I am sorry, too."

Hours later, a story reaches her through Jean. The King had planned to go hunting, but the dogs in their kennels would not come out. The horses, too, were restless and nervous. No sooner was the King's favorite mount brought to him than the horse reared. Even with three strong men to help him, His Majesty could not calm the beast. The hunt was canceled. In their kennels, the dogs bayed. With fresh meat to tempt them, they still refused to be coaxed out by their masters. They howled, as if in the throes of grieving.

◆

THESE DAYS, she walks alone. If once courtiers nodded to her and servants shrank against the wall at her arrival, now they giggle and sneer. At the sight of her limp, her thigh bound in a length of white linen, they whisper behind their hands and stare. Women ignore her; they will not meet her eye but look straight ahead. In a courtyard, at the hour of sunset, she sees the distant figure of the King with his friends. Sometimes she sees La Hire and Dunois with him; once she thought she spotted le Maçon. A raw bruise touches her chest at the sound of laughter, the stray notes of a lute, a voice struggling to remember the words of a song. The pain is here, just here, she wants to tell someone.

A count sends a note demanding the return of the silver belt he gifted her, the one with the jeweled clasp shaped like a seashell. It was his favorite belt, he adds, and after the account he heard of the attack on Paris, he no longer believes she is worthy of it.

Jean reads the note out loud as she is eating dinner. Letters come to her through the Archbishop, who passes along only those he believes she should hear.

"Tell him I no longer have it," she says. "If he feels he cannot live without his seashell belt, then he must appeal directly to the King."

The hole in her leg is nearly an inch wide and at least four inches deep. Whole weeks have passed since Paris, yet the wound still bleeds. Every few hours, Jean or her pages must help her change the bandage. When she tries to run, one foot drags behind. When she attempts to walk normally, her back straight, each step is a knife thrust in her left thigh. Her only visitors are those who have gone to battle with her. At the start of their visits, they are relieved. The spot of red on the bandage is only the size of a thumb. But the more she moves and walks about the room, the larger the spot grows, and by the time they are ready to depart, the stain is as large as a fist. So, they beg her to sit, to stay still. Dunois turns away at the sight of her blood, discreetly, like a man who has glimpsed the breasts of a woman who is not his wife. But La Hire asks kindly, "Have you considered a cane? Just as a temporary solution, of course." He winces when he thinks she isn't looking.

He asks her, What would you do if nothing stood in your way? If there were no Archbishop of Reims or La Trémoille to stop you? If things were as before and the King still favored you?

She does not have to consider her answer. She would raise an army twenty thousand strong and march on Paris before taking back Normandy. She would secure the loyalty of the duchies of Brittany and Aquitaine to France.

And then?

Secure the realm. Keep watch on the borders. Build a standing army. Raise money for ordnance, for guns and cannonry to be improved.

And then?

She has not thought that far. Jump on a ship? Cross the Narrow Sea? She has never seen the sea. Attack England?

But if she were God, if she had Christ's powers to raise the dead, then she would not bother with war. She would pull her sister from her grave in Domrémy; she would resurrect her dog, Salaud, his half-burned body from its pile of ash. She would build a ship and leave the kingdom with them. That is what she would do. If she were God, she would be done with court. My sister. My dog. That is all I need to be happy, to live my life.

When she enters the stables, she catches pages stroking her one horse, making it offerings of fresh fruit. They pay bribes to Raymond and Louis to touch a piece of her armor, any piece.

She does not need to remind them she has failed. "What of it?" Louis protests. To him, she is like the great troubadour Arnaut Daniel. Would she rather be the author of masterpieces that will be sung and praised for all time or the author of very good but average and unmemorable works numbering in the hundreds? True, she has not fought so many battles. She has not embarked on dozens of campaigns. But she is young. And already she is the savior of Orléans! Jargeau, Meung, Beaugency, Patay—these are battles every squire and page wets himself thinking of at night. At her approach, the gates of cities go *boom*! Louis demonstrates the explosion, throwing out his arms. Except Paris. But that is only because she didn't have enough men. Then he whispers into her ear, cupping his hands, "Everyone is aware that you were betrayed by the King, though they will not say it. They see that he is jealous of your fame and your glory, so they must take sides." With her or against her.

She lets her pages go. It is the right thing to do, and they know it, even as they cry and protest. They accuse her of having a hard heart.

"Is that the best you can do?" she asks, trying to smile. "You must learn better insults."

She turns next to Jean, who shakes his head. He is determined.

"Such moments test us," he says, "and let us know what kind of men we are. So, I will be with you to the end, or I will give up arms and never fight again. Even if you led an army of one, I would be at your side, ready to die. I could not live out my life in the skin of a coward, knowing I abandoned you when your fortunes were low. Would you have me be so?"

"No," she replies. She is suddenly tired; she feels that if she lay down, she might sleep for whole days at a time. "But you may change your mind, and if you do, then I will not hold it against you."

At night, she wakes, shivering. The linen around her leg is soaked, and blood drips down the side of her ankle. She changes the bandage herself, as she prepares for a meeting. Earlier, her bowl of watery stew came with a note tied to an extra manchet loaf. It was from Yolande.

She heads for the field where the archers practice. In the ground, she has stuck twelve arrows for shooting. The target is a blurry straw-colored dot, and it is growing dark. But she does not even have to try. She may have lost Paris, but she has lost nothing else.

It is one of those meetings that both parties must deny took place, and if one party insists it did happen, the other will shrug and say, Where is the proof?

The Queen of Four Kingdoms is here, as well as the Queen of France.

There is no time to waste. No pleasantries exchanged, no greeting.

"Officially, I rebuke you," Yolande says. It is late, but she is still resplendently dressed. Mother and daughter match, in gowns of moonlit silver, glowing like fish tails in an enchanted lake. "I rebuke you, as Her Majesty the Queen rebukes you. We shun and forsake you for having gone against the King's wishes in launching an attack against Paris. You knew Charles did not support the attack. And look at the result. Officially, I must say to you, Joan, what you have done is shameful, yet Fortune still smiles on you in some small way. The King, my most generous and forgiving son, has spared your life."

In the dark, the Queen smiles gently at her.

"Unofficially," Yolande continues, "I have berated Charles for giving you only three thousand men with which to launch an attack against Paris when he had more than ten thousand at his disposal. I have asked him why he released those men from service without first paying their wages and when there was still work to be done. And I have found the answer he gave me, which I am not at liberty to share with you, disappointing. The Queen shares my opinions, unofficial as they are."

Beside her, her daughter nods.

"Unofficially, though I admire your courage and your daring—would every man of the kingdom be so willing to meet his death—I must scold you, for you deserve to hear some harsh words. Look at you now!" She clicks her tongue. "I can see the blood on your bandage from here. You should have exercised a little more patience. Returned to Chinon and bided your time, until you returned to the King's good graces. But you are young. You let your love of battle and your emotions win. A terrible mistake. Charles can make mistakes, and he has made several. Men can commit as many errors as they like—within reason. We, however, cannot afford a single misstep."

Joan wants to spit out oaths, but she holds herself back. "That is not fair," she says. "France has lost battles before now. Dunois was wounded at Rouvray and the Duke of Alençon captured at Verneuil. Yet they were never humiliated as I am humiliated. To this day, the Duke of Orléans remains a prisoner in a London tower, composing verses, while the English collect his ransom to fund their army. Yet the court only has kind words to say about His Grace. They pity him and patiently wait for his return. Then why is the court not also patient with me? I have done more in a few months than they have for nearly their whole lives, and I am only seventeen. I am young, and I have more battle scars than all of them, to say nothing of our King."

Even in the dark, Yolande's eyes flash. "You forget yourself, or you have really begun to believe the prophecies we circulated about you, Joan. You are a woman. You are poor. You come from nothing. When you were strong, these were not insurmountable obstacles. We dressed you in the mantle of holiness. We said you came of God."

"And now?"

"Now the cloak that disguised you has fallen from your shoulders. The court sees you are, after all, only human. Which means only a woman. Purse and pockets empty. A peasant. You were useful. Now you are no longer of use. And you have no family to fall back on. You are not even the daughter of a common knight. You forget that at the height of your power, when you enjoyed only victories, people still called you a shepherdess. So, I fear you have failed from the beginning to understand. No one could protect you at court. Only your victories protected you. They were your truest allies, more than le Maçon or the captains of the army. More than any of us."

"They are still *my* victories." She stands a little taller. "And I can still fight. Do not be deceived by this blood. My leg will heal. I have fallen from great heights before and leapt back to my feet."

Yolande draws closer to her. When she speaks, her voice is a whisper, almost tender. "Perhaps we were both foolish to expect any other conclusion than this. You have been permitted to do so much. You were the exception to every rule. But how could you overturn a game that is as old as time itself? I think now you were always meant to fail."

"If you tell me to leave Chinon," Joan says, "I will. I will begin again."

Yolande and Marie glance at each other. They hesitate. "The King will not let you leave," Marie says quietly. Another pause. "He means to make an example of you."

"Then I am his prisoner. I thought we understood each other. We were . . ." It is hard for her to say the words. "We were friends."

A dry laugh escapes Yolande's throat. Even her daughter chuckles.

"The King has no friends," Yolande says. "Just people, like La Trémoille, who will lend him vast sums of money when he needs to borrow. Just people, like le Maçon, who will give up their own horse when a city is under attack, to save His Majesty's life and curry favor. Just people, like you, to raise sieges for him, to win battles, until the day you stop winning. And when you have nothing more to give, you return to nothing. But . . ." She pauses. She looks sad. "I suppose it is not only the King. It is everyone. When you are doing well, you are like a fresh flower, and all the butterflies want to rest on your petals. And when you are wilting, you are plucked and thrown away. No one wants to touch you. They think you are bad luck and pretend they have never known you. Human nature, Joan. It is the way people are. France may be the most Christian kingdom, but people are the same everywhere."

"My next battle may still be a victory." Joan looks from one woman's face to the other. "Why shouldn't it be?"

"Then you must hope God is on your side," Yolande replies. "Because no one else is. Officially."

The meeting has come to an end. They leave, but not before they slip money to her, coins in pouches of silk, because, well, livres are always useful, though if asked they will deny that the money came from them.

Joan returns to her bed and sleeps late. Morning comes. In the field, a small crowd has formed to marvel at the sight of a target. On it, twelve arrows make a single point in the center of the circle of straw.

Some call it a miracle. Others: witch's tricks.

◆

NOVEMBER 1429—A MESSAGE arrives from the King. Joan is to go to La Charité, a town well fortified, and retake it by siege.

His Majesty is forgiving. Hadn't she wanted a chance to redeem herself after the disaster at Paris? So, for her redemption, he gives her an army. And because she has proven that she cannot handle three thousand men, he will spare only five hundred this time, though to make up the numbers, he will also give her several cannons. Yes, the artillery she has such high regard for, so she cannot possibly fail. The cannons have been paid for, he adds, by La Trémoille.

La Hire says, "Tell the King you are ill. Say you have lost your appetite for war, that you have retired. Or that your leg still gives you pain. Do not go, little maid. It is a trap."

"Then people will laugh at me."

"They are laughing at you regardless."

She goes. Weeks in, their supplies are running out. A letter is dispatched, and they must wait several days for an answer. The court's reply: The King regrets he has no funds to spare for what she requires. His clerk scribbles, as an afterthought, Perhaps she should acknowledge her defeat and return to the safety of Chinon? To her friends who miss seeing her hobble and limp around the castle?

When the letter is read out to her, she does not curse. She tells Jean to prepare a separate letter, which will go to the citizenry of a nearby town.

"Please send what food can be spared, saltpeter . . ." She looks down at her fingers, gray-blue with frostbite. Jean is tapping the tip of his pen against the ink, a solid block like a stone. He must hold the inkpot over the fire for it to melt, but his hands are shaking from cold.

He frowns. One hand grips the other to still it. He utters aloud what both of them already know.

"This is ridiculous," he says.

"I gave you the chance to leave. You should have taken it."

He glares at her. "It isn't that. The King knew you would not be able to take La Charité. It is like sending a child into a bull's pen with a stick. Yet he also knew you would not be able to turn down the chance to prove yourself."

"You must be more careful with your words," she says. "Even here."

"As of this morning, we have lost several more men."

"Deserted or dead?"

"Does it matter?" He bites his lip. When he speaks, he blows small puffs of air.

"In the camp," he continues, "they say you have been forsaken by God because of your pride."

"It is their hunger speaking," she answers.

She looks up over his head to the sky, to strike a bargain with her God as she had done that day in the field in Domrémy. But the sky is gray, and the clouds hang heavy with the gathering strength of an unleashed storm. Her own stomach groans. For days, she has eaten nothing. There is no God to listen to her here.

In the hours before dawn, it begins to snow. A hard wind descends on their camp, howling like the cries of the dead. She does not sleep, and her thoughts turn, too, to the dead. The sapper who saved her at Paris; his own wife would not be able to tell who he was, his corpse was stuck with so many arrows. She saw bodies missing limbs, like the stumps of trees with their branches cut off. She saw corpses exhaling their last breath. On the cusp of death, they still possessed the strength to pull apart a few blades of grass. And when she closes her eyes, she sees Catherine.

She steps outside, into the dark. The wind beats her as though she were a flagellant, each gust of air a whip across her face. But she tucks her head down and pushes against it until the hole in her leg burns as if a torch is being pressed against her flesh. Her knee buckles, and she falls in the snow.

She crawls toward a cannon, using it to anchor her body in the storm. Even the artillery has let her down. Most of their store of gunpowder has been ruined by the wet weather, and she has had to contend with thievery on her own side: food and tools pilfered, cases of slow matches and crossbows gone missing.

Another irony dawns on her: you go to war so that you can forget what true pain is. Now she knows: it isn't for glory that the knights-errant go off on their quests. Who would slay a dragon for a mere chest of treasure? But one might risk death to escape memories too perfect to describe, that can never be relived again. It is the loss of such moments that can drive a person to madness. For her, it's the memory of walks with Catherine through the village, of falling asleep together beneath the Faerie Tree, her dreams of cinnamon before she ever smelled or tasted the spice. And later, much later, a day of strolling through a garden, thinking she was on top of the world. Orléans saved. Jargeau, Meung, and Beaugency retaken. Goodness is just as capable of torment; it thaws the heart and fills up the soul, then leaves in its wake a pit so deep it can never be whole again.

She knows she is testing God by kneeling in the cold. "Are you still here? Were you ever here?"

There is no answer.

She thinks, as her vision blurs, as she rests her head against the cannon's hard surface, I have let you down, Catherine. I have not found the three men who hurt you. I have not done what I pledged. And you are dead, while the men I have sworn to kill are still alive.

John, Duke of Bedford, regent of England

Henry, sixth of his name, future King of England

Philip, Duke of Burgundy

I have done nothing I set out to do.

The cold makes her head spin. She is aware of her breathing growing shallow, of darkness falling like a heavy blanket over her. Her heart slows.

In her arms, the cannon becomes soft like supple flesh, and her nose fills with the scent of herbs and wildflowers. She is dreaming. When she opens her eyes, it is not the walls of La Charité she sees but her sister's slender waist. And she is small again, ten years old. She is wearing her dress of red wool, and her hair is knotted and long, in need of washing.

"Pitying yourself, Joan?" her sister says.

"Yes."

"It is not like you to waste time. Did you ever heed our father when he hounded you? Did you let him break your spirit, though he tried? The next morning, you were still running around the village. You were still yourself. So, what has changed? You are the same person. Win or lose. You are a soldier, and I have been watching you all this time. I have loved you from afar."

Catherine bends. Strands of her sister's hair cover her head.

A kiss. A touch of warmth, which spreads from Joan's face to her hands. She feels the pinprick of blood circulating in her limbs, tickling her flesh so it comes alive. In her ears, she hears her heart beating strong and steady. She hears a voice, which seems to rise from deep within her: "Now go, Joan."

She sleeps, though the storm buffets her body. And she sleeps deeply, as if she were lying in a feather bed swathed in sheets of silk. In the morning, her arms are still wrapped around the cannon. But she stands without difficulty. She finds she is only hungry and a little unsteady on her feet. Strength ripples through her. When she touches her thigh, there is no pain, no more bleeding; the wound has closed. She makes the decision to retreat. She will not sacrifice any more of her men.

"We return to Chinon," she tells Jean, and he gapes at the sight of her. Has she spent the whole night outside?

Her body is renewed, but she cannot say the same for her army. Out of five hundred, most have deserted. And they must leave behind the cannons, which are too heavy to take with them, so their artillery will fall into the hands of the enemy and one day may be used against their own. It is her second defeat. She has still failed.

VI

◆ ◆ ◆

CHINON, JANUARY 1430

A WEEK AFTER she has returned from La Charité, the King holds a feast where a jester performs. The jester puts on a woman's dark wig, its hair reaching past his waist. He stuffs his chest, so it appears he has breasts. He wears pieces of armor, gauntlets and oversized sabatons, which he stomps around in, making as much noise as possible, and a backplate but no breastplate. He wears a sign around his neck, one painted like a coat of arms, with fire-breathing dragons and upside-down fleurs-de-lis. But the word "whore" is also scrawled across it in large black letters.

The jester prances. He bats his eyes at the King, blows kisses at the Archbishop, and sighs at Dunois, pronouncing himself in love with all three men while pretending to trip over his long hair. He flails a wooden sword and makes moaning noises, as if he is being ravished, then pulls from his leg a bolt of white linen splattered with red paint, meant to remind the guests of the bandage Joan keeps wrapped around her thigh. He jokes about bleeding. Thigh bleeding, a woman's monthly bleeding, how he has one but not the other.

He tickles two of the Queen's ladies-in-waiting under their chins, then blushes and says he sometimes forgets he is a woman and not a man. To make the women scream, he throws his wig at them, though the Queen herself does not laugh, and she glares at those who do.

It is not wine that turns the King's complexion red but laughter. He is laughing so hard he nearly falls out of his chair, and his wife has to support his arm, to keep him from rolling under the table.

But around the room, there is the sound of chairs being pushed back. La Hire rises; he is first to leave, followed by Dunois.

"Dunois!" the King calls after him. He is slurring; his words feel too large for his mouth. The show continues, yet the air in the room has shifted. His Majesty still smiles, but he does not laugh with the same abandon as before.

After leaving the feast, La Hire and Dunois visit Joan in her rooms. They invite her for a walk under the stars and tell her the story, like boys who feel they have done something good and are pleased with themselves for standing up for their friend. Dunois has brought a sack of wine, which he passes, after several generous swigs, to La Hire. When it is offered to her, she refuses. "What a king we serve, eh?" La Hire says. He belches. "Disgraceful."

"There will be other chances," Dunois says. They slap her shoulder to liven her spirits. How do soldiers comfort each other after their defeats? She has always wondered, and now she knows. Drinking and prancing around. Getting so drunk the memory of one's loss is forgotten by the next day.

To placate them, she smiles. She thinks, There will be other opportunities for you. Even your defeats are chances to learn. Sometimes you treat war like it is a game. But the stakes, they have always been higher for me.

She lets them wrestle and dance away from her. The sack of wine depleted, she watches Dunois wander off to piss against a tree. Soon the hoots and calls of La Hire fade. He has tripped over a bush and is retching into it. Behind him, Dunois is laughing. "Can't hold your drink, old man!" he shouts.

She moves away from them. The night is clear. Above, the stars look down at her like pairs of blinking eyes, watching what she will do next. She is alone.

In the morning, Joan hears a rumor from her squire. Following le Maçon's example, the Archbishop has found her replacement: a young shepherd boy, six years old, another prophet with bleeding hands and bleeding feet. The boy's arrival is meant to insult le Maçon, to ridicule him, and to soothe the worries of the King. It is said the boy has received visions of France's victory over England and Burgundy, that he predicts the deliverer of these victories will be none other than His Majesty.

"On the battlefield?" she asks.

"'On the battlefield, to rival Charlemagne' were the boy's exact words," Jean replies.

Even in such times, there are still occasions for laughter.

◆

DAYLIGHT DOES THE KING NO FAVORS; his long nose is red from the cold, his eyes squinting and watery, the corners veined with pink from last night's heavy drinking. He pulls the furred sleeves of his robes closer to him. Kingship has not fleshed out His Majesty's body; he is still a gatepost, though he stands a little taller.

He expects Joan to kneel, so she does, purposefully slow, to make him wait.

"Orléans feels a long time ago," he says when she rises. He sighs, tipping his head to show the Valois profile at its best angle.

Once again, they are meeting on the banks of the Vienne. But there is no blue-shadowed dusk, no flickering candlelight to obscure His Majesty's features. In the early hours of morning, she sees him with startling clarity, as he is. She takes in the pink tips of his ears, his white knuckles, the soft blue veins of his beringed hands, flashing with lapis lazuli and garnets.

"We could always make a trip to Orléans, Majesty," she says. "And ask the people there if they feel it was a long time ago."

"I know that would suit your purposes very well." He grimaces.

"La Charité," he continues. "Paris. All failures, all disasters. Men lost or deserted. Money and supplies wasted. How do you account for this?"

"You would know better than I. How do you account for it?"

A flash of anger.

"I have had successes, too," she says. "If Your Majesty prefers, we could review those as well. For La Charité and Paris, there is Orléans. There is Patay. There is also every town between Chinon and Reims that threw open its gates and surrendered without resistance. What of those?"

"It has since been explained to me," he replies, "that you were only able to win those battles because of the resources I gave you."

"A soldier must be fed if he is to fight. But I wouldn't give the herring in his belly all the credit."

"*My* soldiers. *My* army."

There is a long silence. The King does not look at her.

"How long, Joan? How much longer?" He stares across the river at the opposite bank. "I will be plain with you. I cannot simply have you removed. You still have support, however limited, at court; though the reason is unfathomable to me, there are some who still believe you are a holy woman. And I cannot let you go. I asked my councillors, Why can we not return her to her former peasant life—what harm could she do once she is back in her village, tilling the fields and watching the sheep? But they said to me, You have seen what happens when you put her in a crowd. She will gather a following. She will raise an army of peasants and turn against you. You cannot trust her. But they did not need to tell me this. It is a lesson I have already learned—to my detriment."

He snaps his fingers, and a servant runs up with something folded in his arms.

"So, I will give you a choice," he says. "Stay at Chinon as my honored guest, where no harm will come to you. Live out your life in solitary comfort. Warm meals twice a day, a servant to look after your needs. Consider this my gift for the services you have rendered us in the past. But you will swear an oath before witnesses—La Trémoille, the Archbishop of Reims, le Maçon, a whole assembly of nobility—and the oath will be as follows: You will never ride into battle again, nor will you speak of any matter relating to the war. You will dismiss your squire and relinquish all of your weapons, including your sword.

You will be barred from setting foot any place the knights or archers train. You will swear this oath, or . . ."

The servant passes the King a garment of red and gold; his hands shake it out.

She recognizes the cloak as his gift to her in Reims. "Or I will have you knighted. You shall have your own coat of arms. The design is already made—simple but, I think, effective. Gold fleurs-de-lis against a shield of blue, with a sword down the middle. It was my own idea."

"And?" she says.

"You ride into battle." He touches the place above his heart. "You do not return."

A pause. She can hear the King breathe. He is patient. He will wait for her answer.

"I am fortunate," she says.

A pause. The King looks carefully at her. "Fortunate?"

"Fortunate because I do not live as you do, always fearful. I think now you do not need Burgundy or England to haunt your dreams, to keep you awake at night. You do that all on your own. It isn't only the outcome of battles that frightens you. It is everything. You are timid of every step, every thought and word. You live through each hour terrified and uncertain of who you are. But I don't." She faces him. "I know who I am. I am a soldier, a godmother to many sons and daughters in this kingdom. I am the protector of dreams. All those in France have only to say my name or think of me, and they will no longer be afraid. They will fear neither England nor Burgundy, for they will know their collective strength is greater than any king's. If you do not believe me, you have only to go to Orléans, knock on any door, and ask. I have kneeled, not to receive a crown, but to receive the wishes of young girls and the last words of dying men. I am not afraid of anything, of anyone."

She takes the cloak, and her arms sweep it over her shoulders. The sound is like the spreading of wings.

He sighs. Relief washes through him.

"Where will I go next?" she asks.

"Compiègne."

A French town, under threat from the Duke of Burgundy. She nods. "How many men?"

"Three hundred?"

She can work with three hundred. "I make no promises," she says. She sees that he thinks she is referring to victory and defeat. She isn't. "I may yet return."

His shoulders stiffen. An involuntary movement. "Tell me, do you believe you will be remembered?"

She doesn't answer. She moves to leave, lets him talk.

"You underestimated me, as others have done. But you do not know me. I, too, am blessed by the same God as you and have outlived all my elder brothers in order to inherit this throne. I have outlived Henry, the great warrior-king of England, and my own father. And I will outlive you, Joan."

She has already begun to walk away. "Are you certain?" she asks, turning. It is the last time they will look at each other. When their eyes meet, he takes a step back. He seems to shrink into himself, and she is willing to spare only a few more moments for this sad man with a crown. In the distance, a sound like a rush of air reaches them. It makes the King jump; he starts, looks over his shoulder, but Joan remains still. From where they stand, she can see birds; the sound had come from their ascension, their flight.

"I am the greatest warrior alive," she says when there is silence again. "I am the performer of miracles." A beam of light touches the top of her head; it picks out the gold thread of her cloak and makes her shimmer. She pauses. "What are you, other than a king?"

◆

MAY 1430, COMPIÈGNE. Her men are retreating. They are losing the battle, but it does not feel like a defeat to Joan.

It feels like—freedom. Behind her, the gate to Compiègne where her soldiers are running for shelter must soon close. Her path to safety will be cut off. There is no way for her to reach the gate in time.

It barely registers: the thunderous clang, as it slides shut.

Yet as her horse collapses under her with a scream, her sword moves like a sickle blade across the Burgundian soldiers, who tumble in neat rows as grass freshly scythed to make hay. She can still cut a straight furrow. Outside the town, her body seems to grow, to fill the space of the field. A steel elbow lands in an archer's eye; the sweep of her gauntleted wrist sends another crumpling to the ground. They bounce against her armor, and all she sees is her blade in her hand, like flashes of lightning in the spring air.

Through a wall of men, she creates an opening, but another wall rises to meet her. She feels arms grabbing her, attempting to pull her down, as she is surrounded. Three more men are sacrificed before her sword is torn out of her grip. So, she uses her hands, her fists, which knock stars into her enemy's heads. She kicks. She steps on an ankle and hears a cry beneath her as the bone breaks. She digs her heel in, so he will not ever run again.

Old arms fall away, but new arms clamp onto her shoulders, which are slippery with Burgundian blood. She strains against them, and for a moment, a horror ripples through the waves of men when they realize she is still fighting and unwilling to surrender. Her arms held, her head knocks against a Burgundian's skull and sends his body flying into the soldiers behind him, like a toppled door. But she is panting. She has been fighting four hours without rest, and it is the first time she has stopped to catch her breath.

Before her, a clearing opens, and a black horse rides into the space. From its back, a man, lightly armored and shining in the late morning sun, dismounts. He hesitates before walking up to her.

"Do you know who I am?" he asks quietly, by way of greeting.

She studies the aquiline features, the thin, bloodless lips. She knows, and her heart leaps—with joy. How does one say, politely, You are number three on the list of people I would like to see dead? I have been waiting a long time for this moment.

She thinks of the rock battle in Maxey. So, this is the man for whom Guillaume died. This is who the redheaded captain of Maxey serves.

He takes a step closer.

"Kneel to the Duke of Burgundy," a voice behind her says. She is kicked, though she only stumbles. She grunts but does not speak.

"What? Is France's famous holy warrior mute?" the Duke asks, and laughter goes up around her. He takes another step closer. She holds her breath and hangs her head.

He is standing in front of her now, so close she can hear him breathe. His gloved hand reaches out, grips her chin to raise her face. It is a mistake. She bites down on the groove between his thumb and forefinger, her teeth sinking into ducal flesh until she hears a crack. She had been storing what strength she had left, and now she lunges. The hands that held her loosen in surprise, though only for a moment. She is pulled back and subdued. She is forced to kneel at his feet.

The Duke wrenches off his glove to appraise the damage, his thumb jutting at an unnatural angle. He stares, his face caught between anger and pain. This time, he does not hesitate. With his good hand, he strikes her across the mouth. It is a blow hard enough to send another man reeling, but her jaw only stiffens. She spits a wad of blood across his polished boots, and then shakes her head, like a horse that has been sprinkled with a little water. Is that the best you can do, Your Grace? She thinks, That was for the boy Guillaume.

The Duke looks at the piles of corpses around them. These are his own men, but his gaze is cold, almost sneering.

"Your skill has not been exaggerated. Now that I have seen you, I believe the stories: Orléans, Patay, the journey to Reims," he says. His hand is held by a servant who has arrived to dab the bite wound with a cloth and water.

"Return my sword to me," she says, "and permit me to show you what else I can do."

Her mind is already thinking ahead—to her escape, to being close enough to the Duke of Burgundy to cut his white, pulsing throat.

"You are proud, but you will pay a dear price for your pride," he replies. He steps away to remount his horse. "Though it may sound strange, I am almost sorry to see you captured. A shame, a great shame, that you did not serve someone better: myself or Bedford. Your gifts are wasted on my cousin the Dauphin . . . pardon—I mean, of course, His Majesty the King."

Mention of the King almost surprises her. She has not thought of him during the whole battle. When she thinks of France, she no longer considers its ruler.

"A warning, my lord," she says, as their eyes meet. "Should I escape, I may not only bite you next time."

It is worth it just to see him flinch.

EPILOGUE

◆ ◆ ◆

THE ROAD TO ROUEN, CAPITAL OF THE ENGLISH STRONGHOLD OF NORMANDY
DECEMBER 1430

En route to Rouen, she is kept in a cage. Crowds gather to jeer at her. They spit through the bars. They throw small stones, as the large ones will not reach, and when they cannot get close enough to the cage, they call her names from a distance: whore, witch, demoness. They believe she has rutted with the Dauphin, for they won't acknowledge him as king, and she has no time to explain to them that she wouldn't sleep with the King, not even for his weight in gold, which, at the end of the day, isn't very much.

Her skin has returned to its childhood shades of blue, indigo, yellow, and green, where the guards have struck her. They tell her a story they have heard, in the hopes of frightening her. A woman named Pierronne was brought before the cathedral of Notre-Dame de Paris. As a sermon was read, she was tied to the stake. And then she was burned. Her crime? She'd had a vision of God, and God had told her Joan was good, her cause just. As the guards share this account with her, they smile. Pierronne was lucky, they add. Her death was quick, the fire built up large, and there was no ill wind to blow the flames away. Her agony lasted only a handful of minutes. So perhaps yours will be the same.

Yet even now there are better moments. There is the time she passed through a town; she has forgotten its name, whether it was Burgundian or English. She held a piece of bread, but her left cheek was swollen from being slapped too many times by her right-handed guards, and it became difficult to chew. As the cart jolted down the roads, a boy ran up to the bars. In his hand, he had a stone with a sharp edge, which he carried like a prize. He threw it at her, and the rock flew through the bars of the cage and cut her across her cheek. When she touched her face, she felt the wetness of blood. A cheer went up, and people began scooping dirt and stones to follow the boy's example. But she reached through the cage to pass him her piece of bread, and he took it. He ate it hungrily, and the crowd forgot about the dirt and stones they had gathered. They stared after her, in silence.

This morning, they are riding along a narrow road, uneven and steep. The wagon and her cage lurch, and she has to close her eyes. She rests, an arm draped around a bar, her forehead leaning against the shaft of iron, and the chains that shackle her wrists clinking gently. The guards are tired—one of them is snoring—so they do not taunt her.

But a sound rouses her, and for a moment, she is confused. It is a sound like thunder, though the sky is clear today, a rosy mist of soft colors: pink, white, and gold. She looks out and wonders if she has died; if so, is this heaven? But not far away, a guard coughs. The cart has stopped; he is pissing into a bush, and she knows she is still alive. She looks around for the source of the sound and finds it. It is the sea.

The sea is flat and calm. Its surface is placid; the current moves as though a sleeping giant breathed across the lapping waves. But one day, she thinks, it will wake. It will storm.

She has been gripping the bars of the cage, and from below, a sound like the scraping of metal reaches her, harsh and grating. In her hands, she sees the bars are now slightly bent. Not by much, yet the gap between them is larger than before. Not enough to slip through. Not enough for anything. Yet it is there; it exists.

Call it what you like. A sign. A miracle. Though she is a prisoner, nothing has changed. And if this is possible, what else may she do if given the chance? So, she will bide her time. She will be patient. If she is tried by the church, she will say what she needs to say to survive.

She thinks, I have become more than just myself. I am here, in this cage. But I have another body, which is unseen. I am the battle cry, the roar of spears, pikes, and poleaxes rattling. I am the sound of a hundred horses thundering down a hill and the wind that ripples through banners, the swing of a catapult, the deafening blast and explosion of cannonry. Every soldier, young and old, who goes to war shall think of me and carry me in his soul. A hundred years from now, the sound of my name will still make the English shake, though my own people will look upon me tenderly, with pride and with love. Before each battle, the foot soldiers, artillerymen, and sappers will bend their heads and call my name. They will say, Joan, give me strength and courage, and I shall hear them, wherever I am. I can never die.

Here is God, in the sky and the rosy mist, ready to strike a bargain. In the roar of the waves she hears the cheers of the people—her people. She hears her sister's laughter and knows it comes from Paradise.

God is listening. Into His ear, she prays. That is, she tells Him: I, Joan, will return. All prayers are wishes, but this is not a wish.

It is a promise.

AFTERWORD

♦ ♦ ♦

I don't know when the idea to write about Joan of Arc first came to me. Only that it did, and for the last four years, she has been my constant companion and most steadfast friend. It is still strange to describe the evolution by which a historical character can become more real than the people in the next room. But that is what happened, and no wonder: Joan is a remarkable individual.

This is a work of fiction. It is important to stress that the Joan who appears in these pages is a Joan intensely personal to me. I'll say first what this Joan isn't. She isn't visited by hallucinations in her adolescence, by visions of the archangel Michael and the saints Margaret of Antioch and Catherine of Alexandria. She isn't told by these visions what to do, which is to leave Domrémy and the protection of her family for Vaucouleurs. The Joan of these pages has a complicated relationship with her God. She is a practical young woman: efficient, hardy, as protective of the few people she loves as she is quick-tempered with those who try her patience or belittle her. The historical version of Joan, as she is commonly portrayed in biographies and in films, is a kind of holy woman, one might even say a religious fanatic, who hears Mass multiple times a day, who decries whoring and gambling in her army (she once broke a sword across a prostitute's back) and encourages her soldiers to confess their sins. She is more or less a spiritual cheerleader to the fighting men—that is, the "real" soldiers. The historical Joan does not shed blood. She does not fight, though she puts on an expensive suit of armor, is skilled in riding, and carries a sword. The historical Joan prefers to hold her banner and rally her men without wounding or maiming a single enemy soldier. I admit: I have never wholly bought this story. Joan did see plenty of action in battle, enough to endanger her life on numerous occasions. In Orléans, she was shot in the neck. The story goes she extracted the arrow with her own hands and then returned to battle after pig fat was applied to the wound. At Jargeau, she was knocked down from a ladder when a rock hit her helmet. She was shot in the thigh outside the walls of Paris. These accounts are all true.

For me, Joan is a soldier first, with no pretensions to beatification or canonization, and I think it is important to note that she wasn't made a saint until nearly five hundred years after her death. I envisioned a Joan inspired by God only insofar that she was gifted with the genius of being a great warrior, a natural leader, and a prophet. A prophet not of a vague and mist-covered future populated with angels, but a prophet of the future of battle, knowing how war would one day be fought, how victory could be concretely attained. In 1453, France would win the Hundred Years' War, twenty-two years after Joan's death in 1431, largely through its usage of artillery. This Joan's version of prayer is talking and, as seen in this book, often bargaining with her God. She is no mild or humble genius. She has a mouth on her. She is hot-tempered. Proud bordering on arrogant. Flawed but charismatic. Full of rage and capable of inflicting great destruction and death but also loving, introspective, hopeful for better days ahead. In other words, still very much human.

It isn't that I don't believe in the power of faith. I do, and Joan comes to see the power of faith, though not necessarily faith in the Almighty—rather, the faith others have placed in her. But faith is, for the very reasons that make it unbreakable, also intangible. I had to take many liberties with Joan's history and with the history of the time to make Joan's journey relatable. This story is a quest. It is a quest of a young woman living in wartime who goes off on an adventure. It is a quest for vengeance and redemption. It is also a story about how a hero is shaped and made, how she is tried and tested, until the final product is something that can't be destroyed by any human hand, until not even physical defeat in battle can break her. In the end, this Joan, like the historical Joan, embodies something far greater than herself, and this *something* has fascinated, entranced, and enthralled us for centuries. There is no one who hears her story who does not also feel a tingle of electricity in the air, a sense of wonder. Centuries later, she continues to stand alone, and though she has been made into a saint, I would argue that she stands quite apart from even that exalted company in many ways. She is, in my mind, utterly unique.

The pitfall of writing a character so monumental, one who occupies such a glorious and, I believe, pure and unsullied space in history, is that the writer inevitably falls in love with her subject. But the irony is: to even embark on the adventure of writing such a character requires deviating from her history. There are many wonderful biographies of Joan. I had the honor of sifting through her incredible life and picking out the pieces that resonated most with me and then honing and polishing them in order to create a story. I had to bring the alabaster Joan down from the pedestal on which we have all put her, and talk to her, one woman to another. "Tell me about yourself," I said, and from the pages of biographies and historical texts, her voice spoke. I listened and considered the entire span of her life. The years of her youth, which are commonly passed over. The months of astonishing glory on the battlefield. The final stretch of defeat, disgrace, and tragedy, which, though she experienced despair, miraculously never completely shattered her spirit. And to make her flesh and blood, I had to imagine—everything from the name of her dog (a curse word) to her appearance. To conclude from this rich material, this astonishing and truly singular life, that she was *only* a servant of God following orders from the unseen and a devotee of the church who kept herself pure through her virginity would be a gross underestimation of the sheer magnetism of her personality, her leadership, and her inimitable courage. Faith makes us strong, but we cannot ascribe everything to faith, at the expense of human works. We must remember that God shows Himself in the world in many forms, and among these is genius, though the manifestation of genius is always in the concrete: in music, in art, in literature, in the sciences, and, in Joan's case, in war. This was my interpretation of her life.

After six hundred years, Joan is still a force to be reckoned with. Many people are drawn to her. And why not? A number of attributes of human nature worthy of admiration and that—we can only hope—may justify our continued existence on this earth are in her: a young woman born in obscurity who fought for what she loved, and who lived her short life to the very fullest.

This book is a reimagining of that life. It is also an offering to the inextinguishable light of her legacy. She, Joan, is never forgotten, but always remembered, admired, and loved.

ACKNOWLEDGMENTS

◆ ◆ ◆

This book was a journey, a quest of its own kind, and I wouldn't have been able to vault the hurdles and navigate the many thorny paths without my guide and editor, Caitlin McKenna. You were to me what, historically, Saints Catherine and Margaret were to Joan: a source of inspiration and a reserve of wisdom, strength, and calm, especially in uncertain and challenging times. It wouldn't be much of an exaggeration to say that the Joan who appears in these pages is really *our* Joan. She simply wouldn't have taken on the spirit and form she does without your brilliant notes, ideas, and encouragement. Thank you for embodying, in your person, a true passion for books and for the written word. This work is dedicated to Joan, but I would like to think of it as an offering to her memory that we have constructed together.

I would like to thank Emma Caruso for her thoughtful, enlightening edits and for providing a fresh pair of eyes at an important juncture of the editorial process. Thank you for always fielding my queries and concerns, whether legitimate or otherwise, with such grace and (saintly) patience.

My thanks goes to Bonnie Thompson for her extraordinarily thorough and perceptive copyediting; Simon Sullivan for his elegant and truly stunning interior design; Lucas Heinrich for creating a powerful and impactful jacket; Cara DuBois and Maggie Hart for the care and diligence they put into this book's production; David Lindroth for a gorgeous map; Melissa Folds for her deft and savvy handling of all things publicity; Madison Dettlinger for her insightful work in marketing; Noa Shapiro for her helpful and intelligent contributions to a variety of matters; and Denise Cronin, Rachel Kind, Jessica Cashman, Donna Duverglas, and Toby Ernst for their dedicated management of subrights. I am also grateful to Avideh Bashirrad, Robin Desser, and Andy Ward for their kind support of this book, which has enabled it to become a reality.

A big thank-you to Elisabeth Weed for the boundless energy and time she has devoted to this book. Thank you for your ideas, your infectious enthusiasm, and for being wonderful.

And last but certainly not least, I would like to thank my mother, whose daily courage in navigating the manifold perils and pitfalls of life, both large and small, made possible (and feasible) this imagining of Joan's journey. When my own nerves get the better of me, thank you for being brave, for being a modern-day woman warrior.

Joan

KATHERINE J. CHEN

A Book Club Guide

Questions and Topics for Discussion

◆ ◆ ◆

1. How much did you know about Joan of Arc before you started this novel? How does the book align with or subvert your expectations?

2. Though Joan of Arc is arguably one of the most famous Catholic saints, Chen's Joan is a largely secular reimagining. What do you think of this approach? What are your thoughts about Joan's status as a saint after reading the book?

3. Discuss Joan's relationship with her father and how it does or doesn't evolve over time. What do they have in common? What are their biggest differences?

4. How does little Guillaume's death affect Joan throughout her life? What does he come to symbolize for her?

5. "Since her birth, she has never known a time of peace," Chen writes of Joan. "Like it or not, she is always thinking about the war" (49–50). How do the circumstances of Joan's childhood influence who she becomes? Do you think she would have been just as interested in war if she hadn't grown up surrounded by it? Why or why not?

6. How do Catherine and Joan protect each other? What, besides a sister, does Joan lose when Catherine dies?

7. "She wonders: Why is it so hard to say what I can do? Why, if I possess strength, must it also be bound up in holiness?" (156). Why do you think the court, the soldiers, and the general public need to believe Joan's strength is a divine miracle? Do you think society is still guilty of this type of thinking when it comes to exceptional and/or powerful women? Explain your view.

8. How do other women in the novel wield power and influence? How do these methods differ from the way Joan employs her gifts? Which approaches do you think are most successful, and why?

9. How does Joan's perception of her uncle Durand change over time—especially after her reunion with her father? What do you make of this character?

10. When does Joan's relationship with the Dauphin begin to take a turn for the worse? Do you think there could have been a way for Joan to avoid her fate—and the eventual trial and execution that followed? Why or why not?

PHOTO: ELENA SEIBERT

KATHERINE J. CHEN is the author of the novels *Mary B* and *Joan*. Her writing has appeared in *The New York Times*, *The Wall Street Journal*, the *Los Angeles Review of Books*, *Literary Hub*, and the historical fiction anthology *Stories from Suffragette City*.

ABOUT THE TYPE

◆ ◆ ◆

This book was set in Fournier, a typeface named for Pierre-Simon Fournier (1712–68), the youngest son of a French printing family. He started out engraving woodblocks and large capitals, then moved on to fonts of type. In 1736 he began his own foundry and made several important contributions in the field of type design; he is said to have cut 147 alphabets of his own creation. Fournier is probably best remembered as the designer of St. Augustine Ordinaire, a face that served as the model for the Monotype Corporation's Fournier, which was released in 1925.